D1012400

"A GENUINE EYE-OPENER"*

PRESIDENT RICHARD MONCKTON
has turned the Oval Office into a chamber of
political horrors—and, if things go as planned, the
world will be none the wiser.

DIRECTOR WILLIAM MARTIN
knows things even the President doesn't know. And
he safeguards the Primula Report—a weapon that
could destroy his career, his agency, the President,
and the security of the nation.

SALLY
is very beautiful, very famous, and very willing to
cooperate with Martin—for reasons both public and
private.

> **"RARELY, IF EVER, HAVE READERS
> BEEN GIVEN SO INTIMATE AND ODI-
> OUS A PICTURE OF WASHINGTON'S
> TOP ECHELONS OF GOVERNMENT,
> MORE PARTICULARLY THE WHITE
> HOUSE, THE C.I.A., AND THE F.B.I."**
> —John Barkham Reviews*

THE ELECTRIFYING PARAMOUNT—ABC TV SERIES
BASED UPON *THE COMPANY* BY JOHN EHRLICHMAN

WASHINGTON
BEHIND CLOSED DOORS

Starring

CLIFF ROBERTSON
JASON ROBARDS
STEFANIE POWERS
ROBERT VAUGHN
LOIS NETTLETON
BARRY NELSON
HAROLD GOULD
TONY BILL
and
ANDY GRIFFITH

Special Appearance By **JOHN HOUSEMAN**

Created By: DAVID W. RINTELS
Executive Producer: STAN KALLIS
Supervising Producers:
ERIC BERCOVICI and DAVID W. RINTELS
Producer: NORMAN POWELL
Written for Television By
DAVID W. RINTELS and ERIC BERCOVICI
Directed By GARY NELSON

A STAN KALLIS, DAVID W. RINTELS, ERIC BERCOVICI PRODUCTION
IN ASSOCIATION WITH

Paramount
Television

Gulf + Western
Company

WASHINGTON
BEHIND CLOSED DOORS

THE COMPANY

A novel by

John Ehrlichman

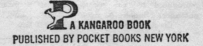 A KANGAROO BOOK
PUBLISHED BY POCKET BOOKS NEW YORK

THE COMPANY

Simon and Schuster edition published 1976

POCKET BOOK edition published May, 1977

2nd printing.........................July, 1977

The author wishes to thank Alfred A. Knopf, Inc., for kind permission to reprint lines from "Asides on the Oboe," by Wallace Stevens, from *Collected Poems of Wallace Stevens*, copyright, 1942, by Wallace Stevens.

This POCKET BOOK edition includes every word contained in the original, higher-priced edition. It is printed from brand-new plates made from completely reset, clear, easy-to-read type.

POCKET BOOK editions are published by
POCKET BOOKS,
a Simon & Schuster Division of
GULF & WESTERN CORPORATION
1230 Avenue of the Americas,
New York, N.Y. 10020.
Trademarks registered in the United States
and other countries.

ISBN: 0-671-81792-2.
Library of Congress Catalog Card Number: 76-2508.

This POCKET BOOK edition is published by arrangement with Simon & Schuster, Inc. Copyright, ©, 1976, by John Ehrlichman. All rights reserved. This book, or portions thereof, may not be reproduced by any means without permission of the original publisher: Simon & Schuster, Inc., 1230 Avenue of the Americas, New York, N.Y. 10020.

Printed in the U.S.A.

Author's Note

This is a story about people, events and the forces that impel them. The people are wholly fictional. But the forces—the stresses, pressures, fears and passions—that motivate the characters are real.

Santa Fe, 1975   J.D.E.

The prologues are over.   It is a question, now,
Of final belief.   So, say that final belief
Must be in a fiction.   It is time to choose.

WALLACE STEVENS, "Asides on the Oboe"

Prologue

The Oval Office was in a shambles—the door to the hall stood ajar, the guard was gone, and the passageway leading to the door was jammed with the chairs, couches, tables and other furniture that had been hurriedly removed from the President's office. The huge three-screen television console had been left but a faded quilted cover had been thrown over it and the family pictures usually displayed on top of the television cabinet were gone. The desk top was bare.

The curving west wall was inset with light-green bookshelves. Long ago some General Services Administration interior decorator had been called in to select sets of books to be placed on these shelves; he had chosen them for the color and design of their bindings, and had placed them, inert, between golden eagle bookends. Three china vases of obscure origin filled the gaps between the sets of books.

Apparently the President's thoughts had rested often on the opposite side of the room where French doors and tall windows opened the view to the White House residence and the snow-covered garden in between. In front of the windows was a totem-like cedar carving, a gift from constituents in the President's home state; it squatted there like a benign house god. Between the northernmost window and a curved door leading to the secretaries' room, columned pedestals held large bowls filled with fresh-cut flowers. On the walls on either side of the windows hung oil paintings of the mountains and forests of Oregon, selected by the President's wife from the National Gallery of Art.

The north end of the elliptical room was dominated by a fireplace of classic design. An oil portrait of Abraham Lincoln hung over it, mounted in an ornate frame a bit too heavy for the wall space. Most winter days there was a fire burning in the fireplace, but tonight there was no fire. The ashes had been removed and the bricks were swept clean.

Behind the desk were floor-to-ceiling rounded windows bordered by faded green damask drapes. Because the windows could be seen from the Washington Monument a thousand yards away, the Secret Service had installed green-tinted glass some five or six inches thick, which in daylight gave the outward view a pale aquamarine cast. Now the curved panes irritated the men in the room as the concave glass reflected the bright lights.

This night the President's room had been given over to sixteen sweating men. They moved grimly about their assigned tasks; most seemed not to care that they were working in a place held sacred by most Americans.

A great black cable, thicker than a man's arm, snaked from a plug in the outer hallway to a square camera on a wide tripod that dominated the center of the room. The green carpet, etched with the great seal of the President of the United States, was covered by a white canvas that lumped and bunched about the heavy cable. A man stumbled across it, cursing.

The French doors to the Rose Garden were open, but the cool evening air drifting in along the floor did not relieve the heat generated by the intense lights. Two silver reflectors, about three feet square, stood on tripods behind the camera. A gray-haired man was turning one of them to cast reflected light on a tall swarthy man in shirtsleeves who sat in the President's chair behind the desk; he grinned as he thought of where he was sitting. A long-haired lighting expert in Levi's and an embroidered jacket darted behind the man in the President's chair to adjust a small spotlight shining up from the floor. "One minute," someone yelled. All at once the frantically moving parts of the scene seemed to fall into some previously designated order. Shouting reduced to murmurs. The man in the chair rose, glanced back once quickly, then hurried out into the hall.

A door that had been built flush to the curving west wall swung open and a tall, raw-boned man in a dark-blue suit entered holding a notebook. He squinted into the lights and nodded to the men standing among the forests of equipment.

"Good evening, gentlemen."

"Good evening, sir."

He was ugly. The nose and ears were too big, the chin wide and thrusting, the teeth mottled and uneven. The knuckles of his huge hands were gnarled. He exuded power, vigor, toughness and, overall, a pervasive, crude inelegance. This was a strong machine with all the seams and rivets showing, built for performance, not looks.

As he sat down in the chair behind the massive desk, a waiting sound man clipped a tiny microphone to his tie and buttoned his coat over the thin wire. The heavy wooden desk had belonged to his predecessor, the late President William Arthur Curry, and recently had been donated to the White House by his young widow. The chair, oversized, extra tall, heavily padded and cushioned, had been especially tailored for Esker Anderson, Curry's successor. It was made to order, one of a kind, just as every President is one of a kind.

"Thirty seconds."

A makeup man moved to the President, dabbed his forehead to remove the sweat, and applied a chemical to inhibit perspiration. He scuttled away as a small loud-speaker on the floor near the door crackled.

"From the White House," the voice said, "a message from President Esker Scott Anderson. The White House has requested this network time tonight to bring his statement to the nation. No advance text has been released but we have been told by the President's press secretary that it will be a statement of historic importance to the nation. Ladies and gentlemen, the President of the United States."

A red light on top of the big camera went on.

The President hunched forward a little in his chair, grasped the near edge of the desk with both hands in a familiar pose and began to read aloud from the notebook lying open before him. The pages were thick, with unusually large holes to permit easy turning. Although Anderson wore contact lenses, the type was five times normal size. Tonight he was going to read it this way, from the notebook. No TelePrompTer, no idiot cards with big printing. There would be no attempt to make the performance appear spontaneous. Tonight it didn't matter. He would look at the camera when he could, marking his place in the text with his index finger when he glanced up. He would speak softly, letting quiet tones carry the emotion of the message to the listener, he thought to himself. Every American would remember this speech. It would go down in history, regardless of the delivery.

"My fellow Americans," he began, "for over thirty years I have been talking to you about our nation, first as a citizen, then as Senator and Vice President. They tell me that as your President I have spoken to the Great American Family forty-one times on television, just as I am doing tonight."

The President was known as a great stump speaker—and he would not lose this opportunity to string out the suspense. For the next ten minutes or so he spoke at length of his deep and abiding love for his land and his faith in America, despite the great rifts in the country caused by the war in Asia. He spoke slowly, with obvious deep feeling.

The President paused, then looked straight at the cameras and cleared his throat.

"Frankly, this is the hardest speech I have ever had to make to you. Some of you may know that I have recently been out to Walter Reed Hospital." The President paused again, reaching for the emotion being felt by his listeners.

"Well, now, those very fine doctors there examined me carefully, and, my friends, they've given me some bad news." His left hand nervously flicked across his face. "They tell me that I am ill and that, as they best can judge right now, I would not survive a second full term as President. They say that if I retire in January, go back home and take it easy, I just might live to a ripe old age. But if I stay here at this desk, someone else would certainly have to finish out my second term. That is, if you saw fit to return me to this house for a second term."

The cameraman shot a look at the lighting man by the door.

"I decided to tell you all this tonight myself. I felt that you should hear my decision from me and no one else."

The President hunched forward and looked up at the camera.

"I want you to understand that my affliction is not painful. Nor does it seem to impair my ability to come to grips with the hard decisions of this office, just as I always have. For that I am grateful. In these past four and a half years the challenges have been grave and the hours long but, because I love my country, I was looking forward to running for reelection next November as my party's nominee.

"Now, given the circumstances, I have decided that it would not be in the country's interest for me to do so, and I will therefore retire upon inauguration of my successor next January. I will, I promise you, do everything in my power to make the transition from my Administration to his a smooth one, whomever you may choose to succeed me.

"When I retire, Marta and I are going back to Oregon, back to our old house on Gleneden Beach. It's a beautiful place and I'll be happy to finish out the remaining days God chooses to give me there. We will look back on our years of public life, particularly our privileged years as occupants of this house, with much satisfaction. I ask for your support and God's blessing to see me through this time.

"Thank you and good night."

The TV camera followed the President as he rose and, looking neither to the right nor left, strode from the room.

Three thousand miles away in San Francisco, William Martin, the Director of Central Intelligence, sat staring at the screen. "Son of a bitch," he muttered.

The door to the living room of the hotel suite opened suddenly. Young Simon Cappell leaned into the bedroom, hand on the doorknob. "How about that, sir? He's quitting! My God, the Presidency is up for grabs!"

"Have the others gone?" Martin asked quietly as he continued to stare at the TV set.

Simon walked to the television and turned down the sound, leaving only the picture of the wrap-up commentator with an Ivy League look, obviously as surprised by the President's announcement as his listeners.

"All three men left before the speech ended, sir."

Martin turned from the set, rose and began to pace the length of the room, nervously cracking his knuckles.

"Simon, get us ready to return to Langley immediately. I want to leave in an hour."

"I'll have to cancel tomorrow's appointments," the aide said. "I may need a little more time if I have trouble reaching the people who were coming from Honolulu."

"You can call from the plane. Also, have the office begin to pull together an analysis of the domestic political situation with Esker Anderson out. I suppose Vice President Gilley will run, but I don't have a real feel for it. I want full files on everyone being mentioned. You're the office politician, Simon, with all your experience." A grin twitched at the corner of Martin's mouth.

Simon smiled broadly. "If I'm the political expert, we're all in big trouble, Mr. Director. I was only an advance man for a Vice Presidential candidate! And one who lost, at that. Some credentials! But I'll ride herd and have it for you as soon as I can."

Thin and wiry, balding before the age of thirty, Simon Cappell had let his dark hair grow out around his ears and over his collar at the back of his neck. His hawklike nose projected sharply from his face, but soft brown eyes and a rounded chin saved the look from being too harsh. He was an honor graduate of George Washington University, who had found his way to William Martin's service through the personal recommendation of a mutual friend. While attending school he had worked part time for the director of one of the regional commissions; it was this well-connected politician who had recommended Simon for his advance man's job during the last Presidential campaign. Simon had worked with enthusiasm for a Vice Presidential candidate for whom he felt no enthusiasm. He had found his candidate weak and unadmirable. But the logistical work fascinated him and he did it well. He was sensitive to the people in the towns and small cities to which his Vice Presidential candidate was sent. He genuinely liked them and although he did not consider himself a party man he got along well with the committees of local political workers.

Simon Cappell's ticket lost to Esker Scott Anderson and Ed Gilley. But Simon had been noticed during the campaign by one of William Martin's closest Harvard friends. The result was a letter of recommendation to Martin, and a job at the CIA.

Now Simon was Martin's aide, staff assistant, executive helper and general right hand. He supervised the flow of paper in and out of Martin's office, diverting and referring all the written work that the Director didn't really have to see. Cappell arranged his boss's appointments, took many of his telephone calls, made sure he was "briefed up" on what his meetings would involve before Martin attended, and acted as a buffer between the Director and his thousands of employees to screen out those who didn't absolutely have to take the head man's time. He traveled with Martin on all out-of-town trips (after making the reservations and arrangements), saw that the trip schedule went smoothly, kept the office back home informed of the Director's decisions and needs, arranged for couriers to keep the out-of-town paper flow coming, and made sure the laundry was sent out on time so that Martin was never without a clean shirt.

William Martin stood up. "And I want Horace McFall to meet me for lunch tomorrow. Tell him it's urgent."

It was more than urgent, he thought: it was critical. With Esker Scott Anderson gone, there could be a new Director of Central Intelligence. And then the hindsight muckraking would begin. By God, thought Martin, that just couldn't happen.

The past must remain sealed in the closed black notebooks in their closed gray filing cabinets in the stainless-steel vault deep under the ground. A new President could make the Primula Report public knowledge. Sensational revelations and double-standard hindsight could make the Primula Report a weapon that would destroy the Company and, with it, William Martin.

could make the Pinball Role ... how many ...
... and ... foreign could
... U.S. Company ... with ... William Weld

1

During the twenty-four years of his Government service, William Martin had served administrations of both political parties.

Though not partisan, Martin was not without personal preferences. At Harvard he had decided that the Republican ideology of his father was too inflexible for his tastes, and he found Franklin D. Roosevelt's show of progressive political initiative exciting. By his senior year he considered himself a New Dealer when he joined the Office of Strategic Services. His father had gone to school with the director of the new foreign intelligence operation, the OSS, and they had remained close friends. The OSS Director had put many of his friends and their sons on his recruiting lists. Martin turned out to be a lucky choice.

High-school and Harvard football and the rigorous OSS physical training had shaped him well. He was a medium-sized man, broad shouldered, narrow at the hips, with thick arms and wrists. In his youth his hair had been bright red, but it had darkened and thinned as he added years and a few inches to his waistline.

His broad forehead, rusty-golden eyebrows, green-flecked eyes and a generously wide mouth combined to make his twice-broken nose less noticeable. The total effect during his Harvard years was rugged, not quite handsome; more than one Radcliffe girl had found his overall appearance irresistible.

Because he spoke Spanish fluently, his first OSS post was in Argentina, where he posed as a junior clerk in the Buenos Aires branch of a New York bank.

In the late 1940s the OSS became the Central Intelligence Group, and William Martin was asked to stay aboard. He recognized the chance for an interesting career and figured he could make the pay stretch with the aid of a little private income.

Most of Martin's years of foreign intelligence service were in Latin America. For nearly a year after V-E day Bill Martin had worked in Buenos Aires as a member of an intelligence team assigned to the pursuit of high-ranking refugees from Nazi Germany. Martin's "cover," to explain his presence in Argentina, was a commission as a captain in the United States Army, and he was assigned to the Embassy as an assistant military attaché. Toward the end of that time Martin was ordered to recruit, develop and manage a string of intelligence agents, most of whom were active on the Atlantic coast of South America.

In the late fifties Martin was recalled to Washington, and before long he had an office in the sprawling, modern CIA "campus" at Langley, Virginia, across the Potomac and upstream a mile or two from the capital city. The seven-story main building covered the equivalent of about two city blocks, and one of its accessory buildings was a geodesic dome that was used as an auditorium. Deep below the ground were the rooms and tunnels that provided vast storage areas for the computer tapes, films and documents which were the grist for the Company's mill.

The Congress had been unknowingly generous in its appropriation for the construction of the Langley campus and the Company's budget people had been unusually adroit in the diversion of available funds to the project. As a result, the CIA's buildings were lavishly decorated and appointed. A privileged visitor would take away an impression of space, marble, glass and polished metal not often experienced in other Government buildings around Washington. But there were not many such visitors. Triple fencing surrounded the hundreds of acres of forest, lawns, and gardens. No buildings were visible from any public roads, and the entry lanes were identified by misleading signs. Guardhouses, patrols of guards and dogs and an elaborate underground grid of sensory wires insured against trespassers. Even invited guests were always kept closely in hand, escorted to and from their destination by a security agent and never permitted to wander in the halls.

Martin's promotions at Langley were rapid. By the time William Arthur Curry, President Anderson's predecessor, was elected, Bill Martin was Special Assistant to the Director of the CIA, Horace McFall.

Bill Martin had never met Senator William Arthur Curry before Curry became President of the United States. But from the political biographies, the magazine profiles and news stories, and the Company files on the handsome, wealthy and articulate young Senator and his family, there was very little about the Currys that William Martin didn't know.

Martin had been attracted to Curry during a bitter campaign in New York State. As a political newcomer Curry had bucked the New York Democratic organization and won the Governor's seat. His storybook upset victory made him the youngest Governor in New York history. Although the son of a rich and conservative capitalist, Billy Curry spoke movingly of the poor, the disenfranchised and the hungry. And he promised change.

Curry was not Governor for long. The senior United States Senator from New York died during Curry's second year in office and William Arthur Curry resigned the Governorship, and by prearrangement with his Lieutenant Governor, had himself appointed to the Senate.

He was elected Senator at the next election by a landslide.

During his first full term in the Senate Billy Curry began to campaign actively in the Presidential primary states. He went to the next Democratic convention with more delegates than any other contender, but he lacked enough votes to be nominated.

Old Esker Scott Anderson had delegates too. The convention faced a deadlock until, in a secret meeting with Curry's father, Esker Anderson blinked first. Some said the elder Curry paid Anderson a lot of money. Others said he just bluffed Anderson out of the balloting. Neither Curry nor Esker Anderson ever told anyone what really took place at that meeting, but Senator Esker Scott Anderson dramatically threw his support to young Billy Curry after the first ballot, and that did it. Curry was nominated on the second ballot and soon announced that his choice for his party's nominee for Vice President was Esker Scott Anderson. It was a logical choice, the anchor men all told their television audiences. Curry was from New York, Anderson from the West Coast. Curry was young, Anderson nearly sixty. Curry was liberal, his running mate more conservative. Curry was rich, Anderson came from humble beginnings. Curry's wife was young and glamorous. Mrs. Marta Anderson epitomized the all-American homemaker.

Curry and Anderson campaigned across the country, in their different styles, with great effect. Curry was devastating on television and in the great halls before friendly crowds. Esker Anderson was the master flesh-presser. He was in his element at the county fair, the fund-raising cocktail party and the small-town rally.

When Curry and Anderson were elected, Bill Martin was pleased. He had developed a close relationship with Senator Esker Scott Anderson and knew he could only be helped by Anderson's elevation. And he admired

Billy Curry in the way he had admired Franklin D. Roosevelt.

Curry was President of the United States for only two years and eight months. On a Friday evening in September a weary manufacturer's representative flying his single engine Cessna home from Boston to Rochester collided with Air Force One as the President's airplane began its descent to Glens Falls, New York. The President's wife, Jenna Curry, had been at Lake George all week, and her young husband was flying to be with her for the weekend. The tail was torn from his great silver-and-blue aircraft and he died in a field of cornstalks near Cobleskill, New York. Others died, too: the military air crew, a doctor and the Secret Service detail, six members of the White House staff, two secretaries, the President's cousin and a white dog named Arty. And a Major General of the United States Army. His name was Alfred Eugenio Primula. At the time of his death he was the Inspector General of the CIA and the author of the Primula Report.

Within minutes of Billy Curry's death, Esker Scott Anderson was sworn in as President of the United States.

It had been on a trip to the Broadmoor Hotel in Colorado Springs, long before Anderson became Vice President, that William Martin had first watched Senator Esker Anderson up close.

By his own admission Esker Scott Anderson was as qualified to be President as a lifetime of public service could make a man. He had been elected Senator from the State of Oregon four times. Before Anderson became Vice President, his phenomenal reputation had been built on a combination of electoral invincibility and monumental self-confidence. He always won by big margins, and each time he won, his belief in himself grew. A reelection, to Esker Anderson, was the ultimate absolution for all past sins. And so, as the pluralities increased in successive elections, Anderson's political horizons and self-esteem expanded in geometric proportion.

Few Roman emperors confidently gathered to themselves more perquisites than did Chairman Esker Scott Anderson of the Senate Appropriations Committee. By the time Chairman Anderson became Vice President Anderson the all-time Senate records for the most staff, the largest committee budget, the prettiest secretaries and the best foreign trips were held, hands down, by the senior Senator from Oregon. It was his view that these trappings were his as a matter of right.

In the official Senate records the Broadmoor trip was booked as an inspection of the CIA's training facility at Fort Collins, Colorado, by the Intelligence Oversight Subcommittee of the Senate Appropriations Committee, of which subcommittee Senator Esker Anderson was also the chairman. And, in fact, Bill Martin and three men from the Company's Division of Plans did take Anderson and two other Senators to Fort Collins by helicopter on two different days during their week at the Broadmoor.

The CIA Director, Horace McFall, had chosen the facilities for the junket with care. No hotel in Denver would have provided the Senators with the luxury, cuisine and resort atmosphere the Broadmoor offered. The suites looked out at the Rockies, looming over a small, brilliant blue lake. The hotel staff, trained in Europe, knew how to care for United States Senators. Lavish luncheons, served on the terraces of the senatorial suites, included Rhine wine, Mexican strawberries and trout from a stocked hotel pond. The waiters hovered in constant attendance, supervised by the French maître d'hôtel himself. The suites, cars, drivers, golf pros, trips to a stocked fishing stream, the ice chests to carry the trout back to Washington, were all designed to promote senatorial happiness. It was no wonder that on his arrival Director McFall found his distinguished guests beaming.

Chairman Anderson was suitably accompanied on the trip by his staff and family. Although Esker Anderson had an established reputation among senatorial colleagues as a raconteur of off-color stories, he was perhaps better known in Washington circles as a clandestine lover on the grand scale. At various times in his Senate career he was believed to be keeping three ladies satisfied, more or less simultaneously.

Apparently deaf to all the gossip, Marta Anderson always behaved as though she'd never heard a single one of the dozens of stories of her husband's amorous escapades that constantly made the Washington rounds. Though gossip linked Esker Anderson with women from all walks of life, his closest liaisons were said to be with the young ladies of his office staff. It was clear that they were chosen for their beauty. Rumor had it that if they presented the Chairman no special problems during their tenure they attained a unique kind of job security. It delighted the powerful Senator to concern himself with the continuing welfare of the young women from his loyal staff even after they had left his little official family. Many were placed in excellent positions with Government agencies as a result of Anderson's sponsorship. Some were given good jobs with the large corporations that maintained public-affairs offices in Washington. And the Chairman took great pleasure in introducing his protégées to eligible young men of whom he approved. Some of the capital's most noteworthy marriages, while not truly made in heaven, at least could be said to have been made under the genial auspices of Chairman Esker Scott Anderson.

Since Marta Anderson and the two Anderson sons had come to Colorado with the Chairman, on this trip he was a family man. Five members of his staff were brought along as well, as a reward for faithful service. It was on the Air Force 707 that carried the senatorial party to Colorado Springs that Bill Martin first noticed a tall brunette with well-turned legs and a long, beautiful face. The pilot's manifest identified her as Linda Winton, secretary to the Chairman. When the plane was airborne and level Bill walked back to the galley.

"Any coffee?" he asked a steward in a bright-blue blazer. "I missed breakfast."

"Yes, Mr. Martin. I'm doing waffles for Senator Mihara. Can I fix you some?"

"No, thanks, Sergeant, I'll settle for two coffees to go."

A complete kitchen had been built into the end of the cabin area. Ovens, a stove top and sink and a large refrigerator-freezer made it possible for the stewards to prepare almost anything on order. This Air Force jet, from the President's fleet based at Andrews Air Force Base in Maryland, was kept in constant readiness for the emergency evacuation of the President's staff in the event of threatened attack on Washington. At times it was loaned for the use of influential ranking members of Congress or the Cabinet. The White House was always pleased to make it available to Chairman Anderson on request.

Carrying two large china mugs, Bill walked past the built-in bunks and paneled office area to the rows of seats where the Senator's staff and their families were sitting. He slid into the empty seat beside Linda Winton and handed her a coffee.

"Courtesy of the management. I'm Bill Martin of the CIA." He smiled.

Her return smile was warm as she took the mug from him. "You read my mind. Thanks, Mr. Martin." There was a hint of Southern softness to her voice. "I'm Linda Winton."

"Yes, I know. I looked at the manifest. We have our sources, you know. And call me Bill, Linda."

She smiled again. "This is my first trip to the Broadmoor. I hear it's quite a place."

Sensing an invitation in her words, Martin offered his services as guide, porter, wrangler and escort, but her response was noncommittal. As the plane sped westward they talked easily about Washington, home towns, Linda's schooling and career, her new apartment in McLean, not far from the CIA, restaurants, food and books.

As the young woman talked, she occasionally moved her right hand from her cup to rest it on Martin's arm for emphasis. Once she grasped his hand in hers in expressing her delight at a book she had read and enjoyed. Martin was immediately aware of her easy sensuality. They got on well; the time passed quickly as they warmed to each other.

Senator Esker Anderson had walked by them twice, glancing first at Linda, then at Martin, saying nothing. On a third pass he returned from the front lounge section with a sheaf of typed pages in disarray. Reaching brusquely across Martin he dropped them in Linda's lap.

"This goddamn report is all out of order. Do you think you can tear yourself away from this handsome young stud long enough to do some work?" The smile that followed the drawled question was cold, the lips tight.

"Certainly, Mr. Chairman," she said evenly.

Bill rose and climbed out into the aisle. "Mr. Chairman, I'm Bill Martin. I've appeared before the Oversight Committee a couple of times but there's no reason why you should remember me."

Anderson looked at him blankly, ignoring Martin's opening.

"Linda," Anderson went on, "when you are done with that report, come into the forward cabin. Marta has some letters she needs help with." He turned abruptly and went into the forward lounge occupied by the other Senators and their families.

"Well, there goes the Company appropriation," said Martin grimly, sliding back into his seat.

"Oh, I don't think it's quite that bad." Linda smiled wanly. "We all have our problems, don't we?" She looked at the papers on her lap. "Why don't I give you a ring after I get settled at the hotel?"

As the days passed, Bill Martin did occasionally see Linda at the Broadmoor, but only during the leftover hours. Senator Anderson clearly had first claim on her attention; he had obviously sensed her interest in Martin on the plane, and it seemed to Martin that her boss was making sure she didn't have much free time during their stay. Martin doubted that there really was all that much work to do on a trip of this kind, but he was careful not to urge Linda to give him time she couldn't or wouldn't freely give.

On brief acquaintance he found Linda to be a charming companion, warm, attractive and comfortable to be with, but if Esker Anderson had any kind of claim to her, Bill Martin wasn't about to get involved. There were two good reasons why he would not be interested. A powerful Senator like Anderson, who virtually controlled the Company budget and legislation, could cause fatal problems for a career Government employee. Who but a Peace Corps do-gooder would want to be stationed in Nigeria? But, on a less pragmatic level, Anderson was physically repugnant and Martin found it impossible to accept a romantic relationship between Anderson and Linda—or for that matter, anyone. If she was his, Martin would look elsewhere.

Late one night, during one of those "leftover hours"

when Bill Martin and Linda Winton were the last remaining customers at a dark little bar in Colorado Springs, studiously ignoring the bartender's broad hints that he'd like to go home, Martin finally probed Linda's feelings toward Esker Anderson.

"There must be something in the man that I don't see. He attracts good people to work for him. But he seems so gross and crude to me. What's he really like, Linda?"

Linda shook her head slowly. "I'm not sure I can answer that, Bill. Esker Anderson is a chameleon. He's one person to his constituents, another to people like you in the Government, still another to his family."

"But what's he like to you?" Martin pressed.

"He can really be very gentle and genuine and charming when he wants to be." She paused, then slowly stirred her ice with a finger. "I think deep inside he's a genuinely good man."

"He buries it pretty damn well when I'm around. Do *you* find him personally attractive?"

"I don't care for his public person at all. That's the side he'd always show around you, I suppose. You may never know him any other way. Some of us see him at unguarded times, and he is really different." She sighed. "I don't think I'm explaining it well."

She had ducked the question. Martin wanted to believe that Linda was only a loyal Anderson employee, nothing more. Why wouldn't she answer the question? It was unbelievable that she was his mistress. But Senator Anderson's deliberate preemption of her time, apparently out of jealousy, made Martin very, very cautious.

After they returned to Washington, the unlisted phone number that Linda had given Martin went unused. He continued to see the covey of ladies already on his active list with whom he could be seen without the risk of incurring powerful senatorial displeasure.

About a month after the Colorado trip Linda called Bill Martin and invited him to escort her to a party. But Martin, still cautious, decided to try to find out more.

"Let's meet for a drink this afternoon and talk about it, lovely Linda. How about Duke's around five?"

"I don't have a car today. Can you run me home to McLean afterward?"

He promised he would. And later, over drinks, he flatly and frankly told her his concerns about Esker Anderson and his own career. "If you're Anderson's girl, you're big trouble for me. I really like you a great deal, Linda. I feel we could have something good together. But I have to know, and I don't know how to be sure except to ask you."

She looked at her drink, stirred the ice with her finger —a habit he had already noticed—then looked up at him with a poker face. "Esker Anderson knows that I'm here now, Bill. And he knows that you are going to take me home tonight. And he knows that I've invited you to the party. I haven't had a chance to tell you; it's at the Andersons' home." She burst out laughing. "He knows I'm after you, you poor man, and that I usually get what I go after. Anderson's been like an uncle to me, not a lover, if that's what's been bothering you. I know all the stories that go around about him and the girls in the office. Some of them are true, I know for a fact. But any stories about me would be outright lies."

Martin set his drink down, a broad smile creasing his face as he covered her hand.

"You have nothing to fear from him, Bill. Actually he likes you. He's glad that I'm bringing you to their place next week—if you'll come. But you haven't really told me that you'll take me yet."

Martin had heard what he wanted to hear. When he

took Linda home that night he parked his car in an all-night zone.

At Senator Anderson's party the host took Martin aside during the evening to bless the new union—in the crudest of terms. Martin was not shocked; he had expected something of the sort.

A few months later Linda moved from McLean to Georgetown, about a block from Bill Martin's place, but she didn't spend much time at her new apartment. From the time Linda moved across the river, she and Bill were an established Washington pair.

Esker Anderson cultivated the young couple, including them in frequent invitations, phoning Martin at work to warn him of hidden problems for the Company which had come to the Chairman's attention. Martin, in turn, began scratching Anderson's back. There was no question that he was one Senator who could advance Martin's career at the Company. And so Senator Anderson began to see copies of confidential reports; he received informal briefings and was telephoned by Martin from time to time with advance information.

Martin didn't consider this leaking information. He rationalized that the then Senator, later Vice President, was, after all, as entitled to the information as the others who would get it. And Esker Anderson knew how to use such information discreetly, always protecting his sources. He avoided the cheap shot and the premature press release characteristic of the Washington neophyte. Rarely did Anderson display his inside knowledge in public. He used it wisely to be ahead of events, to anticipate problems, to avoid pitfalls and to enhance his reputation for invincible power among his colleagues.

As William Martin and the Senator became better acquainted their conversations ranged over the countries of the world and into the shadowed caverns and catacombs of the Federal Government. But Rio de Muerte was one subject never discussed. The Senator knew that Martin had much of the responsibility for planning the disastrous Dominican operation, but he sensed that his increasingly profitable relationship with Martin would be impaired if he asked about it.

Neither the Senator nor William Martin could then foresee the extraordinary events which would force them to talk together about Rio de Muerte and the Primula Report.

The Rio de Muerte was a shallow brown river that entered the Caribbean at the back of a wide cove called the Bay of Glass. Because of the compact white sand and absence of coral reefs, the calm bay was considered an ideal location for an amphibious military landing. An Interagency Planning Committee of men from the Departments of Defense and State, the U.S. intelligence community and two representatives of the Free Dominican Committee approved a CIA staff plan for a full-scale attack there. The plan was carried to Horace McFall by William Martin, since Martin was then Chairman of the Interagency Committee. McFall and Martin took the plan to the President, explained it to him and left with Billy Curry's approval for the entire operation.

It was "Operation Walrus" until it failed. When the death count was released the failure took the name of the muddy little river in the lurid press accounts that followed. Even the official reports and Government memoranda began calling the operation the "River of Death," and the code name was forgotten.

In the same way the official CIA Inspector General's report on how it all went wrong took the name of its author. It was originally entitled "Report of the Inspector General on the Rio de Muerte Operation," but now everyone called it the Primula Report.

It was characterized as a report for the President.

What he would do with it was up to him, the press was told.

About the time the Primula Report came to the Director's hands President Curry was acutely feeling the pressure. In the Congress and the press there were demands that blame be fixed. Esker Anderson, who was then the Vice President, urged that Horace McFall be retired at once to cool some of the heat on the White House. And, after all, Horace was over seventy. By the time McFall handed the Primula Report to President Curry, the President was ready to ask the gray-haired Director for his immediate resignation. When Curry told the Vice President of his decision to turn the old Director out, Anderson immediately proposed Bill Martin as McFall's replacement.

The press correctly assumed that McFall was the scapegoat for the Rio de Muerte disaster, and that was the way they wrote it. McFall cleaned out his desk and was out of the Director's office at the Company in three days. He retired in total silence, refusing to comment on a CBS television report that, in his meeting with the President, McFall had been fired with hard words from William Arthur Curry. The White House press secretary also maintained silence, saying only that a successor would be nominated soon.

Four days later President Curry was dead and Esker Scott Anderson had been sworn in as his successor. And less than forty-eight hours after the sad and hurried ceremony in Anderson's apartment, William received a call from the new President's appointments secretary summoning him to the White House. When Martin's car pulled up at the southwest gate to the White House grounds a policeman went back into his small white guardhouse to telephone for instructions. In a moment he returned and leaned into the driver's window.

"Mr. Martin, kindly back up twenty-five yards and I

will have the south gate opened for you. You are to drive right up to the residence to see the President, sir."

Another policeman walked over and opened a rarely used gate in the fence that was at right angles to the main southwest gate. Martin's car slowly moved along a driveway that crossed the south lawn and curved toward the familiar White House south facade. A black usher in wing collar and tails stood by the diplomatic entrance in the center of the ground floor.

"Mr. Martin, come this way, sir," he said as he opened the door.

He led the way through an oval-shaped reception room brightened with hand-painted French wallpaper. They crossed a broad, red-carpeted and windowless hallway, then passed through a narrow doorway into a foyer at the foot of a flight of steps. The butler gestured Martin into a small elevator.

"The President left word you were to come up to his bedroom, sir. His valet will meet you."

The elevator was very slow. Its walls were delicately inlaid with fine woods and strips of mirror glass. Martin wondered why this exquisite decoration had been obscured by a collection of framed etchings of the White House, arranged on both side walls. At last the door eased open and Martin was greeted by a smiling Filipino in a blue blazer and gray slacks.

"President just waking up, sar. Come, please."

The valet led Martin to a door just across the wide hall from the elevator alcove. He knocked once and Esker Scott Anderson's voice boomed, "Come in."

The plain bedroom, by hotel standards, was not large. The walls and ceiling were painted white; dark-blue curtains covered the windows that faced south across the ellipse to the Washington Monument.

The new President, wearing a light-blue pajama coat, the top buttons open to expose his milk-white chest and belly, had just ended his customary afternoon nap. He reached under his armpit to scratch his side.

"Come in, Bill, come in. I want to talk to you." His voice was still thick with sleep.

"Mr. President," Bill began formally, "please allow me to congratulate you; also, to express my grief at the President's—at President Curry's—death. I am—"

Anderson cut him off with a raised hand.

"I know what you thought of Curry, Bill. And I can tell you the admiration was mutual. He told me so, just six or seven days ago."

The President's comment brought Martin to a sudden sense of deep sadness. He had been shocked when he heard of Curry's death. Curry was, in a way, his only remaining hero. But there had been so many things to be done quickly at the Company that there had been no time then for emotional self-examination. Here in Esker Anderson's bedroom, for the first time Martin was filled with a sense of loss and loneliness so overpowering that he found it impossible to reply.

Anderson's next words jolted Martin out of his remorse and reverie. "Bill, I want you to be my Director of the CIA."

Martin looked at the President sharply.

"Surprised, Bill?" Anderson smiled paternally. "You shouldn't be. After all, we've always gotten on well." He waved at a blue Victorian chair. "Sit down over there— no, pull it over here by me. You had better understand some basic things about how I intend to operate before you tell me you'll accept. I'm a very goddamned different person than Bill Curry was. People may think they know that, but they don't know the half of it. Your old boss Horace McFall is a nice enough man but he couldn't have been my CIA Director. I want someone over there who will be spending most of his time looking out for me, Bill, and by Christ I think you're the man to do it."

Anderson eased himself closer to the edge of the bed

and jabbed a finger at Martin. "Don't look so worried, Bill, I'm going to look out for you, too. I'm not going to let the goddamned Rio de Muerte fiasco become a problem for you. I want you to be an effective Director over at Langley. As far as I'm concerned I never heard of General Primula or his goddamned report."

Anderson smiled thinly. "As Linda's probably told you, I'm a pretty good fellow to work for. I take care of my people. All I ask in return is that they take care of me. Understood, Bill?"

Martin stood up, still very shaken by his delayed emotional reaction to Curry's death, and at the same time fully aware of the implications of the deal the new President had just offered. This crude man who sat on Curry's bed was proposing that Martin deliver up the Central Intelligency Agency to him, for his own purposes. A quid pro quo. Rio de Muerte for complete control of the CIA. Fear and anger swept over him. There was no question of what he had to do. In Esker Anderson jargon, the President had him by the short hairs.

Martin forced a smile. "You've got yourself a new Director, Mr. President. Thank you."

The President nodded solemnly. "I know you'll do a good job, Bill. Be sure to talk to the NSC people about proposed staff changes, but you'll have a very free hand. Just one thing. When you move into Horace's fancy office and get his big limousine, don't forget who you work for. I'll see you later."

"Thank you, Mr. President." The conversation was ended.

As he rode back down in the elevator with the usher, Bill Martin felt very warm. He had begun to flush when Anderson mentioned Primula, his mind swirling with questions. Had Anderson seen the Primula Report? Had McFall left it with Curry for any length of time? Could Anderson have received it from Curry? What did Anderson know—really know? How much of a hold did Anderson have on him?

When his car slid up to the diplomatic entrance Martin reached for the red telephone mounted on the floor hump. He pressed a button on the receiver.

"Sir?"

"Simon Cappell, 1141."

"Stand by, please."

In a matter of moments his assistant's voice came on the line.

Martin's tone told his aide it was urgent. "Simon, listen carefully. I'm on my way to the office. Meet me as soon as I get there. And find out how we reach Horace today. Ask Tony, Jim and Arnold to wait for me also."

"What about your appointments, sir?"

"Cancel all of them. And cancel any personal plans you may have for tonight."

"Yes, sir."

As his car crossed the Potomac, the Director-designate began to make his plans. Simon would stay with him, he thought, but he would have to make changes. And above all, he would have to get hold of the Primula Report and make sure it stayed buried.

The day following his visit with the new President, Martin met with Horace McFall to ask him if Esker Anderson had ever seen the Primula Report. McFall was certain he had not. The late President Curry had read the entire report straight through for nearly an hour, in McFall's presence, and had immediately handed it back to him. No one else had seen it.

"What the hell did Curry say, Horace?" Martin persisted.

McFall lit his pipe slowly. His neat moustache, wire-rimmed glasses and closed face had always made him look both honorable and reliable, like a country lawyer who knows everybody's secrets. "He said only, 'General

Primula was a smart son of a bitch.' Then Curry told me to quit. Immediately. Said he needed a vacancy for someone else. But he was complimentary about me," McFall continued. "Offered me a job with his family foundation if I needed money."

Martin tried to nail McFall down. "Did he say whether he would talk to anyone else about it?"

"No," the Director said emphatically. "I got the impression he wouldn't. He said I must never say a word. He swore me to secrecy. I got the impression he intended to put a tight cork in the bottle."

Martin had begun to sense he was pressing McFall too hard. "Did he order you to destroy it?"

"Odd thing." McFall framed his words slowly. "He asked how many sets of copies there were. When I told him I was sure there were no copies, only the original, he said 'Good. Put it in your safe for your successor. I'll talk to him about what to do with it.' "

"And then?"

"He was dead within a few days of our meeting."

Martin was drawn into more insistent questioning almost in spite of himself. "But you didn't put it in the Director's safe, did you, Horace?"

"Well, no, Bill, not exactly." McFall leaned forward and spoke earnestly. "That is, I put it in there when I got back from the White House that day, but I took it out again. When the President was killed, it changed things. Primula's report was more than an inside assessment then. It was really a piece of history."

"So you logged it into the permanent Company archives." Martin's mind was probing for a gap; how could Esker Anderson have seen the report?

"Yes, but not in the regular way. Only the Director has access to that report, as you probably know. It's under seal and only the Security man has the access combinations. Other hot stuff is kept the same way. Nothing as hot as this, of course, but hot all the same."

"Horace, Curry must have told some people about Primula's report. Could he have told Anderson?"

"I suppose he did in very vague terms—that there was a report. I did too, in fact. The Senate Oversight Committee had me on the pan right after the Rio de Muerte massacre, as you know. I told them the Inspector General was looking into how it happened and that the President would get a report."

Martin let out a sharp breath. "So that's how Anderson heard of it.'

McFall smiled wryly. "That could've been one way. But there's been plenty of talk in Washington about a damaging report floating around—though nobody knows what's *in* it. Only Primula and Curry and I really knew, and, of course, Primula died with the President. He was supposed to talk to the President about the report during that airplane trip, you know."

After McFall left, the Director-designate phoned Dave Ashley, the Assistant Director for Security, to arrange an inspection of the Company vaults. It had been years since Martin had seen them, he explained. It seemed like a good idea to get around the building before the new job had him completely tied up.

And so that same afternoon Ashley led the Director-designate to the rear of the CIA sub-basement storage area. Martin was required to show the guard in the bulletproof booth his plastic lapel badge, then was logged in on the inevitable clipboard, heard the locks release and pushed the turnstile gate on its pivot to enter a hallway three floors below the ground. A combination and two keys tumbled the huge lock on the bank-vault door. Within the safe room were six ordinary metal file cabinets.

When Martin was seated at a table at one side of the vault, Ashley brought him the contents of each file drawer, one by one.

About forty minutes elapsed during which Martin,

feigning deep concentration, made a cursory inspection of the piles of documents, occasionally making notes on a pad. Finally Ashley handed Martin three black note-books labeled "Report of the Inspector General on the Rio de Muerte Operation." Martin tried not to let his emotion show as he reached for the first volume.

The table of contents showed the arrangement of topics, with a separate security classification for each section of the report. The chapters on Scope, Methodology of Investigation, Operation Objectives, Planning, Modifications and Conduct of Operation were all stamped BYEM, an extremely limited Company access classification. This meant that fewer than a hundred people in the country would be permitted to read what was there. Other legends insured that the restrictions on access would never be changed without the CIA Director's personal approval.

Martin saw that some of the headings on the second page of the index were enclosed in a red cross-hatch box and stamped "DCI Eyes Only": to be read only by the Director and no one else.

```
Classification:  BYEM (No downgrade)
     To:         The Director of
                 Central Intelligence
     From:       Inspector General A. E.
                 Primula
     Subject:    Rio de Muerte:
                 retrospective
                 investigations, analysis
                 and conclusions


                 Contents

Volume I
     Scope of Assignment
     Methodology Used
```

Objectives of the R d M Operation
The Original Operation Plan
Modifications Adopted Prior to
    Landing
The Operation as Conducted

<u>Volume II</u> (A) Departures from the
                Plan
          1. Air cover
          2. The death of Fr. Julio
              Benitimes
          3. F-D infantry inertia
              and collapse
         (B) Comparative Analysis
          1. Pre-landing
              intelligence
              estimates and actual
              field findings

<u>Volume III</u>   Assignment of
                Responsibility
         (A) Causes of failure
          1. The White House role
    DCI   2. The murder of Fr.
              Benitimes
    Eyes 3. The actions of the
              Division of Plans, CIA
    Only
         (B) Conclusions of the
              Inspector General

Martin glanced over at Ashley as he pulled Volume
III in front of him. The Assistant Director, back turned
to Martin, appeared to be rearranging the file-cabinet
drawers. As Martin opened the volume to the section
labeled "Conclusions of the Inspector General" and
began to read rapidly, he felt a sudden surge of warmth
through his whole body. Although he thought he was

prepared for what he would read there, he was surprised at the physical reaction he was experiencing. He was excessively warm; his palms were sweating. His nerves were taut. This thing was hitting him hard.

The bond paper was in mint condition; the typing was perfect—clear and black and double spaced. Martin saw his name in the first paragraph, with President Curry's name and Father Benitimes' and Durwood Drew's and Nikolai Menshikoff's.

I have concluded that there is a direct, proximate relationship between (1) the failure of the landing at Rio de Muerte, (2) a number of decisions and instructions by President Curry, (3) the murder of a priest who served as chaplain and inspirational advisor to the landing military forces (Father Julio Benitimes) and (4) President Curry's winter summit conference this year with Nikolai Menshikoff, First Secretary of the USSR. William Martin (SA to DCI) was President Curry's conduit for the instructions given concerning the landing and the murder.

How many sleepless nights had Martin speculated, fearing the ugly words on these pages? He had known that General Primula would criticize him—through four successive interviews the Inspector General's attitude toward Martin had become increasingly hostile—but the text was far worse than he had imagined it would be. He read it and reread it.

I conclude that the R d M landing failed because of the murder of Father Benitimes during the hour just prior to

commencement of the landing. Our interviews with many Free Dominican soldiers
establish that this priest was the
central symbol and inspiration to the
very superstitious and rather simple men
recruited for this landing.

When Fr. Benitimes was stabbed the
word passed among the troops on all
three ships like lightning. Morale
among the officers and men of the landing force plummeted. They were landed
on the beaches no more than an hour
after the priest died. They failed to
mount an aggressive advance, and the
Dominican regime defenders were able to
mobilize and move an entire division of
infantry to Rio de Muerte before night-
fall.

The F.D. officers in charge of the
landing objected to going forward with
the landing in view of Fr. Benitimes'
murder.

Their request for delay was made to
Durwood Drew, acting ops-in-charge for
the CIA, who was aboard the flagship
Duluth Victory.

In view of the extraordinary aspects
of the problem Drew referred the details
and request for delay to Acting Director
of the R d M operation Wm. Martin by
scramble phone. A review of the record-
ings of that call establish beyond
question that Martin immediately rejected the request for delay and ordered
the operation to proceed as planned.

There is likewise little room for
doubt that Mr. Martin gave those in-

structions pursuant to the standing
directions which had been directly given
to him by President Curry in a personal
conversation the previous day.

The writer has not been permitted to
question President Curry about his
reasons for his instructions to Martin
concerning this operation, therefore my
conclusions must necessarily depend on
Wm. Martin's statements and deduction
from extrinsic events which are known.

One can only deduce the President's
motives from what he indicated to
Martin.

The report was hard on President Curry. Hard on
Bill Martin. All together, it was very, very bad.

In extensive interviews with me Martin
said that he had been ordered by the
President, personally, to cause the
death of Fr. Benitimes before the priest
left the ship. The President based his
order expressly on "the highest national
security and foreign relations consider-
ations" and swore Martin to secrecy.
Martin was alone with the President at
the time.

In my second interview with Wm. Martin
I asked how the President knew the
identity of the priest. Martin answered
that President Curry had not designated
Benitimes by name but had asked for the
identity of the "inspirational leader of
the F.D. forces." Martin had replied
with Fr. Benitimes' name. The President
then asked eight or nine questions about

the priest's role in the F.D. movement,
his personal history, and his relationship to the Roman Catholic Church. It
was after Martin had answered these
questions that the President issued his
liquidation instructions.

I conclude that the President had
decided to insure the failure of the
operation while, at the same time, not
calling it off.

William Martin provided President
Curry with the information which led to
Fr. Benitimes being designated by name
to be the victim.

After the President's order was given,
Martin admits, it was not questioned.
Martin promptly called his assistant,
Durwood Drew, on the flagship from the
President's office. Drew was given the
assignment; in the conversation they
discussed methods which might be used.
They agreed that a knife was the most
practical, given the crowded conditions
aboard the ship.

So far as I can determine only Martin,
Drew and the President knew of the
President's orders. With President
Curry unavailable to me, I must rely on
the credibility of Wm. Martin for the
assertion that he acted under an order
from the President. Drew corroborates
the details which involve him.

There is no evidence of Martin acting
for another power or otherwise being
disloyal to the CIA, the mission or the
country.

William Martin was, however, at fault

in his failure to advise his superiors
in the CIA of the President's order and
its execution. The President had no
authority to require Martin's silence
within the CIA; the order to exclude
his superiors from knowledge should have
been disobeyed. In my view Martin's
failure to make internal reports is a
separate, different and very serious
offense which requires disciplinary
action by the Director. There can be
no place in the CIA for a solo per-
former, regardless of his instructions.
I recommend Martin's immediate
retirement.

Martin swore silently to himself as he closed the notebook and quietly laid it on the pile of documents he'd
received. Ashley had taken out another stack for Martin to see. If he left immediately it might be obvious
that he'd come to see only the Primula Report. So he
spent another twenty-five minutes flipping pages blindly
as his mind raced.

"What is your logging system for this stuff, Ashley?"
Martin nodded toward the six file cabinets.

"I have to account for who sees the various pages,
Bill. Many of them have been given restricted access as
to certain parts. So I keep a logbook here to show who
has cast a gaze on what, and when."

"How can you keep track?"

"Oh it's not too hard. No one sees the contents of
these cabinets unless I'm here, personally. I never let
them out of the vault. If I did, it would be impossible to
log access, to say nothing of the Xerox copies we'd have
all over town."

"May I see the log, please?" Martin asked, hoping

his voice sounded natural. Ashley handed Martin a large, bound book with a blue cover.

The last entry Martin read was that day's date, the exact time he and Ashley had entered the vault and an itemized list of the documents Ashley had set before Martin. About halfway through he read:

PRIMULA REPORT—RIO DE MUERTE
3 VOLS. (ALL PAGES)

This seemed to be the only entry in the entire ledger that mentioned the Primula Report. Martin again leafed back in the ledger to earlier dates to be certain that he was correct. No one else had come to the vault to see the Inspector General's assignment of blame for the Rio de Muerte massacre.

Martin stood up, casually stretching. "Dave, this has been well handled. You're to be congratulated. Please consult me well in advance if anyone contemplates changing any of this procedure."

"Of course, Bill." The aide was grateful for the praise. "I don't see any need to change a system that's obviously working pretty well."

As Martin left the vault Ashley asked him to sign the logbook as evidence that the entries for his visit were correct. Bill Martin's signature on that page was the high price he had to pay for knowing. But he had to know.

2

Martin sat in the Director's office at Langley, staring out over the endless waves of barren gray treetops. But the new Director was not concentrating on the view. As he drummed his fingers on the heavy desk, his mind grappled with the problem created for him by Esker Anderson's announced retirement.

He reached for a lined yellow pad, then took a pen from the onyx stand. This thing could overtake him if he was not disciplined. He began to make some notes to organize his scattered thoughts.

1. There would be a new President.
2. There would probably be a new CIA Director.
3. As a result, there would be a new reader of the Primula Report.

Martin put his pen down. The consequences were incalculable. A legion of conceivable possibilities came into his mind. Congressional investigation, newspaper leaks, innuendo, then political charges and accusations. Criminal charges were not likely, but prison might be a peaceful haven in the political story that would surely rage once Rio de Muerte became the lead story on the evening news once again.

If Vice President Gilley became the new President, perhaps Anderson would be able to force him to keep me on, Martin thought. Though the price would be perpetual bondage to Esker Anderson, it might be the least of all the evils.

But could someone beat Gilley? How would a Republican feel about keeping on Director William Martin, friend and protégé of Esker Scott Anderson, admirer of William Arthur Curry, campus defender of F.D.R.? God, I don't even know who the Republican front-runner is right now, Martin thought to himself.

He lifted the telephone receiver and punched a colored button on the console. Cappell picked it up on the first ring. "Simon, where is that domestic political survey? Can't you hurry that?"

"I sent it in with the morning reading, Mr. Martin. It should be there."

Martin leafed through the stack on the walnut desk and extracted a memorandum. "Got it. I should have looked there first. Thanks."

He flipped open the blank cover sheet, settled back and began to read with deep interest.

THE CENTRAL INTELLIGENCE AGENCY

```
Office of the Director
To: DCI            FYI            NODIS
From: S. Cappell
Requested Estimate of the domestic (USA)
national political situation in the two
major parties.
```

The retirement of President Anderson, a Democrat, requires a re-estimate of the probable nominees of the two major parties. The Republicans evaluate Vice President Gilley as a weaker candidate than Anderson would have been. They consider the race "wide open." There-fore there may be greater efforts by

more potential Republican candidates,
and the G.O.P. can be expected to make
a maximum effort to win in the fall.

The President's announced retirement
should be taken at face value. We have
verified that the Army physicians and
their specialist-consultants have diag-
nosed his disease as leukemia, in its
early terminal stages. The President's
home in Oregon is being remodeled for
his permanent residence and medical
care, and all evidence available points
to his certain retirement.

Following is an analysis of the
situation as of this date.

The Democrats

(1) Vice President Edward Miller Gilley

It is generally believed by commentators and political experts that the
Vice President will be the Democrats'
nominee. While he will be opposed by
the liberal wing of the party, his endorsement by the retiring President,
when combined with his home-base Pennsylvania delegation and solid AFL-CIO
support in other industrial states,
should insure his nomination on the
first ballot. President Anderson has
not yet openly endorsed him but it is
believed that he will do so before the
convention.

E.M. Gilley is 60, was formerly a six-
term Congressman from the Eleventh
District of Pennsylvania and Chairman

of the House Labor and Education Committee.

He is married to Alice Mae Brown, of
Denton, Texas, a housewife. They have
one daughter (husband a teacher) and
three grandchildren. A brother is employed by the House Agriculture Committee.

Gilley was President Anderson's choice
for Vice President at the last Democratic convention; he has been given
relatively little in Executive Branch
assignments during his term.

No derogatory file information. A
good CIA voting record while in the
House. (File Ref. R 73710.616.001)

(2) <u>Mayor</u> <u>Tom</u> <u>Dobbins</u> <u>of</u> <u>Indianapolis.</u>
Considered a liberal dark horse. Age
48, in first term as Mayor. Former
Speaker of Indiana Legislature. M.
2C. Although populist oriented, could
be well financed. Unless President Anderson withholds endorsement from Gilley,
Dobbins probably could not carry even
the Indiana delegation. President Anderson might oppose his nomination.

Also mentioned as a Vice Presidential
possibility.

Some international Communist contacts
ten years ago. (R. 23113.606.011)

(3) <u>Senator</u> <u>Harry</u> <u>Lee</u> <u>Rollins,</u> <u>West</u>
   <u>Virginia.</u>
Age 56, M. No C. Conservative,
third-term Senator, Democratic whip.
Small-town lawyer. Wealthy family. A
possible contender if Gilley withdrew

for any reason, but depends on same
general constituencies as Gilley for
support. Good CIA voting record. (R.
19730.606.001)

The Republicans

(1) Richard Monckton.

Moderate to conservative. Age 56,
married to Amy Curtis. No children.

United States Senator from Illinois
for 18 years. Was Chairman of the
Senate Foreign Relations Committee four
years, ranking member two years. Re-
tired from the Senate to run as Vice
Presidential Candidate with James
Dudley, who was the Republican candi-
date for President opposing William
Arthur Curry. When Curry was elected
President, Monckton retired from public
life and became senior partner of one of
Chicago's largest law firms: Monckton,
Carr, Goldwein, Pozzi and Hall.

Believed wealthy, came from farm
poverty in his youth. Director of seven
major U.S. corporations, only three of
which are not his clients. Principal
clients include several multinational
corporations, a mutual investment fund,
a bank holding company, a newspaper
publisher.

Since retiring from the Senate he has
traveled abroad extensively, primarily
on business for his clients. He has
maintained contacts he made with high-
ranking foreign officials while Chairman
of the Foreign Relations Committee. A

file on his recent contacts is attached
as Tab A. (Ref. R 02110.613.110)

Monckton has "campaigned" steadily for
his party since his retirement from the
Senate, appearing on behalf of candidates in nearly every state. He is
known to have received substantial
financial support for these activities
as a result of organized solicitation on
his behalf by a small committee of
Chicago and New York Republican busi-
nessmen. He is known to have received
some foreign funds (see R. 91139.613.
011) from nationals of countries
friendly to the interests of the U.S.

At present Monckton is the front-
runner for the nomination. He is leading polls of probable convention
delegates by from seven to fifteen
percent.

His orientation is toward a strong
national defense; is internationalist,
and while in the Senate his voting
record was generally pro-CIA. (R.
71891.613.211)

No derogatory personal information is
on file. He is believed to have led a
conservative and circumspect, even
"square," life.

(2) Governor Thomas J. Forville of New
    Jersey.
Incumbent for the past 10 years; in
his third term. Age 61, married to
Glenna Forbes. (Third marriage, two
divorces. Five children aggregate. See
personal notes below.)

Sole heir of his late mother, Jeannette Dougherty Forville, reputed to be a billionaire. The Governor has a net worth of over 300 million dollars in his own right.

One of three trustees of the Forville Foundation and sole executor of his late mother's estate.

Orientation is liberal; he is considered an internationalist.

The Forville Foundation constitutes an important and interesting part of the Governor's political assets. Located principally at Princeton University, the Foundation is independent of the school. It employs nearly three hundred experts, ranging from economists and social scientists to geographers and physical scientists. In addition to the permanent staff, substantial cash grants are made to others. These outside experts accept assignments from the Trustees of the Foundation to work on contemporary issues and problems, national and international.

Governor Forville has freely used their work product to further the economic and political interests of the Forville family (including himself) and their companies.

Their extensive foreign operations are supported by a private intelligence capability (called Foretel) directed toward U.S. and foreign government activity and competitors of the Forville businesses in the private sector. (A recent Defense Intelligence Agency

study of Foretel is at A. 10142.469.
227.)

The Forville candidacy is organized to
draw upon the Foundation resources,
apparently within legal limitations.
Issue papers and advice are received
from an impressive expert panel which
includes:

Dunlop Graham
Professor of Economics, Princeton.
Former chairman, President's Council
of Economic Advisors, under President
Curry.
(R. 36792.613.110)

Almon Dressler
Former president and chief executive
officer, New York and Eastern Trust
Co.; former Director of the Budget,
Office of the President of the United
States.
(R. 20012.613.110)

Carl A. Tessler
Professor of International Relations,
Harvard. Special Advisor on National
Security Affairs to Presidents Curry
and Anderson (temporary consulta-
tions).
(See R. 91933.676.001 through .007)

J. Brode Stanley
Nobel laureate in agriculture research. Former Asst. Secy--Agricul-
ture.
(R. 49136.613.110)

Forville domestic and foreign business
interests include minerals and oil,

urban real estate, agribusiness, communications, trucking and timber.

The Governor has been a member of the
President's Foreign Intelligence Ad-
visory Board for four years. Much of
Dr. Carl Tessler's work for the founda-
tion has been in support of the
Governor's work on FIAB. (See a recent
memorandum summarizing Tessler's work
and recent contacts with the CIA at
N. 91934.676.010.) Both Forville and
Tessler are known to be helpful to the
Agency.

Old files reflect the Governor's
indiscreet personal conduct abroad
before entering politics. (R. 99919.
613.111 and .112)

Although he is well-financed and
staffed, his liberal politics and
divorces weaken his chances for
nomination.

(3) Commentary and Polls

A Lou Harris preference poll six weeks
ago asked:

"If the Presidential election were
held today and these were the Democratic and Republican nominees,
who would you vote for?"

The response, allocating the unde-
cided, was:

Vice President Gilley	47%
Gov. Thomas Forville	47%

Vice President Gilley	49%
Richard Monckton	46%

Note that this was a poll of the population generally, not convention delegates. Twelve days ago columnist Robinson said in The New York Times that Republican delegate sentiment was heavily conservative; in his opinion if ballots were cast at a convention today Monckton would win the nomination on a very early ballot.

Collyer held a similar view in the Washington Post the week before.

CIA Considerations

As stated, none of the three major candidates--the Vice President, Richard Monckton or Governor Forville--is believed to be hostile to the CIA, as such.

However, Richard Monckton had been the late President William Arthur Curry's bitter political adversary for over ten years. Monckton was the tough, cutting edge of the campaign against Curry seven years ago but the hatred between the two was legendary before that. As junior Senators they were political rivals and they remained adversaries until Curry's death.

Monckton is reported to have stated that if elected he will make it his business to disassemble the vestiges of the Curry administration which remain in the Federal Government. He considers it too leftist and elitist, according to a source close to Monckton.

He is a highly partisan politician

who believes in rewarding his friends
and punishing his enemies.

To the extent that he sees the CIA or
its management as a vestige of the
Curry administration or even Curry-
oriented, his election could result in
problems here.

William Martin tossed the memorandum aside and
leaned back in his desk chair. In order of preference,
then, Gilley, Forville and Monckton. No; from the
standpoint of the CIA, Monckton's election was out of
the question.

Simon Cappell walked in quietly and cleared his
throat. "Have you forgotten your lunch date with Congressman Atherton, sir?"

"Is he here?"

"He's in the outer lounge having a drink."

Martin slipped the political memorandum into his top
drawer and locked it. "Tell him I'll be right out."

The Director's working office could be divided from a
lounge area by rice-paper sliding doors so that guests
sitting in the low chairs in front of the beige marble
fireplace would not see Martin's desk. A second lounge
was located in a room just off the Director's reception
room. It was here that Congressman Jack Atherton sat
alone, a drink in his hand, looking at the front page of
The New York Times spread out in his lap.

Like the other rooms in Martin's suite the walls were
papered in light-brown grass cloth, decorated with Oriental hangings, subdued paintings and simply framed
etchings. The ceilings seemed lower than those in an
ordinary Government building's rooms. Indirect lighting
cast a warm glow on thick gold carpeting and antique
brass door fittings. The design of the teak and dark
mahogany furniture was vaguely Oriental.

Bill Martin crossed a private hallway to the Director's small dining room, glanced at the formal place settings for two, the Oriental arrangement of iris in a porcelain bowl in the center, then opened a door on the far side of the room, entered the lounge and greeted Atherton.

"Congressman, I'm sorry to have kept you waiting."

"No problem, Bill. It's given me a chance to catch up on today's *Times*." Atherton stood, the paper sliding to the floor.

"How's your time, Jack?"

"I'm due back at three for a subcommittee meeting. If you can get me a ride back I'm in good shape."

Martin pressed a small brass panel on the wall. A tall waiter in a white jacket, black tie and trousers and gleaming black shoes quietly opened the door. Martin pointed to Atherton's nearly drained glass and the Congressman nodded. The waiter took Martin's drink order and disappeared.

Atherton immediately asked the question being discussed by everyone at every luncheon table in Washington that day.

"Bill, what's the real lowdown on the retirement? Most members don't think that Esker Anderson is seriously sick. They think he's being forced out by his failure to win the war."

"No, Jack, he's sick—very sick. I don't think anything but an act of God could force E.S.A. out. He likes the Kingdom and the Power and the Glory too much."

"Do you think he'll last out the term?"

"Yeah, but the question is why he would want to. If he's as sick as he is, why not just quit now and go home?"

Atherton crunched on a piece of ice. "Hell, he wants to be a force at the next Democratic convention, I would guess. If he retired now, in office, Gilley would be the incumbent going into the convention and Anderson would be sitting on his ass out in Oregon watching on television. If he can hang in he can keep them guessing a while. He can trade his endorsement for a deal to ease his transition." Atherton smiled. "After all, he's faced now with becoming a mere mortal."

"What do you call that, terminal politics?" Martin asked wryly as the waiter silently returned with drinks on a round silver tray. "Let's take them in to lunch." Rising, he led the way to the dining room, one wall of which was windows opening onto a narrow terrace and low parapet. Out beyond, as far as Atherton could see, were the leafless gray trees of the Virginia winter forests. They sat down and another waiter brought in their shrimp cocktail.

The meeting had been scheduled so they could talk budget. The Congressman was the ranking Republican on the House Appropriations Subcommittee on Intelligence, and it was a part of the job for Director Martin to cultivate his Congressional alliances. He tried to have as easy a relationship with his ranking minority member as with the Democrat who was chairman. Jack Atherton lacked the power of the chairman but did influence the other Republicans on the committee. And if his party ever got back in, he would be chairman.

Martin had a budget problem. Every year the budget of the National Aeronautics and Space Administration had some CIA money hidden within it. The political bloom was fading from the astronautical rose that season and NASA was threatened with some sharp cuts. Over the grilled minute steak and tossed green salad Martin explained to the Congressman the Agency's particular interest in the intelligence uses of the proposed space shuttle.

He explained in detail how barn-sized doors in the top of that man-operated space vehicle could be opened to swallow up some of the hundreds of space satellites which had been placed in orbit by the Russians to photograph the United States and other countries. A shuttle pilot could bring them back to home base as valuable prizes for the Company's analysts.

Martin reached over to the windowsill and handed Atherton a plastic model of the shuttle, mounted on a pedestal; he opened the doors in the top, dropped in a plastic model of a Russian satellite, closed the doors and handed the souvenir to the delighted Congressman.

"I'd appreciate it if you keep this under your hat, Jack."

"Jesus, I'm glad I know about this. How much of the shuttle program is your money, did you say?"

"About point-nine billion. I'll get you a breakdown." Martin again reached over and pressed a button panel on the broad windowsill. A moment later Simon Cappell opened the passageway door.

"Congressman, you remember my assistant, Simon Cappell?"

Atherton greeted the young man warmly. When he'd been told what Martin needed, Simon disappeared for a moment and returned with a plastic-bound loose-leaf, opened to a graph. Placing it on the table next to Atherton, he pointed to a red bar and the number 935. "Actually, sir, we have 935 million in the coming budget for the Shuttle."

Martin nodded. "Hang on to that book, Jack. It's a summary of our hidden share in programs of all the other agencies."

Atherton flipped the pages. "You even got yourselves some of the Interior budget? If the folks back home knew that Smokey the Bear is a spy . . ."

Martin smiled. "Oh, we have a couple of people who manage international conferences on topics within Interior's scope. Oceans, Arctic seals, environment, stuff like that. It's a nice way for our fellows to get in and out of countries we like to keep track of."

Cappell left the room and Martin closed the budget discussion. "Jack, let's get back to party politics for a moment, OK? Can you fill me in on the Republican picture? I'm somewhat confused."

Atherton snorted sarcastically. "Welcome to the club. When you understand the Republicans please explain what's going on to me."

"How can a dour, colorless fellow like Monckton have the inside track over an able and attractive man like Forville?" Martin asked.

"It's a hare-and-tortoise thing, Bill. Ever since he quit the Senate to run with Dudley, Richard Monckton has been campaigning for the nomination. What is that, five years? Six? All those years of cross-country fund-raising dinners. A million miles, ten million handshakes and a thousand grateful Republican county chairmen who will all be convention delegates."

"Don't those fellows think about Forville's appeal to the Independents and Democrats come November?"

"Sure, but when it's balloting time in Philadelphia next summer the Monckton people will be grabbing each delegate's elbow saying, 'Remember last year when you were in a bind for a speaker at your fund-raiser? Who came all the way to Ashtabula for you. Richard Monckton or that billionaire dilettante Forville? You remember, Mr. Chairman, Old Dick Monckton busted his ass for you.' It can't be underestimated."

"That may be true, Jack, but doesn't Forville's ability count for anything? He's so goddamn well staffed too."

"No question. On sheer ability, mental capacity, it's about a draw. But Forville's backup is extraordinary. He gave a speech at San Diego College, in my district, last spring. It was on foreign policy and it was brilliant."

Martin grinned, rubbed his jaw. "The speech was pure Carl Tessler, no doubt. He could make anyone look brilliant."

Atherton nodded. "Did you know Tessler taught me at Harvard as an undergraduate? It was a great opportunity."

"Do you see much of him these days?"

"Some. Forville loaned him to me for a few days a while back and paid him a good-sized stipend to come down and tell me what I needed to know about the Middle East. Tessler is a rare bird. Insisted on staying at the Madison, nowhere else. We had to lean on the owner to get him a room. They were jammed to the walls. But if he couldn't stay there he wouldn't come."

Martin nodded. "How balanced is he on Israel? I've wondered about his Jewish background getting in the way."

"He's hard on the Israelis; almost too hard, I'd say. Maybe it's compensation, but I don't think so. His wife is the family Zionist. But they have lived apart for nearly ten years and she has virtually no influence over him. Maybe she accounts for his skepticism about other Jews. The Tessler kids are all grown now, but still no divorce for her. She's now a full Professor of Economics up there at Harvard."

"I had forgotten that Tessler had children," Martin mused. "He's not exactly the family-man type."

"You're right. He's totally devoted to his work—it's his way of getting away from all of them, I suspect. He and his wife never speak. The oldest boy is a Ph.D. candidate in Tessler's field, but he's at Yale and they say he hates his old man. His thesis is an attack on Tessler's geopolitical philosophy. *Foreign Affairs Quarterly* is running some of it issue after next, I understand."

"No wonder Carl has no fingernails."

"Yes, isn't that something? Carl really bites them right down to the quick, doesn't he?"

"Jack, how does he survive in that faculty jungle at Harvard?"

"Sheer talent, I'd say. His views are the opposite of everyone's in his department, I'm sure, but he's now so famous that he can write his own ticket. People up there tell me that most of them hate him. It's partly because they think he's wrong on the issues, but it's jealousy too. He pulls down large lecture fees, and all that Forville money comes rolling in for helping dumb Congressmen like me."

"If Forville were elected," said Martin, "do you think Tessler would be Secretary of State?"

"Maybe. But that's not where I'd put him if I were President. I'd want him right down the hall as National Security Advisor, to keep tabs on you and Defense and all those creeps at State."

"Do you think Forville stands a chance, Jack?"

"He's my choice, of course. If we can get him nominated I think he can beat Gilley. Forville can carry New York and New Jersey, probably Ohio. He'd be better against Gilley in Pennsylvania than Monckton would be." Atherton grinned. "With a Californian on the ticket Forville could do well out west, too. Texas would be tough and so would Illinois. But I think he'd win."

"But what will happen at the convention?" Martin persisted.

"It's too soon to read it. If I had to place dough right now I'd have to give it to Monckton on the second or third ballot."

"And it will be Gilley for sure as the Democrat?"

"Almost certainly, unless he bows out for some reason."

Over dessert of melon and cookies Martin brought the talk back to Monckton. "Do you know the Senator, Jack?"

"We were in Congress together for a while and I see him at Republican shindigs occasionally, but I can't claim to know him well. A Harvard classmate of mine who is a partner in Monckton's Chicago firm tells me that no one there really feels he knows him. He's a kind of recluse. Hard to talk to, doesn't socialize well, a brilliant mind, no hobbies. A real grind, as we called them in school."

Martin scratched his head. "How the hell did he get elected to the Senate? He doesn't sound like an Illinois politician."

The Congressman leaned back on two chair legs, balancing with one hand on the edge of the table. "True grit, as the saying goes. He made up his mind to go to the Senate, so he learned everything he needed to know to do it. I'm convinced he can do anything he decides to do and probably do it better than almost anyone else. He's a cold and calculating s.o.b. But at the same time he can be very gut-passionate about some things. His vendetta against Curry was classic. He'd crawl across the Sahara on bloodied hands and knees just to get a chance to throw a rock at someone in the Curry crowd, even today."

"What started that anyway, Jack?" Martin asked.

"That's a typical Monckton story. It happened when he and Curry were both in the Senate. Monckton, from a poor family, just squeaked through the University of Illinois. Financially, that is, working his way, all the way. As for grades, he was straight A for seven years, clear through law school. Bill Curry, of course, was born with the silver spoon. I'm not sure he even finished Yale."

"I think you're right." Martin nodded slowly.

"Anyway, they were both on Senate Banking and Finance, before Monckton went over to Foreign Relations. Curry found out that Monckton was taking heavy honorariums from the bankers—to the tune of two or three thousand a speech. Instead of leaking it to the press, Curry dropped by one day to tell Monckton he knew about it and might have to say something. My guess is the guy was just trying to be decent, but Monckton sensed he was being put down in a patronizing way. He needed money. I guess Monckton probably knew he was dead wrong to be taking from bankers when the committee had their regulatory legislation before it, but he couldn't take Curry's moralizing, you know, as the rich, Ivy Leaguer elite setting the moral tone for the poor common folk from the Midwest. Monckton blew his stack and threw Curry out of his office. They were enemies from then on. Monckton simply hated Curry's guts. I think Curry looked at Monckton as some lower form of life that he couldn't be bothered with. And that attitude just made Monckton madder.

"Then they both began to be talked about as Presidential prospects. Curry's family bankrolled him through the primaries and got him the Democratic nomination. Monckton made his move at the Republican convention but had to settle for second place on the ticket when Dudley put together the heavy Eastern delegations with California and Texas. Monckton learned a hell of a lot from that defeat, I'm sure. He burns to be President, you know. Don't underestimate his determination and persistence. He's dogged."

"What motivates the man?" asked Martin.

"I'm not sure. You always have the feeling he's driven to prove that a poor boy from the farm is better than the elite. And the revenge motive comes through very strong."

"Would he make a good President?"

"Oh, I expect so. Don't you believe the old saw that a man elected to that office rises to it as he sits down in the chair? I think Monckton would be OK. But I hope we never find out."

"Christ, look at the time," Martin said, glancing at his watch and pushing back his coffee cup. "We've got to get you to the Hill. And I've got to be getting to the White House." He pushed the brass square three times. "Let's go through my office on the way."

Simon Cappell was standing by Martin's desk as Martin and the Congressman came in. Simon laid a typed buff-colored schedule card on top of a briefcase on the desk.

"Mr. Director, your meeting has been moved to Secretary Donnally's office in the West Wing of the White House. His secretary called to change the time. You're going to see the President at three."

"I wonder what the hell that's all about," Martin muttered. "Let's get going, Jack. You can drop me off and then go on with the car, if you don't mind."

"Mind? Hell, a poor Congressman is just grateful for any kind of ride at all from the privileged classes in the Executive Branch. In my next life I'm going to be a bureaucrat so that I have a car assigned to me. It's us Congressmen who make the cab drivers rich in this town."

As Martin's limousine moved smoothly along the George Washington Parkway Martin stared out the window. His three-thirty meeting at the White House had been originally scheduled to review South American developments with Carl Tessler's deputy. Now it had been changed. Secretary Donnally and the President. That combination spelled Democratic politics. And some of Esker Anderson's well-known persuasion. It promised to be a long afternoon.

3

The West Wing of the White House is a little white crackerbox of a building, seldom noticed by the passing tourist. The visitor's gaze is drawn by the familiar facade of the White House residence, pillars and flag and curved driveway. Then the eye passes to the next huge structure, the Executive Office Building, that great gray Victorian collection of porches and dormers and Doric columns and ten different shapes of windows in pile upon pile up to slanting gray roofs and chimneys and more chimneys.

Almost no one sees the West Wing tucked between the two structures. It squats close to the ground, its second floor at driveway level, the third floor concealed by a white parapet covered by a low convex roof of neutral green. The Pennsylvania Avenue tourist cannot actually see the President's office on the back side of this little building, its thick bulletproof windows looking south toward the sweeping lawns.

When Theodore Roosevelt first built the West Wing, he didn't need the third floor; he didn't have that much staff to house. But from the time of his cousin, Franklin Roosevelt, the upper floor was used for offices. President Esker Scott Anderson, too, liked to have all his top people close by so they could get to him in a hurry when he called. And White House staff people liked the prestige of being close in the West Wing. At various times in the course of the Presidency, Washington hostesses, journalists and lobbyists have adopted a kind of yardstick principle to determine which White House people are the most powerful. As a general rule, so the dictum goes, the shorter the linear distance from a staff person's office to the President's desk, the greater the occupant's power.

Like most such legends perpetrated by the Washington press corps, it is both demonstrably untrue and believed by almost everyone in Washington.

During Esker Anderson's first year in the White House, belief in the legend raised the population per square foot of the West Wing to its highest in history. The third floor of the building became a maze of tiny cubicles, some of which could only be reached by walking through someone else's office. The staff was provided with certain minimum furnishings including a desk, two chairs, a ten-button telephone, and, in every room, an inscribed and autographed photograph of President Esker Scott Anderson. In the bowels of the huge gray building next door was a modern photo laboratory that produced these color photographs of Anderson in nearly fifty different poses.

The President would stop almost anything going on in his office to give attention to an incoming stack of portraits brought to him for his autograph. Clipped to each picture was a card on which was typed the name of the autograph recipient, a first name or nickname if it was to be used, some history of his relationship to the President (although none was really required in order to merit a handwritten greeting) and a suggested text for the inscription. Middle-level Government employees toiled long hours composing these typed inscriptions for the President's guidance. The White House workshop mass-produced the brown-and-gold wooden frames in which the photographs were enclosed.

A narrow street runs between the West Wing and the looming gray Executive Office Building. At the margin of the White House grounds this street is gated and guarded by the President's own police force. Since it is a one-way thoroughfare, cars must enter by the southwest gate and leave by the northwest gate. As the Director's limousine entered the southwest gate, Bill Martin patted Jack Atherton on the arm and said, "See you, Jack. Let me know what develops on the NASA budget, please."

"Righto," the Congressman replied. "Thanks for the lunch and the lift."

The driver left Martin midway between the two gates, at a basement door to the West Wing. A uniformed policeman at a desk in the cluttered hallway just inside the inner storm doors recognized Martin, smiled and spoke his name quietly into his telephone. As he talked he filled in the blanks on a white printed slip and put it in a slotted tray.

In a minute an elevator door opened across the hall from the policeman's desk. A tall, attractive girl wearing a plaid skirt held the door and leaned out. "Director Martin? Would you like to come up?"

The venerable and very small elevator rose at a stately pace. In due course its door slowly opened to reveal the nondescript third floor. Three wire-service teletypes in a wooden box clattered on the right side of the hall. An old refrigerated drinking fountain was on the opposite wall. A faded green runner served as a carpet. Six or seven doors stood open on the right side. As the girl led Martin straight ahead to the end of the hall he glanced into the open doorways. He received a quick impression of desks piled with papers, big telephones, the colored pictures of Anderson; in one room there was a flag. Phones were ringing; men and women moved about quickly, giving a sense of overburdened urgency—too little space, too little help, too little time.

The young lady in the plaid skirt brought Martin into a room with high windows. There was no view; a white parapet rose from the narrow roof to block any sight of the south grounds. The highest cornices of the White House residence could barely be seen over the top of this wall. There were three secretaries at gray metal desks in what was obviously an outer office. They continued to type, barely glancing up as he came in. Calendars and typed lists were tacked to the pale-green walls. These adornments and three inscribed photographs of Esker Scott Anderson were the only decoration in the room. Since there were no chairs, Martin stood waiting until he was announced.

In a moment a door to his right opened and the Secretary of Labor, Al Donnally, stood in the doorway, his blue shirt rumpled, his tie askew.

Donnally was about fifty-eight, short, twenty pounds

overweight, most of it at the waist and in the face. His curly black hair was beginning to gray, and thin wire-rimmed glasses gave him a professorial dignity that his receding chin might otherwise have denied him. Al Donnally was a child of the Democratic clubhouses of Hartford. Although now Secretary of Labor, he had not found his way to that office through some union hiring hall. As Esker Scott Anderson's long-time political operative, he had labored quietly behind the scenes for years. Recently, with uncharacteristic self-concern, he had finally asked for and been given a seat in the Cabinet. His confirmation by the Senate had come just three weeks before. This suite of office cubbyholes had been his before his confirmation, and he had not yet moved his staff and personal effects to the ornate Secretary's office at the Labor Department. He still handled White House politics, and the only place from which to do that was a room in the White House. The Department of Labor could be run from anywhere.

Al Donnally's Cabinet nomination came about the time the President first went to Walter Reed Hospital, and a few people were beginning to wonder if they shouldn't have read more into the nomination than they did. Now, looking back, it made much better sense, as a farewell present for a loyal political satrap. Though the appointment had been criticized by some unperceptive columnists at the time, the AFL-CIO had not complained. Labor well understood that Donnally's closeness to the President would strengthen their outpost in the Executive Branch.

Martin had never met Donnally, but was characteristically greeted like an old friend. "Come on in, Mr. Director. Sit over here. I'm sorry to rearrange your afternoon like this, Bill, but there are some things that the President needs to cover with you that can't hold."

Donnally walked over to his desk, picked up a page

of heavy bond White House stationery and sat in a chair beside Martin's.

"He has two items he wants to talk to you about today. If you have anything else, let me know before we go down so I can add them to this agenda outline. Number one is a complaint from the FBI."

Bill Martin shook his head slowly. "Good Christ, now what? Why the hell can't Elmer Morse call me directly instead of bitching over here?"

Donnally smiled wryly. "It sounds like your liaison with the FBI leaves a good deal to be desired."

"To say the least," Martin replied, with heavy sarcasm. "We've had a formal process to keep one another informed—and to avoid conflicts if possible—by talking to each other. But about eight months ago Morse reassigned his liaison people to other jobs and just quit talking to us. What the hell's bugging him now?"

"Morse told the President yesterday that the CIA is operating in New York City in violation of the Act. Something to do with a UN Ambassador. He says your people interfered with the FBI management of a double agent they had developed."

"Yes, I know the situation very well," Martin said, then sighed slowly. "In fact we reviewed it at the Interagency Intelligence Board last week. But Morse has refused to send anyone from the FBI to those meetings for some time, so it's no wonder he doesn't know what the fuck is going on. I can give you the lowdown. Or is it better to wait until we go downstairs?"

Donnally smiled and shook his head. "I don't need to know anything about it. Jesus, the last thing I want to do is get between you and Elmer."

"I can't say that I blame you."

Donnally cleared his throat. "The President is really concerned about Ed Gilley's chances, and he expects everyone to help. That's number two on the agenda."

Martin frowned. "Well, Mr. Secretary, how do I

handle that? I'm career and nonpolitical, and so is the Company. The law spells that out clearly. There are just no—"

The only red button of the thirty on Donnally's telephone console suddenly glowed with light, and a bell on the far side of the room began a loud, insistent ringing. It reminded Martin of an old-fashioned doorbell.

"Excuse me," Donnally muttered as he reached to the table to push the red button and pick up the receiver. The bell immediately stopped. "Yes, sir?" He listened and replaced the instrument. "He wants us down there now. I'll meet you in the hall." Before Martin could finish his explanation Donnally abruptly rose, walked through the door into his outer office and opened a closet.

Martin had no choice but to gather his coat and briefcase and follow. He found the Secretary of Labor, jacket on and tie tightened, having a drink at the hall water fountain. Instead of taking the elevator they turned right into a short hallway and went down a flight of narrow stairs. At the ground-floor level they moved into a hallway nearly twice as wide as that on the floor above. The passage was thickly carpeted from wall to wall and the walls were hung with gold framed oils of American landscapes. Halfway down the hall a pedestal held a small bronze bust of Lincoln. The hushed tone in this area contrasted vividly with the rabbit warren one level above.

The hall veered thirty degrees to the left where a policeman sat at a desk on the right side by a white paneled door, listlessly talking into his black telephone. As Donnally and Martin approached him, he reached under the center drawer of his desk. Martin heard the door latch click, and somewhere a buzzer sounded. Donnally pushed the door open and Martin walked into the Oval Office behind him.

Bill Martin had been in this room perhaps a dozen

times before, but it never failed to thrill him every time he entered. There was not much regal panoply to it; only the five tall flags of the Armed Services with their bright battle streamers, topped with big gold eagles. The furniture was ordinary. But it was one of those historic places that grip thinking men's minds and emotions, like Runnymede and Gettysburg's Little Round Top and Westminster Abbey and the bridge at Concord. Simply standing in the Oval Office touched Martin.

To the left he could see through the French doors to the Rose Garden. On high pedestals by the windows were the two huge bowls of fresh spring flowers from the greenhouse.

The President was hunched over his desk, eating from a white china plate on a linen-covered tray. He ate with concentrated energy, as if in a hurry. As he ate, he was reading a folded newspaper propped against the telephone. There were no other papers on the desk, but it was cluttered with a hodgepodge collection of objects of political significance.

Martin's eye roved over the desk-top symbols. A little American flag on a tiny gold flagpole, an American Legion seal on its base. A brass donkey. A china Vietnam elephant. A plastic model of a Minuteman missile. Another model, this one of a lunar module. A fragment of wood, no doubt from Abraham Lincoln's log cabin, encased in a little glass box and identified with a brass plate. A huge marble pen set with a gold clock mounted at its center. A bullet.

The men of Congress (with whom Esker Scott Anderson still proudly asserted his identity when it was to his advantage to do so) were given to such desk-top collections, somehow as evidence of what each believed himself to be, or wished he were, or at the least wanted his visitors to believe he was.

Anderson had not looked up from his paper at the

sound of the door buzzer, so Donnally finally said, "Mr. President, Director Martin is here."

The President then looked up, nodded at the chairs by the desk, wiped his mouth with a napkin and forked the last bite of steak from his plate. As he chewed he looked at his Secretary of Labor. "The goddamned Mayor of New York is blaming me for his fucking garbage, Al. I don't collect his fucking garbage. What am I supposed to do about the son of a bitch's garbage in Bedford-Stuyvesant, will you tell me that?"

"I saw that, Mr. President," Donnally soothed. "It's a cheap shot. There is a Federal program for waste disposal and he can't qualify for it because New York City barges all its garbage into the Atlantic. So now he puts the blast on you."

The President slammed the desk top with a clenched fist. "Are we letting that cheap liberal bastard get away with it?"

Donnally tried for a placating tone. "Let me find out, Mr. President. I just saw the story myself a little while ago."

The President looked straight at Bill Martin. "You think you have bad guys to deal with, Bill? Of the 'enemies foreign and domestic,' I'd prefer to deal with the foreign every time. I just sit here like a goddamned milk cow waiting for every headline-seeking politician in this goddamned country to take a shot at me for some goddamned thing or other. And my staff sits around and doesn't do a goddamned thing about it." Suddenly he seemed to relax. He smiled warmly and looked at Martin. "Thanks for coming on such short notice, Bill. I'll tell you what's on my mind."

Martin cleared his throat. "Mr. President, I want to say, first, how troubled I am to know about your illness. I'm truly sorry and concerned; I regret your forced retirement."

The President looked at him blankly as he spoke, as

if he did not hear. And then, apparently oblivious to Martin's words, he went on: "Elmer Morse was in here yesterday, hopping mad. He says you are jumping his claim up in New York. Bill, if your people are getting in the FBI's way up there, it's got to stop. Morse is doing some things for me and I don't want anyone to screw them up."

"Mr. President, I know—" Martin began.

Anderson hunched forward, leaning across the desk.

"I *know* you know, Bill. Because we've talked about this FBI situation before. Morse is right. It's a god-damned mess when two intelligence agencies compete. I don't really know why the hell we have to have two. Why in hell can't they be consolidated?"

"Sir, if I could explain, the CIA is ready, willing and able to cooperate. But in fairness—"

"Shit! It's not a question of fairness. It's a matter of staying the fuck out of the FBI's way when they have an operation on. It's a matter of results, not of hurt feelings. I'm telling you this goddamn competition has to stop."

"I totally agree there should be no conflict, Mr. President," Martin replied evenly.

"Well then, my boy, there's no problem, is there?" The President leaned back in his huge chair. "The other thing I need to talk to you about is the Vice President's situation, Bill. You know, continuing problems like the organization of our intelligence—the thing we were just talking about—that's not something I'm going to be able to do in my few remaining months here. That's for the next man, Bill. It's awfully important that the next President in this chair be the right one, for many reasons. But I'm sure I don't need to tell you that."

"Of course, Mr. President."

"The question is, who should it be? I'm going to take you into my confidence, Bill. Only Al here knows what I've decided on that. But you should know too, because it's very much in your interest to help to get the best man in here to take over. I know I can count on you."

"Well, on that, Mr. President—"

"I can count on you to keep my decision confidential, can't I, Bill?"

"Of course, sir."

"Bill, I've weighed it. I've pondered it. And it's Ed Gilley. I know his strengths and weaknesses. I think that on balance he's the best man. Don't you agree?"

Martin cleared his throat. "Well, you know, sir, the CIA is not supposed to get into political—"

"Bullshit, Bill." Anderson pounded a fist on the desk. "Everyone in this Government is political and you know it. Politics is what makes it all go round. If everyone just piously folds his hands and says, 'Goodness me, I shouldn't get into all that political crap,' you know what's going to happen? The next man in here is going to be that bastard Richard Monckton, that's what. How would all you purists at the CIA like Richard Monckton over here calling the shots? If you think this is politics, just wait until that son of a bitch gets in here. You'll be eating his political shit for breakfast, lunch and dinner."

Martin nodded finally. "I'm sure you're right about him, sir."

"You're goddamn right I'm right about his. Of course, you know, *I* would be better off, personally, with Monckton in here than Gilley, as far as my personal comfort is concerned. Former Presidents aren't taken care of because their successors love them so much, you know. It's pure self-interest that builds the precedent. That's all in the hell it is."

Martin and Donnally nodded in unison.

"So personally I'm better off with a venal son of a bitch like Monckton who understands that if he takes good care of me the precedent he sets will take good care of him later. Good old simpleminded Ed Gilley probably never would understand that. But *you* aren't better off. And the country isn't, with Monckton here."

"Mr. President," Al Donnally said, "your love of your country and its people is the quality history is going to remember you for."

Esker Anderson pretended not to hear.

"Bill," he went on, "you've got to help Ed Gilley. He hasn't been in on many of the foreign intelligence briefings, you know." Martin looked as if he was about to comment on this, but the President continued. "Oh, I know. He wasn't invited because he's so goddamned indiscreet. But there are things you *can* tell him that will be helpful in this campaign. Stuff he really can't appear ignorant about if he's asked. Good Christ, he is the goddamn Vice President, after all."

"Of course, Mr. President, with your permission, I'll be happy to brief the Vice President." Martin inwardly hoped that this was all he'd be asked to do. "As you say, he is a Constitutional officer and—"

"Fine, Bill, fine. That's a good handle. But be careful what you tell him. Just figure he'll repeat every goddamned thing you say ten minutes after you leave. Now what about what Al needs?"

Martin looked puzzled. "Sir?"

Al Donnally fidgeted. "We didn't have time to get into that before you rang us," Donnally said.

"Al, my boy, you tell him what you need," the President said firmly.

Donnally turned to Martin. "I am told that the Agency has files on all the foreign activities and contacts of Forville and Monckton. I'd like to get a look at those, for a start."

Martin felt his face beginning to redden. "That's pure dynamite, Mr. President," he said slowly. "I don't see how we possibly—"

"Al," said the President, holding up one big hand to

stop Martin, "I think Bill and I can cover the rest of this ourselves. I'll call you if I need you."

"Certainly." Donnally rose and quickly left by a door near the French windows. As he opened it the clack of typewriters could be heard from the room beyond.

The President leaned across the wide desk, hands clasped and held high, elbows resting on the desk. "Goddamn it, Bill, let's take stock. I have been looking out for you for a long time, you know. You are my Director. I haven't let them go after you in all the time I've been here. You *know* that, don't you?"

"I'm very grateful for all you've done for me, Mr. President." Martin was tense.

"All right. Now you can show me how grateful."

"But if a thing like this became known, sir, it could hurt you too."

"Shit, not much can hurt me any more. You let *me* worry about that. I'm concerned now about what could hurt *you*." The President's tone became paternalistic. "That Primula Report is what ought to be on your mind, Bill. That and nothing else. Every jackass in town knows there's a report. But only one or two people know what it says in there. And that's the way we're gonna *keep* it, Bill. But to do that we need our man in here. Monckton would rip your guts out the first week he was here. Gilley will do what I say. So he'll look out for you, too. You can count on me for that."

Anderson stood up, indicating the meeting was coming to an end. Martin, feeling outmaneuvered and helpless, also stood. "Mr. President—" he began.

"Bill, I'm thinking about Linda too." The President's words enveloped Martin like a thick fog. "You know a Congressional investigation of that Dominican deal would be rough on your wife. She shouldn't have to go through something like that. She should be having kids and enjoying life. Listen, son, you aren't getting any younger. When is Linda going to have a baby? Goddamn, I want to be a godfather before I leave this earth."

Martin tried to frame his words to mask his fury.

"Well, sir, there are no definite plans just at present. Now with respect to the files, sir—"

"Plans! Hell, that's the trouble with people these days." The President took Bill's arm in his big hand and began to walk him toward the door. "Everything is so goddamned planned. Linda is a passionate girl. Go home and make a baby! And if it's a boy, name him Esker. I'd like that." By now his hand was on the knob of the curved hall door.

Martin turned to the President but Anderson was filibustering, determined to get Martin out the door before he could object to Donnally's request.

"Don't you worry, Bill. Gilley and I will look out for you. You just do this little thing for us. And give my love to Linda." The door was open, the buzzer sounding continuously. "Thanks for coming by, Bill." The door closed behind Martin and the buzzer stopped. There was only the hall policeman muttering into his telephone. He looked at Martin and stopped talking.

"You know your way, Mr. Director?"

"Yes, thank you." Martin walked to the elevator and pushed the button, furious and frustrated. Revulsion over the transparency and crudeness of Esker Anderson once again overcame him.

As he left through the west basement door, he found his car waiting. The driver handed Martin the reading material brought over by a courier from the office. He opened a large brown envelope and mechanically leafed through the papers but his mind was absorbed with his more immediate problems. He would play ball with Gilley, of course. What choice did he have? The President could ruin him with the Primula Report. And at no cost to himself.

As the car crossed the bridge, Martin methodically

ticked off what he had to do. He could set up briefings with the Vice President that would win his confidence. Gilley had been cut out of things for so long that he would jump at anything.

Martin knew it would be risky to give the Monckton and Forville files to Secretary Donnally. What if either Monckton or Forville were elected? The revenge would be bloody for Martin, and bad for the Company. But how could he tell Donnally "No dice"? His right foot tapped nervously on the gray carpeting of the car. He decided to sit it out and wait.

But did all the obvious concern for Gilley mean that the White House politicians now thought the Vice President could be beaten by one of the Republicans? Martin sensed it was time to begin looking in that direction—to Governor Forville. And to Richard Monckton, too, to the extent that that was possible. Which was probably damn little.

Martin wondered how he could get to Forville. Tessler was the best man around Forville to talk to. Suddenly he saw a way to put it together. He would get Tessler to come down to Washington for the party he was throwing for Jack Atherton. Martin knew that Tessler fancied himself quite a social lion. It was a good guest list. Tessler would come.

The papers rested, unread, on Martin's lap as the car eased to the curb in front of his house. But by then he was feeling more comfortable. He knew that he could feed Tessler better information than Foretel could provide. As the driver opened the door, Martin made a mental bet with himself that the wily Harvard professor could be bought. Briefcase tucked under his arm, he stepped out of the car and walked up the flagstone path. As he turned his key in the lock he stood very still for a moment and prayed that Linda would not be home.

4

Linda and Bill Martin's marriage had begun to lose its way several months before Esker Scott Anderson announced his retirement. Martin had loved other women before Linda moved in with him, but his romance with Linda had been different. Martin had begun talking marriage to her right from the beginning. He was ready to marry again. Although he was in good physical shape and people usually guessed his age to be in the low forties, the truth was that he was nearly fifty. He began to feel that if he was going to marry again, it would have to be soon. And Bill found Linda more responsive, more satisfying than any woman he had made love to in years. At first she spoiled him outrageously and he loved it. Her low-key, Southern-belle style had soon become indispensable in his life. She was a fine hostess and cook, a knowledgeable and skillful conversationalist and a discreet companion.

Even before Linda moved to Georgetown to be nearer him, he had begun suggesting marriage. At first she seemed to resist the idea but the Georgetown move symbolized her commitment to him; before long they were discussing wedding plans. The wedding took place at Williamsburg, with only a few friends attending. President Esker Anderson had sent them a handwritten note to be delivered by a brigadier general just after the ceremony. And an antique gilt mirror, their gift from the Andersons, arrived a few days later.

74

But after the wedding Bill Martin began to sense changes in his new wife almost at once. Before their marriage she had emphasized their similarities and their shared enthusiasms. Once they were married, somehow, their differences were more obvious to her than the things they had in common. Linda's dislike for athletics of every kind became outspoken. Her new husband craved regular exercise. Her constant preoccupation was politics and she was socially ambitious. Martin had an innate dislike of the Washington social scene and always wanted to decline the dozens of invitations to parties and receptions sent to him by reason of his rank and office. Now Linda adamantly insisted they attend most of them. And she began to entertain, often lavishly. Bill's narrow Georgetown house could barely handle eight for dinner. So Linda began looking for a larger place. And she ordered new table settings, linen and silver service.

Soon she resigned her White House job with Esker Anderson to devote more time to her role as the Director's wife. Before long, money became a problem. Martin had never been a saver. His Government take-home pay was about eighteen hundred dollars a month, but Linda had no trouble in running up bills that required him to dip into a very modest inheritance. They began to argue incessantly about her spending.

Martin's long hours at the office inevitably conflicted with the new social role Linda was trying to create for him. He kept a change of dress clothes at his office to save a few minutes, knowing that if he were very late Linda would be in a rage. A few times he didn't get to parties at all. There were some ugly scenes; it began to seem to Martin that he and Linda argued about everything. Linda, who had once been the passive one in the relationship, deferring to Martin when decisions were to be made, became demanding, critical of his suggestions, scornful of his actions.

When Esker Anderson announced to the nation that he was fatally ill, Linda seemed to become remote and withdrawn from her husband. She began to decline coveted social invitations, stopped entertaining, smoked more and drank harder than ever, often mixing her first martini before lunchtime. Her thin body was becoming gaunt and angular. And Martin knew that she was not sleeping much. In the early mornings, when Linda finally fell asleep with the combined aid of sedatives and alcohol, she muttered and tossed.

Linda Martin made no excuses to her husband for her withdrawal. But Martin needed no explanations. The sequence of events made the relationship between Esker Scott Anderson's illness and Linda's moroseness all too clear.

Because she refused to talk to him about it, Bill Martin first felt jealousy and rejection, then anger and bitterness. He had tried to break through Linda's quiet anguish in ways that had won her response after some of their earlier bitter arguments. But now she met his approaches with contempt and harsh derision.

Martin had suspected for more than a year that Linda's relationship with the President had never really ended. His frequent trips certainly offered her every opportunity to have an affair. Whether she was seeing Anderson or not, it was obvious that she still loved him. When Martin was with Linda it became impossible for him to mask how he felt. And Linda made clear to him her growing hatred. It was as if she blamed him for Esker Anderson's illness and the fact that she and the President would be parted. The Martins' estrangement was visible and tangible but its cause was beyond Bill Martin's ability to overcome. He would not compete with Anderson who was both loathsome and overpowering. He would not fight for Linda. If she grieved for Esker Anderson then Martin did not want her.

A month before the President's illness was announced,

Bill Martin and Sally Atherton first met at a large tennis party in suburban Virginia. Both the Athertons and the Martins were guests of the Iranian Embassy for drinks, dinner and tennis at a huge indoor tennis complex. Sally was the wife of Congressman Jack Atherton; when he met her, Martin felt an immediate and total physical attraction. She reached to Martin's chin, her honey-blond hair falling straight, light against a deep tan. She had an athlete's body, powerful, but very feminine, with a tapered and taut waist, round arms and strong wrists. High cheekbones contoured her face and set off her deep brown eyes with a hint of laugh crinkles at the corners.

Almost from the day of his election Jack Atherton had been a prime social commodity in Washington. Old Harvard friends, Congressional colleagues and lobbyists, all had invited the Athertons into the social swim. But the beautiful Mrs. Atherton had declared her independence, often refusing to accompany her husband to parties and receptions.

Sally Atherton was determined to make a life of her own in Washington and it would have almost nothing to do with politics. Although she had never spoken of it to anyone but her husband, she had bitterly opposed his decision to run for Congress. No one knew that a bargain of convenience long ago had been struck between Sally and Jack Atherton. They had agreed that he would run for Congress; she would live a separate life and they would maintain the facade of a marriage. It suited them both to appear to be happy husband and wife.

When Jack ran for Congress, Sally even did some campaigning for her ambitious spouse. She made the public appearances necessary to establish that the candidate was an enviable married man with a gorgeous wife. Jack won his San Diego district by a landslide and had been easily reelected ever since.

Within a few days after his swearing-in they found a town house on a tree-lined street in old Georgetown. With his customary caution, Jack leased it for exactly two years. After his first reelection the Athertons had bought another house in the same block.

Before long Sally met the owner of a Georgetown art gallery and, through her, a number of artists, critics, art teachers and photographers. This group had their own social subculture and Sally found it stimulating. But she was guarded and impersonal, even with the friends she chose, somehow unwilling to commit herself to close friendships.

For his part Jack was publicly delighted with his beautiful offbeat wife and her separate world. He hung her abstract photography in his office and proudly accompanied her to gallery openings on the rare occasions when he invited him along.

On the spur of the moment Sally had agreed to accompany her husband to the Iranian Ambassador's indoor tennis party and the Congressman was delighted. Tennis was one activity she and Jack frequently shared. But, as she discovered, a Washington tennis party involves very little tennis. A buffet and bar were elaborately provided in a glassed-in area between the two huge buildings that sheltered the ten courts. Drinks, food and Washington shoptalk held most of the guests nearby while four professionals gave an exhibition of doubles on Court One. Few of the guests were moved to watch but Sally Atherton refused to stand at the buffet with a drink making small talk. She found a chair by a window and sat alone, watching the players.

A tall, good-looking stranger dressed in tennis whites sat down beside her. He handed her a plate of caviar and hot hors d'oeuvres and smiled easily at her coolness. "I think we're scheduled to play opposite you in a little while. I'm Bill Martin."

"Hi." Sally smiled with reserve, shaking her head at

the proffered delicacies. "Are you trying to slow down my net play with all this food?"

"You figured me out." He leaned toward her conspiratorially. "Between you and me, isn't this lovely, expensive party a crashing bore?"

She replied with an expression that was his answer. "Do you go to many of these fiascos?"

"Far too many, I'm afraid. Do you? I don't recall seeing you before. And I don't often forget beautiful faces."

Sally looked embarrassed. "Almost never. Jack usually goes without me. I thought this one might be fun. I guessed wrong."

"Didn't I read that you're having a show at Alberta's?"

Sally Atherton reacted with surprise. "I have some abstract photography that she's showing now."

"How's it going?"

"Not bad." Sally seemed to relax as she realized this man might share her interests. "Some fairly good reviews, and I've sold eleven. More than I expected."

"Maybe I'd better get over there before everything is sold." He grinned.

She was about to confirm her hunch that he was *the* William Martin, the CIA Director, when they were summoned to play tennis. As they walked to their court Jack Atherton quietly filled his wife in about the Martins. She was mildly disgusted at Jack's innuendo about Linda Martin and her former boss, President Anderson, and yet, somehow, that all made Martin more interesting—perhaps more available. After three quick games the court was claimed by others. The foursome found a table and ordered drinks.

Linda Martin and Jack Atherton immediately plunged into talk of Esker Anderson and the President's opposition that day to the clean-water legislation; to Jack's pending bill permitting wetback labor in California agriculture, Cesar Chavez, then the California senatorial race and Jack's political future. After several minutes of this nonstop political volleying, Sally felt a tapping on her ankle. She looked down to see Bill Martin's foot against hers, then looked up to catch his wink and the sideways tilt of his head. A few minutes later she excused herself from the table.

When Sally came out of the ladies' locker room Martin was waiting for her. "They're still at it," he said with a shake of his head and a grin. "They won't miss us for hours. How about a quiet drink?"

Over champagne they tried to pick up the threads of their earlier explorations. But within minutes the Iranian Minister-Counselor interrupted them to ask if they would fill in for a missing couple at tennis. They played three games as partners, then went back to Linda and Jack to find their political chatter still going on unabated. As they parted Sally realized that she had genuinely enjoyed Bill Martin's company.

Driving home, Sally and Jack talked about the Congressman's arrangements for his trip to Asia. A weekly Saturday tennis game with Congressman and Mrs. Albert Dunney would have to be rearranged. When Sally asked Jack if he would mind her inviting Martin as his substitute, Atherton's eyebrows went up, but he had no objection. So the next day Sally phoned Bill Martin with the invitation. Martin was anxious to see her again. When he heard Sally's voice he realized how much she had gotten to him. He agreed to pick her up Saturday at noon. As he hung up the phone he made a note to have Simon switch a staff meeting with the Assistant Directors from Saturday afternoon to the morning.

It was on that Saturday that Bill Martin realized he was falling in love with Sally Atherton. As they drove from her Georgetown home to the Riverbend Club they reminisced about the Iranian party. Linda and Jack would make a great political couple, they agreed. Linda hated tennis, in fact most athletics, and Jack's political wrapup had been the answer to her prayers. He had saved the evening for Linda.

"You were my deliverer, too," Sally smiled at Bill. "I was never cut out for this Washington social life. I literally suffocate at one of those parties."

"I've been here nearly fifteen years and I still haven't figured out how to get through an evening of small talk without oxygen," he replied. "In fact I didn't accept any of those invitations at all for a long time."

"What started you again—the Director's job?"

"No, my wife. Linda is impossible if we don't go to our quota of parties— She seems to thrive on them."

"So does Jack; but I refuse to go. He goes alone or takes his sister or someone. Do you have to go with Linda if she insists on going?"

"The bitching and grief I take when I don't go is far worse than the party. It's a question of the lesser of two evils."

At Riverbend Martin played much better tennis than the rest of the foursome and tried to hold back to equalize things. Nevertheless the Dunneys lost straight sets and apologized for not giving Sally and Martin a better game. When the Congressman suggested they all drive to the Dunneys' apartment in Arlington for drinks, Sally declined, saying she had promised to return Martin to his wife at an early hour.

As Sally and Bill drove out of the Club parking lot he said, "I just can't take you straight home. You really don't have to deliver me back so early. Linda won't be home until late. How about drinks and a little dinner? We're not far from Leesburg, are we?"

"No, it's close by. But let's just make it drinks," Sally replied. "I want to be in early. And from what I know of Linda Martin, I don't want to have to explain why you were out past curfew." They rode the rest of the way into Leesburg in near silence.

At the back of the taproom of an old inn they found a secluded wing-backed booth. Hand-hewn timbers crossed the low ceiling. The pewter fixtures and brass hardware had served the inn's guests since the eighteenth century, providing an atmosphere that compensated for the kitchen's indifferent cuisine. Candles and polished brass reflectors provided dim lighting at the wooden table. Bill sat down next to Sally on the highbacked bench, rather than across from her; their bare legs touched as he turned to look at her.

"Are you sure you won't let me ask for a table for dinner?"

"No, really, Bill, thanks, but I can't. With Jack away I think it's best I go home. Just a gin and tonic, please."

Martin gave the drink orders to a young waitress dressed in colonial costume.

"Do you always stay in when Jack travels?" There was a faint edge to Bill's voice.

She paused before answering.

"No, this week is a little different. Jack and I are balancing on a delicate marital tightrope and I don't want to do anything to destroy the equilibrium."

"Equilibrium?" Martin looked puzzled.

"We've had more than our share of problems lately, I'm afraid. His trip actually came at a very bad time. I was in hopes that we could get everything settled before he left, but we didn't. He'll be back in three days. Then perhaps I'll know the score."

"How are you voting?" Bill smiled to soften his probing as the waitress brought the tall, cool drinks along with a crock of Cheddar cheese and a basket of crackers.

"Some days I'm for a quick and friendly divorce. But it's so complicated I just don't know what is right to do.

We aren't bitter with each other. It's not that kind of situation. Jack is an easy person to be married to in many ways. He makes absolutely no demands."

She put her elbows on the table, reached for a paper napkin and began to fold it into small squares.

"Have you been married long?"

"Forever, it seems. We met when I was seventeen and we were married on my eighteenth birthday. Jack was at Harvard Law School and I was a freshman at Radcliffe. We met in a little cafeteria where we both used to eat a lot. When I met Jack I desperately needed a friend and an emotional refuge, and he was both. I was pretty good-looking in those days and men used to follow me home in droves." Sally looked quickly at Martin, then back down at the folded paper napkin. "My sheltered Manhasset home life hadn't prepared me to handle the Cambridge onslaught. Jack simply became my protection."

"Doesn't sound terribly romantic," Martin said wryly.

"It wasn't, but I had had a hell of a lot of romance from the time I was fifteen. Sex and the works. More than I needed or wanted, really. Jack was a blessed relief from all that pressure. We must have had eight or nine dates before Jack even kissed me. No sex until the honeymoon." Sally laughed wryly. "Jack's not exactly your average oversexed American male. And right then I wasn't burning up for it, either. I was convinced there were no thrills in it for me." Sally paused, turned her glance to a young couple in the booth across from them, then went on in a very low voice. "It wasn't until a year after we were married that I found out how great it could be."

"Did Jack read a book?" Bill's question was tinged with sarcasm.

"Hardly. It wasn't Jack, I'm sorry to say." She turned back and looked directly at Martin. "Right after we were married Jack took the California bar exam and immediately left for Korea with his Marine reserve unit. I just went back to the dorm in the fall like everyone else at Radcliffe, except that I had a shiny new wedding ring."

"Didn't that frighten off those predatory Harvard studs?"

"Not all of them. There was a section man in my English Lit section who didn't let it bother him very much. Jim looked a great deal like you, come to think of it, except he had a fine moustache. He was about thirty."

"Did you fall in love?"

"I guess infatuation is a better word. I wasn't as insecure, once I was married. The pressure was off and I felt more at ease. And at the same time I was more curious. So I went out with Jim a few times. He kept telling me how great it could be. And I kept telling him how awful it had been. All of my experience with sex, including those weeks in California with Jack, had been zero or worse. Finally I let Jim show me."

Martin put his hand on Sally's and gently caressed it. She pulled her hand away as if their contact was a distraction from what she wanted to say to him.

"And was it great?" he said softly.

"He was the first man who ever dedicated the lovemaking to me rather than himself, and he did wonderful things. I guess I owe him a great debt. But I suffered such guilt that finally I sent him on his way and climbed into a cocoon to wait for Jack to come home from the wars. All the same, I'll never forget that beautiful man."

"And when Jack came back?" Martin pressed her to continue.

"He had a chest full of medals and was a big hero, but as a matter of fact, our 'happy' reunion in San Diego was ghastly." Sally's face reflected her memory of a distasteful time.

"What happened?" Bill asked.

"Well, by then I wasn't the callow little Cliffie he'd left behind. I had done a lot of thinking and growing and I had developed some very definite ideas about the kind of life I wanted to lead. And about the kind of person I wanted to be, too. It was going to be peaceful and nonthreatening to be back under Jack's wing, but I was determined that he and I were going to live as equals. Kind of early Women's Lib." Sally attempted a laugh.

Bill smiled. "Was he surprised to find you so independent?"

"I'd been writing to him a lot, and he could have seen where my head was at from my letters. But he didn't. Jack had decided for both of us where we would live, who he was going to work for, and he'd made up his mind that he was going to run for Congress. He never even bothered to ask me what kind of life I'd like us to lead. He'd already taken a job with the big corporate law firm in San Diego. He had even picked the house we were going to buy in La Jolla. His folks were helping with the down payment. They'd left the choice of shelf paper up to me. But damn little else." Her voice had the slight tremor that goes with bitter memory.

"That must have made a big hit with you," Martin said dryly.

"I announced I was leaving; he could stick La Jolla, Congress and the new house right up his ass. There was crying and a lot of arguing and pleading for me not to leave him. Finally he made some promises and said I could set my own terms for staying. I took him up on it. We called it the Treaty of North Island. We were at the Coronado Hotel on North Island for a reunion holiday when all this scheming and screaming took place. As I look back at it now, I probably wouldn't have walked out. All my bravado was a bluff. I was still pretty insecure, but he didn't know that."

"So you wrote your own ticket then?"

"Almost entirely. I agreed to stay and he agreed I could lead my own life, as long as I would never embarrass him professionally or politically. Otherwise, what I did, how I did it and with whom was strictly up to me. He promised never to dictate or even criticize. And he's lived up to that pretty well, bless his heart."

Martin cleared his throat. "Did that emasculate him? Could he still see himself as a husband after that?"

Sally ran a finger around the rim of the glass. "Sex is definitely not the cement that binds Jack and Sally Atherton. We're together because Jack wants to be President of the United States and, believe it or not, I've been scared to be single. It's as simple as that. Jack's missionary ancestors had a strong influence on his attitudes toward sex and marriage, I guess. What we do, we do for him. So we don't do much."

Martin traced the grain in the scarred pine table with his fingers and spoke softly. "He wants you to stay, of course."

"Yes, but he's ambivalent about it. Pride and *macho* and what the fellows at the House gym will say all impel him to insist that I stay. But he is beginning to realize he is never going to be the Republican front runner for President, and these days divorce is not all that big a deal in San Diego. He can be reelected to Congress without me. And he's really not at all comfortable with me any more. He thinks I'm laughing at him a lot of the time."

The waitress brought their second round of drinks.

"And are you?" Bill asked.

"Not really. I would never intentionally do anything to hurt him. In spite of all my bitching, Jack's probably my best friend in the world. We just haven't made a marriage. In many ways it will—would—be hard to leave him." Sally's tone changed. "But you wouldn't know about all that, would you, Bill? Isn't Linda your first wife?"

"No. I was married before, for a short time during the war, but she was killed."

"I'm sorry," Sally said softly.

"It's a long time ago." Martin's tone was matter-of-fact. "My wife was Argentinian. I met her there. She was killed in an automobile accident."

"How awful for you."

"It was hard for a long, long time."

"It sounds as if you were really happy with her," Sally said.

"Yes. We only had six months together, and it was a very fragmented life. I was gone a great deal and she worked. But it was good, and I believe that it would have been very good." He turned the subject back to Sally. "If you leave Jack, what will you do? Stay here?"

"I don't know. I guess I'll go wherever I can earn a living. But let's not get ahead of ourselves. I haven't decided what I'm going to do." Her manner suddenly turned businesslike. "Which is why we have to go home now, Mr. Martin, and why you have to let me out at my front door and then quickly drive away."

"I don't understand all this circumspection, Sally. What's the matter with me?"

"Other than the fact that you are a conspicuous—and conspicuously *married*—Government official, there's not a thing wrong with you, Bill. In fact, there's a great deal right with you. But I've made up my mind that while Jack and I are in the midst of this big decision I'm not going to complicate things. I almost didn't call you for tennis just for that reason, but I talked it over with Jack and he approved. I wouldn't have called you otherwise." She paused. "Let's see, weren't you with someone named Linda Martin at the Iranian Ambassador's party?"

Sally's wry reference broke the tension and Martin chuckled.

"I seem to recall the name. A dark-haired girl?"

"That's the one."

"If you could spare a few more minutes maybe I could explain that particular situation," Bill said.

"Afraid my time is up, Mr. Martin. Save your sad story for next time. This was exclusively my turn. It's the first time I've opened up this way to anyone. Thanks for listening." Sally reached into her pocketbook for her compact and lipstick as Bill raised a hand for the check.

On the drive back, winding along tree-lined Georgetown Pike, they didn't talk much, but Bill took her hand and held it lightly.

As they passed the CIA campus at Langley, Bill decided to press a few more questions.

"What kind of married life did you have in California, Sally? Before Congress."

"Jack and I pretty much went our separate ways. I wanted to do my photography and so I took courses and built a great darkroom for myself. We lived near the beach and I got a board and learned to surf. And I painted some, just for fun. Jack politicked and practiced law and kept up the Atherton family bonds."

"Did you campaign for Jack?"

"I hated it, but I did. And I still do. The coffee hours and door-belling and all that. To all appearances, out there I'm the candidate's beautiful, different, artistic wife. That's part of the deal as long as I'm married to Jack."

"It sounds like a business contract."

"I'm afraid it is. Quid pro quo. I'm not proud of it, but I guess I'm not the first woman who has made a marriage of convenience."

She looked straight at him and smiled as Martin

turned the blue Fiat into a street lined with handsome brick-and-shingle houses.

"What a hell of a time for the Atherton house to appear. When can I call you, Sally?"

"Let's see how this week goes, Bill, please," she said.

"Do you mean 'Don't call me, I'll call you'?"

"Sort of, I guess. Don't worry. We'll see each other again." She quickly brushed her lips against his cheek, a kiss that might mean nothing, or everything. Then she ran up the driveway, unlocked the door and waved at Martin.

He waited until her front door closed, then drove away, more alive than he had been in a long time.

5

A few blocks west of the White House, at 1839 G Street Northwest, an old frame house, reached by a long flight of stone steps, sits high on a corner lot. Like a dowager Washington hostess, it is unable to hide the ravages of advancing age, despite its fresh paint. Its Victorian turrets are firmly corseted and rise superior to the encroaching apartment buildings and the ordinary life of the street below. The old Club exudes social standing.

Half of the front door is a lace-curtained window. In the middle of the lower panel is an old-fashioned round brass doorbell with a winged handle in its center. When the bell rings it is answered by a small man in his seventies, gray and balding, dressed impeccably in white serving jacket, black tie, black pants. He is joined in the narrow hallway by a gray-haired woman in a starched black-and-white maid's uniform of some bygone vintage.

The G Street Club offers comfortable old rooms and excellent food and drink to its members and their guests. Washington parties are often given there by hosts and hostesses whose homes and apartments are smaller than their social aspirations or obligations. No such Washington party is complete without a guest of honor. Often the honoree is not the real reason for the gathering; but neither he nor his host would ever unmask the pretense.

Bill Martin had intended for months to have a party, in part as repayment of past invitations but also to maintain informal contact with influential and important Congressmen, White House people, lobbyists and diplomats. Jack Atherton was an ideal guest of honor for the dinner, since many of the people Martin wanted to invite were friends of Congressman Atherton. And of course it would be a way to be with Sally Atherton. Since Atherton was ranking Congressman on the Oversight and Appropriations Committees, the Company would pay for a good party from the "legislative relations" budget—not a minor consideration for one living on Martin's government salary.

And when Professor Carl Tessler accepted his late invitation, Martin had added a very political motive to his other, private reasons for the party.

Several weeks before the party, Simon Cappell had prepared a drawing of the dining room of the 1839 G Street Club, locating on it the large round tables, each surrounded by ten chairs. Martin went over the final guest list and every detail of the seating arrangement with great care, taking it home with his evening reading. The following day, engraved invitations were mailed from Martin's office.

The Director of Central Intelligence
and
Mrs. Martin
*request the pleasure of your company at*_____

A calligrapher in the cartographic section of the CIA was instructed to set his mapmaking aside to fill in the blanks. The words "Black Tie" set the dress: long gowns for the ladies, black ties and dinner jackets for the men.

As the RSVPs came in, the guests' names were either erased or confirmed in ink on Simon's seating chart, then crossed out or checked on the master guest list. When an invitee declined, a standby invitation was quickly dispatched to the top name on the reserve list. Seating then had to be juggled to conform strictly with diplomatic protocol.

Four days before the party, the seating chart was finalized and the names of each of the guests were engraved on stiff little white seating cards. They, in turn, were placed in small white envelopes that would repose in a wooden rack in the Club hallway. Each seating card displayed a numbered circle portraying a table, an inverted U marked "door" and a thin red X with a legend repeating the guest's table number. Without these cards, Washington society might well lose its way.

The experienced Washington party-goer knew how to find his table simply by matching his card with a large number placard temporarily standing by the flower centerpiece on his or her table. A waiter would quietly remove the number signs as the last guest was seated.

The invitations, place cards and handscripted menus bore the four-color embossed seal of the CIA. Out-of-town guests slipped them into purse or pocket as a coveted souvenir. A few passed the menu around the table and asked their dinner companions to autograph the back in memory of the happy occasion, especially if the table included a particularly desirable political autograph.

An hour before the first guests were to arrive, Simon Cappell had double-checked arrangements, then turned the seating chart, cards and guest list over to the butler in the foyer. A few minutes later Linda and Bill Martin arrived and gave their coats to the maid. As Bill walked through an open arch into the old living room, Linda turned into the mahogany and plush parlor where another septuagenarian tended a tiny bar.

Linda wore a black lamé gown with full sleeves and a square-cut neckline. Her dark hair was gathered severely at the back in a knot, adorned and held with a rhinestone clip. She wore no other jewelry. Her eyes were heavily colored in shades of blue makeup. The sleek dress seemed to accentuate her protruding collarbones. She appeared gaunt and tense, her movements nervous and impatient.

The bartender handed her a martini, which she took without a word to him. She found Martin in the dining room among the six tables, adjusting a place card.

"Who did the flowers?" she asked.

"The Club got them, I think. Do you want them afterward?"

"Are you kidding? I want to forget this rotten evening as soon as it is over. You and your goddamned dancing. I thought we had agreed on an early evening. We'll be here until two, now that you've added the dancing. Who the hell are you trying to impress?" she asked acidly.

Martin refused to be baited. "I just think it's a nice touch; our guests will enjoy it." He moved close to her. "Try to relax and have a good time."

Martin had added the dancing at the last minute. He calculated that, while the others were dancing in the terrace room—a twentieth-century addition to the venerable house—he could take Professor Carl Tessler aside for a serious talk about Governor Forville's Presidential prospects. But Martin was not confiding his motives to Linda Martin because, in fact, he was no longer sure that whatever he might tell her would not shortly be known in every detail by Esker Anderson.

Martin straightened the place card to the right of his place at the table and smiled. He had not seen Sally Atherton since their tennis date and Leesburg talk several weeks before. To Sally's right would be seated Congressman Atherton's former Harvard Professor, Dr. Carl Tessler, and on Tessler's right Madame Ritaka, the wife of the brand-new Finnish Ambassador. She had been carefully chosen for this particular seat. If the vast resources of the Central Intelligence Agency were correct, Madame Ritaka spoke only her native tongue, and Carl Tessler spoke no Finnish. Martin hoped to have Tessler's complete attention at dinner by fair means or foul.

When Simon Cappell came into the dining room to cue Martin that the guests of honor were just arriving, Martin sent Simon to find Linda and bring her to the door.

The Athertons had shed their coats and were coming through the arch. Sally looked stunning in a simple white silk strapless dress, which outlined her ample breasts and dropped straight to the floor. Her only jewelry was a wide gold mesh bracelet on her wrist.

Martin had wanted Sally before. Now that she was here, beautiful, tan, graceful, Martin coveted her with a hollowness in his chest, a physical urgency. He now knew without a doubt that his marriage was over, and, knowing that, somehow there was a new quality in his desire for her.

As Martin led the Athertons into the G Street living

room Linda emerged from the parlor with a fresh drink in her hand.

"How nice to see you, Congressman." She leaned forward and placed a cheek against his. Then she turned to Sally. "That dress certainly was made to show off your tan," she remarked coolly.

"Jack and I were at Palm Springs during the Easter recess. It was heavenly," Sally smiled.

"I'll bet," said Linda. The drinks were already beginning to reach her, and her voice sounded thick. "I haven't sat out in the sun since forever. The Director here has just been to Florida; business, strictly business, you know. He keeps up his tan, never fear. But I never get out of town."

Jack Atherton chuckled. "You sound just like a Washington wife, Linda. It is certainly wonderful of you two to do this for us tonight. Before the others get here I just want you to know we're thrilled that you've invited so many of our good friends."

"We're delighted we could do it," said Martin, steering his wife by the elbow. "Simon tells me we're to stand here in front of the piano to receive as they come in. Hope you don't mind the formality."

A waiter brought them a tray of drinks. About ten glasses of different sizes were filled and ready. Scotch, Bourbon, orange juice and martinis arranged in little groups.

"Scotch, please." The waiter turned the tray to point the Scotch cluster at Jack Atherton. He took a glass. Martin took another. When it was Linda's turn Martin raised an eyebrow and nodded toward the orange juice. She paused, glared at her husband, then reached for a martini.

Nearly all of the guests arrived within a few minutes of one another and most of them had been received, furnished with a drink and begun pre-dinner chatter within twenty minutes. Jack Atherton then left the Martins and Sally to talk to a Congressman he had been trying to reach on the telephone. Linda Martin moved to Professor Carl Tessler's side to overhear what he was saying to the Undersecretary of State with such animation.

Most Washington cocktail hours eventually achieve a noise level that forecloses meaningful communication. The crescendo increases with the passage of minutes along a predictable curve which is the algebraic function of the room size and temperature, the number of people, their occupation and gender. There was another variable which accelerated the upswing of the decibel curve at the G Street Club that night, and that was the impending retirement of Esker Scott Andreson.

The cocktail chatter of many of the knots of people focused on the imponderables in the months ahead. There would be a new President. Jobs would be transferred, reorganized, downgraded, held vacant. Policy would be reexamined, budgets scrutinized. Like the inhabitants of an anthill that hear footsteps approaching, the Washingtonians at the Martins' party were sounding the alarms for one another.

As the din increased, Martin took Sally Atherton's bare left forearm gently in his right hand and steered her through the half-open door to the dining room. He held her arm loosely, caressing it gently as they walked. She appeared not to notice. Four waitresses in white uniforms were putting the finishing touches on the tables. They ignored the couple standing in the corner inside the door.

"Tell me, my dear tennis partner," said Martin, "how would you like to do something for your country tonight?"

"What do you mean, Bill?" Sally sounded puzzled as she smiled at him.

"It's important that I talk with Carl Tessler tonight before he leaves. I've put him on your right at dinner and I hope the combination of your charms and the good wine will make him mere putty in my hands. Will you watch for a chance to steer him to me after dinner? I'm sure he'll be your lapdog by then."

"You have an exaggerated idea of my capacity to lure men to their doom, my friend," she said with a laugh. "But I'll do my best in the cause. I suppose I shouldn't even *ask* what's up?"

Martin's voice turned serious. "I wouldn't mind telling you, Sally, but it's a long story. In fact, I want you to know. Just make Tessler a contented man tonight and perhaps it'll all have a happy ending."

"I'd really like to know about it, Bill." Sally placed a hand on his arm and looked at him evenly. "Things are better and I'm pretty free the rest of this week. Can you call me?"

"Can I? The first possible moment." Bill gave Sally a long look. "You look absolutely marvelous tonight, Sally. I am knocked off my feet."

"Stay on your toes, Mr. Director. We can talk about all that later."

"The sooner the better." Martin smiled, pressed her hand and led her back to the noisy living room.

The dinner, served at beautifully appointed candlelit tables, went flawlessly. Conversation flowed easily between the courses of mousseline de solé Breton, Chateaubriand with grilled mushroom caps, and endive salad served with a perfect soft Brie. The accompanying wines were superb, the service unobtrusive and thoughtful. The G Street Club knew its business.

Carl Tessler was enchanted by Sally. He leaned forward often to speak to Martin and Sally together and found nothing to distract him from their company. Madame Ritaka sat in stoic, diplomatic silence, smiling occasionally at the man from the Department of Transportation on her right. Martin in turn did his bare conversational duty toward the lady on his left, but no more. Sally and Tessler claimed most of his attention.

After dessert of meringue puffs piled with fresh raspberries, the champagne glasses were refilled and Bill Martin stood for what Sally had just referred to as the host-toast. Simon Cappell had written out a short toast, but Martin had decided not to use any of it. That afternoon he had written a few notes of what he might say. They were in his pocket and would stay there. He would wing it, making it short, faintly humorous and without any real content.

"Congressman Atherton, my charming dinner partner Sally Atherton, your Excellencies and our other distinguished and delightful guests": The room fell silent, all heads turned to the Director. "Linda and I are truly pleased that you can all be with us tonight to honor the Athertons. Most of you are their friends of many years' standing."

Martin went on to mention Jack Atherton's intelligence and diligence and his vital role as a member of the Appropriations Committee. His few witticisms were received with smiles and polite laughter. And he made it short. There is a formula for winding up a formal toast and Martin came to it with decent speed.

"Ladies and gentlemen, I call upon you—" chairs scraped the floor as the dinner guests started to rise "—to join with me in toasting the distinguished Member from California, Congressman John B. Atherton." It was a nice little toast, he thought.

By then everyone was standing, raising their champagne glasses. They muttered various responses:

"To Jack." Or "The Congressman." "Congressman Atherton." "Hear, hear," said an Ambassador.

After everyone had a sip of champagne, the chairs scraped again and the guests reseated themselves amid a low buzz of post-host-toast comment.

Jack Atherton immediately stood up to make his required reply, buttoning his dinner jacket. He was of medium size, heavy and round-faced. His dark hair was receding; where hair had once been, his skin was pink from the sun of the Palm Springs recess. He smiled easily, dimples creasing his cheeks.

"Mr. Director, Linda, Honorable Ambassadors and Members, distinguished ladies and gentlemen: I thank Bill for his generous toast."

The reply toast that followed was warm and funny; Atherton was a clever and experienced speaker and he could turn a phrase. He said a few kind words about Linda Martin, duly complimented Bill on the great job he was doing, and gracefully found his way to the ritual ending with time to spare.

"And so, please join me; I toast a dedicated American public servant, Bill Martin." Again the raised glasses, the subsiding murmurs, and some applause for Jack Atherton's wit and brevity.

Bill Martin stood again. "Ladies and gentlemen, I am entitled to the last word, I think. For your pleasure there is a small orchestra out in the terrace room—"

Sally Atherton stood up beside Martin and put her hand on his arm. "Bill, before we dance, on behalf of the women here tonight, I would like to propose a toast." Her voice was even and strong. She tossed her blond hair, smiled at the guests and reached for her glass. Murmurs were heard at some of the tables, a few commenting about a woman making a toast, others remarking on her striking beauty.

"The women in this room have a right to envy me tonight," Sally began. "By the luck of the draw I have been seated between the two most interesting men in the room." She paused for a second or two. "Other than my husband, of course." A little polite laughter. Bill Martin looked across the room at his wife. She was grimly scoring the tablecloth by her wineglass with a fork, drawing deep lines in the heavy linen as she looked at Sally Atherton.

"Jack has told you all," Sally continued, "about Bill Martin. What Jack couldn't tell you is that Bill Martin is probably the best dancer in the room. Ladies, I hope Linda is going to let us cut in tonight for at least one dance."

Some of the guests turned to look at Linda Martin. She quickly smiled, raised one hand toward her husband and shrugged a "couldn't-give-less-of-a-damn" gesture.

"But it is to the distinguished statesman on my right that I want to propose a toast tonight." Carl Tessler looked up at Sally sharply, hesitated, then broke into a broad grin. "Since I was a student at Radcliffe, I have heard about Professor Carl Tessler. My husband was his student. 'Brilliant' is the word most people use to describe Dr. Tessler's lectures. But I would like to contribute two or three additions to the Tessler legend tonight, based on my own observation during the past few hours." Sally paused, her timing faultless.

"Girls, he's a pussycat." Carl Tessler began to chuckle, chin down, looking at a spoon he held in his left hand, as laughter swept the room. "You probably suppose we've been sitting here discussing state secrets or Greenland's strategic significance? Well, friends, you're dead wrong. I have discovered that Carl Tessler knows a great deal about modern art and I have been learning things about Modigliani from a *real* art connoisseur." Tessler was obviously pleased to be characterized as a man of interests broader than his professional reputation. Behind his thick glasses his eyes sparkled. "He tells me that he sketches and paints when allowed the time. In fact I have just acquired an original Tessler tonight, his sketch of the centerpiece of our table, on the back of my menu. I will treasure it always.

"I have dined tonight with the true Renaissance man, ladies and gentlemen, and I think I'm falling in love."

Sally smiled and raised her glass. "Please join me in toasting Dr. Carl Tessler."

When the toast was completed, many of the guests, especially the men, remained standing to applaud Sally. She sat down, flushed and smiling. Carl Tessler leaned to her and, placing a pale hand on her shoulder, lightly kissed her cheek.

Bill Martin sat down, still applauding, turned to Sally Atherton with a broad grin and reached with his right hand to take her left hand in his between their chairs.

Carl Tessler leaned forward and said to Bill, "Mr. Director, I am forever in your debt for the seating arrangement this evening. How could I have been so fortunate as to have this beautiful and witty lady for a companion? I have never been so flattered by a toast or so willing to believe what was said about me!"

Martin had not released Sally's hand, now resting on his thigh; the coupled hands responded to one another in discreet pressures as Tessler went on: "As I was saying, and I want to finish the point I was making before the toasts, the key is Israel. I am suspect, I know, because I am a Jew. But I am first, and, I believe, exclusively, a geopolitician. Israel is the pivot. As you well know, it sits astride Russia's way to the riches of Africa. It intrudes Westernism into pan-Arabia. Its air power dominates the Suez Canal. I hope we are as careful in our acquisition of intelligence in and about Israel as we are about the Communist countries."

"I will never underestimate you, Carl," Martin replied quietly, but his mind was racing in two directions. Tessler's comment was a message, perhaps meant only for him, perhaps intended to convey some hint of information which had come to the Professor about the Israelis' plans or intentions. Was something going on there that the Company had missed? Bill Martin strained to classify and retain the message.

But near the hem of the tablecloth he was receiving another message, one of passion and need and magnetic attraction. Sally had curled a finger inside their hands and was scraping her fingernail along the inside of his palm with a regular, throbbing rhythm. She was pressing her hand into his thigh and moving it back and forth imperceptibly in harmony with her finger. Martin looked at Tessler but at the same time he caught Sally's moving finger with two of his. He squeezed it in the rhythm she had created for them.

"Carl, before you leave I must talk to you for about ten minutes. Just let me get the dancing started and then I'll come find you," said Martin.

Tessler nodded. Bill squeezed Sally's wide, tan hand, lifted it and kissed the finger that had caressed his palm. Then he stood and led her to the glassed-in terrace at the back of the dining room. The four-piece orchestra had begun to play "You're the Top," but only two couples were on the floor. One of them was Jack Atherton and Linda Martin.

Bill suddenly realized that he had never danced with Sally. It felt strange to hold her. Linda was thin, narrow, small-boned and light. Sally was larger in all ways, not so easy to lead, but God! how exciting it was to hold her and feel her close.

He leaned back and looked at her as they danced. Their legs touched. "Lord, you are great!" he said quietly. "That toast to Tessler was magnificent. I've got to get to him now, but I really have to see you, talk to you. Can we be together tomorrow?"

"I don't know, Bill. You'll call me?"

"Do you really want me to call this time?"

"*Very* much. Things are clearing up. I meant what I said, but I wasn't really talking about Carl Tessler."

Martin's right hand quickly brushed the length of Sally's hair. "I'll call you."

As he led Sally off the floor, the Finnish Ambassador

blocked their way, offering his hand, palm up. Martin released Sally to the Finn, then moved alone among the tables, nodding and speaking to several of his guests. At the living-room door he stopped to look back at Sally, dancing slowly, head back, talking enthusiastically. When she saw Bill they exchanged a long, locked gaze, then her partner turned between them.

Smiling in spite of himself, Martin walked through the overstuffed Victorian living room, across the hall into the empty parlor. Carl Tessler sat alone on a small horsehair loveseat, a demitasse of coffee balanced on his knee, the cup held steady by his delicate fingers.

Tessler was a physical anomaly. His head was large, though not out of proportion to his neck and shoulders, nor his broadening girth. But his arms and legs were thin, his hands and feet small, almost dainty. He had short, thin fingers with raw pink tips; all the fingernails had been torn away again and again by his teeth in some continuing uncontrollable private agony. The middle knuckles of his third fingers were red and enlarged, another result of constant nervous chewing.

Tessler's face was perfectly round. Dark hair, curly and unkempt, almost hid his ears. Riding on his large nose were round, heavy glasses with thick lenses. The mouth was small, almost cherubic, made the more so by fat cheeks and three layers of chins. His facial skin was young and ruddy, making him look younger than his years. He smiled easily and often, showing even but yellowing teeth.

Tessler had been born in Vienna. His family had fled the Nazis when he was a boy. He spent the war years with his refugee parents in England and came to the United States to do graduate work at Harvard. The University was a congenial if not perfect environment for his brilliant mind, and he'd been there ever since. His deep voice could have been guttural if it had not been leavened by the tones of the English midlands and Cambridge, Massachusetts.

At times his reactions were quick, at other times long delayed. He seized ideas, sorted them out deep inside himself, then selected what he brought back to the surface with care and calculation. He usually presented himself to others under rigid self-control. Only the fingernails, knuckles and shy mannerisms gave reliable, unvolunteered evidence of the hidden man.

"You were good to wait for me, Carl. First, let me assure you I'll follow up on your suggestion regarding Israel. I appreciate it. It's getting late and I'm sure you'd like to be on your way." Martin, sitting on a small plush chair next to Tessler, motioned a passing waiter to bring them more coffee. "I want to talk to you because you know Governor Forville so well. Obviously the CIA Director never gets involved in partisan politics, Carl, but I'm legitimately worried about the Company and its future, particularly if the election goes wrong. Perhaps there are things I should be anticipating." Martin spoke smoothly, easily. "I thought you might help me understand the current situation among the Republicans so that I'll be better equipped to go about my job."

Tessler's thick eyebrows rose. "Mr. Director, I don't know very much about domestic politics. I do work for Forville now—actually for the Forville Foundation— but only on issues of *foreign* policy. They don't talk to me much about the convention or the election."

Martin nodded.

Tessler began to talk faster, with latent enthusiasm. "Frankly, Mr. Director, I'm as concerned as you are. Vice President Gilley seems to me to be a talkative fool with no real background, in spite of his years in Washington. Maybe he's a good domestic politician. I don't know. Senator Monckton is very intelligent and knowledgeable in my field; I've recently corresponded with him a little. But he's a terribly unattractive person, anti-intellectual, I think; a pragmatic politician and not a statesman. In my opinion his performance on the Senate Foreign Relations Committee was largely irresponsible. He is the master of the cheap political shot. One would anticipate that if he were President his foreign policy would always be the servant of his domestic political interests. Forville lacks *Sitzfleisch,* but he is certainly the best of the three."

Martin caught Tessler's reference to the Governor's lack of the scholar's ability to study a problem through to the end. Was this a signal that Tessler was not altogether Forville's man, or was it just an intellectual's cool, objective assessment of a politician's personality?

He leaned forward. "But can Forville be elected?"

"I'm not competent to say. As I said, I don't follow domestic politics that closely. Forville has enough money, God knows! And good help, also. But he is a liberal in a conservative party, isn't he? I know he's more worried about the Republican convention than he is about the November election. In fact, he's told me so," the Professor admitted, with a smile.

Martin leaned forward again and lowered his voice. "Carl, I'm going to say something now that you must never repeat. I am relying on your discretion."

"Of course."

"I not only like you, but I *admire* you, Carl. It would be a good thing for the country if Forville were President because he would bring *you* in to look after foreign policy."

Tessler nodded slowly, unconsciously, in agreement with Martin's premise, not so much out of egotism, but as if it were an objective, obvious fact.

"You know I can't be of help to you and Forville in any overt way," Martin continued. "That would be bad for the Governor and fatal for me. But I do want to help in any way that I can. Does that shock you?"

"Mr. Director," Tessler replied, "I am realistic about such things, as I know you are. I know the CIA and also the FBI are influential to some degree in domestic politics and they always have been. I am not dismayed by that. It may even be a very good thing for the country that they are. But I will not mention it to Forville or his people. It should remain an understanding strictly between the two of us. Don't you agree?"

Martin looked at the Professor. "I most certainly do," he said. "What kind of information would be most helpful to you, Carl?"

Tessler closed his eyes and paused for a second. Then he came to life and ticked off his requests one by one on his fingers, as he often did in his lectures.

"Obviously, any intelligence about the war that Gilley or Monckton get, we would like to have. And, since I am now working on a paper on international economic policy, I would like as much as I can have that's unpublished information on the Finance Ministers' meetings this year. Russian gold, Mideast oil production and atomic electrical generation technology are subjects I am having trouble getting reliable data on. Relations between Iran and Russia. President Anderson's meeting with the Egyptians. I could give you a list as long as your guest list."

"Why don't you make a list, Carl?" Martin said. "That would help me."

Tessler looked at him with surprise. He seemed astonished that Martin was giving up so much so quickly. "How can I get a list to you without causing trouble? The mails, of course, are out—should I bring it to your home?"

"No, that would be unwise." The Director paused, then felt the tumblers of the combination fall into perfect position. He leaned further forward, again speaking very softly. "I have a suggestion, Carl. Let's choose a go-between who has no apparent connection with either of us, and no political interests. A courier. Someone nobody would suspect. How about our dinner partner, Sally Atherton?"

"That would be most pleasant," Tessler said, smiling. "Most pleasant indeed. But would the wife of a Congressman do such a thing? Her husband is a Republican, isn't he?"

Martin nodded.

"Do we tell her what she's carrying? She looks like a lady who would insist on knowing."

"Perhaps. She could be trusted, I'm sure," Martin replied. "She is very independent of her husband. I don't know about her politics, but I'll find out. Still, there's no reason to tell her everything, is there? Why don't I talk to her and let you know?"

Tessler stood, pulling down his rumpled dinner jacket. The point of his left collar protruded over his lapel. "Thank you, Mr. Director, for this evening. I will look forward to your call. Please say good night to Mrs. Martin and thank her for me."

Martin walked with Tessler to the hall and waited as the Professor rummaged through several pockets to find his coat check. As he hunched into the overcoat with the help of the butler, he looked at Bill Martin and said, "Don't forget what I said about Israel, Mr. Director. I hope the lady didn't distract you too much. I meant what I said."

"I heard you, Carl." Bill grinned as the door closed. The *Herr Doktor* didn't miss anything. It was a delight to find himself dealing with a first-class mind.

Martin returned to the dancing and did his duty as host by waltzing a few of the older wallflowers. Within a half-hour most of the dancers had quit the floor and come over to the Martins to say their thanks and good night. Among the last to leave were the Athertons. Jack

Atherton was excited, warm and profuse in his gratitude. Sally extended her hand to Bill, and as their hands joined there was an eloquent and private statement in the look that passed between them.

The Martins left the Club soon after. His car and driver were double-parked directly in front of the steps, blinkers flashing. Linda had said almost nothing to her husband all evening. When the car door slammed she looked away from him, out the window, and said sarcastically, "You certainly had a lovely evening. I'm happy for you."

"Home, Rudy," said Martin quietly to the driver as the car eased forward. Rudy was an employee of the Company. Though not really a bodyguard, he was armed and a good shot. He had been Horace McFall's driver when McFall was Director. Martin assumed Rudy's loyalty and discretion, as countless Washington passengers relied on the rectitude of their chauffeurs. Many private things were said and done in Washington limousines.

Rudy was therefore considered unlikely to betray his passengers' confidences. And he was tactful. As soon as he caught the bitter, personal tone of the Martins' back-seat talk he asked if they had any objection to his turning on the radio. It always made passengers feel better to imagine that the driver couldn't hear their conversation from his seat.

Martin turned to his wife. "As a matter of fact, I *did* have a good time. What's wrong with having fun at your own party? And what about you? Did you enjoy yourself?"

"It's so nice of you to ask," she said between clenched teeth. "It might have been nice of you to dance with your wife, too. But I realize you were preoccupied with Sally. Who am I to compete with all that tan skin and blond hair?"

Martin ignored the barb. "My dear, I was only paying very proper attention to the wife of the guest of honor. And how did you and the Congressman get along at your table?"

"Since you ask, he's a fat bore. Why in hell we gave an expensive dinner party for him I don't for the life of me understand. It doesn't make political sense—he's only ranking, not a chairman, and he's very unattractive. What was the real point of all that—his wife?"

Martin sighed. "Sometime I'll explain it to you, Linda. It had nothing to do with Sally."

"Bullshit, Bill. I'm not blind. You thought that little toast she gave was marvelous, didn't you? If I had tried something like that, you'd have never quit reminding me of my place. And, I hope you noticed, we were practically the only people who danced. What a waste of money!"

Martin finally exploded. "OK, you didn't like the goddamn party, you can't stand Jack, you're jealous of Sally, I was wrong about the dancing—any other friendly little thing you'd like to say before we get home to our happy love nest?"

"Screw you, Martin," she said, moving over to the corner. "You make me sick."

They rode the rest of the way in silence, the music of the radio counterpointing their unspoken hatred and disgust.

Later, in bed, Martin lay on his back in the dark. Linda was on her side, turned away from him. He was thinking about Sally Atherton—more than thinking, he was reexperiencing her. Her husky tone of voice, that finger caress, her way of looking at him from the corners of her eyes, challenging, provocative. He knew he must have her, and soon. The idea of making her a courier was a good one, and convenient. It was something they would do together, something beyond the physical thing they both obviously felt for each other. Yes, he would get the Tessler channel started tomorrow.

A few minutes later Martin's regular deep breathing told his insomniac wife that he was sound asleep.

6

William Martin and Simon Cappell stood quietly at the fringe of the crowd at the Park Avenue entrance to the Waldorf Astoria Hotel. Some were typical summer tourists; some were New Yorkers diverted by curiosity from their daily pursuits to gather behind the white wooden barricades. But the majority had come by bus from Suffolk County on Long Island; they were loyal Republicans whose trip to Manhattan that day insured a friendly welcome for one of their party's candidates for President. The police had placed big sawhorses on the sidewalk a few inches from the curb along the entire block from Forty-ninth to Fiftieth streets, with only a gap where the barricades blocked off the sidewalk, creating a clear passage from the curb to the main door. Martin estimated that there were about two hundred people on each side; those at the back of the crowd were swaying and craning to see. The Director remained conspicuously aloof from the crowd. It was important to him that he and Simon Cappell not appear to be a part of it. Three policemen stood in the street giving the vehicles a get-it-moving motion, but the cars and taxis all slowed to see what was happening.

A few feet from the curb stood a young man in a

double-breasted dark-blue suit, wearing a conservative-
ly striped red tie; he looked as if he had just stepped
from behind a desk in one of the big banks across Park
Avenue. He was a freshly scrubbed thirty-year-old with
a sincere and friendly look. Clipped to his belt was a
heavy walkie-talkie radio, causing his well-tailored
trousers to sag to the left. A thin gray wire disappeared
under his suit jacket and emerged at his collar, ending
at a transparent plastic plug in his left ear. Another
wire passed from the walkie-talkie inside his coat sleeve
to his left wrist, where a brown plastic microphone
about an inch long dangled freely. The political advance
man pressed two fingers over his earplug for a moment
to hear better, then walked a few steps to his right,
where a second man stood.

This man was more muscular, a little older and less
polished. He, too, had the plastic earpiece and sleeve
microphone, but his suit was single-breasted and obviously less expensive. In his left-lapel buttonhole he
displayed a round enamel button divided into red, yellow and blue segments of irregular design. As he talked
to the advance man he looked intently at the crowd on
the south side of the entrance. His hands were clasped
in front of him, arms extended, in a kind of fig-leaf
pose, one foot slightly ahead of the other, suit coat
fastened with one button. His revolver rode high on his
left hip under his coat. The candidate's stop at the
Waldorf was his assignment; he was the Secret Service
agent on advance security detail.

For two weeks the two men had been working together, covering the routine check lists required for a
political hotel stop. They had selected the hotel rooms
to be used, the route the candidate would take to get to
the rooms from his car, the one elevator he would use.
The names of all hotel employees had been listed and
run through the Secret Service computer. The elevator
had to be inspected and a city police detail assigned to

keep it secure during the visit. Near the rooms to be used by the candidate, the Secret Service and local police established round-the-clock guard posts. The Technical Services branch inspected the candidate's rooms for bombs or "other threatening materials," sweeping the area with their high-frequency receivers, checking for "bugs" or other transmitters. At least twelve hours before the candidate arrived, agents began to guard his rooms, excluding anyone not on the cleared list, until the Secret Service detail assigned to travel with the candidate took over the post at the door to the suite.

In the street the two advance men talked in low tones. The political man, a member of the Monckton campaign organization, looked at his watch, then down at his clipboard. "Christ, we've lost seventeen minutes somewhere."

The agent never took his eyes off the crowd as he replied, "What difference does it make? You've got a two-hour cushion once he gets here before he even has to start getting dressed for the fat cats. Relax, Charlie."

The political aide had been taught to live by the printed schedule. "I just like to see things run on time, I guess," he said a bit sheepishly. He was new at this. "But at least he's on the ground and driving. He'll make the reception without a hitch."

The agent smiled, thinking that this young fellow would work out. He was not as officious as some of them. When the campaign got into full swing and he was setting up three stops in three different cities all in the same week, sleeping on planes and eating on the run, he'd loosen up even more.

The agent's earphone came to life with a whoosh. The words were loud in his ear.

"Szabol, Szabol, this is Dunnam. I am one minute your location. Do you read me?"

Agent Szabol slipped the tiny microphone between

thumb and forefinger, pressed its side, the old feeling of excitement involuntarily coming to life.

"Roger, Dunnam, read you."

The agent turned to his companion and snapped, "One minute." At the same moment a green-and-white police car, its red light flashing, turned the corner at Forty-ninth Street. It was followed by an ordinary sedan carrying a New York police official, a Secret Service man from the New York City field office, and Frank Flaherty, Richard Monckton's top staff man. One by one the eleven cars of the motorcade made the turn and came slowly toward the two men at the entrance. The agent pointed at the spot where the candidate's car, the third in the motorcade, was to stop.

The white Continental pulled up smoothly where the agent pointed. The right front door opened, an agent stepped out and swept the crowd with an experienced glance as he put his hand on the rear-door handle; his eyes ran over the crowd again, then he opened the door. The young advance man leaned in and said something to the passenger. The candidate, sitting alone in the back seat, looked at his watch and struggled forward to emerge from the deep leather seat. He held his large head low, as if looking for something in the gutter, then straightened up stiffly. He stood for a moment, apparently disoriented by the cheer that went up from the crowd behind the barricades. Then he looked back at the people emerging from the other motorcade cars, carrying briefcases, typewriters and cameras. The huge press bus was disgorging its sixty-two journalists at the Forty-ninth Street corner.

That wily bastard's not confused, Martin thought to himself. He's vamping, waiting for those cameras and the press to catch up.

As Monckton's eyes flicked over the crowd his gaze met Martin's for an instant, but the Director sensed no contact or recognition. The advance man with the clipboard held his fingers to his ear again. He looked ahead to where Frank Flaherty was standing by the lead car. Then the young man nodded and moved to Richard Monckton.

He spoke rapidly in the candidate's ear. "Senator, Frank says there is plenty of time if you want to shake hands. It will be the only New York crowd photo opportunity of the day."

Monckton did not look at him and the young aide wondered if he should repeat Flaherty's message.

Suddenly Monckton's blank expression changed. His eyes and mouth seemed to widen, he broke into a half-grin and he looked at the first rank of the crowd on his right. Purposefully he walked to them, extended his right hand to a man leaning over the barricade, then another, then to a woman holding an Instamatic camera in her left hand. The candidate reached over to the people behind, raising his elbow high, awkwardly grasping and releasing, touching, grinning. "Nice to see you." "Great of you to come." He began moving to his left. With him moved a hurtling semicircle of photographers, motion-picture cameramen, sound men with microphones on long silver booms, reporters, Secret Service agents shoving and blocking to maintain their manual-prescribed positions beside their Principal, all careening off one another, cursing and sweating.

Richard Monckton was grinning fixedly. "Hello. Hello there. Hi ya. Hello. Give that little girl a pen, Tom."

An aide reached inside his coat, handed the ten-year-old a cheap green-and-rust-colored ballpoint pen bearing the legend "Richard Monckton" and pressed to re-enter the moving melee. He was supposed to keep close to the candidate.

At the hotel entrance the young political advance man stood beside the general manager of the Waldorf Astoria. The schedule called for a brief welcoming statement by the manager, for which he was suitably attired in morning coat and gray trousers. As members of the Monckton staff walked up to the hotel entrance, ignoring the familiar bedlam that swirled around their candidate, the advance man handed each one a mimeographed information sheet from his clipboard.

Monckton neared the door, continuing to reach for the hands being thrust at him. The people behind him along the north barricade shouted at him, "Over here, Dick." "Hey, Dick, look at us." "Come here, come here, oh, please!" Monckton's head turned woodenly. He looked over his left shoulder at them as photographers snapped the picture which would be carried over all the wires that day. The shouting became louder.

Monckton grasped one more hand, then turned, lifted his right hand high above his head, lowered it to the horizontal and leveled it at a middle-aged lady in the front row at the north barricade. Caught off guard by the sudden change of direction, the hotel greeter retreated into his doorway. The crowd surged, grouped and began to move closer to the building. Richard Monckton was "working the fence," as he liked to call this handshaking routine. When he was in the mood, he did this political chore well. It often resulted in good pictures on the evening news.

Monckton never thought of handshaking as a personal contact with the electors. Sometimes people said things to him as they shook his hand, but he never replied. He grinned, repeated the same perfunctory greeting, then reached for another hand.

It was a political stratagem, a performance for the the press to photograph, nothing more. Real contacts with real people were made at dinners and cocktail parties and were more painful; their small talk, intimate chatter and friendly questions made him want to withdraw.

When Monckton finally reached the inside end of the barricade, he turned, held his right hand high and waved it shoulder to shoulder like a trainman signaling. The crowd cheered. In the hotel doorway, he turned to wave again, then turned back to the young advance man, who introduced him to the manager. Monckton quickly pre-empted with a few words of his own whatever welcoming address had been prepared by that distinguished hotelier, then moved into the ground-floor lobby.

A red-carpet runner had been laid from the door to the Towers elevator, and the pathway was bordered by red velvet ropes set on silver stanchions, as prescribed in the Monckton Campaign Advance Man's Manual. People stood two or three deep along the ropes but Monckton did not stop to shake hands or talk. He walked briskly, muttering "Thank you" from a set grin as the lobby crowd applauded.

The elevator door was open; Frank Flaherty and Szabol, the Secret Service agent, were flattened against the back of the cubicle. The advance man stood just outside until his candidate was aboard; then he moved inside, the agent nodded and the woman elevator operator closed the door. Richard Monckton's face changed as though he had suddenly broken out of a trance; his smile collapsed, his eyes darkened as if a light had been extinguished. He stared forward, remote from those pressed around him.

It was very quiet. No one spoke.

When Monckton entered the main hotel entrance Bill Martin and Simon Cappell turned away, rounded the corner of Fiftieth and Park Avenue and entered the Waldorf Towers by another door. Simon had taken a suite for Martin on the twenty-eighth floor. The small Towers lobby was crowded with uniformed New York City policemen; each appeared to be trying to find a safe and permanent place for himself in the disorder. Martin and his aide had a long wait for an elevator.

Eventually, as they were riding up alone, Simon said, "Quite a circus, Mr. Martin."

"Did you watch Monckton closely during all that handshaking?" asked Martin.

"Frankly. I was really more interested in the Secret Service's techniques."

"Monckton wasn't even there most of the time," Martin said with a tone of wonder. "He was doing all that crap on autopilot. What in hell do you suppose he was really thinking about during all of that?"

As soon as they were in their rooms, Simon picked up the phone to call the Monckton suite on the thirty-third floor. As Martin came through the connecting door from his room, Simon shook his head.

"No dice, boss. The hotel operator says all their house phones have been cut off, at their request."

Martin's reply was impatient. "What the hell? Then call through the Signal board. The Secret Service details must be hooked into the White House system."

"I'll have to find out how to get that Signal number, sir," the aide said nervously.

"Call the White House—456-1414. They can damn well put you through directly."

It took a few minutes for Simon to identify himself to the White House operator and to be switched to the Army Signal switchboard. Meanwhile Martin paced their rooms and smoked. His thoughts passed through what he'd just seen of Richard Monckton—to a comparison between Monckton and President Esker Anderson. Comparison revealed many similarities and few differences. He wondered how an unattractive, withdrawn man like Monckton, without a commanding presence, could become a front-running Presidential candidate. His thoughts then slipped to the threat Monckton was—then to the Primula Report—to the

Carl Tessler approach to Forville—to Sally Atherton—
to the golden skin, the feel of that sensual woman.

Martin had seen Sally two days after the G Street Club
party. It was a bright, clear day; when he telephoned, he
suggested going for a drive, because he had something
important to "assign" to her if she was interested. Sally
was obviously intrigued but Martin would give her no
clues on the telephone. She laughingly agreed to meet
him, appropriately attired in a trench coat.

Martin suggested that Sally pick him up in her car in
front of the Concert Hall of the Kennedy Center, about
three thirty that afternoon. Neither wanted to be noticed.
Martin's taxi had just pulled away when Sally Atherton
drove up. Martin slid behind the wheel and drove her
sports car to Manassas in the Virginia countryside.

Sally Atherton was everything he wanted in a woman.
And it was clear that she shared his desire. It was more
than physical, he told himself. They could happily
share every moment and every event of the rest of their
years. Yet she brought a sense of freedom to their relationship that was a blessed relief for him; she was intoxi-
cating, fresh, alive and full of promise.

They parked overlooking the Bull Run battlefield,
and talked. Martin found it easy to talk to this woman,
but his ingrained caution prevailed. He told her only
enough to get her to agree to carry a few envelopes to
Carl Tessler. Martin explained that he wanted to help
Tessler and Governor Forville. Since the Governor was
seeking the Presidential nomination, Martin could not
openly give aid but he and Tessler had agreed to enlist
Sally because they both had confidence in her. He made
clear that she could tell no one, not even her husband,
what she was doing; and that he and Tessler trusted her
completely.

It had been years since anyone had asked Sally Atherton to do something that could really make a difference.

Bill Martin and Carl Tessler valued her as an individual, a person. Her subdued response masked a deep gratification. Of course she would agree to help them out.

When the sun finally went behind the trees that afternoon, they drove back slowly to the city; Martin got out at the Statler Hilton and took a cab home.

Simon Cappell's apologetic and uneasy tone interrupted Martin's pacing. "I can't get you in to see the Great Man at all today, I'm afraid. I got a flat turndown from Flaherty himself. But we can settle for a meeting with Bob Bailey, if that's all right with you."

"Who the hell is Bailey?" Martin snapped, stubbing out his cigarette.

"He was Monckton's press secretary for a while when he was a Senator." Simon handed his boss a tan folder. "Here's the Monckton file if you want to read about Bailey. Tab eight or nine, I think. He's editor of one of the Denver papers. He is on leave from his newspaper for the campaign, supposedly to be the candidate's press secretary, but something happened after he came aboard and he lost out in the infighting. Anyway, Bailey stayed on the staff; probably to save face with the boys in the city room back home."

Martin flipped the pages of the file. "How high up is he?"

"It's hard to tell in Monckton's outfit. Our people say he's a 'confidant,' but that could be just press talk or window dressing."

Martin sighed. "It doesn't sound too promising, Simon, but as long as we're here, if that's the best we can do, let's try it. Where do we go?"

Simon led the way back down the quiet hall to the Towers elevator. When the door opened on the thirty-third floor, the narrow foyer was nearly filled with the two heavy men who faced them. The older man extended his hand and smiled.

"Mr. Director, my name is Tallford. I'm on the Senator's staff."

"Hello, Mr. Tallford." Martin wondered if Tallford had been sent to the foyer as a greeting committee and, if so, why. Maybe Monckton intended to see him after all.

Tallford was a Washington, D.C., legend at the age of forty. In the lexicon of Washington journalists he was variously described as a "political operative," "hatchet man," "partisan," "Republican political expert," or "Washington denizen," depending on whose copy one read. When Monckton decided to add Tallford to his campaign staff, Frank Flaherty had ordered that there be no press release; but almost immediately Len Archer of the Washington *Post* had written an exclusive Sunday story on Tallford's new campaign role with Monckton. Some of the old Monckton staff hands suspected that Tallford, bridling at the decision not to publicize his campaign job, had leaked the story himself to Archer. Although Flaherty considered Tallford among the two or three most effective political operators of either party, he was also aware of Tallford's downside reputation as a ruthless and excessively ambitious predator. T.T. Tallford was not squeamish about the means he selected to carry out his assignments. Accounts of the scurrilous last-minute advertising Tallford used against opponents had become political campaign legend.

Five feet eight inches tall, Tallford was one of those strongly built men who somehow give a false impression of flabbiness. His long nose offset his full cheeks and round chin. His hair was long, black, shiny and slicked straight back, his forehead deeply carved with worry lines. His eyes were coal black, cold and expressionless; the broad, bluish bands under them contrasted with his sallow complexion.

"Mr. Tallford, this is my assistant, Simon Cappell."

Simon shook Tallford's hand with scarcely disguised distaste.

Tallford gestured to the other man. "I understand you're going to see Bailey. The agent here will take you to him. I must ask you to excuse me. I'm overdue downstairs. It was very good to have seen you, gentlemen."

The Washington Hedge, thought Simon Cappell: he uses "seen," not "met" or "been introduced." "Good to have seen you!"

"Nice to have seen you too," said Simon wryly.

Leading Martin and Cappell a few steps away from the elevators, the agent pointed to the first room down the hall. Scotch-taped to the open door was a large card with "Robert Bailey" printed on it. Down the hall, some of the other doors also had name cards.

Simon Cappell's experience as an advance man for the unsuccessful Vice Presidential candidate during the last campaign had made him wise in the ways of handling room assignments for political hotel stops. And so he understood more about Bob Bailey now, about his relationship to the candidate, and the quantum of his clout. Bailey's room was virtually in the elevator shaft; thus he had evidently been relegated to the job of outpost hack, stationed there to achieve an early interception of "locals" who inevitably make their way to the candidate's floor. The security people are supposed to get rid of nuts and cranks, but in a campaign a candidate hates to see any bona fide potential supporter rudely rejected. So men like Bob Bailey are supposed to gently but firmly explain the gratitude of the candidate, his total unavailability, and the impossibility of a personal hand delivery of all gifts, messages and memoranda for security reasons.

Simon Cappell knew that the Company file was wrong about Bob Bailey. A deflector is seldom a "confidant." Bailey's door was open. Cappell knocked and Bailey waved them in. He was standing between twin beds at the right side of a narrow room, talking on the telephone. One bed was covered with an open suitcase, a disarranged pile of handwritten notes and papers, a mountain of dirty laundry waiting to be listed and bagged, and a pair of shoes. He gestured Martin and Cappell to sit at chairs around a small table by the only window, at the end of the room. As he talked on the phone Bailey rummaged in the suitcase, finally extracting a fresh pack of cigarettes which he opened and jabbed in Martin's direction.

As he waited for Bailey to finish his call, Cappell read the mimeographed sheets taped to the mirror over the dresser. One was a staff schedule. One was a rooming list for the campaign traveling party; Simon noticed that Richard Monckton was not listed.

The third paper was a memorandum from the advance man to the traveling staff, giving them hints for survival in the Waldorf Astoria Towers.

Welcome to New York!

Although your stay here will be brief, should any of you desire <u>tours, tickets to shows or help in shopping,</u> please contact my secretary, Sherrie Liebowitz, in room 1512, the main hotel.

We have six staff <u>automobiles</u> available but taxicabs are cheap and plentiful. For cars call room 1512.

A 24-hour <u>bar</u> and <u>snacks</u> service is set up in 1512, my office. <u>Please do not order from room service</u> without Mr. Flaherty's specific OK. If you do you will be personally charged for it. <u>No Room Service.</u>

<u>My office</u> is at Room 1512 in the main hotel, down the elevator to the lobby.

Take the main bank of elevators to the
15th floor, walk north.

Laundry: 24-hour pickup. Must be
sent before 2 P.M. Thursday to be back
by baggage call Friday morning.

Valet: One-hour service. Closes at
10 P.M.

Room Service: 24-hour service,
at your expense.

Newspapers: Will be put in your room
as they come in.

Press Room: The Empire Suite, mez-
zanine floor, main hotel. Phone: Ext.
127.

Baggage Call: 6:45 A.M. Friday. All
bags outside your door. Be sure your
tags are on your bags.

Have a good stay; let me know if I
can help.

                    Charles T. Ferris
                    Advance Man Ext. 1512

CTF/sl

Bailey was trying vainly to bring his telephone conversation to a close.

"Yes, sir, Mr. Clausen. I know. I'm sure Dick wishes
he could. The schedule here is a killer. I've never seen
it so tight. I know. Of course. Dick understands that,
Mr. Clausen. I know he appreciates that. Yes. Yes, sir.
I'll tell him right now that we talked and that you no
longer feel that way about Texas. I know he'll want to
know. I will count on it. Yes, sir. He'll be delighted you
called. Thank you."

Bailey cradled the phone, stubbed out his cigarette
hurriedly and turned to Martin, smiling broadly. His
age was hard to peg. He had that sandy hair that lightens
into grey without fanfare. He had been a well-built

handsome man twenty years before. Now he was somewhere the far side of fifty and well beyond two hundred
pounds, puffy and pale. His fingers were cigarette-yel-
low, his teeth showing signs of systems failure.

"Mr. Director, I'm Bob Bailey. I'm glad you could
come by." The voice was deep, almost husky.

Martin introduced Simon and stood up to shake
Bailey's hand across the bed. "I'm staying at the Towers myself, as it happens, Mr. Bailey, and called on the
spur of the moment in the hope there might be a few
minutes for me to renew an old friendship with Senator
Monckton."

Bailey exuded friendliness. "By George, I'm sure he'd
like that, Mr. Martin. How long have you two known
each other?"

Martin replied in a flat tone, intentionally dampening
Bailey's ebullience, "We had a trip to Russia together
in the fifties."

"As I was saying on the phone, Mr. Director, our
schedule here is a killer. I just know I'm not going to
be able to even get in a minute for you this go-round.
When he hears we couldn't work it out, I know Dick is
going to be most unhappy. But there just isn't any way
to work it. I hope you'll understand." Bailey sounded
sincere.

"Of course," Martin murmured.

Simon Cappell repressed a grin. When he was an advance man, his Vice Presidential candidate insisted on a
long nap every afternoon. He'd put on pajamas, pull the
curtains and sleep, politics be damned. And his down-
the-hall deflector used the same line Bailey was giving
Bill Martin. Right now, Simon was sure, Richard
Monckton was less than sixty feet down the hall, in a
typical Waldorf Towers suite, probably sleeping or
twiddling his thumbs with nothing important to do until
time to dress for his fund-raising dinner at eight.

Bill Martin was already moving toward the door to

leave. "Mr. Bailey," he said, "please tell the Senator that I strongly believe that he and I could spend a very profitable hour together some day soon. Will you do that?"

Bailey grinned and nodded. "I sure will, Mr. Director. Count on that. Listen, is there anything you and I could discuss now? Anything I could pass along to Dick—to the Senator?" He gave a little laugh. "I'm still cleared for secrets, I think. You can rely on my discretion."

Martin nodded coldly. "I'm sure I can, but for now, just give the Senator my regards and say that I need an hour alone with him some day. Thanks for your offer anyway."

As Martin and his young aide entered the elevator their departure was logged by a different Secret Service agent.

In the elevator Martin gave vent to his anger. "How fast can we get out of here?" he said grimly.

"Ten minutes, sir. We're all ready," said Simon quietly.

"Then let's get going. I should have known that goddamned Bailey was just a flunky. And I'll bet Monckton knew I was there. What a collection of two-faced bastards."

Richard Monckton sat deep in a large, low chair, his back to the darkened windows, his legs extending straight, heels resting on the floor. He held a glass in his hand, about half full of whiskey and ice. Occasionally he shook the glass a little to jiggle the ice cubes.

The Monckton hotel suite was furnished with a Japanese motif. A golden screen dominated one wall of the living room. The tables were square and of dark wood, the chairs and couches low. A fine Oriental rug provided most of the color in the room. There was only one lamp burning. The shades and drapes were drawn to dim and block the New York City noise.

As Director William Martin left the Towers, Frank Flaherty walked from room 3334 to the door of the suite at the end of the hall. The agent on guard at the door nodded and pushed the door open for him. A hotel key was in the outside lock. Flaherty had ordered all advance men to follow the key-in-the-lock procedure wherever the Monckton campaign went. No time lost with check-in at the desk, no confusion in passing keys out to the staff on arrival, no chance of mislaying a key. Just stick them in the locks. Simple and logical and efficient.

Flaherty was that unique American hybrid, the efficient Irishman. The black-haired Celtic appearance and name he took from his father. The efficiency was rooted in his Milwaukee mother's Swiss and German ancestry, polished at the Harvard Business School and nurtured at General Motors. He was the youngest Buick Regional Zone Manager in GM's history when he was given the job in St. Louis after only a few years.

When Frank Flaherty came in Monckton did not look up. "Hi. What's going on?"

"William Martin of the CIA just left. Bailey got rid of him."

"What the hell did he want?"

"Said he was staying here and dropped by for a 'mutually profitable chat.' He says he needs an hour with you sometime."

"I'll bet he needs an hour with me, the son of a bitch," Monckton snorted. "Mark the bastard down. He's one who is through when we get in. I know him. They put him on one of my trips to Russia. There's one goddamned bureaucrat who has gotten where he is purely on ass-kissing. Nothing else. Anderson made him Director but he's basically a goddamned Curry man. He's a goddamned Curry man, and that means that he's out."

"Bailey says he's a pretty smooth article," Flaherty added.

"What the fuck does Bailey know? I suppose Bailey wants us to keep him, is that it? Why the hell do we put up with a jerk like Bailey, Frank?"

Flaherty replied in a low tone, "He's a good buffer out there, and he's good with the press, Senator. He collects three or four reporters and takes them for drinks every afternoon, and it's one helluva good way to pump out the Monckton party line."

"I suppose we need people like that," Monckton grumbled, taking a long swallow of his drink. "But Frank, do me a favor. Keep Bailey away from me. He thinks he's a great politician. He's full of advice. Keep him the hell away from me."

"No problem, Senator," said Flaherty. He nodded toward the bedroom. "Are you going to have a nap today?"

But the candidate was deep in thought and did not answer. Flaherty was accustomed to Monckton's periods of total silence. At first he had mistaken them for fits of depression, but now he understood Richard Monckton better. The man was capable of deep and total concentration. No noise or movement in the room could distract him during those times. Unlike any other person Flaherty had known, this man needed to be able to shut out the world and go to some inner well for renewal. Flaherty tried to structure the campaign schedule so that every afternoon included at least two hours of "staff time" before dinner. If asked, he explained that Senator Monckton needed that interlude to handle his extensive correspondence and deal with major policy questions. In fact he needed the time for sleep or, at least, quiet in a dark room.

But occasionally bad weather delayed a flight or something else went wrong with the schedule. Then there was hell to pay. When Monckton was denied his "staff time" he could become mentally bedraggled, superficial and careless. He tired easily. Ironically, when he became very fatigued he found it impossible to sleep without pills, and at those times a normal dosage was not enough. Sleeping pills always made him feel dull the next day and, when he woke up, coffee alone wouldn't pick him up. So he had to have a drink or two to get things started. Unfortunately he became intoxicated quickly, leading him to become morose, bitter and belligerent. If he was tired it took only one or two drinks to turn Monckton the intellectual statesman into Monckton the offensive slob.

At age thirty-eight Frank Flaherty held the title of Chief of Staff, but actually he was Richard Monckton's keeper. He now knew all the symptoms and physical warning signs. Both Flaherty and his boss realized that this cycle of exhaustion, pills and whiskey could surely defeat Monckton in his bid for the Presidential nomination.

Seven years earlier, when Senator Monckton had made his Vice-Presidential bid, Flaherty had written to Monckton to offer his services: as a result of that letter and an interview with Bob Bailey, the young Flaherty had been given a job in the Monckton campaign as an advance man. Although Monckton was defeated in that election he did not lose track of the able young Buick man. He obviously could be useful in the future. He was the best detail man Monckton had ever seen. Flaherty's father had left him well fixed financially, his wife was beautiful and wealthy in her own right. Unlike most campaign workers, Flaherty had no personal political ambitions or demands. He was the answer to a Presidential candidate's prayers.

The General Motors brass were happy to give Flaherty a leave of absence to help in Monckton's Presidential campaign; they assured him that he would not lose his place in the intramural race up the GM ladder. The Monckton-for-President finance committee agreed to pay Flaherty seventy-five thousand dollars plus expenses, including an apartment in Chicago. He would select the campaign staff, subject to Monckton's approval, and run it. But Flaherty and the candidate agreed that everything in the campaign would have only two goals: to capture the lion's share of evening network television news for Monckton and to keep him from fatigue. The strategy necessarily minimized events on the schedule that wouldn't win the television-news coverage, but carefully contrived press handouts would give an adequate appearance of feverish campaign activity. At all costs Richard Monckton must avoid the cycle of fatigue = sleeplessness = alcohol which could carry him into certain disaster.

After a few moments Monckton broke his reverie. "Imagine that Martin coming here to see me! So transparent."

"Has the CIA anything to offer us? Could you get anything from Martin?" Flaherty asked.

Monckton grunted derisively. "He's worried about his career, that's all. We can get the usual CIA briefings after the nomination. We don't need the son of a bitch. I don't want to see him. Keep him out."

It was true that Bill Martin was worried about his career. But, as he rode in his car that afternoon from National Airport to his home, he was more concerned about what might happen *after* he was fired than about whether or not he would be fired by a new President. He mentally ticked off the possibilities. If he "retired," his knowledge and background would be highly valuable to the multinationals doing business around the world and he'd surely be offered good jobs in business or finance. The salary would be high, with perks and prestige.

He'd be safe until President Curry's newly elected enemies began to move in on the old records and files. But once the Primula Report began to circulate, Martin knew, he would be the key witness. He would be used to destroy the memory of a great, dead President. And William Martin would be thoroughly destroyed in the process.

Fact after agonizing fact would be hammered out of him, probably in nationwide televised hearings. It would be sensational stuff. The source stories and opinion pieces would echo and re-echo the questions. As his driver eased the Mercury through the heavy late afternoon traffic along the river, Martin could actually hear how the Senate barrage would go.

Q: You say, Mr. Martin, that the President gave you a direct order?

A: Yes, Senator.

Q: Who else was present?

A: We were alone.

Q: And what did you say?

A: I simply said "Yes, sir."

Q: But, Mr. Martin, didn't you know, didn't you fully realize that you were being asked to commit a murder —to kill a noble hero of the resistance, a priest? Didn't you ask why you were being asked to do such a terrible thing?

A: No, Senator, I didn't question the President's instructions.

Q: You say you realized you were to murder a priest of the Church?

A: The President identified a man—by name, Senator.

Q: Mr. Martin, did you know or later learn he was an ordained priest of the Roman Catholic faith?

A: Yes, sir.

Q: The President's own church?

A: I believe the President was of that faith, sir.

Q: Are you a Catholic, Mr. Martin?

Relentless questions that would be asked over and over again, and for years, maybe decades, to come. Had there been a direct Presidential order? Was it lawful under the circumstances? What is a subordinate's legal duty when given such an order? Does he have a higher moral duty to disobey? How is that duty defined? Was William Martin a hero or a vile murderer? Was President Curry observing some higher morality in ordering the action? Was the larger interest of the nation involved more important than the life of a man? Could an act be moral for a President and immoral for a subordinate at the same time?

One thing was crystal clear. These questions must never be asked. The Pandora's box must remain closed, for both William Martin and the historical integrity of President William Arthur Curry. Only Horace McFall shared this heavy burden with Martin. From one cryptic conversation with his predecessor, Bill Martin knew that McFall believed President Curry had made the right decision and that Martin had had no choice but to carry out the President's order. McFall had carried out a number of direct Presidential orders himself when he was Director. He, too, knew no alternative to such an instruction. Horace McFall could be relied upon.

But no one else must know. And Monckton certainly must not be the next President. Governor Forville probably would not be a problem if Carl Tessler came in with him. Tessler could control the situation. But obviously the Vice President was the best alternative, if only he could win, because Gilley would be totally controllable. Esker Scott Anderson would keep him in line.

Martin reached behind him to the shelf of the back seat and flicked the switch for his reading light. As he picked up the *Evening Star* his eye caught a headline on the bottom half of the front page.

SENATOR AHEAD OF GOVERNOR FOR NOMINATION

Monckton leads poll of G.O.P. convention delegate probables by two-to-one margin

Martin dropped the paper and stared out the car window, a tightness beginning to form in his stomach. What in the hell would he do if Richard Monckton couldn't be stopped?

7

Martin had every reason to believe that he was buying Governor Forville through Carl Tessler. And Tessler repeatedly expressed his gratitude and satisfaction.

Because their surreptitious meetings had a purpose that transcended the conspirators' romantic interest, both Martin and Sally Atherton found their actions easier to rationalize. They were helping Carl Tessler, Governor Forville and, arguably, the Company. And they were doing something of importance—together. The gentle aroma of danger and the need for secrecy added spice to their meetings.

Sally Atherton delighted in her courier role as she carried the manila envelopes in her large leather purse from Washington to Boston on the Eastern Airlines shuttle. The deliveries were usually made over an elegant lunch at the Ritz. A good lunch with the witty and well-informed Tessler made the trips a pleasure.

Carl Tessler devoured the information and greedily hungered for more. It stimulated his thought processes, reshaped his hypotheses. As a result a new quality of assurance and authority was to be seen in Governor Forville's campaign speeches and position papers on foreign affairs and international economics.

The half-joking code name for their caper was the "Cambridge Channel." The flow of information continued unabated until the Republican convention that August. Then Richard Monckton defeated Governor Forville for the Presidential nomination and the Cambridge Channel abruptly dried up.

William Martin had never before watched a political convention from beginning to end. But that year he saw virtually every minute of both the Philadelphia conventions. The Democratic convention, in late July, was divided and bloody. Martin hoped and believed that Vice President Gilley would be nominated and would go on to defeat either Monckton or Forville in November; but within a few hours of the Democratic convention's opening fanfare Martin's wishful belief had begun to fade.

Back in Washington President Esker Scott Anderson knew that Ed Gilley was in trouble even before he was nominated, but, unlike Martin, Anderson knew why.

It would take a broad ethnic-city-organized-labor coalition to elect a garrulous, likable political hack like Gilley. And the Democratic convention showed stark evidence that there could be no such coalition. Vice President Ed Gilley would be nominated, with the help of President Esker Scott Anderson's videotaped endorsement speech to the convention. But before the nomination was made the Democrats' serious ideological battles over convention reform and the platform thinned Gilley's nomination into a hollow anticlimax.

By the end of the second day of the convention the Democrats were being portrayed by the commentators as a fatally divided political party, probably incapable of electing any candidate. And the President, who sat in the Oval Office with Al Donnally, agreed with their diagnosis. He watched, shook his head and began to do what had to be done to salvage something for his party and incidentally for Ed Gilley.

Over at the CIA in Langley, Bill Martin also watched and began to live with the possibility that Richard Monckton could defeat Edward Gilley in November.

Philadelphia's tough police department was kept busy dispersing the organized crowds of young demonstrators who had come from all over the country to protest Vice President Ed Gilley as the predicted Democratic Presidential nominee.

The young demonstrators had "no candidate, no political party, no name" for their movement. Their young press representative blandly assured the few reporters who asked such questions that the demonstrations resulted from "spontaneous" disillusionment.

On the second day of the Democratic convention the networks moved additional cameras to the exterior of Convention Hall. At dusk, as the television lights were turned on and the cameras were manned, a serious battle erupted between demonstrators and Philadelphia police, and a number of young people were badly hurt. The evening session, which was to feature the Presidential nominating speeches, was postponed for ninety-five minutes while the tear gas used to break up the demonstration was blown out of the hall by large fans brought in by the fire department.

That ninety-five minutes of prime television time was devoted to full accounts of the fighting, tape replays of the police hitting young people, and pictures of correspondents being gassed.

The Democratic party leadership, already politically bruised by the intraparty battles of the previous two days, never did overcome the horrified public reaction to the brutality of the police against the demonstrators. By the time Vice President Ed Gilley, who was not a great orator, made his acceptance speech to the convention on the final night, vast political damage had been done.

William Martin's peace of mind had been based on good odds that the Vice President would be elected President, under Esker Anderson's continuing control. But during those long July nights Martin saw that assumption fracture, fade and disappear. For the Director, the problem clearly became centered on whether the Republicans would choose Forville or Monckton.

Three weeks later, in the same City of Brotherly Love, Richard Monckton received his party's Presidential nomination. And the contrast between the chaotic Democratic convention and the orderly, well-managed Republican gathering foretold the outcome of the election as well.

From the beginning it was Monckton's convention.

For three days and nights Monckton people virtually monopolized the network television coverage from Convention Hall. A Monckton television team had been on the scene in Philadelphia for nine weeks. One member of the advance group was Tony Allen, a veteran network television news producer who understood how news assignments and editorial decisions would be made by the network producers over in the television control booths in Convention Hall Annex. The former producer worked with a member of the Monckton TV staff, alongside logistics and advance men and a convention-arrangements expert. They were working from two large house trailers, moved to the parking lot behind Convention Hall next to the large rear door, three days after the Democrats left town. The trailers bore no markings or signs. Three uniformed officers guarded them around the clock. Thousands of miles of telephone cable were laid from these trailers to floor command posts, phones in the spectator galleries, and to each of the network control booths. Direct lines ran from a small switchboard in one trailer to a huge six-operator switchboard at Monckton headquarters in the Sheraton Hotel downtown.

One trailer was a political command post for T.T. Tallford and those responsible for recruiting and wooing convention delegates.

The other was exclusively for the Monckton television team. It was Frank Flaherty's theory that the convention offered Richard Monckton two unique opportunities: one was to be nominated; the other, of equal importance, was to dominate national television for three full days and nights, at virtually no expense to the campaign. With some planning and adroit execution, Richard Monckton should be able to capitalize on the presence of all those cameras to enjoy television exposure he could never buy. And Flaherty was right.

One astute contemporary historian recorded that the Monckton people in their television trailer played the three television networks like a harpsichord during that convention. The only detail the historian missed was perhaps the most important: the director of the television operation was Richard Monckton himself.

In an ornate suite on the top floor of the Sheraton Hotel, Monckton and Frank Flaherty sat side by side in overstuffed chairs. Four large television sets displayed the three networks and the pool feed from the convention floor. Flaherty held a telephone which was connected directly to a telephone on Tony Allen's desk in the television trailer. As the convention proceeded,

Flaherty tore off pages from a thick script that lay on his lap and dropped them to the floor.

```
8:07        Music by Troubadors or Martins-
            ville, Ky.  (Note:  Nets will
  to        want only first 30 sec.
            Our trailer will offer a
            2 1/2 minute interview.)
8:10        End musical interlude
8:11        Chairman introduces Senator
            Harly Parton, Chairman, Conven-
            tion Platform Committee for
            report.
8:12        Senator Parton reports.  (At
            4 p.m.  Our trailer offered
            Bob Bailey, Dorothy Wilson and
            Congressman Curtis to sit with
            net anchormen and summarize
            platform from Monckton stand-
            point as report drones on.)
8:30        Trailer notify nets of Mrs.
            Monckton move toward Hall.
8:34        Mrs. Monckton depart Sheraton
            Hotel.
8:44        Mrs. Monckton arrive Hall at
            Gate 2.
8:45        Mrs. Monckton enter Door 2.
8:47        Mrs. Monckton seated, Box 11,
            Section 2.  Joins Alma Coving-
            ton (astronaut's wife), Melissa
            Connaught (wife of Governor of
            Massachusetts), Rev. Sherman
            Smith (Pastor, First Congrega-
            tional Church, Chicago).
9:00        Platform report ends.
            (Network station break and
            commercials.)
```

```
9:03:30   Film:   "Toward a New Era of
          Progress."  (Nets will carry
          only 1 min 30 sec of film then
          cut to booths.)
```

Monckton and Flaherty knew where their strengths and weaknesses were among the delegates. The bandwagon psychology they wanted to build was helped by favorable television interviews with delegates who had switched from Forville to Monckton.

"Sherm? This is Tony in the Monckton trailer. Thought you might be interested; Senator Allwyn says eight of the Forville delegates in the Ohio delegation are now going for Monckton on the first ballot. The Senator is over at station twenty-one on aisle three. He'll give a short interview if you want him."

"Bob, this is Tony. Mrs. Monckton is going to leave the Sheraton in three minutes. She'll be entering the hall at gate two at eight forty-five exactly. Right. Glad to be of help."

"Mary, this is Tony at the Monckton trailer. Fine, how are you holding up? I have an advance text of the Monckton nomination speech that Governor Connaught will give. It times out to five minutes, forty seconds. Right, five forty. The last two minutes is very controversial stuff. I thought you ought to know. You're welcome."

Monckton and Flaherty were calling the shots, goading Allen for better results, criticizing flawed efforts, passing along praise, demanding the impossible every minute the convention was on the air.

In Governor Forville's trailer, parked at another door to the hall, little attention was given to television coverage. Forville's delegate strength had begun to erode about ten days before the convention in scattered and insignificant numbers. As the days passed, the reports from Forville field men assigned to "head-hunting" delegates were of more and more defections. The Monckton people were putting heavy personal pressure on Forville delegates all around the country. Each delegate and alternate had received a long personal letter from Monckton, many with handwritten postcripts when there had been a previous personal encounter with the candidate. Some were even getting personal phone calls from Richard Monckton. Before leaving for Philadelphia, each convention delegate and alternate had received, at his home, an elaborate kit of convention gifts, each emblazoned with the big blue Monckton "M." The bandwagon had begun to roll long before the delegates left home.

Monckton hosts and a Monckton band greeted every delegate as he or she stepped off the airplane at the Philadelphia airport. Free Monckton buses delivered the delegates and their luggage to their hotels. Aboard the bus were flowers for the ladies, Monckton pens and cuff links for the men, and drinks for all. Two channels on every Philadelphia hotel television set were Monckton closed-circuit channels featuring convention news, Monckton campaign films, tour and shopping hints and live interviews with Monckton supporters.

The Forville organization was simply outgunned on all fronts. By the end of the opening session of the convention it was assumed by the press that Forville's strength had ebbed so low that he could not deny Monckton on the first ballot.

On the second morning the Forville effort totally collapsed. At a house in Bala-Cynwyd, a posh Philadelphia suburb, Governor Forville held a secret meeting with Richard Monckton. Later that day Governor Forville announced, through his press secretary, that he would be one of those seconding the nomination of Richard Monckton. The rest was pure formality. That night

Monckton was nominated by acclaim. Next night he made a stirring acceptance speech, was loudly cheered, then flew off to a quiet retreat in Arizona with his staff to put the final touches on his campaign plans.

At the CIA, Bill Martin watched every minute of the Monckton triumph with a growing sense of fear. Richard Monckton was strong; Gilley and the Democrats looked pitifully weak. The odds would favor Monckton unless Esker Scott Anderson could somehow rescue Gilley.

In the White House, even before Richard Monckton's acceptance speech had ended, Esker Scott Anderson and his Secretary of Labor, Al Donnally, were diligently at work on that repair job. Donnally devoutly believed that most voters cast ballots against candidates, not for them. Thus the tactic of a Donnally campaign was always to attack; its only goal was the demolition of the opposition. Al Donnally had been placed in firm behind-the-scenes control of Gilley's campaign from its first day. The target was Richard Monckton. The orders that went out were to attack, immediately and often.

The Donnally staff became Monckton experts. No event of his life was unimportant, no potential source of information could be overlooked. President Anderson gave Donnally a free hand to seek Monckton information from the Internal Revenue Service, Federal law-enforcement agencies and other Government sources.

A couple of days after the Monckton nomination Donnally called William Martin at his office at the CIA with a low-key reminder that "the President has been looking for those Monckton files." But within a week after Monckton's nomination Donnally's demands became blunt. It was a stifling Washington summer day. A sticky haze hovered over the trees at Langley when Simon Cappell buzzed the Director to tell him that Donnally was on the phone.

"Christ almighty, again?" Martin jabbed another button and said tightly, "Hello, Al, how're things?"

The Secretary of Labor was no longer genial. "Bill, the President feels there has been more than enough time for you to gather your Monckton stuff and get it over here. Somebody there is dragging his feet."

"I assure you that's not the case, Mr. Secretary," Martin replied firmly. "But you know as well as I that Monckton has made many trips abroad and has had a thousand contacts. It's damn slow work to put that kind of a package together."

Donnally exploded. "Why the hell can the FBI do it and you people can't? Monckton's all over this country, more than he's been abroad. The difference is that Elmer Morse is cooperating and you aren't, and I want to know why."

The temperature in the Director's office was a pleasant seventy degrees but Martin was feeling the heat. "That's very unfair. I hope you and the President don't really feel that way, Al. What you've asked me to do is probably against the law. Of course I want to serve the Vice President. But it's got to be done very, very carefully. You'll just have to bear with me. I'm sorry."

"I'll tell the President what you've said verbatim, Bill," said Donnally. "And I can promise you he's going to be goddamned upset. But it's your ass, not mine."

Martin chose his words with care. "Al, please tell him I want to serve the Vice President. I've given him two briefings and he now has background reading from us, too. I'm really trying."

"Not hard enough, I'm afraid," Donnally replied. "He wants me to have those Monckton files and he wants them here fast. It's up to you to deliver." The Secretary slammed down the phone.

Martin pressed his secretary's intercom button. "Alice, that was Secretary Donnally; write the call up, please." Martin knew that they would press harder and harder; with these tapes he would have it down in black and white that he was actually forced to turn over the confidential CIA file material under direct orders of the President of the United States.

In the last few days a new CIA struggle with the FBI had developed, and Martin had been under too much pressure to sift through the files personally. The Monckton review had been left to Simon Cappell in the hope that if there was nothing derogatory perhaps Donnally would give up.

During the lame-duck slack since Esker Anderson had announced he would retire, the venerable FBI Director, Elmer Morse, had been maneuvering on many fronts to gain political ground. Martin discovered in checking around that bureau and agency heads all over the Government were having invasion jitters as the FBI deliberately trespassed on their prerogatives and functions. Martin knew that Elmer was a master of bureaucratic tactics, but little in his experience had equipped him for the pressures that Morse brought to bear that summer. Morse well knew that Esker Anderson had no desire to referee territorial, bureaucratic battles among the FBI and its competitors at Treasury, Defense, State and over at the CIA. With the President out of the fight and the FBI's Congressional flanks secure, this was the time for Morse and the FBI to make their move—and it was clear that they were on the march.

On the same day that Secretary Donnally made his final threatening call to Martin, a directive from the Assistant to the President for National Security Affairs advised Martin that the President had approved a 200 percent increase in the number of "legal attachés" (FBI agents) in the European and Western Hemisphere Embassies. The CIA was directed that thereafter it was to coordinate all its foreign surveillance of U.S. citizens in those areas with the FBI.

The following week the FBI Director attacked the CIA in an exclusive interview with *U.S. News & World Report*.

The interview had been shown to the CIA press officer in advance of publication by a magazine reporter who hoped to build the story with a tough response from the Company. When Martin read the interview he called a meeting of the CIA press officer and three Assistant Directors to talk about what to say and do in response.

It was obvious that there was very little the Company could do about Morse's attack. Although galling, it was probably better to make no reply. As his staff rubbed this salt in the wound Bill Martin afforded them one of his rare displays of rage. He first eviscerated the CIA press officer, the messenger who brought the bad news. He then engaged in a shouting match with an Assistant Director who tried to defend the press officer. The meeting ended when Martin stalked from the conference room in a blazing fury.

The Assistant Director for Plans, Bud Corelli, followed him into his office. "Bill, I've noticed something I feel I should mention to you."

"Not now, Bud, I'm too goddamned mad," Martin barked.

"That's part of it, boss. You are showing some battle fatigue these days, you know. Are you getting any relaxation?"

The Director laughed sarcastically. "Relaxation! How the hell can I relax? I haven't been able to let down for a minute. I'm surrounded by idiots. No, I know that's not true. But I am keyed up; I guess I just proved that. I'm not sleeping very well, I'm afraid." Martin sagged wearily into his chair behind his desk.

Corelli walked over to the desk and spoke earnestly. "Look, Bill, why not use the place at Tobacco Landing this weekend? It's empty and it's quiet as hell down there. You're sure to relax."

Martin looked up with a faint smile. "That's a helluva good idea. Thanks, Bud; I really appreciate your concern. A couple of quiet days away from this place would help."

Martin pushed a buzzer and Simon Cappell came in as Corelli left the office. "Simon, I'm going to use the small house at Tobacco Landing tonight and tomorrow night. I'm going to try to get some rest."

"Good idea, boss. What about staff and services?"

"I'll eat at the big house with the permanent staff. You don't need to come. I'm just going to try to get some sleep."

"Right. I'll set it up. When do you want to fly?"

Martin shook his head. "No, I'll let Rudy drive me after work today. Phone Linda and say I've been called away but don't say where. I don't need her on my back. No one needs to know where I am."

Simon Cappell went into his office to telephone the Agent-in-Charge at the CIA's secret transaction house to tell him about his guest.

Tobacco Landing, Maryland, slumbers on an inlet of Chesapeake Bay twenty-one miles south of Washington. Its one general store serves the small farms and large estates bordering the bay. Eighteenth-century stone houses, still in use, dot the county; some are handsomely restored weekend retreats and summer homes.

In the mid-1950s the CIA quietly purchased a two-hundred-and-eighty-acre estate in the name of a nonexistent industrialist's nonexistent widow. This determined but fictitious lady demanded total privacy. Fences, gates and guard dogs were installed soon after the purchase, and the local residents began to lose track of what went on at the old place. None of the household help came from the area. Because of the location of the gate to the property it was nearly impossible for arrivals and departures to be chronicled by the neighbors. A few yachts were seen to dock there briefly, but that was not unusual thereabouts. Once in a while guests came and went in little helicopters. That was extravagant, even for estate people. But almost anything might be expected of rich, eccentric old ladies. Even helicopters.

William Martin was deep down and he was being brought up on a chain. The chain that was pulling him up made a great clashing noise as it fell to the steel deck. No, it wasn't a chain. The sound was wrong. It was a bell. As he came up slowly they were ringing a bell. It was a telephone bell. He had to answer a telephone. He reached out in the dark but there was no table. Disoriented, Martin reached toward the persistent sound and found it.

"H'lo?"

"Director Martin?"

He struggled to awaken. "Yeah."

"Sorry to disturb you, sir. This is the White House operator. Are you awake?"

"I guess so. What time is it?"

"Five ten A.M. The President placed a call to you at one fifteen this morning but he retired before we could locate you. He is awake now and on another call. As soon as he is through I'll ring you again. Will that be all right?"

"I guess so." Martin was still half asleep. "What's up?"

"I have no idea, Mr. Director. I hope you'll keep your line clear so we can get through to you."

"Right, OK, 'night." He replaced the receiver and rolled over. The telephone was on the wall, next to the bedpost. The bedside table and lamp were on the other side of the bed. It seemed a strange arrangement.

He had taken a couple of sleeping pills when he had finished unpacking and he was groggy. The sedatives had put him out cold as soon as he had settled into the big bed in the guesthouse. And Martin quickly lapsed into sleep again. At 6:20 A.M. he was once more jarred awake by the ringing telephone.

"Mr. Director? This is the White House operator. The President is ready now. Are you awake?"

"Yeah. I guess so." He reached over to switch on the light, then pulled himself to a sitting position and shook his head. "What time is it now?"

"Six twenty A.M., sir. I'll put you through."

There were several faint clicks and then a loud one.

"Mr. President, I have CIA Director Martin for you." Esker Anderson's voice boomed up through the receiver.

"Did I wake you up, Bill?"

"Yes, sir, but that's no problem."

"Look, Bill, I've been talking to Al Donnally this morning. I guess I need to see you later on today. I'm flying to Oregon at ten. Will you meet me on the plane at Andrews?"

Martin slammed a fist into the mattress. "Of course, Mr. President."

"Thanks, Bill. See you then."

Wearily Martin sank back into the pillows to measure the situation. Then he reached for the phone to get things rolling. He would have Simon Cappell bring his synopsis of the Monckton files to Andrews Air Force Base just before takeoff time. He would also have Simon arrange for a helicopter to pick him up in time to make the departure. Cappell could round up things he needed: a briefcase of urgent papers from the office and a change of clothes.

Martin couldn't call Sally Atherton at that hour. She had agreed to one last campaign appearance for Jack and had gone West with the Congressman the previous Sunday. It wasn't quite 3:30 A.M. in San Diego. Perhaps he could arrange to see her while they were both on the West Coast, Martin mused. At least there might be some pleasure in what otherwise promised to be a very unpleasant journey.

8

The CIA helicopter flew low, between gray clouds and the green, humid Maryland countryside. Fields and farms yielded to close-packed houses, then became red brick apartments and wide highways. Dozens of military aircraft were parked in rows on the wide ramps of Andrews as Martin's helicopter banked around the concave concrete control tower. Air Force One was parked in front of the Operations Building. Like a champion prizefighter on his stool between rounds, the great silver-and-blue airplane was being ministered to by a swarm of seconds. A huge truck pumped refrigerated air through a plastic duct into the side of the plane. Another generated electricity. Air Police guards with conspicuous sidearms were posted in pairs at the two stairways. Men in white bustled at the lower cargo doors.

About one hundred feet from the airplane's front stairs, temporary metal barricades formed a square pen some twenty-five feet across. Inside this enclosure cameramen were erecting tripods and mounting motion-picture cameras. A few reporters drank coffee from Styrofoam cups and watched as Bill Martin alighted and shook hands with an Air Force colonel.

They walked to a car parked just inside the ramp-area fence where Simon Cappell waited. A suitcase and briefcase sat on the ground on the driver's side. Simon's chauffeur lounged against the fender.

"Hello, Simon. Any problems?"

146

"Good morning, sir. No, we got the work finished and it's in the briefcase. The trick will be to get the luggage on board the airplane, I guess."

"What's the matter? Aren't I listed?"

"Yes, now you are. The President forgot to tell anyone that he'd invited you, but we finally got that straightened out. But the luggage can't go aboard unless you vouch for it. You'll have to personally assure the Secret Service that it's yours. I'll go get an agent."

The baggage was identified, inspected and marked with round stickers bearing black stars and a code word. As Martin and Cappell walked toward the front stairway of the aircraft they talked briefly about appointments that would have to be canceled or rearranged.

The guard with the clipboard ran his white gloved finger down the manifest. "Mr. Martin, you are listed for the rear stairway, please. Go around the end of the wing. Do not walk under the wing, please."

Martin smiled at his aide. "Hmmm. What kind of ticket did you buy me, Cappell? Am I going steerage?"

Simon played along. "There's really not much difference except the seats are narrower. The food's all prepared in the same gleaming kitchens. And you save so much money."

The guards at the rear stairs had Martin's name on their load list. One of them snapped a salute. Martin waved to Simon and started to climb the long stairway. As he did, the engines of the airplane began to whine; the President's helicopter was landing on the ramp about a hundred yards away. Martin stood at the top of the stairs and watched the helicopter taxi to a red-painted circle near the nose of the 707. A doorway in the side of the gleaming olive helicopter, hinged at the bottom, dropped down to become stairs bordered on each side by flexible railings. The Air Force colonel who had greeted Martin moved to the bottom of the stairs and saluted. A Secret Service agent emerged, ducking his head. He was followed by a Navy doctor in civilian clothes, then the President's press secretary and another aide. There was a short pause and then Esker Scott Anderson bent his long frame through the door and straightened up on the stairs.

A few people standing along the ramp fence applauded and one yelled a greeting. Anderson smiled and waved to them. He shook hands with the colonel, then walked briskly to the front stairway of Air Force One. The Air Police saluted stiffly.

At the top of the stairway Anderson turned and waved in the direction of the newsreel cameras. He knew, and the newsmen knew, that the pictures of that wave would never be broadcast unless Air Force One met with an accident. But everyone cooperated, even early in the morning, so that the public would not be denied a last picture of the President boarding "just before the terrible event," should an accident occur. There had been such a filmed sequence of President William Arthur Curry that was shown on all the special network news shows, along with floodlighted scenes of the crash the night of his death. Farewell-wave shots and Presidential death watches were in the finest tradition of American television news coverage and American politics.

The President was closely followed through the door by two Air Police guards. The two guards at the rear stairs came bounding up beside Bill Martin as he watched the front door close. "Let's go, let's go! Let's button it up!" Martin moved inside as the two large sergeants jostled and pressed against his back. The stairs were wheeled away, the plane began to taxi and the rear door was swung closed by a steward—all appeared to be one fluid, practiced motion.

"Sorry to hurry you, sir, but Mr. Esker Scott Anderson don't like to sit around on the ramp waiting for folks."

"That's okay, Sergeant," Martin said. "I hope I didn't hold things up."

The other Air Policeman smiled. "No chance of that, Mr. Martin. We might have trampled you and left half of you hanging outside, but Colonel Armbruster would have pulled away just the same. When the President comes aboard we go. Pronto!"

The steward took Martin's elbow. "Sir, you are sitting in the next compartment forward. We'll be taking off immediately. Please belt up."

Martin quickly walked forward as the airplane lumbered along the taxiway. In the rear compartment were the guards and Secret Service agents and a few empty seats. The second compartment contained six rows of the type of wide seats found in the first-class section of a commercial airliner. Martin took a window seat alone in the rear row. When he had fastened his belt he looked around him. It was his first time aboard Air Force One and he sensed an atmosphere, an esprit, different from that in any airplane he'd ridden before.

The upholstery was heavy and expensive. The carpeting was luxurious, selected for color and texture rather than durability. Cabin decoration and lighting were handcrafted and elaborate. Separating the seats were upholstered arm rests with an inset wood table surface. On each little table was a ceramic tray about eight inches long, embossed in gold leaf with the legend "Air Force One" and the Presidential seal. Candy, cigarettes and matches were neatly arranged in each tray with great care. The cigarettes were in a special blue wrapper. The matches bore the seal in gold. All the wrappers said Air Force One, even the cellophane on the candy.

There were only three other passengers in Martin's compartment. Each had a window seat. Two were women, probably secretaries. Martin did not recognize the man. Once they were airborne, everyone read; no one spoke. A blue-blazered steward offered food and drink, serving the coffee in white plastic cups that also bore the Presidential seal.

As soon as the plane leveled off, Martin opened his briefcase and pulled out Simon Cappell's memorandum on the Monckton file. Since he expected to be summoned into the President's cabin at any moment, he turned to the last page of the memorandum to read the conclusions, then went back to the beginning to skim the review. When Martin had hurriedly read through the report he made a few penciled notes on a pad. Then he slowly read all the pages again. Forty-five minutes later the steward served a very large breakfast: strawberries, pancakes, eggs and bacon. Martin began to wonder when he would be summoned. The breakfast trays were removed and Martin had glanced at the *Post,* the *Times* and a long report on Chinese-Russian border fighting before the President's appointments secretary stopped, as he was walking through the compartment, to say that the President expected to see the Director in about an hour.

Martin had only begun to reread Cappell's memorandum when another steward opened the door at the front of the compartment. He leaned from the aisle and said in a low tone, "Mr. Martin, the President would like to see you now."

Martin followed the steward forward through a compartment similar to the one he shared, except that every seat was filled with reporters. They were the "pool," selected by the press secretary to ride on the President's airplane to represent all of the press corps. The rest of the White House press, too numerous to be taken aboard Air Force One, were riding to Oregon in a chartered plane. The pool would write up everything they observed; mimeographed copies of their report would go to every reporter who wanted one. The pool report would state that, as Air Force One sped westward, the President had worked on heavy matters of state as evidenced by the fact that he had summoned the Director of the CIA to his compartment.

In the small partitioned section ahead of the press compartment there were only three rows of seats; the President's doctor and men on the White House staff occupied all of them.

The steward knocked on the door at the front of the staff compartment and immediately opened it; turning, he beckoned Martin into a long open area dominated by Esker Scott Anderson. He was seated in a very large chair mounted on a chromium-plated column that disappeared into the carpeted floor midway between the cabin walls. To the right of his chair was a massive curved table, heavily upholstered and mounted on two chromium columns that appeared to telescope into chromium sleeves just above the floor. A large telephone console dominated one end of the table. Couches had been built in along the cabin walls behind the table and along the opposite wall.

Beyond the President's chair Martin could see a built-in bed, paneled bar, chairs and an elaborate dressing room and bathroom. This area could be partitioned and made completely private from the rest of the cabin by pushing a button that drew a heavy curtain on a track.

President Anderson was talking on the telephone and at the same time absently playing with a panel of buttons built into the wide arm of his chair. When he pushed a white button his chair rose slowly. When he pushed the black button he gently descended. The red button swiveled the chair to the left. The green button rotated him to the right.

Martin was waved to the couch behind the table. He slid around the curve of the table until he sat opposite the President. The steward brought him a cup of coffee and left.

Anderson continued to rise, turn, turn the other way, then descend like a great, slow Presidential Yo-Yo, all the while talking on the phone to someone about Ed Gilley and the election.

"It's the unions, Jack. They're going to have to do it. I hope your union leaders know that. They can't just print up a bunch of leaflets and expect Ed to get elected. This time it's going to require a helluva lot of hard work! Do you know that? You've got to keep hammering at it, and they've got to spend a pile of dough. You tell those union sons of bitches in Kentucky to get off their fat asses or they're going to get Monckton. We're counting on you, Jack. Fine. Just do that. 'Bye."

The great chair turned, facing Bill Martin, with the President's head some forty inches above Martin's. The President pushed the black button and descended slowly to Martin's stratum. Martin couldn't restrain a grin.

"Do you like my chair, Bill? I suppose you think it's a toy. Well, by Christ, it's not. Y'know what it's for? Suppose there's a goddamned attack and all of the Cabinet and Joint Chiefs and everyone make a getaway from Washington with me on this plane. All those partitions back there come out. The big goddamned brass all sit there in those rows of seats, see? But if I'm here at the console they can't see or hear me, right? But they can if I'm up higher, see? So the chair and table go up. Watch."

This time he pressed two white buttons; he and the table rose simultaneously. Martin sat back in surprise to avoid being hit by the tabletop.

"Now when I'm up here I've got to be heard, right?" The President reached under the right arm of the chair and produced a silver microphone on a retracting cord. He punched a button on his telephone console. "Get the idea, Bill?" His voice boomed from ceiling speakers along the cabin.

Esker Anderson turned off the speakers, clipped the microphone to the chair arm and descended.

"Bill, I need to talk to you. The election is top priority now. Only Gilley's election—that's all we should be thinking about." The President leaned his long body across the table and put his hand on Bill Martin's forearm. He squeezed as he talked, to emphasize his points.

"You know, Bill, a President is only as good as the goddamn advice he gets. There is just no way a President can find out everything he needs to know in a day. Shit, you know that. On some things I don't even know the goddamn questions to ask, much less the answers. I must depend on my people. Every President must. Roosevelt did. Truman did; and it got *him* into a lot of trouble. Goddammit, Bill, a President without good helpers is like a turtle on its back. He can make a lot of motions but he can't go anywhere. Take Billy Curry, for example." Martin began to see where this long monologue was going. He sat back on the couch and folded his arms. The President leaned back in the great chair and looked at the ceiling.

"Billy Curry knew nothing about the Dominican situation except what people told him. He'd probably never been to that two-bit swamp in his life. And although he'd been in the Navy, he was no military man. He was just a kid in a sailor suit in those days. When the damned Joint Chiefs told him something, he relied, goddammit. Right?" No answer was really expected and Martin remained silent.

"And when Rio de Muerte came along, he relied, sure as shit, on the Joint Chiefs and that no-good bunch in the State Department. And he relied on the CIA—on Horace and you. I know damn well he did. He told me. And it was a flaming fucking disaster, wasn't it? How many patriots killed? Eight thousand? About nineteen million goddamn dollars blown. The shit-ass Russians laughing at us in every corner of the goddamn world? It was no coincidence that they got that treaty with India that year. You know goddamn well it wasn't. You of all people." Anderson leaned across the table again, lowering his voice. "So who got blamed for all that mess? You know goddamn well who gets blamed. The fucking President gets blamed, that's who. Bad advice from all sides. But those shits don't get blamed. There are a lot of people who think the history books ought to put the blame where it really belongs for Rio de Muerte, Bill."

Anderson paused and looked steadily at Martin. Then he went on: "Of course, that's not that goddamned Monckton's depraved motive. That's not what he thinks. He wants to blacken Billy Curry's name forever, doesn't he? I wonder who he would have for advisors if he was sitting in this chair? Certainly not you or me. Probably shits like that Connaught. No—maybe not. Monckton is a loner. Connaught might be too damn strong for him. Monckton would want errand boys to do what he told them, not real advisors. He'd be one to make his own mistakes."

The President stabbed a button on his telephone and in seconds the steward appeared. "I'm going to have a drink, Bill. How about you?" Martin, sensing real danger in all this rambling talk, requested another cup of coffee.

As the steward built a drink at the President's bar, Anderson went on.

"Goddamned Monckton will make some big mistakes if he gets in here. He's too alone. He'll make assumptions and won't check them with anyone because he doesn't trust anyone. He'll be erratic; he'll have to back off as the facts come in. If that bastard gets elected it'll be very bad for you, very bad for the country. I'm the only lucky one. I'll probably be dead." A wave of self-pity passed quickly across Anderson's face and then was gone.

"So how do we stop him, Bill? We elect Gilley, that's how. That's the only sure way, goddammit." He took a gulp of the drink and set the glass down hard. "I understand you've been horsing Al Donnally."

Christ, here it comes, thought Martin, but he only said, "Horsing?" with a smile.

Anderson's face darkened. "You know goddamned well what I mean, Bill. You know what Al wants and you haven't done a goddamned thing to help him. You've horsed him."

Martin chose his words carefully. "Mr. President, Al Donnally's request for those files puts me in a tough spot. If I turn them over to him I violate at least four Federal statutes." Martin turned to an inside page of Simon Cappell's report and pointed to a paragraph near the top of the page as he spoke.

Esker Anderson began playing with the red and green buttons, swinging the chair slowly from side to side. "Out home, Bill, we raise a lot of sheep and a lot of goats on the lee side of the Coast Range." The President's voice was so low that it was masked by the jet engines' roar; Martin had to lean forward to hear him. "The old farmers come in to the county seats for the summer fairs and they have wool-shearing contests, better than any in the country. Some folks think a goat's harder to shear, others think the goddamned sheep are. Personally I'll take a sheep any day to a stupid-assed goat. But the shearers have a saying that sort of applies to your situation, Bill. It used to be that it was a hanging crime to steal sheep and goats thereabouts. Some fellows thought that was unfair; sheep had better meat and wool. But the punishment was the same. So a fellow with theft on his mind would go after the goddamned sheep. They'd say, 'I'd just as soon be hung for a sheep as a goat.' That's kind of where you are, isn't it, son? If you're going to be hung either way, why not go for the lamb chops?" The chair swung so that Anderson was facing the Director. "Now, what do you have for Donnally?"

Martin picked up the report. "Mr. President, here is a synopsis of what is in Monckton's files. But I doubt that there is much that Secretary Donnally would be interested in. Monckton has been in some deals in Australia and New Zealand that Al may not know about. And there's some evidence that he's taken campaign money from Asians. But it is not conclusive. Why don't you let Donnally read this and let me know?"

Esker Anderson smiled warmly and took the report out of Martin's hand. "That's a good idea, son. I'll just give it to Al and have him call you. And, Bill, there is one other thing I'd like us to talk about briefly. If you have time?"

Where the hell does he think I'm going? Martin wondered, but he replied, "Of course, sir. I'm at your disposal."

"Well, Bill, it's this. Once a President retires, the goddamn Government tends to forget him, you know. It's hard to get help for worthwhile projects and all. So I'd like you to tell your CIA people to give me a hand now and then when I ask for it, after I'm out of the goddamned office. It won't be much. But I'll be traveling some. And I'd like to continue to get the intelligence summaries. And from time to time a little special information. That won't be too hard to arrange, will it?"

"I can do that, sir. No problem. But if it's Monckton, I'll be retiring too. I don't know how long it might be before he'd cut you off."

"But," retorted the President quickly, "if it's Ed Gilley, you'll be there for a goddamned long time. So why don't you set me up with your people now, and then it'll all be done? And, Bill, if you do retire, let me give you some goddamned good advice. Let's just be sure that when we go we take all the paperwork with us. Those big trucks are just going to back up to the White House and I'm going to take out of there every book, every file, every piece of paper in the goddamned place. It's all going to Oregon where I can keep a goddamned eye on it. And you should do the same when you leave, Bill. It's the secret to a happy retirement." Esker Anderson had what he wanted and his point had been made—the conversation was clearly ended. Martin returned to his seat and tried to do some reading but he was unable to concentrate. Occasional gaps in the thick banks of white clouds gave Martin glimpses of small towns set in endless plains of farmland. Those voters down there, poor bastards, are in for a rough campaign, the Director mused as he nursed a Scotch.

History seems to have vindicated Al Donnally's postulate that the American electorate votes against its Presidential candidates, not for them. When he decided to become President of the United States, Richard Monckton, characteristically, became an accomplished student of Presidential elections. He read everything he could find. There were lessons in history and Monckton was determined to know them better than anyone else. He had his researchers assemble all the public-opinion polls on Presidential issues and candidate popularity from the publication of the very first poll, together with the politicians' memoirs and the biographies of the candidates. In the paneled den of his Kenilworth home he read quickly, sifting out everything that did not teach him what he must do and what he must avoid.

Donald Suede and the other television commentators called in vain for a sober debate on the great issues facing the nation. But Richard Monckton's research and Al Donnally's political-clubhouse appenticeship led them both to give the electorate what it wanted and deserved: a battle to the death with no holds barred.

Ed Gilley's Congressional career had been a lackluster snail creep to seniority. But at the hands of Richard Monckton and T.T. Tallford it was displayed as a rape of the public purse, characterized by slothful absenteeism and consistent pandering to the Special Interests.

The political-action units of organized labor hammered at Richard Monckton relentlessly. His Senate voting record was described as cruel and inhuman, in exquisite detail.

By election eve dozens of charges had been made, countered, restated and denied. Last-minute polls gave Monckton the election by 3 or 4 percent. The contenders gathered themselves for one last effort in their respective home towns, something upbeat, positive, Presidential and dignified.

And in the Oval Office Al Donnally and Esker Scott Anderson realistically faced the facts, as only practical politicians can. Ed Gilley was beaten; that was obvious before a single ballot was cast—and it was time for them to begin packing for the exodus.

9

The polls were closing in Washington as Rudy drove Martin from Dulles Airport to Georgetown in a cold, sleeting rain. Martin had been in England in early November. He voted by absentee ballot before he and

Simon Cappell flew to Ipswich for one of Martin's periodic countryside meetings with Sir Evans Ritter, long-time head of Britain's intelligence service, M-I Five. The quiet and secluded old Tudor manor house at Flixton, near Bungay, where they met had no television set; thus Martin was spared the election eve efforts of Ed Gilley and Richard Monckton.

Gilley and his family were shown in the middle-class living room of their old home in Pennsylvania; Richard Monckton wound up the campaign at a huge rally in the great lakeside meeting hall in Chicago. Then the television commentators sat around tables in New York studios and sadly conceded the election to Richard Monckton.

The first scattered results could be heard in the background as Sally Atherton opened the door to her home and gave Martin a warm greeting. A three-log fire crackled in Sally's den, a platter of cheeses, cold meats and bottles were set on a low table. Another time Martin would have been totally captured by the intimate atmosphere and this beautiful and passionate woman, dressed in a simple white silk blouse and long quilted skirt. But that night there was the insistent intrusion of the television, already beginning to say what he could not tolerate hearing.

"My darling." Sally put her hands on his shoulders and looked at him intently. "Do you know how I have missed you? The telephone is simply not enough. Are you exhausted? Was it a hard trip?"

Martin ran his fingers through her thick blond hair. "No, love, I'm fine. You look marvelous. Was California bad?"

"Well, I did what I said I would for Jack. The coffees and television and all that. He knew it was a sham; but he was a gentleman throughout and I'm sure he will continue to be. I've paid for my divorce in full, I guess."

A commentator's voice commanded Martin's thought:

. . . and the early returns from New York indicate Richard Monckton has won not only the upstate districts but the New York City area as well.

"Are you hungry? There's cheese and stuff there." She nodded toward the butler's table in front of the fire. "Another drink?"

"No thanks, I'm fine for now." He walked over to the low beige tweed couch set at right angles to the fireplace and patted a cushion. "Come sit here by me."

Scattered precinct returns from Philadelphia suggest that Vice President Gilley may be having serious trouble even in his home state.

Sally curled her feet up and put her head on Bill's shoulder. "Are you looking at that damn television over my shoulder? I thought you were nonpolitical."

Martin nuzzled her softly. "You have one magnificent neck, sweetheart. I'm sorry if I'm distracted. There's an enormous stake riding on Gilley tonight."

"Money?"

"Much more than that: lives, careers, reputations, at least one man's freedom, perhaps. Heavy stuff."

"Can you tell me about it, darling?" She sensed his tense concern.

. . . First returns from the Midwest, although scattered, make it Monckton country. He is running ahead in key precincts in Illinois, his home state, Minnesota, the Dakotas, Kansas and Missouri. More returns appear to give Monckton Ohio, a state once thought to be in the Gilley column. The NBC computer now projects a national Monckton victory by four percentage points with the polls still open on the West Coast.

Martin walked over to the bookshelves and switched channels. "If Gilley wins," Martin began, "he'll keep me on as Director. That's arranged. If Monckton gets elected he'll go through the Company like Attila the Hun. He'll be looking for records of President Curry's mistakes. And sooner or later he'll find the Primula Report on Rio de Muerte."

Sally spoke softly. "Will that hurt you, Bill?"

Martin walked back to the couch and, cupping her chin with his hands, looked straight at her. "Perhaps more than either of us could guess right now. There was an in-house investigation at the Company after Rio de Muerte, when the smoke had cleared. There is only one copy of that report. And it's bad."

. . . The rural areas are voting for Richard Monckton, as we expected. The big news tonight is the heavy vote Monckton is getting in the cities, especially in the industrial states of the Northeast and Atlantic regions. Donald Suede, how do you account for Monckton's success in these traditionally Democratic areas?

The assured voice of the commentator delivered his doctrine as if it were knowledge.

. . . It appears, Walford, that we are seeing a disintegration of the old Democratic coalition forged by Franklin D. Roosevelt in the 1930s. The blue-collar voter has ignored his union leaders this time. Monckton's stand on central issues—national defense, busing and abortion—has drawn millions from the Democratic fold, it would appear. There are powerful new political and social currents running just below the surface tonight that may not become apparent until all of the returns are in and have been analyzed by our computer. We will continue to watch...

Martin lay on his back on the floor, his head resting on Sally's lap, his feet toward the television set. Her hand was cool on his cheek. "Curry called me in just before the landing at Rio de Muerte. He asked me for the name of the Dominican rebels' inspirational leader. He was a legendary young Spanish Jesuit priest who apparently had fought in the resistance and then escaped. Anyway, the invasion troops idolized him. He was their chaplain, but he put the fire in their bellies, too. After one of his sermons they would go anywhere, do anything. Curry knew about him but didn't know his name. I told the President the priest's name when he asked me. There was no confusion; he had heard of the fellow —of his reputation—but he didn't have his name. So I told him. Father Benitimes."

"And?"

"And Curry told me to have him killed."

"Oh, Bill. My God. Why did the President want him killed? What did you do?" Sally pressed her hand into the carpet.

Martin spoke slowly. "No one knows why he wanted him dead. President Curry was probably trying to work out some kind of deal with the Russians at the summit; he was under pressure to destroy the landing, Primula guessed. It was too far along to just call off. And politically it was impossible for Curry to call it off. So I suppose he had no option. He let the landing take place, but cut its heart out to make sure it would fail."

Sally's voice was low. "Couldn't you have just refused to do it?"

Martin shook his head. "It was a clear, direct order. Curry obviously knew what he wanted to do. He didn't ask anything except the priest's name. And he ordered me to tell no one except the agent I picked for the work. I couldn't tell Horace McFall or anyone."

"You didn't kill anyone though. You were only a conduit, weren't you?" Sally asked defensively.

Bill shook his head. "The knife was held by someone else. But he was my man. Benitimes was killed on one of the troop ships, just an hour or so before the landing. It's pretty clear that most of the fight went out of the troops when that happened."

. . . Richard Monckton has taken a commanding lead in the first hour returns in our selected key precincts in Denver. The computer gives the State of Colorado to Richard Monckton with 54 percent of the vote.

"Poor darling. You've been living with this all these years. How really terrible for you. But still, you *didn't* kill that man. You were just a go-between from Curry to the murderer. Can't you explain that to people?"

"That's where Monckton's election fits. He'll want me out, of course. He wants to end forever the Curry legend, raze the Curry temple brick by brick, leave nothing standing. He'll want to do it spectacularly, on television; stamp it indelibly in the mind of every American. His line will be that Billy Curry murdered a priest in cold blood. I was his arm and Durwood Drew was his hand, holding the knife. But the murdering brain was Curry's. What a vile business that will be! How many people will acquit me after all of that shit hits the fan?"

"Oh, Bill." Sally cradled his head tightly in her arms.

"You *know* Monckton's elected. The television has been saying so all evening. What will you do?"

. . . Edward Gilley is the political protégé of President Esker Scott Anderson, and here, in Oregon, what Esker Anderson wants he usually gets. Even tonight as Richard Monckton scores upsets elsewhere it looks as though Vice President Gilley will carry Oregon and the neighboring State of Washington by generous margins. The proud old Northwesterner who is retiring from the White House knows tonight that he has delivered his home state once again for the party he has led for all these years.

Sally's telephone rang loudly; Simon Cappell was calling to report to Martin that Linda Martin had telephoned Simon, demanding to know where she could call her husband. Simon had told her nothing.

"Jesus, all I need is an argument with Linda tonight," Martin groaned.

"But I should call Jack and congratulate him," Sally replied. "There should be enough precincts reporting out there by now." She placed the call to Atherton's California headquarters; the Congressman sounded pleased to hear his wife's voice. He told her he was winning by a large margin. It was a good year for Republicans. No majority in the House, of course. But much better odds. And stronger committee ratios. Sally smiled and made faces at Martin as she listened.

"I'm so glad for you, Jack, dear. Give everyone my love. Night." Sally turned to Martin, smiling. "I just had a complete political analysis from the Congressman. He's standing there, phone in one hand, champagne in the other, a grin from ear to ear. Never happier. He could care less where I am, what I'm doing. But there'll be more Republicans on the Congressional committees, so it's a great night. That's my Jack."

"I'm glad someone's celebrating tonight," said Martin grimly. "I'll bet Richard Monckton is drowning in champagne. That son of a bitch."

At that same moment, Richard Monckton was seated alone in a huge, brown overstuffed chair in the dimly lit living room of a suite in the Blackstone Hotel in Chicago. Three large television sets were lined up against one wall, dark and silent. The President-elect hunched forward in the chair, a yellow legal pad on his knees, a telephone held close to his ear.

The room was heavily carpeted and draped in gold and brown. The dark wood, high ceiling and strong old doors were vintage Blackstone. Only one of the floor lamps was on, at low level. Richard Monckton wore a faded blue brocade dressing jacket tied at the waist with a tasseled belt of the same material. The broad velvet lapels were worn and water-spotted. His gray trousers, knife-creased, were hiked to his shins, revealing red garters holding up sheer calf-length blue socks. The black shoes gleamed. His white shirt was heavily starched; its wide collar framed a large necktie knot patterned with tiny dots.

At that moment, by order of the computers of all three television networks, Richard Monckton was the President-elect of the United States. It rankled him to have to accept the bestowal from the hated networks. Bu he had won, as he knew he would, and he was the next President of the United States. The President. The President of the United States of America.

The President-elect waited for his long-distance connection, and he thought about his appearance. The best barber would be obtained to give him a trim. And he would try to get a real suntan in Scottsdale this week. That would help. Real sun was better than that sunlamp he used. His hair seemed to be receding faster in front. Perhaps the sunlamp caused baldness. And although his body was spare, all the fat seemed to have gathered in his face. He wasn't handsome; he knew that well. The cartoonists loved to exaggerate his cheeks and jowls, his broad nose and dark brows. The Presidential medal for his inaugural would be etched in profile. From that angle, less of the bulge of his jaw would show.

Of average height and build, Monckton's appearance was not remarkable. His brown hair and heavy eyebrows were flecked with gray. Deep vertical lines scored the wide area between his gray eyes. No humorous reactions played at the corners of his mouth when he was amused. When it came, laughter was extruded in short barks. His voice was an orator's, his face a poker player's that never tipped its owner's hand.

The operator rang. Monckton strained to hear his elderly mother's faint, tinny voice through the telephone. It helped to press the receiver hard against his ear, but even so he could barely hear her. She was a thin woman, but her voice had always been strong. Now she was in failing health and probably dying slowly; but she had lived to see her son do well. Her mind seemed alert. She understood he had won, thank God.

The President-elect enunciated clearly. "I want you to come to the inauguration, Mother. There will be a warm place for you to see it from."

The voice was faint. "No, Richard, I'm sure they won't let me come. But I suppose I'll see you on television. They are very good to me here. They always turn on the television when you are on. Are you at home tonight?"

"No, Mother. We are all at the Blackstone Hotel where you stayed that time in Chicago. I'm glad you're feeling better."

"Yes, I am, Richard. The pain in my arm seems to be better."

"I'll be coming down to Sullivan to see you before long, Mother."

"Fine, Richard. Be my good boy, now."

"Good night, Mother."

As Frank Flaherty walked into the dim room he heard the telephone receiver smashed into its cradle and he could not resist a smile. Another telephone instrument has met its doom at the hands of the Mad Monk, he thought. Monckton always ended telephone calls with a smash, even when he wasn't angry or upset. For years this unintended punctuation had brought him some subjective affirmation of his superiority over those mechanical and technical empires which he neither controlled nor understood. He had no interest in how a telephone worked technically, but he did not ignore the existence of all the technology it represented. Rapid communication was a powerful force. He intended to dominate it. Somehow, the harder one slammed down telephones at the end of a conversation, the better it felt.

"My mother," muttered the President-elect to Frank Flaherty.

"She must be very proud and happy," the aide replied. "All three networks' computers now have you winning, but they disagree on percentages. CBS says fifty-six percent; the others may go higher. No concession by Gilley yet."

"Christ, I should think not. The polls have only been closed an hour in California. I won't go downstairs for a statement until the California count is pretty well in. It must really gripe West Coast voters to be so taken for granted by the shit-asses on the networks. Is the draft statement ready?"

"Yes, sir," said Flaherty. "The writers have come up with a pretty good draft, I think."

Monckton put one hand up for the draft as he put on a pair of horn-rimmed glasses with the other. Flaherty sat quietly as the President-elect rapidly flipped the pages.

He looked up, anger darkening his face.

"Frank, this speech is simply unusable. You must find me some goddamned writers with a little style and flair; 'Help me knit together this divided nation,' for Christ's sake! It's been the same all through the campaign! Anything good that was written I did myself. Now you know, Frank, we cannot continue to have this kind of crap coming in, especially for the moments of high drama. I simply will not have time to do the speeches myself once we get down there. Is that clear, Frank?"

"Yes, sir," Flaherty said nervously.

"I'll work on this one myself, now. But you've just got to take hold of this, Frank. Do you see what I mean?"

"Yes, sir."

"I just finished all the phone calls; no one else could do those either, of course. I don't object, understand. But I won't always have the time, Frank. We must begin to staff ourselves so that the President isn't personally writing every goddamned pissant speech that has to be given. There must be some good writers somewhere who would like to write for the President. Or am I wrong, Frank?"

"No, sir. You're right."

"It took nearly an hour to do the phone calls, you see. Not counting my mother. You didn't have her on the list, by the way." Monckton reached down to the floor for his telephone-call list. "Our illustrious Vice President-elect tells me tonight that we're carrying the states he campaigned in. I should by God hope so. Have someone give me the breakdowns, Frank. The states Oldenburg went to and the percentages, the states I went to, and the overlaps. I told Oldenburg to make no statement tonight until he hears from you. I think we should tell the networks to let him introduce me. Let them show him first, from Boston. Have him spend his television time doing a lead-in to my taking the stage here. What do you think of that?"

"That's great, if he'll do it," said Flaherty.

Monckton compressed his lips in anger. "Why the hell shouldn't he do it, if we tell him to?"

"He's a pretty proud man—a former Governor and all that. He may want to do his own statement."

"Wait, Frank. Let's settle that one thing right now. He's Vice President for only one reason: I picked him and put him there. Doesn't he know that, Frank?"

"Yes, sir. I'm sure he does."

"Then there should be no problem. Just tell him that's what I've decided, Frank. Cold turkey. He'd better begin to get used to instructions. Right?"

"Yes, sir."

Monckton sat back heavily and picked up the yellow pad from the floor. "Understand, I don't *want* to rewrite this speech, Frank. But it's no good the way they've sent it to me. Believe me, I'd rather spend my time in other ways—even seeing my campaign manager and those other miserable politicians. But we just don't have the writers to do the job, Frank. So I'll have to do it. Did you have something else before I start on this?"

"You asked a while ago about the plans for tomorrow. The President will furnish a Government plane to take you to Phoenix. You need to decide a few things so I can get them in motion tonight. The Blackstone will give us a floor. Do you want to run the transition from here, for sure?"

Monckton nodded. "I think that's best. I don't want to go to Washington until Inaugural Day. Chicago is as good as anyplace if we aren't in Washington. Let's firm up the Blackstone."

"Fine. Here is that Government-personnel paper you

wanted. As you see, you can only change about four hundred people right away. The others will take time. All told, you can reach about fifteen hundred. I thought it would number in the tens of thousands."

Monckton grunted. "That's the miserable goddamned Civil Service. About two thirds of those protected were put in there by Curry and Anderson. We'll be years getting rid of those little bastards. And they'll fight us from their holes in the woodwork; they'll fight us every day that they're there. Frank, I want you to put our sharpest man on the personnel thing. I want him to be smarter than they are. His assignment is to figure out how to root those Curry people out of there. It's got to be done quickly or they'll keep anything from happening. What about the top jobs?"

Flaherty reached for a blue folder on the end table. "I know you're tracking with Carl Duncan on the Cabinet. Here is the rundown on the Federal agency and commission jobs we can fill." He handed a paper to Monckton.

The President-elect shook his head and pointed to the left side of the paper. "The Chairman of the Federal Reserve belongs on this other list. I want him out of there, too." Flaherty made a note on a letter-sized yellow pad. "So, we get vacancies at CIA, Civil Service Commission . . ." Monckton looked up. "Who do they have for Chairman of Civil Service? I want a tough son of a bitch over there who can follow orders."

Flaherty reached for another folder, flipped it open and handed Monckton a paper. "That's the biography on one of the three present Commissioners. He is the top candidate for Chairman."

"Shit, Frank! Look here. He's another Harvard. Went in as a Curry appointment. Don't your little personnel boys understand what we're trying to do, Frank? Can't we find a tough bastard who is for us? Maybe a graduate of Tulane or Kansas State or Illinois? Are our personnel people all Ivy Leaguers, Frank?"

"No, sir." Flaherty sounded grim. "This man was recommended because he *is* for you. Price Monroe thinks very highly of him. Price is sure he'd be loyal."

Monckton grimaced. "It's starting already, Frank. I knew it would. You and I must be tough about this, even with our friends, like Price. No one is going to look out for the Monckton Administration except us, Frank. Our so-called friends are all out to pay off their old debts. We can't let them. Take this bastard off the list, Frank, and never again, *never* again bring me a name from Harvard. And no more Curry holdovers. They are out. Understood, Frank? *Out!*"

Monckton sailed the biography toward where Flaherty was sitting. It landed between them and Flaherty got up to retrieve it.

"What about national security, Frank? Have we heard from the Ambassador?"

"No, sir. Not yet."

"That's the vital spot, Frank. That's where I've got to be spending my time. What is being done?"

Flaherty handed the President another folder, this time with an orange cover. "In addition to Ambassador Murray, we've worked up this list from a raft of names that your friends have given us."

Monckton pursed his lips and steadied his glasses as he read. He looked up at Frank Flaherty sharply. "Carl Tessler? Is there any reason to think he would work for me? He's been on the Forville payroll for years. He probably hates my goddamned guts."

"Well, that may be," said Flaherty, "but Carl Duncan got a lead on Tessler yesterday that may be worth following up. Duncan was interviewing one of the Cabinet prospects—the HUD fellow, I think—when Tessler's name came up. Did you know that Tessler had done work for Curry and Anderson?"

"Yes. He's been a consultant from time to time on special problems. But would he come with us full time?"

"I'm not sure; but here's what we've picked up: Tessler thinks of himself as a sort of universal Man of the Age in foreign affairs. He fancies that he is not a partisan or the protégé of any particular person. He'll take Forville's money but he's not indentured. He told this other professor that he fully expected to work under every President elected during his lifetime. In other words, if a President has good sense, he'll just naturally hire Tessler to take over foreign affairs."

Monckton smiled wryly. "So he figures he's destined to shape the twentieth century? I wonder if the White House is big enough to house the son of a bitch's ego?"

Flaherty nodded. "That's the problem, of course. As good as Tessler is, can anyone work with him? I've made a few calls to check on him and it's unanimous: He has a terrible temperament. People use words like childish, egomaniac, limelight hog and petulant. But these people I called also agree with the HUD fellow: Tessler will come in a minute if you ask him. I don't know how loyal he'll be. He'll be absolute hell to work with. But he's the best man in the field, and you can get him if you want him."

"I don't know, Frank. He's a theoretician—a Harvard professor. He's done a little negotiating, but my NSC man will also have to run State and the CIA and Defense. He'll have to wheel Cabinet officers. Can Professor Carl Tessler do those things?" He sneered the word Professor. "We don't know. But then again, we have to realize that no one on this list can do everything. When you pick anyone, you always get less than you need."

"What about his temperament?" Flaherty pressed.

"Frank, that is up to you. If you think you can handle him, we'll take him on. But all the arguments about what office he gets in the White House and how long his car has to be and all that crap will have to be yours and not mine. I won't waste my time with a goddamned prima donna."

"Yes, sir. From what I know about him I think I can get along with Carl Tessler. Shall we get him in for you to talk to?"

"First I want you to call Elmer Morse at the FBI. Tell him I need to see him out in Scottsdale the day after tomorrow. Have him bring everything he has on Tessler. But don't tell him we're looking at Tessler for the White House staff." Flaherty made more notes on his pad.

"I should see Morse right away, anyway, Frank. He is someone I want you to get very close to. He and the FBI can be of enormous help to us. Have him spend the night in Scottsdale; he can ride back to Chicago with us the next day. When the press sees him on our airplane, that will send some skyrockets up in Washington. It's good to let the country know that I intend to keep him on at the FBI."

"Mr. President," said Flaherty, "when will you want to go down for the victory statement?"

Monckton suddenly grinned his instant grin. "By God, Frank, that's the first time anyone has called me Mr. President. You may want to make some little note of that; the question may come up later. The press likes to know those little things. Footnotes to history." Monckton stood and moved restlessly toward the window. "Where do we go for the statement?"

"We have to cross the street to the Conrad Hilton. There wasn't a big enough room here at the Blackstone."

"That street's full of crazies out there, isn't it, Frank? They were yelling a while ago."

"There are demonstrators, Mr. President, but they'll be a long way from you as you cross."

"Why not do the statement from here? They can bring cameras up, can't they? A quiet, dignified statement, with just my wife here. I kind of like that."

"You have a ballroom full of people over there, sir. Senators, Governors, all of the campaign people. There would be a lot of broken hearts."

"How about security, Frank? How does the Secret Service feel about me crossing the street?"

"Why don't I get the agent in charge? You can talk to him direct. He's told me they will move the demonstrators over a block away. You won't even be able to see them."

"I don't need to talk to the agent, Frank. I'm thinking of the television coverage. They'll show us crossing the street and you'll be able to hear all those little shits in the background shouting their terrible obscenities. It will be a bad picture, won't it?"

"But the ballroom enthusiasm—"

"Frank, can't we fill the street with our people, cheering? Move the hippies a block away and fill in the block with our kids; get a couple of loud bands, the Moncktonettes, flags and banners. Drown out those faggots. Can't you do that, Frank?"

"I can do at least some of it, sir. It will take a little time, though."

"Why don't you go and start that in motion? Frank, you see, someone should have been thinking of that hours ago. If anyone had been thinking of the picture they would have already prepared the street, Frank." Monckton dropped into the big chair with an I've-got-to-do-everything-myself air of resignation.

Monckton put his glasses on firmly, unscrewed the cap of his fountain pen and put the cap halfway into his mouth. He stabbed his pen at the typewritten speech copy, x-ing out the first three paragraphs. On the yellow pad he began to scrawl the opening lines of his victory statement.

The movement of the President-elect from the bedroom of his Blackstone suite to the stage of the grand ballroom across the street began as a trickle of motion and ended in a torrent. Monckton walked slowly into the living room, eyes downcast, deep in thought about the speech he had just rewritten. Frank Flaherty waited near the door with a Secret Service agent.

"Well, all set?" Monckton said too loudly, looking up.

"Mrs. Monckton will be here in a few seconds, sir. She's just leaving her room."

"Let's wait for her in the hall," said Monckton.

"No, sir," Flaherty contradicted respectfully. "She'll come through the connecting door; that hall out there is full of lights and cameras. You'll be on camera from this door until it's all over. The cameras outside the hotel are on platforms on both sides of the Hilton's doors. We have bands and people in the streets. It should be a good picture."

Monckton was impatient, now that he knew what he would say. He began to pace back toward the bedroom. Then a door opened and his wife came into the room with two men from her Secret Service detail.

The Moncktons greeted each other perfunctorily. Amy Monckton wore a dark red Mainbocher dress with long sleeves and modest lines. Her gray hair was simply arranged. An angular woman, long-faced, she wore no jewelry or accessories. She squeezed her husband's hand as they walked to the door, blinked involuntarily at the glare when the door opened, constructed a broad smile and held it in place as they moved through the hot overcrowded hallway.

The procession that walked to the elevator included the President-elect, his wife, Flaherty and four agents. At the lobby they were joined by eight more agents and Bob Bailey, T.T. Tallford, Carl Duncan, Tom Shelby, the campaign manager, a Governor and two United States Senators. Monckton walked rapidly through the lobby, intending to set a pace that would carry him across the street before the demonstrators knew he was there.

The narrow street between the hotels was blue-white shadowless brilliance. Echoing, clashing sounds dashed like waves against the walls of the buildings on either side. One hundred yards away several thousand demonstrators were held on the far side of a wide boulevard by deep ranks of Chicago police in riot helmets. The protestors' chants were partly masked by a twenty-piece brass band which stood in the street just east of the hotel doorways loudly playing Monckton campaign songs and Sousa marches. A Monckton advance man stood beside the bandleader to ensure loud and continuous sound.

The President-elect's entourage hurtled through the glare and noise of the street into the Conrad Hilton. The cavernous lobby was solidly packed with the Monckton people who could not get into the ballroom. As Monckton entered, the huge room was bright and dense with crowdroar. The men moving with the President-elect and his party found themselves surrounded by a phalanx of Chicago police who formed a wedge of blue. Frank Flaherty fought his way to the Deputy Chief of Police who led the detail. "What the fuck do you think you're doing?" screamed Flaherty over the roar of the lobby crowd. "Nobody asked for uniformed police here!"

"Who the hell are you?" yelled the officer in a brogue.

"Never mind that. Just get those men away from the President and out of the picture. We don't need them and we don't want them." Flaherty reached out and grabbed a Secret Service agent. "Tell this son of a bitch to get these blue-jackets out of here, Tom. I don't want them in the picture," Flaherty shouted.

The Secret Service agents on the Monckton detail were more than familiar with the problem. Richard Monckton did not like to give the appearance of being protected by police. It implied cowardice. And city police sometimes panicked in close crowd situations, striking out at the people who were the voters. So the general rule was: No uniformed police around the candidate. Actually, most Secret Service men felt cops weren't needed; they added no protection and they were a political liability to the Monckton people. But all those lights and cameras were simply irresistible to the Chicago police. It was nothing new. The agent nodded at the Chief and yelled, "Please clear them out, Chief. Don't let them come into the ballroom with us."

At the ballroom door Monckton paused, enveloped by the enormous sound, waiting for the scheduled televised introduction by the Vice President-elect from a similar ballroom in his home state.

"Ladies and gentlemen, the President-elect of the United States of America," boomed a voice from inside the ballroom. A surge of happy screaming, cheering and applause, the thumping of a band, a thousand balloons released from a net above the chandeliers and the focus of lights on his doorway were Monckton's signal. Monckton looked at Flaherty. Flaherty nodded. Holding his wife's hand high, the President-elect began to move down an aisle through the crowd. The fixed, plastic smiles so long held by the Moncktons seemed to be melted by the genuine joy exploding from this packed throng. As they walked through the crowd of screams and waving hands and straw hats and flags and banners, the President-elect and his lady said their thanks and pleasure and greetings in brief gasps as they moved, with the twelve agents, through the tangible, throbbing pandemonium to the steps and up onto the stage. There the noise more directly engulfed and battered them. Monckton let the crowd shout and scream until he sensed that the volume was subsiding a little. Then he walked a few steps to a speaker's rostrum and held up his hand. As he knew it would, his gesture renewed and regenerated the noise. He looked behind him at the ranks of hangers-on who had gathered on either side of his wife, at the broad smiles and self-satisfied expressions. Holding up both hands, Monckton finally quieted the crowd.

"My fellow Americans," he began, "I thank you for your friendship and support." There were loud cheers. "My wife and I have come over here to see all of our hometown friends and thank them personally." More cheers came from the Chicagoans. "But I also want to say a few words to all the other good Americans watching television tonight and the peoples of the other countries who may see this telecast.

"This has been a hard-fought campaign, perhaps one of the toughest in the history of this country. But when an election is over and the American people have made their choice, the divisions and differences are put aside and we are once again a united people; no foreign government should misunderstand this."

Applause thundered through the ballroom.

"It will be my task to organize the Executive Branch of the Government in the next two and a half months. I want this to be a diverse and open Administration, a Presidency of all the people. I will be asking for your help in making it so." He turned and reached back to draw his wife to his side of the rostrum for the conclusion of his speech.

"To each of you who has made this victory possible, our sincere and heartfelt thanks. To every American, I ask that you join me in a prayer tonight for our nation and its people. With God's help this can be a time of peace, of progress and of prosperity for every American.

"Thank you, and good night."

The cheers were more subdued than they had been at his entrance, but they were nonetheless loud and sustained.

After waves to the crowd and ritual handshakes with most of those on the stage, the Moncktons were led backstage to wait for a few minutes. The very largest financial contributors were being assembled in a room upstairs to have a quick drink with the President-elect in their moment of triumph.

Frank Flaherty moved to Monckton and shook his hand. "A great speech, Mr. President. Really fine. I noticed you took out all the conciliatory stuff about Ed Gilley. Will you want a meeting with him if he asks?"

Monckton's eyes narrowed. "That dismal son of a bitch? Never, Frank. Never."

10

THE CENTRAL INTELLIGENCE AGENCY

```
Interoffice memorandum
From:   Asst. Dir., Operations
To:     The Office of the Director of
        Central Intelligence
          Attn: S. Cappell
At your request, this is written con-
firmation of my call to you this
morning.  Following is the text of the
conversation recorded beginning at 1042
hours today between
Calling party:  Carol Carlson, secretary
                to Dr. Carl Tessler (our
                asset:  code name
                MARGARET TWELVE)
```

<u>Call taken by:</u>	Morton Sturdevant, manager, Electronic Factors, Inc. (code name SAILCLOTH TWELVE)
<u>Sailcloth:</u>	Hello?
<u>Margaret:</u>	Hello, this is MARGARET TWELVE. I am in a phone booth across the street from Harvard in Cambridge, Mass. 617-227-3001. This call is code 9.
<u>Sailcloth:</u>	Yes, MARGARET?
<u>Margaret:</u>	I took a call this morning at 0920 from a Frank Flaherty F-L-A-H-E-R-T-Y. He is chief of staff to President-elect Richard Monckton.
<u>Sailcloth:</u>	Was he calling Tessler?
<u>Margaret:</u>	Yes. But Tessler is on vacation in the Virgin Islands. So Mr. Flaherty gave me a message for him.
<u>Sailcloth:</u>	What is it?
<u>Margaret:</u>	Monckton wants Dr. Tessler to come to see him at the Blackstone in Chicago on Friday. The President-elect wishes to offer Dr. Tessler a position with his Administration. I am to tell Flaherty the arrival

time; Monckton also arrives in Chicago Friday, so Tessler should not get there too early.

Sailcloth: What position is he offering?

Margaret: He didn't say and I didn't ask.

Sailcloth: Have you given Tessler the message? What will he do?

Margaret: Dr. Tessler is using one of Governor Forville's homes in the Virgin Islands. Since there is no direct telephone I can only reach him by Marine Radio at nine every morning and I will call tomorrow.

Sailcloth: Exactly where is Tessler?

Margaret: The place is called Reef Villa. It is on the western tip of Jost Van Dyke, a Dutch island.

Sailcloth: Better spell the island.

Margaret: J-O-S-T V-A-N D-Y-K-E. Three words.

Sailcloth: After you have called Tessler, either call me or SANDPAPER TWELVE and report, please.

Margaret: I will.

Sailcloth: Anything else urgent?

Margaret: No, the rest is routine
                      and I'll send it along,
                      as usual.

Sailcloth: Very well, MARGARET.
                      Thank you.

          --end of recording--

"Margaret Twelve" had been hired as Carl Tessler's secretary in April, the week after the party at the G Street Club. She was an attractive, competent secretary with impeccable, although entirely fictitious, recommendations and credentials. It had not been too difficult to induce Tessler's venerable secretary to retire a year early. And when she left suddenly Tessler considered himself truly lucky to have found "Carol Carlson" so quickly, through a mutual friend.

The Company had penetrated Foretel, the Forville family intelligence apparatus, several years before. One of its second-level men was a Company asset. But Martin needed more assets close to Governor Forville to monitor the Forville-for-President campaign. And Carl Tessler—he had some good foreign contacts of his own. There was a need to gauge whether Tessler was under control, too.

When the Forville Presidential effort collapsed, Martin left "Margaret Twelve" as Tessler's secretary for whatever might come to hand on foreign subjects. But no one anticipated that the lovely redhead would be sending in such urgent information about President-elect Richard Monckton.

Simon Cappell could not reach William Martin immediately to tell him about Monckton. That morning Martin left the office early to attend a meeting of the Foreign Intelligence Advisory Board in the old Executive Office Building, next to the White House. When that august gathering of senior citizens had broken up for lunch, as was its custom, Martin stayed for a brief meeting with the FIAB chairman. It was not until Martin was in his car, moving slowly through noontime Washington traffic—its usual congestion compounded by a sleeting rain—that Simon reached him on his car telephone.

The car phone buzzed insistently, but Simon Cappell would not talk to Martin on the car phone; he requested a return call on a land line. Martin told his driver to pull up close to a telephone booth at a service station; it was raining hard.

Simon picked up his telephone on the first ring and his voice was urgent.

"Sir, Margaret Twelve phoned in from Tessler's. There has been an unbelievable break. Monckton wants to give him a job!"

"My God. Tessler? What job, Simon?"

"We don't know. Secretary of State, I suppose. But there's more. Tessler doesn't know about it yet, and won't until tomorrow morning. He's on an island and can't be reached."

"Do we know where he is?"

"Yes, sir."

"Hold everything. I'll be right in. I'll want to work on this when I get there."

Head down to avoid getting drenched, Martin ducked into his car and told the driver to get him to Langley as quickly as possible. He looked out the window at the gray downpour. My God, what a blockbuster! It was as if a totally blank and unsurmountable concrete wall had begun to show the outline of a hidden doorway. Monckton and Tessler! It was beyond belief. By Jesus, this Monckton had brass, if nothing else. Martin realized that in the next four years Monckton would even deal with an enemy if it could create an opportunity. And Tessler would be a tremendous asset; with all his background and talent, with his good press rapport, Monckton would get an open door to the intellectuals and a bridge to Forville and other Republican liberals. Monckton must not be underrated.

But if Tessler went with Monckton, would he help William Martin? The Director mused that it was worth a try; there was no other good alternative in sight, God knew.

Simon Cappell was waiting at the Director's private elevator when Martin emerged. He handed the telephone transcript to Martin and followed him into his office as Martin walked and read. When the door was closed the Director sat down and looked at his aide. "Can we reschedule my testimony at the Oversight Subcommittee tomorrow, Simon?"

"That may be tough," Simon said thoughtfully. "We've put them off once."

"Tell our legislative section it's urgent. I simply won't be in town."

Simon moved toward the phone. "I'd better call them now."

"No, Simon, wait. Here's what I want done: The station chief in Puerto Rico is to locate Tessler on that island. I want him to deliver the message from Monckton; don't have Tessler's secretary do it. Our man is to provide Tessler transportation to Florida tomorrow morning." Martin began to pace the wide room, then turned back. "No, I will send my plane; then it can pick us up at Opa-locka and take us all to Chicago. You and I will go to Florida tonight after work. Will you put that together?"

"Yes, sir. Right now." Simon gathered his notes and stood.

"Oh, one other thing, Simon. In the reading the other night I had that synopsis on T.T. Tallford, remember? That creepy fellow on Monckton's staff? In the package on the new White House staff?"

"Yes, sir. I returned it to files. It was in your outgoing stuff."

"One of our assets was mentioned in the Tallford memo. Do you recall that? Some old school friend of Tallford?"

"Right. Tallford was at Yale with one of our people and they are still social friends. Someone in the Western Hemisphere Division, wasn't it?"

"Right. Check to see who that is. I would like to see him this evening at Opa-locka. Very quietly. Unless he's on the other side of the world, of course. But bring him in quickly from wherever he is. It's important." Martin nodded a dismissal to Cappell and sat back in his chair to stare at the ceiling. He would talk to Carl Tessler. What he said to Tessler could salvage everything. It must be carefully thought through. It had to be right.

Opa-locka Naval Air Base had an air of genteel decline and disuse about it. A few patrol planes still flew in and out but the Navy lacked the budget to maintain the grounds and buildings on such a low-priority installation.

Within the seven-foot fence that surrounded the entire naval base was a CIA enclave protected by its own fence, higher and stronger than the Navy's. In addition to aircraft hangars and support facilities the Company maintained a complex of low buildings used for living quarters, training and storage. Most CIA operations in the Caribbean area had been managed from this site at one time.

As William Martin and Simon Cappell were eating dinner in a guest cottage somewhat apart from the other buildings, but within the Opa-locka CIA Station, a call came in from the Company station chief at San Juan, Puerto Rico. The caller reported that Tessler had been difficult to find. He had gone for an all-day cruise and picnic in one of Forville's outboard runabouts with only a native boatman for company. An agent had finally found him as he was eating his lunch on Green Cay, a tiny uninhabited island. The Monckton message had been delivered and Tessler had immediately agreed to go to Chicago the next day. He was delighted to be furnished with CIA transportation. The agent would boat him to Tortola in the morning and the plane could bring him directly to Opa-locka by noon. Tessler had assumed that the CIA was assigned to find and transport him, but he was a little surprised that Martin himself would meet him in Florida. He asked that the Director be told of his gratitude; he would look forward to their flight together to Chicago.

As the waiter cleared away their dinner dishes Simon took a second telephone call. The Company employee, T.T. Tallford's friend, known as Symphony Nine, was at the reception desk. Simon directed that he be brought to the bungalow.

"Your Lars Haglund is here, Mr. Martin. His 201 file folder is on the desk in the study."

"I want to see him alone, Simon. I'll talk to him in the den. Hold him here until I can look at one thing in his file; I'll call you."

Simon chatted with the visitor as they waited. Haglund looked like a Scandinavian stereotype; ruddy, blond, blue-eyed and stocky. According to his file he was forty, but he looked younger. He moved about as correspondent for a monthly travel magazine published by a credit-card company. Simon's call had found him preparing an article on Mexico City's night life for the magazine and an analysis of Japanese economic espionage in Mexico for the Company. He had taken the first commercial flight leaving Mexico City for Miami when his control officer called.

William Martin talked to Lars Haglund for nearly two hours in the den of the Opa-locka cottage. After Haglund left, Martin closed the bedroom door, stretched out on his bed and called Sally Atherton.

She answered sleepily. "Bill? Where are you, darling?"

Martin's reply was necessarily cryptic. "Out of town."

"Oh, I see. Will I see you again this week?"

He hedged. "I'm not sure. But I'm going to see an admirer of yours tomorrow, sugar."

Sally laughed. "Who's that? I thought you were the only one."

Martin teased, "Do you remember a pudgy Harvard professor?"

"Oh, him! Will you tell him I dream of him all the time?"

"I thought you dreamed of me all the time, sweetheart. Since when are you dreaming of Tessler? I'm jealous."

Sally's reaction was languid. "That's a very good sign. Tell me, Bill, am I going to start having lunches with Carl again? Will you be sending him things?"

Martin sounded cautious. "I don't know. He may go to work for Monckton, Sally. If he does, I *may* be able to hold on. It depends on how much authority Monckton will delegate to him."

"Oh sweetheart, that's terrific. You mean you could stay at the Company?"

"It's just a possibility. I will be talking to Tessler tomorrow. Then he has to decide whether he wants to work for Monckton. And it depends on what job he's offered. A great many things would have to fall into the right slots to do me any good. So don't get your hopes up too high."

"Oh, Bill. Wouldn't that be wonderful? You just tell Tessler that if he takes good care of you I'll give him a big, sexy kiss, just like in my dream."

"So that's the kind of dream it was, eh? Hell no, I won't tell him, my love. If I do, he'll decide his personal interests require him to sink me so that he can get you."

Martin dropped his bantering tone. "Seriously, dearest, are you all right?"

"I'm fine. I ran errands in the rain all day but I'm feeling good. I miss you, though, terribly. Will you call me tomorrow?"

"Of course. After I see Tessler. Sleep well, my darling. I love you."

"I love you too, Bill. Good night."

The next morning at 11:30 A.M. an unmarked Jetstar cut its two port engines and rolled to a stop in front of a CIA hangar at Opa-locka. Before Carl Tessler had time to unfasten his seat belt, William Martin had settled into the seat facing him and was fastening his. Simon Cappell moved up the aisle to take a seat near the forward bulkhead, out of earshot. The airplane immediately began to taxi toward the runway.

"Good morning, Carl. A good flight?"

"Oh yes, Mr. Director. Thank you so very much for sending your airplane for me. A great kindness." Tessler was tanned. He wore a rumpled tropical-weight gray suit and a wrinkled blue necktie. His shoes were grayed and stained from walks on the beach.

Martin put a large manila envelope on Tessler's lap. "Here is more reading, Carl. It may have some interest. There is an unusual report in there on the Greek situation."

Tessler tore open the flap eagerly and flipped through the nine documents. He selected one report, glanced quickly at Martin, and, as the plane took the runway and accelerated, began to read. In minutes Tessler had consumed the documents, reread the Greek report and made some notes in a small leather notebook. He stuffed the papers back into the envelope and handed it to Martin. "Thank you, Mr. Director. Your people do nice work. That is partly the reason I am going up to talk to Monckton, you know? Or do you know? I am being offered a post with his Administration." Martin nodded once. Tessler tapped his finger on the envelope. "Information. Facts. That's what one needs for the work to go on. You have it all, in the Government. We have so little hard information on the outside. And, too, in my field, the State Department is where the action is. I can sit at Harvard and write but I can have very little effect from there. It's all in Washington." Tessler waved an arm. "And there is so much that could be done. What a challenge! There is so much more State could do. The Department has not kept pace with world changes, you know. I really look forward to what might be done there."

Martin leaned forward closer to catch Tessler's words; he was confused. Either Tessler knew something about Monckton's intentions that Martin didn't or Tessler was making an unfounded assumption that he would be Monckton's Secretary of State. From the first moment he'd heard about Monckton's call, Martin wanted to believe that Monckton would ask Tessler to be Assistant to the President for National Security Affairs, to run the National Security Council staff and apparatus. Tessler would be of no earthly use to Bill Martin over at the State Department. All Company problems came to the President through the NSC. The National Security Advisor could have great influence in keeping Martin in the job; but as Secretary of State, Tessler wouldn't even be consulted.

Martin decided to see if Tessler's ambition could be steered a little. "How about the NSC, Carl? Does it need to be changed much?" he asked casually.

"The NSC? In my view that depends on Monckton. If he intended to take a strong hand, the NSC would have to be rejuvenated. Anderson and Curry let it slide into disuse."

"That's true, Carl." Martin nodded.

"No one has ever really used the NSC correctly, in

my view," began Tessler. "That is where the policy work should be done, not in the Departments. Let the Departments gather the facts, make recommendations and carry out policy. The President should make his own policy in his own office. But most of them, most Presidents, don't know enough." As he warmed to the subject Tessler seemed to raise his voice. "The NSC should shape Government-wide policy in all aspects of national security and foreign affairs." Tessler's big head bobbed and nodded as he spoke.

Martin asked questions to draw Tessler out, then adroitly turned the conversation, as he had planned, to bring Tessler to a consideration of Martin's tenure at the Company. He first offered the Professor a measure of his admiration for Tessler's ability, with just a dash of flattery. Then Martin shared a tidbit of international political gossip known only to a few. Tessler was both delighted and titillated. Martin asked his advice on his growing problems, what should be done about Elmer Morse and the FBI? Tessler sidestepped by saying that he believed the White House should intervene to prevent such conflicts among the security agencies. Congressional relations must remain placid. The budget should be increased. Martin laid down one more layer of flattery, then garnished the dish with a portion of Washington insider gossip. It was all served with discreet urbanity and consumed by Tessler to the last morsel. As the Jetstar descended over Lake Michigan, Tessler took the bait.

The Professor leaned forward. "Tell me, Bill, have you talked to Monckton? Will you be staying on?" To Tessler, the question seemed a natural one, in the setting of their intimate chat. But his unconscious use of Martin's first name, for the first time, revealed to the Director how effective the afternoon's blandishments had been.

"I don't know what Monckton plans for me, Carl. I really don't have a clue."

"Do you want to stay?" Tessler's tone was warm and confidential.

"It's my career, Carl. I am a career man; no politics, you know. I've served four Presidents so far."

"But why wouldn't he keep you, Bill?"

"I don't know. I'm told he thinks I'm a Billy Curry protégé; but that's not true, you know. Other than that, I don't know."

"If I go to State, Bill, would you be interested in a slot there?"

Martin shook his head. "Thank you, Carl, but I don't think so. The CIA has been my life. If I couldn't stay with the Company, then I guess I would try to find something on the outside." Martin took the opportunity to steer the conversation back to Tessler. "Do you really think it will be State, Carl? I would have bet Monckton would want you closer, at his right hand in the White House."

The Professor blinked behind the thick glasses. "Well, I only have the short, relayed message from Monckton, and I don't know what he has in mind."

But he wanted to be Secretary of State; it was first in rank, senior among all Cabinet members. Tessler knew that because he was foreign born he could never be President; but still, the job was in the line of Presidential succession. He knew, too, how all those jealous bastards on the Harvard faculty would burn if he got State.

At the same time Tessler wondered what Martin was hinting at. What would he reply if Monckton only offered him the NSC job? His colleagues on the Harvard faculty must not think that he was running away from the University. He blinked again at Bill Martin as the plane turned on final approach to the small lakeside airfield. "I want to do what I can to help you, Bill. You have been very decent to me. Shall I say something to Monckton?"

Martin had Tessler! He nodded. "If you find yourself in a position to recommend me, Carl, I would be most grateful. I can serve Monckton very loyally, but I don't think he knows that. And you and I would make a damn good team. If you can give him some confidence in me, it can only help me."

Tessler nodded, and his tone lightened as the plane dipped to touch down. "I will see what I can do. Who knows? Maybe he wants me to take over the Weather Bureau? If so, I will put you in charge of naming hurricanes. You will meet a lot of nice girls that way."

As Carl Tessler squeezed up the narrow aisle to the stairway, the only welcoming committee was the black civilian driver of a small green Chevrolet sedan, with "For Government Use Only" lettered on the front door. At the door to the plane, Tessler turned, shook hands with Bill Martin and clumped down the stairway and into the automobile. Martin watched the car until it left Meigs Field, then turned back into the airplane. The day had gone well.

11

As he left the car and entered the Blackstone Hotel, Carl Tessler could sense that the old hotel was pridefully re-experiencing its role as a historic and exalted place. It was not because there were police all over and huge flags on poles over the marquee. There was something about the building itself, the marble lobby, the venerable registration desk and the way people stood and moved about the beautiful public rooms that reminded him of the feeling in some great buildings he knew in France and England. Once again a President of the United States was a guest there and the Blackstone was the center of the nation's attention.

They had been expecting Tessler. A young man met him at the curb and steered him through the lobby to the elevator. When they reached the sixth floor, young men in business suits were standing near the elevator, in the hallway and at several of the doors; it was a heavy guard. Tessler's escort moved him easily along the hallway. Inside the first open door, a young woman sat at a Louis Quatorze table and a secretary typed at a scarred gray metal desk near the window. There were papers everywhere, piled, collapsed and stacked on every level surface. Telephones rang, unanswered. The receptionist's antique desk held a room-service tray, the club sandwich and coffee untouched. She smiled a thin, distracted welcome, although she apparently had no idea who Tessler was. Just four days before she had been a secretary to the campaign-office administrator in the Monckton campaign headquarters in Washington. When Flaherty had called her boss for girls to staff the Presidential transition office in Chicago she had taken the call. Now here she was, the receptionist for the President-elect.

"Mr. Tessler, just move those papers, please, and sit down. Mr. Flaherty would like to see you for a few minutes before you go in. I'll tell him you're here."

Frank Flaherty quickly appeared, freshly tanned, smiling and enthusiastic. He shook Tessler's hand warmly and drew him through a connecting door into his room, from which all of the hotel furniture had been removed. Deep carpet marks indicated that twin beds had once rested where Flaherty now sat at a battered wooden desk. There were two wooden office chairs directly in front of the desk and a large wooden table against the wall near the hall door. The table was piled high with bundles of telegrams and letters tied with string. Flaherty's desk top was nearly clean. A brand-new leather folder concealing a letter-sized yellow pad was embossed in gold at the lower right corner: "Franklin R. Flaherty, Assistant to the President of the United States." It had just arrived by mail from his mother in Milwaukee. Behind him on the wall, centered between the absent beds, hung a gaudy oil painting of a gondola cruising a canal in Venice, a lone remnant of earlier furnishings.

"Dr. Tessler, this is a particular pleasure for me." Flaherty spoke like a student to a professor. "I apologize for the mess and confusion. We just flew in from Arizona about two hours ago. The President-elect will make his office here until the inauguration, you know."

Tessler nodded.

"Where did we find you, Doctor?" Flaherty went on. "Your secretary said you were only to be reached once a day. You were in the Virgin Islands?"

"Yes." Tessler's manner was cautious. He wasn't sure how the name Forville would be received. "An old friend allowed me to use his place to vacation and do some writing. I have no classes this quarter."

"That sounds marvelous. God knows when I'll get any time off. Doctor, as I told your secretary, the President-elect would like to talk to you about your availability. But I wanted to speak to you first; obviously, if you are not at all interested there would be no purpose in taking up his time."

And no purpose in my leaving the sunshine to come to this bitter cold and windy place, thought Tessler, wryly. "I understand," he said. "Frankly, Mr. Flaherty, I am very surprised to be asked to come to Chicago. I did not support Senator—that is, the President-elect—

when he was running. To be candid, I don't know whether our respective philosophies of world affairs will fit; I must say his campaign statements confused me."

Flaherty smiled. "I think you will be pleasantly surprised, Doctor. The President-elect is a student of your writings."

Tessler's downturn of the mouth showed surprise.

"In fact," Flaherty continued, "he recently finished one of your books, *Global Policy for the Century,* and was very impressed with your ideas. I personally have heard him discuss it."

Tessler was skeptical of people who said they read his books, but he was determined not to register anything except availability to this shiny, clean young man. "Well, naturally," he began, "I would always wish to make a contribution if I were convinced that I could be useful. I have served both Presidents Curry and Anderson as an advisor; you probably know all that. It is my belief that the next six months will be critical in the nation's foreign affairs. Relations in Europe are in disrepair. Our own hemisphere has also been ignored. And the war must be brought to a conclusion on a proper basis. There are great needs and, I believe, even greater opportunities. I would say, if the President wants me, I will come. But I still wonder that he truly would want me."

Flaherty stood up. "I'll leave that for him to talk to you about, Dr. Tessler. Will you excuse me a minute?"

Seconds after Flaherty walked out into the receptionist's room, she came in with a cup of coffee in a paper cup set on a small tray. Tessler took a swallow and set it down. It was harsh and tepid. The girl went out briefly, then returned to the doorway. "Will you come this way, Dr. Tessler?"

She just found out I'm a doctor, Tessler mused. Maybe she read my book too, since I got here.

They left the reception room, went another ten yards

along the hallway past a small desk manned by a large Secret Service agent to a dark wooden doorway to which had recently been affixed a large, carved and gilded wooden eagle rampant on a furled American flag. A brass plate designated this the Presidential Suite. There was no key in the lock; the campaign was over. The agent standing by the door opened it as Tessler neared.

Frank Flaherty was standing alone at a window gazing out at Lake Michigan. He turned and said, "Come in, Doctor. Sit down here." Tessler looked about; characteristically the President-elect was not in the room. In the years to come, Tessler would, on countless occasions, stand with a high-ranking foreign visitor in Monckton's empty office waiting for the Leader of the Free World to emerge from his lavatory to greet the dignitary with a slightly damp handshake.

When the President-elect entered the room he didn't shake Tessler's hand. Instead, Tessler heard what was to become Monckton's habitual conversational opening. "Ah, Frank tells me," it began. In his deep timbre Monckton said, "Frank tells me you would consider joining us." At the same time that Monckton was speaking, Tessler was offering guttural election congratulations and expressing his pleasure at being invited to this meeting.

Flaherty quickly cut through the garble and led them into the anticipated conversation. "I think Dr. Tessler was glad to know that you read and liked his latest book, *Global Policy for the Century,* Mr. President."

Monckton sank deep into an old brown easy chair that seemed out of place among the French antiques the hotel had assembled for the suite. "Yes, Doctor. I was particularly interested in your theory about war between China and Russia. One of the reasons I've asked you here is because of your flexibility and open-mindedness. I think it's time for us to change our policies toward China, and I think you agree."

"I do, indeed, Mr. President," Tessler said as he sat on a straight chair.

"Would you have problems in leaving Harvard for a while?"

Tessler grinned. "No, sir, I would not. In fact I suspect it would occasion quiet celebration."

"I know you've worked part time for other administrations," Monckton went on. "How much experience have you had with the National Security Council?"

Martin was right, Tessler realized. It's NSC he wants me for, not State. "I was a consultant to President Curry's NSC Director for a year. But I had very little contact with the NSC staff and machinery, as such. Perhaps it's none of my business, Mr. President, but have you decided on a Secretary of State?"

"It doesn't matter, Carl," Monckton said flatly. "It doesn't make a goddamn who is at State."

Tessler looked surprised. "Perhaps I don't understand—" he began.

"Then let me explain, Carl," Monckton said with slightly exaggerated patience. "I will make foreign policy. At the White House. I will tell those little shits at State what to do and when to do it. If you come in your job will be to make sure they do it. You and I will call the shots, make no mistake about that." Monckton was grim. His eyes narrowed and he spat out the words with passion.

He really hates the State Department, thought Tessler. That speech came right from the spleen. "I understand, sir," said Tessler smoothly, "and I concur; foreign policy should be made by the President, not by Foreign Service officers. But the NSC is in serious disrepair. It will be a major job to reconstruct it."

"Oh, I totally agree, Carl. And I would like you to begin immediately. Why don't you go out with Frank now and discuss details? I have someone else waiting for me." It appeared that there was nothing to do but leave. Tessler rose, muttered his thanks and followed Flaherty into the adjoining office.

"Frankly, Mr. Flaherty," Tessler began as they entered Flaherty's room, "I had come here prepared to accept the Secretary of State job. I know very little about the White House job beyond our conversation with the President."

Flaherty spoke as though his reply had been rehearsed. "That's easy, Doctor. It pays forty-two thousand five hundred dollars. It's one of four top jobs on the staff. You will have a car and driver, as you need one. You will remain here in Chicago until January and then have an office near the President in the White House. The NSC has a very large budget and a staff of about one hundred and sixty. You will run the NSC apparatus, approve all foreign policy and national security work before it goes to the President, and convey his decisions to State, Defense, CIA and the other agencies involved. It will be your job to make sure his orders get carried out. Will you do it?" Flaherty smiled at Tessler.

Tessler almost said yes, but something held him back; in truth he was cruelly disappointed that he was not to be Secretary of State, and he was not completely sure he wanted the White House job. Would he be seen only as Richard Monckton's puppet, or could he carve out an independent identity? What would the Harvard faculty reaction be? Would the press write that he had been passed over for Secretary of State?

"Mr. Flaherty, I would like to sleep on the President's offer, if you don't mind. Could I call you tomorrow?"

"I'll tell you what we'll do, Dr. Tessler." Flaherty was determined to clinch the deal. That was his job. "Let's get you a good room here. Then if you have any questions, I'll be close by."

Tessler nodded his thanks but spoke cautiously. "That will be just fine. I hope you understand. I am sure the President would want me to deliberate thoroughly before giving him my decision. I feel the need to do that."

"Of course, Doctor. Call me in the morning after you've had breakfast. Good night."

When Carl Tessler opened the door to a spacious room on the fourth floor he realized how exhausted he was from the strain of the day. He undressed and got into bed, ordered a steak dinner and fell asleep watching a cowboy movie on television. When the dinner arrived he ate quickly and went back to sleep again, in spite of a climactic cattle stampede that filled the screen. He awoke at three fifteen in the morning and turned off the whistling and empty video screen but he couldn't fall asleep again.

He knew he was trapped. On the one hand he had to leave Harvard. The atmosphere was pure poison and his wife's animosity was not helping the situation. And on the other hand, he wasn't being offered State. So the choice was between a downgrade to a lesser university or to the White House job with Monckton. Tessler knew he could do a good job for Monckton if the man would not interfere. But Monckton appeared to be as odd as he was portrayed in the stories about him. He could be very difficult to work for. But what President wasn't? Anderson was a pluperfect egomaniac. And Curry had been a stylish and handsome weakling, buffeted by a swirl of advisors each trying to get in the last word. If one is destined to serve Presidents, then one must be prepared to take them as they come. Still, he thought, Monckton was a very strange man.

It was two weeks before Christmas when William Martin was summoned to the Blackstone by the new Assistant to the President-elect for National Security Affairs,

Carl Tessler. From his office on the closely guarded sixth floor Tessler spent his days and evenings interviewing prospects for his staff and assembling policy reading for his new employer. Fortunately, the Forville Foundation people were feeding him both people and material to help him. Tessler found that his ability to turn out work was hampered in part by the makeshift working conditions. But he was chiefly plagued by Richard Monckton's frequent interruptions.

Richard Monckton was relaxed. The campaign was over and he was elected. He was working out his own personal transition from perennial candidate to President by turning his thought to broader subjects, leaving the day-to-day work to others. And his Harvard professor was his vehicle of transport. The President-elect would call him down the hall to the Presidential Suite at all hours for long, rambling conversations ranging over hundreds of subjects.

Tessler was in his makeshift office when William Martin was ushered to the door. The Professor was wearing the same rumpled gray suit he had worn on their flight from Florida. In the intervening weeks the Blackstone valet had done his best, but it retained the appearance of lumpy poured concrete.

The hotel had resurrected a Queen Anne desk for the Doctor's use and Tessler had piled it high with message slips, mail and work folders. Still awaiting a desk chair that had been on order for days, Tessler sagged over the margins of a high-backed Italian chair.

"Mr. Director—Bill! Come in!" Tessler said with genuine pleasure, closing a folder and standing. They shook hands cordially. "Sit there, Bill. It is all I have to offer you. It threatens to collapse, like everything else about this place, but I believe it is safe. How are you? I have missed seeing you. I see no one. This transition is like a salt mine."

Martin sat gently on a folding metal chair cushioned

with green plastic. "I read that you're making some real progress in rebuilding the NSC staff, Carl."

Tessler shook his head. "It's slow going. Some of the good people I cannot pay enough; a few I cannot get cleared."

"You mean they are security risks?"

"Oh, no," Tessler chuckled. "They are Democrats. I am forbidden to hire Democrats, especially Curry Democrats, homosexuals or Ivy Leaguers. If you know any Republican graduates of Ohio State who like girls will you send them to see me? At this juncture I don't care if they know anything about foreign affairs."

"Is it really that bad?" asked Martin.

"They are determined to reward their friends, you know. Perhaps one can't blame them, as a general proposition. But I am trying to find experts. I had a great deal of trouble in convincing the President-elect that you should be kept on, Bill." Tessler's voice was low and confiding.

Martin's face did not change expression. "And?"

"You were not Monckton's first choice, let us say. But circumstances worked in your favor. The leading candidate declined yesterday. And I was able to catch the President in a very good frame of mind."

"He's agreed to keeping me on?"

"Yes, I have vouched for your loyalty and willingness to cooperate, as well as your good work. He is, frankly, skeptical." Tessler leaned forward and placed a hand on Martin's arm. "So be on your best behavior, Bill. Give him no excuse to be unhappy."

"Have no fear, Carl. I'm very grateful to you. I hope you know that." Martin sounded sincerely grateful, very relieved and even a little surprised. But he had known everything Tessler had just told him since the previous day. Margaret Twelve had come with Carl Tessler to the Blackstone transition and she continued to make her reports to her control officer, Sailcloth, every evening.

Martin knew Tessler had gone out on a limb for him with the new President. It was now important that Tessler number Martin as one of those who bore personal loyalty to Tessler, rather than Monckton. And so Martin labored it, repeating his gratitude and personal admiration. Tessler looked somewhat pained and embarrassed at Martin's assuring pledge, but nonetheless pleased.

Tessler's secretary came into the doorway and said, "He'll see you now, Dr. Tessler."

Tessler nodded and turned back to Martin. "The President-elect would like to talk to you, Bill. Let's go down the hall."

The tall CIA Director and his rotund escort walked across the elevator foyer to the Presidential suite. They passed four security posts, receiving approving nods from each of the young agents as they reached them. The agent on post at the door pushed it open for them and they found Frank Flaherty seated alone in the over-furnished living room. He rose and smiled. "Mr. Director, welcome." Flaherty turned to Tessler and greeted him in a mock German accent. "Ah, liddle Klaus Tesselheim! *Vas hast du?*"

Tessler shook his head doggedly and smiled. "You see, Mr. Director? No respect. Ethnic humor is all I get from these politicians."

Flaherty stood up as Monckton came through an archway from another part of the suite. The President-elect was holding his hands out from his sides, fingers spread apart. "Frank, goddammit, there are no towels in there. My hands are all wet."

"Mr. President, there are no towels on the whole damned sixth floor." Flaherty laughed.

Tessler shook his head. "What profiteth it if you rule the whole world," he intoned, "and do not have a towel to wipe your hands?"

Monckton did not look amused; he dropped awkwardly into a large chair, propping his elbows on the chair arms to hold his damp hands up in front of him. "They tell me, Bill, that you are willing to stay on with us." Before Martin could reply, Monckton went on, more loudly, as if to preempt the possibility of any conversation, "The intelligence establishment must do better, Bill. I'm sure you know that. Its record is not exactly, shall we say, unblemished, is it? When I was in the Senate, I know, we were caught flat-footed over and over. Venezuela is an example. We were completely surprised by that coup, weren't we? China is worse. We spend billions and billions for intelligence and we get results like Rio de Muerte. You have those thousands of people sitting on their asses over there at Langley doing nothing. Well, we're going to do better. Oh, you people aren't the worst, are they, Carl?" Tessler looked startled, shook his head once and repressed a grin. Flaherty shook his head in a negative.

Monckton, oblivious to any reactions, went on. "No, the little shits at the State Department are infinitely worse, Bill. As you know, they sit over there and worry about their appropriation and who is in charge of place cards for the next state dinner, while they leak all kinds of secrets to the press. They don't do one constructive goddamned thing. At least you fellows do a few things. But you'll be the first to admit that on the whole our intelligence gathering is a piss-poor effort, won't you, Bill?" Flaherty nodded in agreement; Martin kept an expressionless face, waiting for his cue to speak. Monckton went on. "I'm determined that we will do better, Bill. The first thing to do is fire about forty percent of those people who just sit there and read newspapers all day. I want all that deadwood cut out—right away. Oh, there will be some squeals, but we're going to do the same thing at State, aren't we, Carl? Except that it should be sixty percent over there. Let the little pissants shriek. Our people in the country will love it. Most of them hate the State Department, you know."

Monckton had been looking at Martin as he talked. Then he turned his head and gazed out the window at the sky above Lake Michigan. "Have they talked to you about the Deputy Director at the CIA?" Monckton asked. It was a question that needed no answer. "I've decided to name Arnie Pittman your Deputy for the military slot, Bill. I know you'll get along well with him. He was in my ship during the war. He's an easy fellow to get along with. And he may be of considerable help to you. He has spent a lot of time in the Pacific and knows that theater pretty well." He turned his head back to look directly at Martin. "I'd like him put in place just as soon as you can do it."

Monckton slapped his thighs with his hands and leaned forward so that his forehead nearly touched his knees. He lurched to his feet and moved toward a door without looking at Martin again. "Frank, I'd like to see you," Monckton said as he opened the door and went into the next room. Flaherty looked at Martin, smiled apologetically and followed Monckton; he closed the door as he left the room.

Tessler was smiling broadly; he was deeply amused. "That was undoubtedly the most ungracious job of recruiting since the press gangs roamed the streets of London. But welcome aboard."

Martin was not amused. After decades in Government work, he valued the worth of the thousands of bureaucrats who did mundane tasks day after day. Monckton's attack on these Company people was not only unfair, it was cheap and boorish. And, more personally, Martin was offended by the insensitivity and indifference of Monckton's invitation to him to serve. He wasn't a day laborer, for Christ's sake. He was Director of the Company. For Monckton to show so plainly that he took him for granted, and was so obviously indifferent to Martin's feelings, sickened him. As they left the suite he asked Tessler, "Who the hell is Arnie Pittman?"

"Captain Arnold Pittman, U.S. Navy. He's a destroyer flotilla executive officer in San Diego. We're having him brought East to you immediately. I have no idea if he is any good, but he's your brand-new Deputy."

Martin left Carl Tessler in the hallway and doggedly headed for the press secretary's office on the second floor, where he was to appear at the afternoon press briefing for the announcement of his reappointment. As he rode down in the elevator he changed his mind about returning to Washington that night. He had planned to celebrate his appointment with Sally over drinks and dinner. After this shabby episode with Monckton he didn't feel like celebrating. He needed a hot, cleansing bath and a few stiff drinks. Alone. He knew he had to try to come to grips with some questions about himself and his future. The Monckton episode had dredged up doubts long buried.

As he lay back in a hot bathtub, steam enveloping the bathroom, he began to take stock of what having Arnie Pittman as his Deputy would mean, and he chuckled to himself. If Monckton thought he was getting a pipeline into the Company by putting his old buddy in as Deputy he didn't understand how things worked at Langley. Martin would see that Pittman would be hermetically sealed; he would have the cleanest desk in the place. Stepping out of the tub and wrapping himself in a thick terry bath sheet, Martin exploded, "Fuck you, Captain Pittman!"

When the call came, Captain Arnie Pittman was in the barber shop at North Island where one of the barbers gave a very fine facial massage. He could have retired from the Navy two years before, but because of Dick Monckton he had stayed in, even though he knew he would never again have a command of his own. An admiral at the Naval Bureau of Personnel had made it clear when his captaincy had gone through that if it hadn't been for Dick Monckton he'd have been passed over and retired out at commander. The guy was really bitter; he called it a political promotion. Pittman knew that was really unfair. All Dick did was make sure Pittman's promotion came through when his number came up, along with the rest of them.

Arnie Pittman had barely made it through the Naval Academy. He never discussed his class standing, but there were plenty of fellows around who would tell you that he was number 389 in a class of 399. He was a man who knew he was not brilliant.

But they could put him anywhere and he would always do a job for the Navy. And, by God, Richard Monckton knew that. When he had been a United States Senator, Dick had the Navy assign Arnie Pittman to the staff of the Senate Foreign Relations Committee for nearly two years. That had turned out to be a good job, mostly spending time with Dick when he wanted someone around who could be quiet, looking after him on trips abroad, that sort of thing. The soft life and all that good food had played hell with Pittman's fitness during that tour. Ever since then he'd had a weight problem.

But although he was large he could be unobtrusive, he could hold his liquor, and he could keep a confidence.

Arnie Pittman and Richard Monckton had played a lot of nighttime cribbage together as lieutenants j.g. aboard the U.S.S. *Caribou,* a supply ship that made long anchorages in the atoll harbors of the South Pacific. During the day Pittman and his smaller shipmate would sit side by side in the shade for hours, neither one saying anything. Then Monckton would talk and Arnie would listen, nodding occasionally. Monckton talked about the world and about Illinois and his little home town, Sullivan. He had become a lawyer and wanted to go to Chicago to practice. Pittman was career Navy and intended to stay in. When the war ended they parted, but Monckton kept track of his big, quiet friend. It was painful for him to drop the barriers and admit a person to friendship. But once admitted to that lonely circle, his friend received Monckton's unstinting loyalty and trust; and when Monckton gained seniority in the Senate he helped his few friends generously. As President, of course, he would continue to help them. Arnie Pittman was a friend; it was not a question of qualifications or ability.

Arnie Pittman was not surprised that Dick Monckton was making him Deputy Director of the CIA. Once he knew that Dick Monckton was elected President he knew there would be something good in store for Arnie Pittman. That's just the way their friendship worked.

12

The Director of the Federal Bureau of Investigation, Elmer Morse, was surely the most wily and skillful of all of those who toiled in the labyrinths of the Congress of the United States. The results for Elmer Morse and his bureau were immeasurable in terms of power: vast appropriations, new buildings, exemptions from Civil Service laws and freedom from some of the troublesome restrictions imposed on other Government agencies were the produce of their toil.

For example, Elmer Morse knew the special needs of the venerable chairman of the subcommittee of the House Appropriations Committee that was given charge of the FBI's annual appropriation. Everyone had needs. Elmer Morse and the FBI had needs, too. It was simply a matter of two people looking out for each other—that's what the Congressional process was all about. Clearly Chairman Thomas Grimes needed a chauffeur. A veteran FBI agent was dispatched to drive Congressman Grimes's modest Chevrolet; his principal duties were to take Mrs. Grimes from their apartment house to the Safeway several times a week and to sit patiently in Grimes's office until the old appropriator was ready to go home at night. But the chauffeur-agent was not lonesome while waiting. He could talk shop and baseball with the other FBI agents working or waiting in the office of Chairman Thomas Grimes. One served as a guard and receptionist in the outer office. Another, listed as a legislative assistant, primarily worked on the FBI's complex and extensive appropriation. At the Grimes's modest apartment in Bethesda, Maryland, the young man in a white butler's jacket and black bow tie who greeted visitors at the door was also an FBI agent. They were all on assignment by order of Director Elmer Morse.

All of this perception and thoughtfulness paid and paid well. Legislation which Elmer Morse needed usually received early favorable attention when he let his needs be known. And legislation that Morse opposed generally lost its way in a maze of parliamentary sidetracks.

Richard Monckton was well aware of Elmer Morse's clout in the city of Washington so it was not mere chance that Morse was the President-elect's first official visitor in Scottsdale, two days after Monckton's election. The friendship went back to Monckton's first months in the United States Senate years before. As time passed they fought Washington battles side by side. Every alliance needs an enemy to keep it strong, but few observers accurately assessed the strength of the link that was being forged between Monckton in the Senate and Elmer Morse at the Bureau. They continued to collaborate quietly for fifteen years, at first to expose and root out Communist agents of the International Communist Conspiracy, later to attack and destroy anyone else they considered to be a political enemy of the FBI, Elmer Morse or Richard Monckton.

The two men thought alike; Elmer Morse was convinced it would be good for the country and good for the Bureau if Monckton were elected President. When Monckton was nominated it seemed right and natural to Elmer Morse that he should help; and because Morse and the FBI were indistinguishable, it followed naturally that when Elmer Morse helped, the FBI helped. During the campaign Monckton and Morse talked often, and the FBI Director's information was put to good use against Vice President Ed Gilley in that vicious campaign.

On Al Donnally's advice, the Democratic candidate was walking the perennial Democratic civil rights tightrope during that time. On the one hand he wooed and cultivated black leaders in private meetings in Chicago and New York, extravagantly promising them favorable legislation and big-dollar Federal programs; on the other, Gilley soon found himself in a public dilemma. About a month before the election, accurate, almost verbatim accounts of Gilley's talks with Northern black civil rights militants began to appear in Texas newspapers and were widely reprinted. Gilley supporters in the South, traditionally Democrats, were demoralized when Ed Gilley would not or could not deny the stories. Faced with an impossible choice, Al Donnally preferred to let the destructive stories ride without reply. The Southern vote was important but the Northern states were vital. Without the blacks Gilley was dead; without the Southerners there still would be a slim chance.

Old Elmer Morse was never identified as the source of the information, but of course Richard Monckton knew. Some of those black faces at the private Northern meetings with Gilley had been Bureau informants, long planted in the civil rights movement.

Elmer Morse was not a good man to have as an enemy. And he had been the CIA's enemy since the days of the OSS and its regenesis in 1949. He was convinced that an independent intelligence agency, reporting directly to the President, would develop an existence of its own, virtually without control, and he fought hard to prevent its creation. Elmer Morse was a master bureaucrat and he knew the realities of the bureaucratic jungle; the FBI was a branch of the Department of Justice under the Attorney General, and he knew that the CIA, as a free-standing agency, would threaten the FBI's turf and primacy. When he lost the fight to put the CIA within the military departments and it was placed under the President's direct control, Morse shifted the site of the bureaucratic battle to the President's desk. There for years Morse fought an implacable guerilla war against the CIA to contain its jurisdiction, cut its budget, reduce its manpower and call out the CIA's blunders so loud and clear that they could never be overlooked by any President.

In the first ten months of the Monckton Administration Elmer Morse continued to win contests of bureaucratic skill and strength at the expense of the CIA and, in some cases, at the personal expense of William Martin as well. Morse had easy access to President Monckton; a telephone call could cause a rearrangement of the President's schedule to provide a same-day meeting between the President and the Director of the FBI. William Martin had no such direct access; in ten months he had not been invited to one private meeting with the President. His White House contact was always through Carl Tessler, usually made in writing, whenever he thought he had information the President should know. Martin's relationship with President Monckton was diseased at its heart, poisoned by President Monckton's preconceived dissatisfaction with the CIA and with William Martin himself, constantly weakened by Elmer Morse's relentless subversion of the President's waning confidence in the CIA, and only barely kept alive by Carl Tessler's occasional interventions with the President.

One of the symptoms of the President's attitude toward the CIA was the overt hostility of the President's Bureau of the Budget.

In the old days the Bureau of the Budget had generally been willing to let the CIA work out its budget problems with the Congress, within its very broad Presidential guidelines.

Richard Monckton quickly changed all that. He insisted on having mountains of CIA budget detail in a hurry; he demanded to know how much money the entire intelligence community was getting, where the dollars were hidden in the budgets of the other departments and the number of employees who were engaged in intelligence for the CIA and the other agencies. All this information was clearly a foundation for future deep Presidential cuts. Monckton had campaigned on a platform promising no new taxes, but advocating a strong defense and some expensive new domestic programs. The President needed to find tax money to do the things he was committed to do, and he would not and could not consider reducing the defense budget. But clearly he could cut the multibillion-dollar budget of the intelligence community. Monckton also passionately believed that the CIA employed too many people; he was convinced that they were, to use Carl Tessler's cynical term, "chronic under-achievers."

Bill Martin had a good budget man of his own at the Company. Howard Walter had been the state budget director for one of the mid-Southern states for ten years before he'd gone to work for the CIA. Walter became Bill Martin's buffer in the daily battles with the sharp pencils, narrow lapels and wire-rim glasses from the President's Bureau of the Budget. It was the rare evening when Bill Martin's reading did not include a memorandum from his budget man warning of some new assault on the Company's planned appropriation for the coming year.

Martin knew that it was true that the CIA was spending more heavily than ever before, especially for space hardware; it was also true, and also part of the problem, that intelligence gathering is not a science but an art requiring enormous sums of money, and therefore does not lend itself to precise cost measurement.

President Monckton was quick to seize on any surprises and mistakes as evidence of the inadequacy of the Company's results. There had been a few unpredicted foreign coups, some political shifts and territorial grabs. And there would be more. No intelligence service is good enough to predict them all in advance. But President Monckton's morning Intelligence Report in its blue notebook with the gold seal on the cover would sometimes come back to Bill Martin annotated with marginal Presidential acid, especially when the report described unforeseen foreign political events.

"Why weren't we on top of this?" the unmistakable scrawl would slant along the margin. "Give me a report by tomorrow noon on what went wrong"; "Where was the CIA?"; "Terrible work. Someone should be fired."

And Elmer Morse adroitly fueled the President's displeasure. Growing numbers of FBI agents assigned to U.S. Embassies abroad as "legal attachés" were required to report any intelligence community failures, no matter how minor, directly to Morse. Morse occasionally asked for private meetings with the President to report the other agencies' failures in graphic detail. The FBI Director's seeds of bureaucratic poison fell on fertile ground. Monckton delighted in such back-channel reports. The number of FBI legal attachés was increased by nearly one hundred in the first ten months by specific order of the President to the Attorney General.

Bill Martin felt the sting of Elmer Morse's Congressional clout several times in Richard Monckton's first year as President. There was only one victory, and even that episode had its price. At the end of a long day, as Simon Cappell reviewed the day's paperwork with his boss, he held a one-page memorandum out to Martin. " 'Fly-eye' is stuck in Appropriations, our legislative boys say."

"What's holding it up, for Christ's sake?" Martin demanded. "Timing on that one is critical. Haven't they the brains to explain that to the Appropriations members?"

"It's through our subcommittee, all right," Simon said as he scanned the memo. "But Congressman Grimes is holding up full committee action, demanding further hearings. Hearings of that kind couldn't be completed before the summer recess, they say."

"Shit, Simon! That makes no sense. What the hell does Grimes care? Fly-eye has nothing to do with him or his district. What do our people say about Grimes?"

Cappell shook his head slowly, somewhat baffled. "That's it, they don't. There's nothing here about his motives."

"Goddamn, find out what's behind that roadblock, and fast!" Martin exploded.

In a few days he had answers from the Company's Congressional specialists. All the rumors were that Grimes was dancing to Elmer Morse's tune. To get the Fly-eye appropriation moving again Bill Martin either would have to make some kind of deal with old Elmer or somehow blast Morse out of the way.

Martin knew from bitter experience that he lacked the clout to beat Morse by himself. But this time Morse might have made a mistake. Carl Tessler wanted the results of Fly-eye as much as Bill Martin wanted the appropriation to put the satellite cameras up there. Martin could never win an eyeball-to-eyeball fight against Elmer Morse in the President's office. But Carl Tessler might. Everyone knew Tessler hated bureaucratic controversies. Martin had learned early that the Professor would try to shuffle such troublesome problems to the lower strata of the mountain of paper on his back table, never to be seen again. But, above all, Tessler needed Fly-eye. It was programmed to hover over the People's Republic of China, and the Professor was pressing for the information that only Fly-eye could give him.

Seizing the opportunity to join battle and win, Martin reached for the telephone to explain to Dr. Tessler the appropriations blockade Elmer Morse had erected. "It could cost us a full six months' delay in getting Fly-eye up, Carl."

Tessler sounded puzzled. "I don't understand, Bill. What would Morse gain from interfering with our satellite?"

Martin's tone was patient. "Carl, this is part of a continuing vendetta. Elmer Morse will demand some concession from me—he's been bitching to the President again about getting a veto over our UN activities. If I give in he'll call off his trained poodles at the Appropriations Committee. Otherwise it's clear you don't get your China pictures."

Carl Tessler prided himself on his pragmatism; he was fond of saying that it took a great deal to shock him. These kinds of Government maneuvers differed in degree but they were of the same genus of wheeling and dealing he had encountered among the distinguished members of the Harvard faculty. As a young assistant professor Tessler had decided that, if Harvard was to become his life, he must master the game rules and learn to play them better than any of the others. He had finally understood the faculty politicians and therefore he now understood Elmer Morse.

"Bill, can you afford to deal with the old bastard on this?" asked the Professor.

"Not without endless delay, Carl. It could take months. And if I do cave in we'll just have something else held up next month. It's time the President moved in to stop this kind of thing. Remember what you said in my plane going to Chicago last winter?"

Tessler sounded grim. "Let me see what I can do, Bill. Keep me posted on this one regularly if there are any changes." He had to have the Chinese pictures and intercepts. Elmer Morse would have to be trumped.

That Friday, White House lobbyists fanned out to buttonhole every member of the large House Appropriations Committee to say that the President had put a high national security priority on Fly-eye. The CIA Appropriations subcommittee had held the necessary hearings; further delay for more hearings could harm top-secret operations, the White House men argued. At five o'clock Monday afternoon, the President's principal legislative assistant called on Congressman Grimes. After sipping the ritual glass of tepid Bourbon and branch water and passing a little light shoptalk, the White House man unfolded a tally sheet and handed it to the veteran Congressman. It showed that he was beaten. The White House had the votes to roll over Grimes and move the appropriation out of committee.

Within minutes Elmer Morse also knew that Carl Tessler and Bill Martin had beaten him. He told himself it didn't matter. Grimes was his man in any case, and that would not change. But he would have to make sure that Tessler bore him no malice. Tessler was too close to the President for that. On that score Elmer Morse worried needlessly. Once Fly-eye was back on the supplemental appropriations track Carl Tessler totally forgot about Director Morse's maneuver.

Tessler's long days quickly became short months, consumed by Richard Monckton's insatiable demands on his time. The results of some of Tessler's long talks with Monckton would shape the world's destiny. But some were of such trivial and nonsensical substance that were Monckton not the President of the United States Tessler would have curtly insulted him. The central fact of their relationship was that the President totally controlled how his distinguished Assistant spent his time. And Monckton was capricious in the way he disrupted the Professor's meetings, summoning Tessler at will to wait upon his desires. The President showed no awareness that others bore heavy responsibilities and work loads. He was the President, and when he wanted to visit with Carl Tessler he exercised no restraint.

Tessler soon began to suspect that Monckton's pervading indifference to the personal problems of others was actively reinforced by Frank Flaherty's earnest, almost sycophantic, deference. Flaherty organized the logistical side of the White House so that the staff responded to a Presidential whim with immediate, unquestioning service. A helicopter? In five minutes. A yacht? In ten. A movie, a car, a videotape recorder? Instantly. Tessler could imagine Flaherty sitting in the Oval Office reminding the President over and over that no one on the staff was doing anything so important that he shouldn't be summoned at will. It seemed that Flaherty didn't give a damn whether any substantive policy work got done, as long as Monckton looked good and got reelected. Flaherty had made himself a philosophical eunuch, Monckton's instrument, efficient, always in equilibrium, devoid of bias. That was the way Richard

Monckton wanted it, but a man like Tessler couldn't work that way.

The President's bell would ring day after day and Carl Tessler would leave his visitor or his staff meeting or his paperwork and catapult his corpulence down the hallway to the Oval Office.

"Hi, Carl. Come in." Monckton was fond of slouching in his chair, his heels on the corner of Theodore Roosevelt's carved desk, a cup of coffee always nearby. Sometimes he would open with "I wanted to talk to you about . . ." That was a good signal to Tessler; it meant the President had something specific on his mind. They could discuss it, perhaps dispose of it, and Tessler could get back to his office. Some solid work was done in those sessions.

Other times he would be greeted by "How are you? Busy?" or "Well, what big problems do we have today?" That meant that the President didn't have anything to do—at least anything that he wanted to do—and so they would discuss whatever subject came up. In these long sessions Monckton would ask hundreds of questions; he was curious about the governments of other nations, the personalities of some of the foreign leaders he had not met, the problems of American universities, Billy Curry as Tessler had observed him, Tessler's progress with State Department reforms, domestic politics, anything that came to mind at random. If Tessler lacked an answer, he would often be asked to research it and send in a memo.

The war in the Far East was no nearer to a conclusion than it had been at Monckton's inauguration. As soon as the weather warmed up huge organized antiwar marches and rallies were held on the wide grassy mall near the White House. The President refused to see representatives of the protesters, but he knew they were out there. And Monckton knew that the combined pressures, the military pressure of the enemy in the Far East and the political pressure of the militant protesters, magnified thousands of times by the television networks, could ultimately frustrate his foreign policy and defeat him if he permitted them to. He had to move, quickly and vigorously.

Monckton and Tessler agreed that the only way to bring the military enemy to the bargaining table was through the coincident insistence of China and Russia. One without the other was no good. Otherwise either China or Russia would seek to gain from the apparent weakness of the other.

Monckton had been to Russia and knew many of its leaders. But China was an enigma to him. Tessler had read voluminously of the new China and its people but he had never been there. As they developed their China strategy both men began to bombard the intelligence community with queries about the Chinese economy, China's political institutions and its military. Tessler bore responsibility for the intelligence gathering, translating the President's questions into assignment specifications, deciding on the timetable and ruling upon the quality of the work product. When some aspect of the effort was complete, Tessler became the President's translator, digester and monitor, passing to him what he needed to know in a form and quantity that would inform without strangling. That was the established process, but, as Tessler's orderly mind made a frontal assault on the problem, Monckton's was the cavalry, dashing in at the flanks, taking wide-ranging detours, developing a full attack upon a tiny aspect of a question. And all the while Richard Monckton continually prodded, asking Tessler questions, giving assignments, carping, hurrying and insisting.

Carl Tessler would clump back to his office after a session with the President holding pages of scribbled notes to be transcribed into more questions of the divisions, agencies and bureaus of State, Defense and Central Intelligence, all marked "for immediate action and reply."

In the first weeks of the Monckton Administration William Martin had routinely insisted upon being shown any memoranda that came to the CIA from the President or Carl Tessler. In the second month, the President had decided to tour eight European countries. Almost immediately that prospect produced a roaring river of paper. Psychological profiles of national leaders were urgently needed. Political intelligence estimates were given top priority. The Secret Service needed estimates of possible danger to the President on the tour. The advance team required briefing books on all eight countries within a week. One day Tessler sent Martin sixty-one questions asked by the President about West Germany. Answers were needed at once.

When the President returned from the European trip the focus shifted to China and the drumfire of demands continued. The Company maintained an elaborate China watch in Hong Kong, staffed by experts, most of whom had formerly lived in China. But what they sent back to Washington was principally secondhand information from newspapers, refugee gossip and radio intercepts. Its control officers had almost no success in running agents within China itself, despite countless attempts.

From the day of the first CIA summary report to President Monckton on China, Bill Martin knew the President was dissatisfied. His critical preconceptions about the CIA were only confirmed by the gaps in what the Company was able to tell him about the Chinese. Monckton complained bitterly to Tessler about the quality of the CIA's work. Never one to bear responsibility for the faults of others needlessly, Professor Tessler agreed with the President and passed to Bill Martin the Presidential anger undiluted.

The unremitting White House pressures and hostility

were very different from those Martin had known during the days of President Esker Scott Anderson. He had been Anderson's boy. But Martin and the CIA would never have any of the benefit of Richard Monckton's doubt. The work must be produced quickly and correctly, free of mistakes. Under ordinary circumstances Director Martin would have assigned CIA final review of any White House work to a highly competent subordinate, perhaps one of the Deputy Assistant Directors. But of necessity he began to read everything addressed to the White House before it left the Company. When the volume became too vast he delegated some of the final review to Simon Cappell. But the pressure of the White House paper flow, added to his other problems, often stretched his late-afternoon paperwork sessions beyond 9 P.M.

One evening, as he reviewed the China information to be sent to Tessler, he felt the tension at the back of his neck and behind his knees and in his upper arms. The door from the conference room opened and Arnie Pittman came in, dazzling in Navy whites and campaign ribbons, complete with sword and brocaded captain's hat.

Martin had maintained correct and friendly personal relations with the President's old shipmate, but he had made certain that Deputy Director of Central Intelligence Pittman was given absolutely nothing of any consequence to do. Simon Cappell was responsible for knowing what went in or out of Pittman's office and he continued to report that Pittman spent his time reading routine, nonsensitive intelligence reports, and the daily newspapers. Pittman attended a daily staff meeting on administrative problems but was not invited to staff meetings on operations or intelligence. Simon reported that there were no complaints; years of intellectual inactivity in the Navy had ideally prepared Pittman for such vacuous days in his new office. Arnie Pittman was a man who knew a good deal when he saw one. If he kept to himself and didn't make a fuss, Dick Monckton would make sure that he retired an admiral. Who would complain about inactivity under such circumstances?

Martin looked up wearily. "Hello, Arnie."

"Hi, Bill. Aren't you going to the Joint Chiefs' party? It's nearly eight."

Martin shook his head. "I've got to get through this goddamn China stuff for the White House tonight. I may not make it."

"That's too bad, Bill. I've been pretty busy too, but I wouldn't miss the Chiefs' party."

Martin looked up sharply. "Really, Arnie? What have you been working on?" His staff had assured him that Arnie Pittman had no assignments.

"Protesters," Pittman said with a puff of pride. "Order came right from the top. High priority. Remember when I said I was invited to Newport News with the President on Air Force One last month? That's when I got it. He called me in to his little room on the plane and told me to get into all this antiwar business, so I've had the Intelligence Division putting together a report for the President."

Martin took off his glasses and looked sharply at Pittman. "You don't say? This is the first I've heard of it. I'd like to see your report before it goes to the President." He tried to maintain a casual tone.

Pittman, looking flustered, sat down near Martin's desk and fingered his braided captain's cap. "Well, Bill, Dick—the President—said he wanted to have it from me direct. He said not to send it over through regular channels, see? Maybe I shouldn't have said anything."

"Oh, that's all right, Arnie," Martin said, brushing it off. "I understand completely. Have you come up with anything good?" Martin would make sure he saw a draft of the report before the President himself did.

Pittman brightened. "As a matter of fact, yes. Some

of those long-haired bastards arrested last month near the White House are directly linked to the Russians through a control in Sweden. And we think there is a money flow to the antiwar movement from the same source."

"How will the President use that information, Arnie?" Martin asked gently.

"I don't know. It shouldn't be too hard to leak out, though. Christ, everything else leaks right out of there, doesn't it? The Monk—the President—is really upset about all the White House leaks, I'll tell you that."

Martin nodded. "Some of the press have really got a pipeline over there, haven't they?"

"Yeah, but he says it won't last much longer."

"Who says—the President?"

"Yeah. He told me on the airplane. He's going to know soon who's feeding all that stuff to the press. He thinks it may be someone that works for Tessler."

"Oh, really? How will he find out, Arnie?"

"He's got old Elmer Morse and the FBI on it and they are going balls out. Tapping and following guys and everything. Dick really set fire to their tail feathers, I guess."

Martin sucked in a breath. "Arnie, is the Company involved in all of that? Are you?"

Pittman shook his head vigorously. "Oh, no sir. On the airplane he just told me about it, is all. I'm only investigating the antiwar rioters and demonstrators and that kind of thing. Say, I've got to get going. My wife is going to kill me. Excuse me, will you, Bill?"

Martin grunted and put his glasses on. When Pittman closed the door, Martin pushed aside a thick memorandum on the Red Chinese Army. Maybe it was time to use DDCI Arnie Pittman to solve a few Company problems, including the problem of Captain Pittman himself. He reached for the microphone of his dictating machine.

"To DDCI Captain Pittman," he began. "We are receiving a flood of White House requests regarding the People's Republic of China. The volume is so great that I am simply unable to give our outgoing work my personal review any longer. Therefore, will you please consider yourself the point of initial and final contact with the White House (President, Tessler, NSC, *et al.*) on all incoming memoranda and outgoing work product relating to the PRC? This is an internal arrangement. Nothing need be said to Carl Tessler at this time about who is responsible for what over here. Signed, Martin." It's time, Martin thought to himself, that the President had all the remarkable talents of his confidant, Captain Pittman, exclusively devoted to Monckton's number one subject. And it would be interesting to see how many days passed before the shit hit the fan.

13

Washington newspaper society reporting is a unique journalistic art form, found nowhere else in the country or, for that matter, in the world. In New York, or even Kansas City, tea parties, benefits, receptions and dinners are defined as "social" and the local society columnists dutifully grind out the names of those who attend, the color of the ladies' gowns and sometimes even the names of the couturiers. But the aggressive ladies in the nation's capital who write society copy turn out material that would be considered front page news anywhere else. At a Washington social reception the women columnists buttonhole, badger or cajole the guests; their prime targets are the famous or controversial personalities who are inaccessible to the ordinary reporter. The *Post*'s Diana Dangerfield was the queen of them all. She looked for an unguarded or casual remark; if her victim was cautious, she'd build a column around a hint. Lacking anything as substantial as a hint, she'd write a column on a hunch.

Bill and Linda Martin were the targets of a Diana Dangerfield column on the front page of the "People" section of the *Post* one Sunday, and it created serious problems for Martin. Until that Sunday morning following the Turkish Embassy party, only a handful of people were aware of Bill Martin's impending divorce from Linda and his discreet romance with Sally Atherton. Martin had even talked to Linda about how the divorce should be announced; he proposed a brief, dignified statement by the press officer at the CIA. "The Director and Mrs. Martin have agreed upon an amicable separation and divorce." But whenever he raised the subject with Linda, she turned and walked away, refusing to discuss it.

Bill and Linda Martin had not gone to parties together for a long time. Linda had moved out nearly five weeks earlier, after a raging argument. Linda had been drinking, Martin was tense from the growing pressure of his work; their volatile emotional tinder blazed when Martin demanded to know what, if anything, was still going on between Linda and Esker Scott Anderson. It was a shot in the dark but it inflamed something in Linda. She hurled a glass that narrowly missed his head. Bitter and cruel remarks flew back and forth, and within thirty minutes she was gone.

A week later, one day while Martin was at the office, Linda came by the house, took some clothes and left him a scrawled note with her new telephone number. When he returned home he called and they talked, but it was obvious that neither of them wanted to try to put the pieces of their marriage back together. They both agreed that they were happier apart than either had been for weeks. Their conversation then turned to practical matters such as money and bills and cars, and to Linda's seeing a lawyer about a divorce. But they agreed to go together to Ambassador and Mrs. Yaman's farewell party for their Washington friends at the Turkish Embassy. The Martins had grown to know and like the Yamans. The couples often were paired at parties and they had become genuine friends. Their invitation simply could not be refused, so it was agreed that Martin would pick up Linda at seven forty-five and they would arrive together.

At seven-thirty on the night of the party, Martin had his secretary phone Linda to say he'd be late and to suggest that she take a cab. Bill would get to the party as soon as his meeting ended. It was pouring and cabs were scarce. Dispatchers refused to take telephone orders. Linda walked to Wisconsin Avenue, hiking her gown up to clear the puddles, ruining her favorite pair of silk shoes. At last she nailed a taxi. When she finally arrived at the Embassy she was very wet and very angry at William Martin; as usual, he had failed her. She left her sodden cape with the butler, repaired her limp hair and streaked makeup in the powder room, and climbed the wide marble staircase to the paneled reception rooms on the second floor. The first person she saw was her husband, dry and debonair, drink in hand, talking to a beautiful blonde in a lovely green silk dress.

Linda Martin was so furious that she did not really see Ambassador and Mrs. Yaman, although she smiled at them, shook the Ambassador's hand, brushed cheeks with his wife and said something appropriate. Nor did she see Diana Dangerfield, the aging doyenne of the *Post*'s society column. But Diana Dangerfield saw Linda Martin from the moment she came into the room.

She watched Linda take a drink from a passing tray and belt it down. She saw Linda, her face set, stride across the room to her husband. And she observed the startled look on the face of Joyce Duncan, the blonde in the green dress, as she quickly turned and walked away from the Martins.

It was not unusual for a husband and wife to arrive at Embassy parties separately, he from the office and she from home. But from the moment Linda came in, Diana Dangerfield sensed the current of tension between the Martins and she knew how her next day's column would shape up.

The Embassy had been built by a nineteenth-century railroad baron. Ceilings were high and paneled and the dark wood walls were covered with Turkish tapestries. Most conversational sounds were deadened and lost in the rooms. Thus the *Post*'s columnist could not hear what the Martins were saying as they stood by themselves before dinner. But she could see Linda's face. The Director of the CIA was catching merry hell.

During dinner Linda Martin appeared moody and distracted. After dinner the men remained at the table for cigars and brandy while the ladies retired to a parlor for demitasse. Linda talked to Mrs. Yaman briefly, then excused herself. She did not reappear when the ladies rejoined the gentlemen for after-dinner drinks. Martin was talking with Carl and Joyce Duncan as Diana Dangerfield moved quickly to Bill Martin's side. The Duncans nodded at the columnist. Martin did not.

"Excuse me, Mr. Director," Diana Dangerfield purred. "Has your wife gone home? I haven't seen her for *hours!*"

Martin turned and looked directly at the reporter, smiled and turned back to the Duncans. "Joyce, tell me about Sun Valley. We've often talked about going there."

Before Joyce Duncan could reply, Mrs. Dangerfield

swiftly broke in. "Is it true that you and your wife aren't living together?" The columnist had heard no such rumor, but it was worth a try. Even a denial would be printable.

Martin smiled at her again with effort, shook his head with resignation and took Carl Duncan by the upper arm. "Carl, shall we go somewhere where we can talk without being interrupted?"

But Martin had not denied that he and Linda were separated. A few minutes later Diana Dangerfield left the Embassy for the *Post* building to craft her column for Sunday. It was good enough copy to command a double-column head on the first page of the "People" section.

THE DANGERFIELD DIARY
By Diana Dangerfield

TURKISH AMBASSADOR SAYS FAREWELL; EX-FRIDAY AND SUPERSPY SPLIT?

All was grape leaves and old world charm Friday night as the Turkish Ambassador, Amin Yaman, and his charming wife hosted many of their Washington friends. It was a farewell party because the Yamans, one of the diplomatic corps' most popular couples, will soon be posted to Peking.

The guest list was a testament to the Yamans' broad spectrum of high-ranking American friends. Prominent among the guests were the Presidential Assistant for Domestic Affairs, Carl Duncan, and his charming blond wife, Joyce. They were telling CIA Director William Martin about their fishing vacation at Sun Valley, Idaho. Director Martin's wife, Linda, who was a secretary to former President Esker Scott Anderson before marrying Mr. Martin, was the last to arrive at the Turkish Embassy for dinner last night and she was the first to leave. The Martins did not appear very happy to see each other. Sources close to the Martins confirm that Linda has moved out of the couple's fashionable S Street town house and that a divorce suit is imminent. Friends say the charges Mrs. Martin will make in her divorce action against the CIA Director may sensationally involve another prominent Washington woman.

The column then went on to describe the lavish dessert served wrapped in sugared grape leaves, and to list more of the prominent guests.

On Monday Linda saw a lawyer and on Friday he filed her divorce action against her husband alleging "conjugal unfaithfulness" as an element of "extreme cruelty," but no corespondent was named. In less than a week, the Martins' fractured marriage had moved from the "People" section to the front page of the *Post*. Martin, like most Washingtonians, seldom read the Saturday *Post*. But it became evident that this was not going to be like most Saturdays.

On the following Monday, at the close of a National Security Council subcommittee meeting in Carl Tessler's conference room in the basement of the White House West Wing, Martin was quietly asked to remain. When he and Tessler were finally alone in the small room the Professor moved to the chair next to Martin, leaned forward on the conference table and cleared his throat several times.

"Bill, the President called me last night about your divorce." Tessler's voice was low and apologetic. "He is upset because your wife is charging you with adultery. He says he will not have anyone in the Administration who is involved in a moral scandal." Martin had expected something like that and had carefully prepared his reply.

"Well, that's not quite correct, Carl. The ground for the divorce is only cruelty—a standard ground—not adultery. Linda's lawyer threw in something about unfaithfulness, but we think that was only to help her bargaining on a property settlement. It is not really a ground of the suit."

"Well, Bill, I must tell you how the President feels. If it is going to be a messy divorce case, you will have to resign. That's what he says, and I guess he means it."

"I can promise you it won't be messy," Martin said firmly.

"I hope not. I would hate to see you put out, under a cloud, for something like that," said Tessler, blinking several times behind his thick glasses. He had taken this subject as far as he decently could with Bill Martin. There was no use in trying to describe the strident moralism and harsh judgment in Monckton's telephone call. It was enough that he had forewarned Martin that the President would swiftly, intolerantly remove an adulterer from his Administration, whoever he might be. In the pause Martin adroitly switched to another topic. "I hear the President is also very upset about information leaks."

"Ah. Indeed he is, Bill. Very upset. And so am I." Tessler rose and began to pace up and down the small map-lined room. "As you know, I am talking to the Romanians and the French about China. Someone is feeding information about my talks to the press."

Martin sounded surprised. "Is it someone here, Carl?"

"It may be someone on the NSC staff; or it may be someone at State. It could be one of a hundred people."

"Are you getting enough help from our people?" Martin asked.

"To the extent that we need it, yes." Tessler stopped

walking and leaned on the back of a chair. "In the view of the President, this is an extraordinary problem calling for extraordinary measures. I know the CIA involves itself in some security breaches. But we have devised other measures in this case, Bill. Frankly, this one is entirely being handled from here."

"Enough said," Martin replied. "I understand."

"Come in, Bernie," Martin called. The small, thin young man with the curly blond hair closed Martin's office door and moved to a desk chair.

The Director looked up from his papers and motioned his visitor to be seated. "Bernie, I've decided that it's time we invested some Company time and manpower in finding out what certain people in the Government are up to, and I need your help. I will want you to follow out some leads I'll give you and to report back to me as soon as you can."

"Yes, sir?" Bernie Tibbitts rubbed his chin quizzically.

"You are not to talk to a goddamned soul about this project, Bernie." Martin's voice was grim and his eyes were steely. "I will tell Simon Cappell about it so that you can funnel reports or questions to me through him. But no one else. Not the Deputy Director of Central Intelligence, not your boss in Plans, no one. Understood?"

"Yes, sir," Tibbetts said with equal vigor.

"And I want nothing at all circulated in writing. Not *one* word!"

"I understand."

"All right. Here's where we start." Martin leaned across the desk and spoke in a very low tone. "The White House suspects some of its people of leaking its secrets to the press. Someone, possibly the FBI, is conducting some kind of surveillance for them. I don't know who they are watching or how. But this thing's getting priority treatment. I want to know who they are covering and how they are going about it. And I don't want anyone asking the FBI. What can you do for me, Bernie?"

"I'm not sure, Mr. Martin." Tibbitts paused for a moment and unconsciously lowered his voice. "Do you think they are going in on telephones?"

"I really don't know. But isn't that a fairly typical FBI procedure?"

"Yes, sir. I think that's the place to begin. We'll canvass the telephone companies on some pretext and see who the FBI is covering through the central switching rooms. Who can I check names with?"

"You'd better develop a list and bring it to me. I don't know if they are covering White House staff or press or who. As you get into this, Bernie, watch for interceptions that are not FBI, too. I have no goddamn idea where this will take us."

"I understand, sir. Shall I talk to Simon about manpower?" Tibbits asked.

"It's all arranged. You'll have a special section of fifteen people, housed out back in the 121 building. Draw anything you need from Technical Services. You'll have a DCI project number which Simon will give you. Don't worry about cost on this one; just get what you need."

"Right, sir. I'll get started at once. You'll hear from me as soon as I have something."

Martin pressed a call-director button and Simon Cappell came in. "Simon, you know Bernie Tibbitts?" he asked.

Simon looked at Tibbitts and smiled. "Yes, sir. We play squash sometimes. I can vouch that he's meaner than he looks."

Martin went on, "I'm investing some time, money and manpower in a special project that Bernie is going to do for us. He'll contact you when I'm not available.

Be sure he has whatever he needs. I'll see him whenever he wants to see me. OK?"

"Yes, sir," Simon Cappell replied, smiling. "When Merrill Lynch, Pierce, Fenner and Tibbitts call about your investment I'll make sure you know about it."

Tibbitts laughed. "Not bad. How about just calling us the Merrill Lynch boys? That should be obscure enough."

"OK," said Martin. "Just don't forget that I'm expecting some *big* dividends."

The call came in two days; Tibbitts needed a meeting with the Director as soon as possible. Simon pulled the Director's appointment book closer and ran his pencil down the many entries for the day. Martin was eating most of his dinners at the office. Bernie could join them and they would talk over dinner.

At about eight thirty Martin and Simon Cappell wearily laid aside the unfinished stacks of day-end paperwork and joined Tibbitts in the Director's dining room. When the waiter asked for their drink orders Martin ordered a tomato juice in recognition of the seriousness of the business at hand and the others followed suit.

Martin got right to the subject without preliminary small talk. "Well, Bernie? What have you got?"

"Your leads sure paid off, Mr. Martin. There is a lot of domestic tapping going on and it looks like dynamite. Very touchy stuff."

"Is the White House involved?" Martin asked in a level tone.

"Up to their ass. And in a strange way. There's a lot about this I don't understand, but let me tell you what I've got so far."

Martin raised a hand. "First, let me ask one thing. Does it reach the President?"

"It evidently does, Mr. Martin. So you may want to just drop all of this when I get through."

Conversation ceased while the waiter took away the juice glasses and passed a platter with grilled steaks, string beans and baked potatoes. When he left the dining room the Director returned to Bernie's question about the President's involvement and how to handle it.

"Maybe, Bernie. Go ahead."

"All right, sir. We canvassed telephone centrals in six major cities and wrote off five of them. The FBI has a lot of stuff going but it's routine: organized crime, tax evasion, that kind of crap." Tibbitts put down his fork and his tone became more intense. "But in Washington, Maryland and Virginia they have a massive coverage right now; some White House people, a couple of career State Department employees, and at least fifteen reporters and bureau chiefs! And none of them are covered by warrants or Justice Department paperwork. Our man inside the Attorney General's office swears none of this ever came through them."

"What is it supposed to be, national security?"

"Mr. Martin, I just plain don't know. That was the first thing that occurred to me because of the leads you gave me; I assumed that it was designed to catch the guys leaking classified stuff. So I set up the computer to display the correlations; you know, reporters' bylines on the leaked stories, possible Government sources—who had access to the secrets—obvious data of that kind, together with our file stuff on each of the people being tapped."

"How was the correlation?"

"Generally terrible. Oh, there were the obvious tie-ins with the reporters who wrote the leak stories and their bosses in the Washington bureaus who OK'd them; but I still can't account for about sixty percent of the people on the list. They appear to have nothing at all to do with the published leaks, at either end of the pipe."

"What kind of people are they?" asked Cappell.

Tibbitts reached to the floor for a file, opened it and handed Bill Martin three lists. "You see," Tibbitts said, "every major bureau chief in the city is covered— *Times*, *L.A. Times*, the news magazines, the networks —the national editors at the *Star* and *Post*, and two columnists. One syndicated columnist just made the Chesapeake and Potomac Telephone Company tap list yesterday morning; they evidently still are adding people. The White House people tapped are mostly on Tessler's staff, but a couple are political types who were carried over from the Monckton campaign. There's no true correlation among the White House people either."

Martin put down the lists and looked straight at Tibbitts. "How the hell did they do all this, Bernie? Who gave the authorization?"

"I can't pinpoint that yet, Mr. Martin. But our Justice and White House sources have given me enough to form a hypothesis that is consistent with the names on these lists."

Martin again held up his hand to stop Tibbitts. "Before you tell me your assumption, let me add what I know and see how it fits. I was told that the President was personally involved in this and that he was doing it to stop leaks. Does it fit?"

"No, not the part about his motives; at least not entirely. Because I can't connect some of the people on the list to leaks. No way. But there may be more than one motive. Try this on for size." Tibbitts put his fork down and leaned forward intently. "Suppose there are a couple of bad leaks to the press and Tessler charges into the President's office and raises hell. He shouts that there are traitors on his staff and at State and maybe Defense. He claims they are in league with traitors at the *Times* and *Post* and CBS. Tessler and the President discuss what they should do. Now up to here we are pretty sure that this is what happened. Apparently the President pushed some buttons and got old Elmer Morse over from the FBI in a hurry. What else? You got traitors, you call Morse, right?"

"Shit," grunted Simon Cappell.

"The President, Tessler and Morse huddle for about a half hour," Tibbitts continued. "About thirty-six hours later, Carl Tessler's deputy, General Castle, goes to see Elmer Morse. Within a day after that, the first taps go on in the central switching rooms at the C and P Telephone Company. The first eight taps are all on White House people. The next six are reporters. Then come the bureau chiefs. Then the columnists. They go on in that order over a period of three weeks."

Martin sounded impatient. "So, what's your hypothesis?"

"That the President and Tessler decided to tap their own people to find the source of the leaks, and Morse was told to do it very secretly. He's not to tell even the Attorney General. Tessler sent Morse the names to start on via his man Castle. But the President couldn't leave it there. Monckton has a notorious burr up his ass about the press, you know, so he decided to expand the coverage. Maybe, at first, he thought he could overhear the leaker and the leakee and catch them red-handed, passing a secret. I don't know what he thought. But he told Morse to expand the coverage to the reporters carrying bylines on the leak stories. It's just a short step from there to covering the national editors and bureau chiefs who boss these reporters. From here on I'm really guessing, but here's where I come out." Tibbitts paused for a moment and then plunged on. "They began to get some really juicy stuff from these taps that had nothing at all to do with the leaks. But imagine the choice dirt a national editor gets on his home phone—about Con-

guessing, but here's where I come out." Tibbitts paused drunk, who's screwing whom. Maybe what some Republican big wheel said off the record about Monckton. Really ripe gossip of the kind that both the President and Morse would love to get; so they decided to see what was going on with the other news bureaus, and now, with some of the political columnists. Who would ever know?"

Cappell sounded puzzled. "But the C and P people know, don't they?"

"No," Martin interjected. "There is one man there who knows, because he's the FBI liaison, but he's an old-timer and in the Bureau's pocket, right, Bernie?"

"Yes, sir. And the C and P fellow wouldn't have any idea why a tap goes on or who ordered it. There is one thing about that which I haven't mentioned, though. One columnist has not only been tapped at C and P; his office has also been bugged. Someone has gotten into his office and planted it—thoroughly."

"How did you discover that?" Martin asked, afraid of the answer.

"You guessed it," Tibbitts chuckled. "I had someone go in and do a little checking around. I can tell you it's a very professional job, but our man's opinion is that it's not a typical FBI installation. It's more like one of ours."

Martin looked at Tibbitts sharply. "What are they getting from all of this?"

Tibbitts shook his head. "I really don't know, Mr. Martin. I thought I'd better talk to you before I moved in to intercept their take. After all, it looks like they're doing this for the President himself. That is very big medicine. I was not about to intercept the Head Man's take on my own, I assure you."

Martin nodded. "But you can get it?"

"Yes, sir. I think I could take it off for you without

detection, but it brings up some very real problems. Can I legitimately do a thing like that, Mr. Martin?"

Martin tapped the lists idly with his forefinger, looked at the tabletop and thought. It appeared that Richard Monckton and Elmer Morse had their most tender parts caught in a veritable vise. And Martin's hand was on the vise handle. If Tibbitts' theory was proved correct, he could squeeze Morse and Monckton so tight that all of Martin's problems of budget and FBI encroachment and the Primula Report and hassle over the divorce and Arnie Pittman might simply disappear. God knows all of Martin's White House and FBI problems could not be solved on a careful step-by-step basis. Martin suddenly realized that this might be the one bold stroke he needed; the one counterthrust that could get them off his back for all time.

He looked up at Tibbitts sharply. "You said a minute ago that the President is involved. How do you know?"

"It's circumstantial, Mr. Martin, but I believe it's obvious. Not even Elmer Morse would tap the media and White House staff on his own. He always covers his ass. So who gave him the order? I'm almost positive it was not the Attorney General. As you know, we have a line into his office—a very good person, very reliable. So that leaves either Tessler or the President. You know Tessler—I don't. But I don't think it's likely that he would authorize Morse to do a huge job like this without the President's approval. Our liaison man at the NSC is positive Tessler and the President discussed it. He also knows that General Castle took the first list of names to Morse. Castle's aide told him so. So it's either Tessler alone or Tessler and the President together. Do you think Tessler would take the risk, tapping his staff and the press, without the President's backing?"

Martin chose his words carefully. "All right, Bernie. I understand your argument. But it's still very possible that the President doesn't know. I think we must go ahead on the assumption that he does not."

Simon Cappell looked at Martin unbelievingly. Then he looked at Tibbitts. Bernie Tibbitts wasn't buying Martin's rationalization either.

"I'm just not willing to accept it, gentlemen; you haven't persuaded me that the President would permit Elmer Morse to run amok like this," Martin said flatly. "We owe it to the President to get to the bottom of this. As far as my legal authority is concerned, Bernie, you can rest easy. The DCI is authorized by statute to prevent compromise of the classification-and-secrets system. I think what you are being asked to do is well within my authority."

"Well, Mr. Martin, I see what you are saying but, frankly, I'm having trouble with it." Tibbitts looked worried. "You may be right; the President may know nothing about it. Then if we get the evidence for him we'll all be pinned with big medals. But I'm sorry, sir, I think he must already know about it. All the signs are pointing straight to him. And if this is his operation, and you tell me to snaffle the President's proceeds and we get caught, the vultures will be picking our bones for the next twenty years."

Simon Cappell nodded. "There is the larger risk, sir. The whole Company would get it broadside if someone discovered that we were penetrating surveillance by another counterintelligence agency which had been secretly ordered by the White House, if not by the President himself. The risks are enormous."

"I think I understand." Martin was curt. "Let's talk about how to minimize the risks. Bernie, I'm sure you've been thinking about how you would go about it; I'd like to have your ideas. But let's understand the objectives here. I don't want to appropriate the proceeds. I'm not interested in the content of what they are picking up. I want proof of who is doing the job, how and under whose orders. How do you get that with a minimum of risk?"

"Well, sir—" Tibbitts cleared his throat and began again reluctantly. "Well, we can establish that the Bureau is tapping in at the C and P switching room. But the way the Bureau does these things, I doubt that you could pin that on anyone above the third level at the FBI. You could never show that Morse ordered it, or even knew about it."

"So?"

"So you would have to get out ahead of the operation and be set up to watch them expand it."

"How do you mean?"

"They seem to be adding to the list every day. I don't think they are about to stop right now. What we might do is try to predict who they will hit next and get there ahead of them."

Simon Cappell shook his head in dissent. "What will that get you? Just pictures of an FBI team opening some guy's bedroom window. What good is that?"

Tibbitts leaned back, shoved away his dessert dish and pulled his coffee closer. "I don't think that's what you're going to get, Simon. As I said, the entry work is not a typical Bureau job. Someone else did the bug work on that columnist. If we knew who he was, who hired him, where his money came from, we'd have a better trail to follow. But he's a careful worker. No prints, nothing telltale. A cold trail. We'll have to get ahead of him if we're going to have a look at him."

Martin took a brandy from the silver tray passed by the waiter, waited until the pantry door closed and said, "Have you asked yourself why they would go outside the Bureau for an electronics man? Why not use Morse's people?"

Tibbitts shrugged. "I don't know. Maybe they don't entirely trust Morse. Tapping in at the C and P is routine at the FBI. Black bag jobs in journalists' offices must be fairly extraordinary, even for old Elmer Morse. Maybe he refused to do it, or maybe they were afraid to ask him; you know that Morse would have a hell of a hold over Tessler if he did a job like that for him. Or over the President, for that matter."

"Hmmm." Martin was noncommittal. "So how would you lay a trap for this second-story man?"

Tibbitts was sure of his groundwork and spoke confidently. "Division T down in Plans Division has done a lot of work in predictions and probabilities. Given the pattern to date, I think Division T's computers can be programmed to give us a rough forecast of their next moves. Once we have a computer projection we'll have to sit down and exercise some judgment about it—it's not foolproof. I think they'll go after more journalists and maybe some Government employees. But I don't understand what they're after; I can't see the pattern, the true motive. That's where computer analysis might help."

"How long will it take to produce a forecast?" Martin asked.

"A day or two, I think. I'll have to recruit someone from Division T to work with Merrill Lynch if we're going to do this."

"And the more people you involve, the greater danger of a leak," said Cappell.

"You mean from here?" asked Martin. He looked as though he didn't believe it.

Simon nodded. "Remember, in this one we are asking our people to work contra the President. That's a big conflict. I don't think everyone would feel that the normal secrecy pledges would apply."

"Now wait a minute." Martin was intense. "As far as any of us knows, this investigation is *not* contra the President. Goddammit, it is just as reasonable to assume that Tessler and Morse are doing what *they* are doing contra the President. I don't want to hear any more talk about this being adverse to President Monckton. Our working assumption is that we are serving his interests in getting to the bottom of a very smelly situation. If anyone raises that particular question, I want to know about it promptly. There is no reason why it should be raised by anyone if the assignments are properly compartmentalized; there is no reason for anyone to have an overview except the three of us. Is that clear?" He looked from Tibbitts to Cappell.

"Yes, sir," Tibbitts and Simon Cappell chorused quietly.

"All right, let's get on with the forecast, Bernie. I assume you'll continue to keep track of what happens at C and P in the meantime?"

"Yes, sir." Tibbitts stood, gathering up his file. "Thanks for the dinner. I'll be calling you for another meeting tomorrow or Saturday."

The next meeting, on Saturday morning, was moved to the Director's conference room so that Martin, Simon Cappell and Bernie Tibbitts would have a large table on which to spread the computer printouts.

Tibbitts handed the Director a short printout and spread the four longer computer sheets across the width of the big table.

> ### Synopsis of analysis.
> There is no apparent corre-
> lation among the eleven em-
> ployees of the White House,
> six reporters, nine bureau
> chiefs, two State Department
> employees and two columnists
> being surveilled except that
> all listed Government em-
> ployees have a clearance for
> access to classified documents

and all reporters, bureau chiefs and columnists are news disseminators.

There are four possible motive patterns to be derived from the programmed information about the persons listed, as follows:

Pattern #1. National Security.

Purpose: To determine who is passing national security secrets and to whom they are going.

Class of origin: All Government employees with access to secrets. This class cannot be limited since some listed Government persons do not have access to secrets involved in specific leaks you have programmed in this analysis.

Class of destination: All journalists. No list given due to size of classes.

Pattern #2. Politics.

Purpose: To gain information not otherwise available upon which to base decisions which have some effect on elections, Congressional action, or other political events.

Class of information: source: All of the journalists listed write on some aspect of the political scene. A time trend is observed: The later additions to the jour-

nalist list are domestic
political; the earlier subjects are diplomatic-defense-
foreign affairs specialists.
The most recent subjects are
both syndicated columnists who
write primarily about Federal
politics.

The content of the recent
intercepted conversations is
largely concerned with
politics and the Federal
Government.

Pattern #3. Blackmail.

Purpose: To extort money or conduct in
return for non-disclosures of
embarrassing facts.

Some minor percentage of the
content of intercepted conversations is classified as
romantic/sex. Other topics
include financial problems,
drug use, planned job changes
and deception. Knowledge of
embarrassing secrets could be
bargained for money, or
certain prescribed performance
by the blackmail victim.

Class of victim: A probable
blackmailer must be assumed to
know in advance of the victim's
potential vulnerability and
that the victim can perform
some financial, political,
journalistic or other act to
the blackmailer's advantage.
List #3 of probable future

objects of surveillance includes only present Government
employees and journalists
living or working within the
30-mile radius whose WALNUT
data retrieval file shows
derogatory information making
them susceptible to blackmail.

Pattern #4. Early warning.

Purpose: To gain advance knowledge of
significant events which will
occur in the future which are
privately known to the subjects of the surveillance.
Advance warning would permit
one to gain or lessen loss by
reason of special information.
See also Patterns #1 and #2.

All of the surveillance subjects are in possession of
advance knowledge of various
future events. There is no
correlation. They do not all
share the same knowledge or
same class of knowledge.

After reading the printouts for several minutes Martin
asked, "How many different names do you have on
these lists of probables?"

"Eliminating the duplicates, there are one hundred
and twenty-seven. Forty-one are in Government, sixty-
five in the news business in one way or another, and
the rest are miscellaneous—at the Brookings think tank,
for instance. All live or work within thirty miles of
Washington."

Martin got up and walked along the table, running
his finger down the printout lists. "How does the Merrill

Lynch hypothesis hold up, now that you've seen the computer work, Bernie? Is it your opinion that they are still after columnists now, for the political pay dirt they'll get?"

"Yes, sir, it is. Look at the National Security list— number one—over there. For one thing the computer won't say that all of the past-action taps correlate with national security. But when you force it to go ahead and assume that national security is the only motive, it gives you such a long display of new names that are equally probable future suspects that you might as well just use a Press Club directory. The political list is much more logical and has the added advantage of being manageable. There are only six highly probable columnists and one seems the most probable—Arthur Perrine."

Martin sat down, rubbed his hand over his face from forehead to chin, and looked at Simon Cappell. "What do you think?"

"By a process of elimination I agree, sir. Whoever is doing this is taking a risk. All the furies of American journalism would come down on him if the press ever discovered what's going on. Even Carl Tessler, as much as he's been successful in currying favor with the *Times* and the *Post*—even he would be destroyed by something like this, I think. So what's the great prize that justifies the risk? Not just early warning, certainly. And I can't believe blackmail is even a remote possibility. A blackmailer would have to disclose what he has going on in order to cash in on it. He would be in deeper than any of his victims; he couldn't win. So it's either national security or politics, and the past pattern makes only one perfect fit: politics."

Martin nodded. "I agree. Let's go over the forecast on that second printout and figure out who might be hit next."

Two of the six columnists on the list were eliminated

quickly. They were known to be wide open to Monckton and his staff; anything they knew they would be telling the White House anyway. There was no need to tap their phones or bug their offices for political information.

"Arthur Perrine is the biggest name left on the list, sir," Tibbitts pointed out. "If we're going to focus on one target, I'd bet on his office."

"Wasn't he a Monckton supporter during the campaign?" asked Cappell slowly.

"Yes, but he isn't a whore like the two we just struck off, Maestrano and Pulaski. He'll blast the Administration if it's news. And he has excellent sources that the White House doesn't have. He is a better political reporter than the two that already have been tapped, in my opinion." Martin smiled. "If I'd been doing it I'd have hit him first."

Tibbitts coughed nervously and cleared his throat. "Is it settled, then?" he asked.

The door to Martin's office opened and his secretary took a step into the conference room. "Excuse me, Mr. Martin. Carl Duncan calling from the White House; he has a message from the President."

Martin shrugged, stood and walked to the window ledge at the end of the long room. He lifted the receiver on a white telephone; the dial held a disk on which the White House south facade was etched.

"Carl, Bill Martin. How are you?"

"Fine, Bill. I know you're in a meeting so I'll make it short. Sorry to interrupt things. When I was with the President a while ago he asked me to tell you that he has made a decision on declassification. He wants to release a large number of classified documents and files that are now just ancient history; he's had us doing a review of how this ought to be done; and I was going over it with him this morning."

"Well, if any of the CIA's files are involved, I'd certainly like to be consulted," Martin said warily. "You could jeopardize the lives of a great many people abroad if the wrong things were declassified."

"I realize that, Bill, and so does the President. You and Elmer Morse and others would be consulted before anything goes out. But, at the same time, the President is going to be the one to make the final decision on what is released. Rest assured, he would be the last one to compromise any truly secret matters."

"Sure, Carl." Martin kept his tone noncommittal. "What is the process he has in mind?"

"I have here quite a long list of files the President wants to glance through next week. He would like me to come by and pick them up from you this weekend, if possible. He'll look at them, decide on a tentative list for declassification and then hear from you or anyone else who has any objections."

"Well," began Martin, "old files will have to be dug out of the archives. That will take time. Why don't you read me the list quickly to give me an idea of what's involved. Then I can guess at how much time we'll need."

Duncan agreed and began to read a list of subjects rapidly. The third item on the list was the Primula Report. There were perhaps thirty-five in all. "I realize that sounds like a lot of paper but we are told that it will all fit in two apple boxes," Duncan said.

"Oh, who told you that?"

"I don't recall," the President's assistant said quickly.

"Well, that's something *I* can't tell you for sure," Martin said wryly. "I think the best procedure is for you to send the list over by messenger today. I'm sure it can't possibly be put together before Monday, maybe not even then. Some of that is really old stuff. What have you got, about two pages of items?"

"About two and a half," Duncan said.

"All right, you send it over and we'll get right at it,"

Martin said. He replaced the receiver, then paused for a second before he turned to the others in the room. The conversation with Duncan had made clear what must be done. "Bernie, let's go on the assumption that it will be Perrine. And don't worry about the President being involved. The more I learn about it, the more certain I am on that score. I'm sure that some day you'll be thanked for what you're doing."

"Thanks, Mr. Martin. I apologize for raising those objections, but I've never played in these big leagues before."

"Perfectly understandable, Bernie," Martin replied. "Let me hear from you."

When Tibbitts had gathered his printouts and files and closed the hallway door behind him, Martin turned to his aide. "Simon, Carl Duncan is sending me a list of files to be delivered to him for the President. I want you to go over the list. Put together copies of all the files that predate the Curry Administration; do that quickly and let me know when they are ready. *Do nothing* on files involving the Curry or Anderson years. Understood?"

"Yes, sir."

"We are in a strange and rather deadly race, my boy. You must be certain that Mr. Duncan's file search proceeds very, very slowly. And we must be sure that Merrill Lynch, Pierce, Fenner and Tibbitts bring us some dividends very, very quickly."

14

The Central Intelligence Agency presents a monolithic external appearance to the outsider. But a surgical cross section of the Company exposes a honeycomb of cells and compartments, divided from one another by a rigorous system of regulations, procedures and controls. Even the very building that houses it is designed to prevent an employee from wandering from his authorized area into someone else's bailiwick where he doesn't belong. It is not apocryphal that the employees at the Langley campus cannot telephone one another with ease; there is no Company-wide telephone directory. One seldom hears the familiar bureaucratic clichés that refer to coordination and routine exchanges of information; Company people are discouraged from "cross-fertilizing," "getting a mix," "circulating the options."

Arnie Pittman was the subject of a compounded compartmentalization; the Deputy Director of Intelligence was embargoed. His CIA colleagues quickly understood that Pittman was the White House man who had been planted on the seventh floor; he was the enemy. Pittman was to be told nothing, shown nothing, without the approval of the Director or his assistant, Simon Cappell. What Pittman did, whom he saw and what he read and wrote were faithfully reported to Cappell each day by Arnie Pittman's loyal new assistant, Sid

Lindsey. In his absence Pittman's secretary kept the watch.

Pittman's handsomely furnished office was a box within a box, and he was kept completely ignorant of what William Martin was doing.

He did not keep long days at the office. About four in the afternoon he routinely folded the morning paper, neatly restoring the sections of the *Post* to their original sequence, and dropped it into the special "to-be-burned" wastebasket. Then he shrugged into his coat, snapped shut his empty attaché case and walked to the elevator in a Navy manner. The evening newspaper would be waiting on the seat of his limousine.

One day as Arnie Pittman made his lonely descent from the seventh floor, the President's Assistant for Domestic Affairs, Carl Duncan, was about fifty feet away in the fortieth minute of continuous, exasperating debate with the Director of Central Intelligence.

"But, Bill," Duncan was saying, "you know damn well that the President is on my back for this stuff. I can't and won't go back to the White House and tell him that it takes two weeks for the CIA to find its files. I don't believe that and he won't believe that. If you're telling me that, you're bullshitting me."

"That's not what I'm telling you, Carl. As we went over the list I showed you how many of the items we will have for you later this week. But, goddammit, some of these other items can be very touchy. As Director of Intelligence I have a statutory responsibility to discharge. If I were to ship a lot of these files out of here simply wholesale, CIA operations could be compromised and people could get killed. I can't do that. And I won't."

"I'm not asking you to do that; neither is the President," Duncan said with some heat.

"Well, I've got to insist on the right to go through some of these things personally before they are copied and sent out of my custody," Martin said with equal passion. "For example, this third item on the second page. We are running a hundred agents in India right now. He wants the Kashmir file. That file identifies some of our assets—agents—in the Parliament, the Cabinet, in Indian newspapers. Who the hell is going to see that stuff? You have some bastards over at the White House who I wouldn't want handling that information. I don't trust them."

Duncan stabbed the list with his forefinger. "This is for the President, goddammit. Who he might show it to is up to him, but it's my understanding that he intends to read the stuff personally. Ultimately the question of who to trust or not trust with the nation's secrets is his, not yours."

"Well, Carl, that's fine, but I think I need to talk to President Monckton personally about some of this." Martin tried to keep his voice low. He didn't want a showdown yet. "Why don't you take what's here, now? That will get him started. The Lebanon material alone is six inches thick. And then, whenever he'll see me, I can tell him my problem with the rest of it. How does that sound?"

Duncan's voice was harsh: "Well, what you're saying is that the President of the United States has requested Government files on the war in Asia and Rio de Muerte and the Hungarian uprising and twenty other things but he can't have them because you don't trust his judgment. But you'll talk it over with him. Right?"

"Look"—Martin's reply was crisp—"I have an obligation to a lot of people who could end up dead if this stuff got to the wrong people. If the President personally tells me that he has to have certain information, he'll get it. Always. But if a bunch of his helpers are going to paw through our raw files and jeopardize our people and operations, the answer is going to be No. I hope you can convey this to the President just as I've said it to you. I want to tell him personally, if I can get in to see him. But I'm beginning to suspect that he doesn't care to see me—ever."

Duncan's voice was ice. "I think an appointment can be arranged, Bill. In fact I suspect the President will especially want to talk to you about this. He'll want to, quite a lot." Duncan was carefully placing crosshatched folders in a black suitcase, checking them on the request list one by one as he did so. "Eleven items, right?"

"Yes," said Martin. "Eleven."

"Eleven out of thirty-four that were requested," said Duncan grimly. "Someone will damn sure call you about the appointment. I think it will be very soon." Duncan rose, turned and walked into the reception room without shaking hands. He was joined by the young CIA employee who had met his car at the door, escorted him to Martin's office, and would return him to the great marble lobby.

As Duncan left, Simon Cappell entered Martin's office by a side door. "How did it go?" the aide asked.

Martin was tense. "No better than I expected, I guess." He lit a cigarette. "He probably took back more than he thought he'd get. But he's a relentless son of a bitch."

"Is it Duncan or his boss who is pushing so hard?" Cappell suggested.

"Oh, I'm sure you're right—it's the big man. Duncan is just Monckton's errand boy. I'm going to get called on the carpet, I guess, so that Monckton can personally beat me up for not producing the files on Hungary and Rio de Muerte and Korea and the rest. The pressure is really on." Martin stabbed out the cigarette. "Simon, I've got to be in a stronger position when I go over there. I need a detailed memorandum on each one of these requested items—reasons why they should not be declassified, why we shouldn't let anyone see them, that kind of thing."

"Is our position that no one can see them? Not even Monckton?" Simon asked.

"I know," Martin said, "you can't tell the President he can't see them. But shit! You know he won't read all that stuff himself. And neither will good old Carl Duncan. It will be sent express to T.T. Tallford and the political ax murderers over there. You know it, I know it, and Monckton knows it. And they will wring all the political juice out of that material without caring how many of our people they kill in the process. We just can't let that happen."

"I've got most of those memos roughed out now," Cappell said. "We can make a pretty good case for leaving the classification on every single one. Won't Carl Tessler help you with Monckton?"

Martin looked up at Cappell with disbelief. "Do you really think he'd buck the President on something like this? Tessler is talented and brilliant but he's basically a coward when it comes to a fight. And Richard Monckton knows it. No, we've got to win this one all by ourselves."

Martin lit another cigarette. "How is Bernie Tibbitts coming? That is our top priority, Simon."

"Merrill Lynch is in place at the Perrine office, waiting. There is only a little to report. Arthur Perrine lives in the house where his office is. He's in town now. And Bernie is sure Perrine has wind of some FBI surveillance of journalists."

Martin stood and began to pace. "Damn. That makes it more binding. Tibbitts' information is no goddamn good to me if Arthur Perrine has it too. And what if the Bureau or the White House thinks he's on to something? They'll never risk covering Perrine if they suspect he's aware of what's going on. We may have bought the wrong investment from our Merrill Lynch boys, Simon."

"Do you want to cover the second choice?"

"I think so. Have Bernie duplicate his coverage on that other columnist—Krasnak. We can't afford to guess wrong."

Three hours later William Martin glanced up from his vodka martini to see Tom Krasnak sitting at a banquette across the restaurant talking excitedly to a small, gray-haired woman. There was nothing unusual, of course, about seeing a political columnist at dinner at Sans Souci. The restaurant had been a favorite eating place for White House people since the Billy Curry days, and the journalists in the White House orbit were drawn to its tables by some celestial law of political and gastronomic attraction. Krasnak had every legitimate reason to be there. But the coincidence jarred Martin's already jangled nerves. While he would watch the man eat, Bernie Tibbitts was setting up the surveillance of Krasnak's office.

This was to have been a happy occasion for Martin. He and Sally Atherton had been talking on the telephone every night while she was in California. They had planned this special evening at Sans Souci for days. She had just arrived at Dulles Airport at five o'clock, a divorced and available woman by order of the Superior Court in and for the County of San Diego. When she telephoned Martin from the airport, she even sounded free, and she was obviously eager to see him.

Martin had arrived first, direct from his office. Paul, the suave but enthusiastic maître d', was engulfed in customers in the tiny foyer when he arrived, but Martin caught his eye; Paul nodded and beckoned him with his handful of menus. The Director dined at Sans Souci frequently, and this evening Paul had selected the near-corner banquette on the left side on the main floor. A bit quieter for Mr. Martin. A waiter in a crisp white jacket soon produced a drink. It was while relaxing over that drink and anticipating Sally's arrival that Martin discovered Krasnak across the room. His second drink was nearly a memory when he saw Sally following Paul down the entrance stairs and to the table.

Martin stood and smiled as Sally gave him both her hands. They were cold; her cheeks were flushed under her tan. She wore a light-blue dress with short sleeves; the wide gold bracelet that was almost her trademark gleamed on her tanned arm. He noticed that her hair was shorter. When she came into a room she never disappointed him.

Paul pulled the table away from the banquette for Sally to slide in beside Martin and murmured, "Madame graces my house. Bon appétit," then, after taking Sally's drink order, bustled up the stairs to charm a new group of arrivals.

Martin suddenly needed to touch Sally. He laid his hand on the back of hers, on the bench beside him, then emphasized his need with pressure. She turned her hand over under his and scraped his palm with a fingernail.

"I like the haircut," he said.

"It's too short. I wasn't watching; he got scissor-happy. Notice anything else new?"

Martin pretended deep thought as he rested his chin in his hand. "I've seen the dress before. It's lovely. So is the lady. No. I give up."

"Look." She held her left hand above the table, palm down, fingers wide. A white band of skin marked the absence of a ring on the fourth finger.

"Very becoming," he smiled. "Was it rough?"

"Oh, some photographers and reporters were outside the courthouse. But it was all right. I had expected that. In the courtroom the judge just zipped it through with only two or three questions. It was a breeze."

"God, I wish mine were over," he said grimly. "Linda seems to be making it as slow and difficult as possible."

Her voice was tender. "How much longer, Bill?"

"They say at least ninety days. We have to be awfully careful until then, Charley says. He and Linda's lawyer are close to agreement on the property settlement, but she'll use any excuse to blow it up, I guess. She may be having one or both of us watched, darling."

"That bitch." Sally stirred her drink, thought of something and smiled. "Shall I go out with some other men to throw her off the trail?"

Martin made his tone mock-threatening. "You'd better not, my love! I think I'll have you followed, too."

"Sure. You probably have plenty of creeps over at Langley with nothing to do," she laughed.

"You sound like the President. That's the kind of shit I get from the White House all the time."

Sally's voice became serious. "It's still going on?"

"More every day. Now they're running barefoot through our old files looking for political dirt. I don't know how much longer I can hold them off."

She drew in a breath. "Rio de Muerte?"

"Yes, that's the worst from my standpoint, of course, but thirty other things too. I used to think old Esker Scott Anderson could put on the pressure, but he's an amateur compared to Monckton."

Sally raised a hand to Bill's cheek. "Poor angel. You do look beat."

"Between this latest rape of the files and some tough budget hassles and a few new international problems, I've really been feeling it. I'm not surprised if it shows. Having you away hasn't helped much either. I've really missed you, sweetheart."

Over dinner they put their problems aside. The sole véronique was tender and piping hot. Paul's choice of a vintage Montrachet was unusually fine. By the time the wine was gone many of the tables in the little restaurant were vacant.

"Will you let me come home with you tonight?" Martin asked quietly.

Sally looked at him quizzically. "You just told me that Charley Jones said we had to be careful until your divorce settlement is final. Would that be sensible?"

"Look, darling. I love you. I don't care how many private detectives know it. Goddamn it, I need to feel you close to me tonight. What can Linda do, anyway? She can't stop the divorce from going through."

"You know the answer to that, Bill. She can pluck you like a chicken; house, inheritance, everything. And she can wreck you with Monckton. Why give her the chance?"

"We don't have to go to your place or mine. We can find a quiet hotel somewhere."

Sally made a face. "Sweetheart, I want you tonight as much as you want me. But no one-night stands in Baltimore. Neither one of us needs that kind of scene. Besides, we just can't take the risk."

"Shit," Martin said quietly.

"I'm disappointed too—" Sally began.

"No. It's not that," said Martin. "My pocket vibrator has just started. The goddamn telephone pager. I've got to call in. Please excuse me, darling."

"Sure. I'll get my coat while you're calling."

They slid out of the banquette and walked across the dining room. The pay phone was on the wall near the kitchen door. Martin dialed from memory.

The phone was picked up after the first ring and a voice said, "789-2301."

"DCI. Am I being paged?"

"Yes, sir."

"Code Strawberry."

"Thank you. The message is: Please call Mr. Carl Duncan, 456-1414. It's urgent."

"Thanks."

He replaced the receiver and strode to the foyer. Sally was standing in her mink coat eating mints one at a time from a large silver bowl. She held out Martin's coat.

"Can you stay out and play or is your mommy calling you?" she said, attempting lightness.

"Ha, ha. Very funny. As a matter of fact, it's not mommy, it's big brother calling. And I'm going to be very bad. I'm not going to call the son of a bitch back. Come on, I've got an idea, and it's the best one I've had in months. Have you ever been to Tobacco Landing, Maryland?"

15

Arthur Perrine's middle name was originally given him as Thomas, but he had affected a new middle name, Standish, at about the time he left the New York *Herald Tribune*. He was glad he had changed it. He would have preferred a better first name as well, but his career as a journalist by then was too far along. The name Arthur Perrine was becoming known. He rarely used his middle name or initial but it was good to know it was there; it somehow buttressed his specious, unspoken claim to distinguished colonial roots.

On the other hand, the old white frame house on the southeast corner of Thirtieth and N streets in which he lived and worked was genuine. The authentic 1785 farmhouse had been purchased by Arthur Perrine in

1948, but Arthur's visitors were permitted to assume that it had passed from one Perrine ancestor to the next over the centuries. Ancestral portraits in simple gilt frames graced the entry hall, living room and dining room. Arthur Perrine had never been heard to claim that the dour colonial ladies and gentlemen portrayed in these cracking oils were of his lineage, but neither did he ever disown them. A guest was always allowed to draw his own conclusions about Arthur Standish Perrine's early American origins.

In fact, Arthur Perrine was born in a Chicago ghetto, the only child of Jewish immigrants. In time, the family moved to Washington, where Arthur's father became a minor employee of the Government Printing Office. He was a stern and demanding disciplinarian who seemed to realize that his son was to be his only accomplishment. He died quietly when Arthur was in college, leaving his widow a pension, the little house in the northwest section of the District, debt free, and enough money to see the boy through school. Arthur Perrine became an able and well known newspaper reporter, whose successful political column he not-too-seriously named The Federal Ferret and from which he enjoyed wide readership and a handsome income. When his column was syndicated to two hundred newspapers across the country he felt secure enough to buy the old Georgetown house. Arthur Perrine lived alone in the house in a generous measure of subdued splendor.

The old house had once been two houses, joined at the corner and combined sometime early in the nineteenth century. The older wing faced Thirtieth Street and was remodeled by Perrine to provide a colonial living room for himself and spacious offices for the Ferret Corporation, with its own business entrance off the Thirtieth Street sidewalk. The N Street house had a small inset porch and an ornate colonial front door with a fan of glass panels at its top. The entry hall led straight down worn wooden steps into the living room. There a large colonial fireplace dominated the right wall. Two ancestral oils were hung above the mantel. Sliding glass doors opened the left wall to a terrace bordered in topiary bushes, carefully nurtured and pruned by Arthur Perrine himself. A high wall at the back of the yard was broken by a gate that opened onto a narrow passage, dividing the N Street properties from the ones fronting on Olive Street. Three narrow two- and three-story Olive Street houses showed their backs to the Perrine yard.

Although the living quarters upstairs were small they were adequately elegant for their single occupant. The cook and yardman came in by the day; there was no need for servants' quarters. And Arthur Perrine hated the very thought of guest rooms and house guests.

Arthur Perrine had never married. There had been times when he had chosen to share his bed, but in the past four years those times had been few and far between. Earlier there had been a lover, but Arthur and his lover had always agreed to live apart. Even then, Arthur Perrine knew that he needed his privacy.

In the late forties Arthur returned from a long foreign trip with a European wardrobe and an affected style of speech. As the years passed, a tired, almost cynical drawl modulated and deepened its tone.

At sixty-one Arthur did not often feel physically fit; his state of health, by now an obsession, became an unavoidable topic of conversation, and he moved like a nomad from one doctor's prescribed diet to another. Although required to abstain from most rich foods, he took great pride in the cuisine of his table. A long-suffering cook had come to him seven years before to provide his guests with the sauces and dressings that Arthur Perrine's progression of doctors denied him. Unlike most Washington hosts, he had an encyclopedic knowledge of wines; and he could be seen on Fridays at the French Market, haggling with the butcher in French over the thinness of the veal or the freshness of the calves' liver.

2990 N Street N.W. was furnished to Arthur Perrine's laboriously cultivated taste, no doubt influenced by his calculated prediction of the effect the display of furnishings would have upon his guests. Museum-quality early American antiques, Chinese vases, paintings and objets d'art were arranged for the visitor's eye, regardless of their utility or comfort. Only a tiny den hideaway displayed Arthur Perrine's personal treasures: two handwritten notes to him from President William Arthur Curry, signed "Billy," incongruously framed in red Chinese-lacquered wood, hung on the wall. First editions lined the bookshelves. Family pictures and mementos covered the leather-topped desk.

But Arthur Perrine did not do his writing in the den. If a straying guest should try the old and slightly crooked door at the far corner of Arthur's living room and discover it unlocked, he would abruptly enter the reception room of The Federal Ferret, a room usually occupied during the day by two secretaries, one young and beautiful, the other in her fifties and merely efficient. Three doors in the far wall led to the offices of Arthur Perrine and his two legmen. A fourth door, on the side wall, was the one that opened onto Thirtieth Street.

Arthur insisted on composing every column himself. No assistant had ever met his exacting standard for grammar, syntax and accuracy, nor had he ever had a partner.

Arthur Perrine's days were largely spent on the telephone and he often worked on the column alone at night. As he grew older he left the white frame house on N Street less and less. He declined the dozens of bids from Washington hostesses, with one exception. He did accept any First Lady's White House invitation to the intimate dinners in the family dining room. No more than twelve could be seated there; and the food was always better than that served at the big dinners. Journalists like Robinson and Collyer were invited to the big dinners. He and one or two others were a cut or two above all that.

It was not really that he was a snob, he told himself. He merely preferred his own food and his own surroundings and, God knows, it was better when one could determine one's own guest list.

Arthur Perrine was no longer a reporter who pounded the pavement for an exclusive story. He would make a grudging excursion to the West Wing at the White House if it was absolutely impossible to obtain a Presidential staff source any other way, but he much preferred to invite knowledgeable men to the dining room of the N Street house for lunch and leisurely talk. He would sit with his invited source at a corner of the very old dining table or, perhaps, have trays served on the terrace if the weather was decent; he would begin by talking of the food and the wine, gossip a bit, and at last, when his guest was at ease, focus upon the subject he was writing about. Arthur Perrine rarely asked a source a question. Some of his guests left, well fed, with the belief that the Ferret column had already been written in advance of the interview. It often appeared that Arthur Perrine's only object at lunch had been to confirm a few things in a completed story, just before it was mailed to the syndicate.

"That veal was absolutely delicious," the guest would remark.

And Arthur Perrine would say, "Farley's is the last decent meat market, y'know. On Wisconsin. It's getting so hard to get good veal these days. It's also the pan. It must be hot. Most cooks don't know that. Mine was the French Ambassador's, y'know. Hmm, Title Two programs, they've failed, haven't they?"

"Title Two," the guest might ask, "of the Vocational Education Act?"

"Yes, it's a total waste, isn't it?"

"Well, I wouldn't go that far."

"Anyone who's ever studied them concludes they've totally failed. The NEA study, the Rand study."

"Well, the Rand study isn't published yet, of course."

"But it will say that Title Two's a failure, won't it?"

"It's confidential until it's published, Arthur. Still, there's no denying that we've had our problems with those programs."

"More wine? There's nothing to be done for them but shut them down, throw in the towel, is there? Title Two isn't even in the draft budget for the Office of Education next year."

"Oh, yes. There will be about five million proposed." Perrine's quick mind would close upon that newly won and important fact and move on. From the nuances of his guest's reactions Arthur Perrine would craft a thoughtful column on vocational education and the weaknesses of the program's administrators without once mentioning his guest's name or hinting at his identity.

In his public encounters in the food stores of Georgetown, and on the rare occasions when some inescapable errand forced Arthur Perrine to go downtown, he was seldom recognized. He wore his thinning brown hair slicked straight back and he moved his robust, middle-sized frame with exaggerated delicacy. He carried a lighted cigarette during all his waking hours, held in the continental fashion with the thumb and two fingers. His choice of clothing ran to waistcoats, bow ties, foulard scarves, silk shirts, British tailoring, even a cape at times, and always handmade shoes.

Unlike some columnists, he thought quite a lot about what he wrote; he would debate often and long over the content of a column before he sent it to his syndicate for publication. His ability and effort yielded financial success and much "influence" in the city of Washington; as a result he became feared by those in the capital who believed that the Perrine column could and would make trouble for them.

Newspapers editors and publishers bought the Ferret column for their papers because it was lively, thoughtful and balanced, knowing that Perrine was going to advocate a healthy defense establishment and would be critical of the Federal bureaucracy and slightly to the center of most other columnists. Few readers stood in doubt of Perrine's contempt for Ed Gilley during the campaign against Richard Monckton but no one was surprised when the column began to criticize the early domestic mistakes of Richard Monckton's new Administration.

Perrine had developed reliable sources of information within the Federal bureaucracy over the years; even high-ranking Government employees would bring him tips and leads. Arthur Perrine well knew that his informants' motives ranged from the most lofty concern for the nation's welfare to the basest desires for revenge against a colleague or a superior. But The Federal Ferret column was less concerned about the reasons than about developing leads into good, full-blown stories based on a reasonable measure of corroboration.

From such a source Arthur Perrine received a skeletal tip that the FBI had recently begun an investigation of several members of the White House staff and at least two newspapermen, all unnamed. From the nature of the source Perrine hoped and believed that he was the only newsman who had the information so far, and he moved with speed to learn more. Within twenty-four hours an Assistant Director of the FBI, Peter Gould, was flattered and then intrigued to receive a gracious invitation to lunch with Arthur Perrine before the lovely fireplace in the N Street dining room.

Gould told Arthur Perrine the truth when he said he

really didn't know of any current investigation of anyone on the White House staff. But before the main course of veal scaloppine and sautéed baby zucchini was removed, the Assistant Director of the FBI had been led to five points of philosophic agreement with Arthur Perrine and heard himself agree to check into Perrine's FBI tip; but depending on what he found out, he might call Perrine; and possibly he might not. Arthur Perrine maneuvered skillfully; he would not ask Gould to do anything Gould should not or would not wish to do.

The following morning Arthur Perrine's secretary telephoned Mrs. Peter Gould to invite the Goulds to "a little dinner party" Mr. Perrine was giving for his old friend the Chief Justice of the Supreme Court. At the second-string level of the FBI, the Peter Goulds rarely received social invitations of that kind. Mrs. Gould accepted with obvious delight and began making plans for the purchase of an elegant long gown. Among Arthur Perrine's eleven guests at the intimate dinner were the Deputy Attorney General, the Director of the Secret Service, the Italian Ambassador and a former Secretary of Defense. Arthur Perrine was careful to include the Goulds in the dinner conversation. Mrs. Gould was given a conducted tour of the kitchen restoration by her host while Pete Gould was locked in close shop-talk conversation with the Deputy Attorney General, the number two man at the Justice Department. Never before had Gould had an opportunity to talk law enforcement with one of his superiors in such a relaxed atmosphere. The career implications of the evening were deep in his thoughts as he and his wife drove home. Mrs. Gould couldn't get over how natural and friendly the wives had been, especially the Chief Justice's lady. They were going to trade recipes. Imagine that!

Four days later, on Saturday afternoon, Pete Gould called Arthur Perrine. "There's more to this than you thought, Mr. Perrine. I think we should talk."

"It's Arthur, Pete. Please. Can you talk now? Did you learn who ordered the investigation?"

Gould's voice sounded strained. "I don't want to talk on the phone. We should meet."

Arthur Perrine was gracious and relaxed as always. "Fine. Can you come here later today?"

"I don't think I should come to your place—er—Arthur."

"There's a rear entrance through a gate in the back wall. There's a little path between the houses. Comes off Thirtieth Street. Come in that way."

Gould was insistent. "No. I don't think so. It would be better to meet outside of Washington; somewhere no one will recognize either one of us. This thing is hot, Arthur."

"Out of town?" Perrine was obviously put out. "My God! I don't go out of town! Where could I go that I wouldn't be recognized? Certainly not New York. It would have to be some godforsaken, terrible little place like, um, like Pittsburgh! Surely you're not . . ."

"All right," Gould broke in quickly. "I've got to hang up. Make it the lobby of the Pittsburgh Horton Hotel at eight thirty tonight." The telephone went dead in Arthur Perrine's unbelieving ear. As he hung up the receiver he called through the open office door for his secretary. There was no answer; it was Saturday afternoon and she had gone.

"Good God," Arthur Perrine said aloud to the empty rooms, "how does one get to Pittsburgh?" If it weren't such an important story he absolutely wouldn't consider going. Jimmy, currently his only legman, was in California doing the gubernatorial roundup research, so if anyone was going to do the story it would have to be Arthur. Perhaps he could head off Pete Gould. He telephoned Gould's home. There was no answer. The FBI switchboard reported that the Assistant Director was out of town on assignment.

Pittsburgh! Well, he had only his silly sarcasm to blame for the selection of the place. After two phone calls Arthur Perrine found an airline that flew there on Saturdays. He made a reservation on a 6:30 P.M. flight, called a taxicab, hurriedly changed his suit, selecting his most nondescript gray tweed and a plain dark blue mackintosh. By ten minutes to six Arthur Perrine had withdrawn an umbrella from the entry hall closet and was standing on his small front porch. When the taxicab pulled up, he slammed his handsome colonial front door, tugged on the handle to be certain that it was securely locked and glanced at the lighted upstairs window. He had methodically left lights burning in the den, the entry, his bedroom and the rear yard. There had been some burglaries in the neighborhood recently and he disliked leaving the house dark and empty, even for a few hours.

At 6:55 P.M. a blue Ford sedan drove slowly past the Perrine front door, turned south on Thirtieth Street, turned east at the next corner on Olive and made a left turn into the cramped garage that occupied the entire ground level of the third house from the corner. Three men quickly left the car; two walked into the narrow house through a door at the back of the garage. The third hurriedly closed the garage doors from the inside and joined them, but not quickly enough to prevent a man with a camera in a window across the street from taking seven frames of his face.

Six minutes later the three men, dressed in dark-blue coveralls, crossed the high-walled yard of the Olive Street house to its rear gate. The tallest of the three turned to the others and said something in a whisper. As he whispered, his face was imprinted on slowly reeling video tape of the camera that he could not see concealed in the shadows of a screened porch at the rear of the third-floor apartment next door. A shadowed cameraman locked his camera at the "on" position and his zoom lens followed the three as they crossed the narrow path between the rear yards. He saw them open Arthur Perrine's gate soundlessly with a small pry tool and walk quickly to Perrine's basement steps near his kitchen door. As they disappeared down the outside stairs, the cameraman turned his taping unit off and waited in the dark.

Lars Haglund quietly opened the door from the basement and stood in Arthur Perrine's front entry hall. The house was silent. He snapped his fingers softly and the other two men came up into the entry and followed Haglund across the living room to the office door. The short, swarthy man with the suitcase quickly tumbled the old lock with a small tool and pushed the door open. He entered the secretaries' area; as he looked about, his full face appeared, centered, on a television monitor in the third-floor apartment at the top of the narrow house behind Arthur Perrine's. Then Lars Haglund and the third man, thin and pale, moved onto the screen and across it as they walked into Arthur Perrine's own office and switched on the desk light. There they did their work swiftly, without conversation. A piece of the wooden molding that topped the wall paneling was neatly cut away and placed in a cloth bag. A small metal tube was placed where the wood had been, and plastic was molded around the tube to replace the wood. The pale man shook a small bottle, opened it and reached high to paint the plastic with a camel's-hair brush. It was not guesswork that the quick-drying color was a perfect match. It had been prepared from a color chip that had been obtained from behind Perrine's leather couch six days before by a telephone repairman who was "routinely checking the installation."

The short man had removed the plastic cover from the telephone on Perrine's desk; he made a slight change in the arrangement of the wires, clipped a disk the size of a dime to one of them and replaced the cover. Haglund checked for sawdust, brushed the chair beneath the cut molding with his gloved hand, looked at the telephone, moved it a little to his right, switched off the desk light and closed the office door. The automatic Leica still camera in Arthur Perrine's furnace grill silently received the "discontinue" signal in the same way that it had been electronically ordered to intermittently photograph the office with its wide-angle lens as soon as the desk light had been turned on.

In a few minutes Lars Haglund and his partners were back in the house on Olive Street. Their passage across Arthur Perrine's lighted yard had been taped by Bernie Tibbitts' hidden third-floor cameraman, this time in full face. He also photographed the first of the three to leave the Olive Street house. That thin pale man left by the rear gate, dressed in brown slacks, green ski parka and stocking cap. He was followed as he turned east and walked the rough path behind the houses to Twenty-ninth Street, turned right to Olive Street and hailed a taxicab. Two men in a green car stayed right behind his taxicab all the way to National Airport. One of them flew with him to Newark and followed him home.

The short, dark man, dressed now in a tweed sport jacket and gray slacks, opened the garage doors thirty minutes later, started the blue Ford and drove it to Baltimore Friendship Airport. Another of the Merrill Lynch men flew on the same airplane with him to the Raleigh-Durham Airport and followed him to his home on a small farm near the outskirts of Durham.

In the third-floor Olive Street apartment, another Tibbitts man sat in front of a table on which he had placed a large radio encased in black steel. He wore heavy earphones, one of which he lifted as he turned to look at his partner. "All right, let's try it with the telephone."

His partner dialed the number listed for The Federal Ferret. After two rings an automatic answering device clicked and a tape-recorded voice announced that the office was closed, then invited the caller to record a message. As the secretary's recording spoke to the man on the telephone, the agent with the earphones fine-tuned a dial on his receiver.

"Hang up," he said.

"Did you find it?"

"On the button. It's at 185.2. Not a very strong signal either. They must be receiving next door or close by. Better call Bernie and let him know we're on it. Tell him they may be close. See if he wants someone to go in for the camera film. It might be risky."

Bernie Tibbitts took the call as his office assistant was entering his office with a pile of still-damp photographs made from the video tape. As he leafed through the pictures of Lars Haglund and his men, Tibbitts was told that his third-floor team had found the frequency on which the bug was transmitting from Arthur Perrine's telephone. He decided not to risk removing the hidden still camera yet. And he asked for frequent reports from the surveillance. There might be other transmitters in there; the other columnist had been double-covered. They were to try to pick up any office conversations. Tibbitts wanted everything taped this time. Above all, he wanted frequent reports.

"Who are these people?" Bernie Tibbitts asked the man who brought him the photographs. "Do we know?"

"One of them was easy. The big blond fellow is from Western Hemisphere Division. Lars Haglund. Code name there was Symphony Nine."

"A Company man?" Tibbitts' voice showed his surprise. "Who the hell is he working for?"

"Personnel says he's recently retired. He is now a Government employee at the White House. Staff assistant."

"My God. The others too?"

"We don't think so, but we aren't sure. One is flying north, the other south, and we have people on them. We should get something fairly soon."

Tibbitts reached across the desk and picked up the top photo from the pile.

"Have this one of—what's his name?—our man—the White House man—have it enlarged and mounted. You can see Perrine's name on that wall certificate, can't you?"

"It should show up very well."

"Who does he work for at the White House—Tessler?"

"No, he's deputy to T.T. Tallford."

Tibbitts looked puzzled. "Is Tallford on the national security side over there?"

"No, Bernie, you remember him, don't you? There was a big story on him in the *Post* a while back. He's the political hatchetman at the White House. He does Monckton's dirty work."

"Jesus Christ! Get out of here, will you? I've got to make a phone call."

Tibbitts discovered that the CIA switchboard had instructions to deflect all calls for Director William Martin to Simon Cappell for the rest of the night. Such instructions caused the five middle-aged CIA telephone operators to smile at one another knowingly. They had tracked Bill Martin to the Atherton number often enough on other nights to be able to guess where he was. And from gossip around the building, they could guess what he was doing there. When you're on an important switchboard for a long time you learn that even the big brass is only human. So you smile and keep your mouth shut, if you expect to get along.

Sally Atherton's telephone rang four times before she untangled herself from the leg thrown across her body and her groping hand lifted the receiver. A moment later she handed it across a pillow to Bill Martin. "It's Simon, darling," she said groggily.

Bill came awake immediately.

"Sorry to disturb you, sir, but we have Merrill Lynch problems that won't keep."

"Never mind, what's up?"

"They went into Perrine's tonight and Bernie has some incredible pictures."

"So, that's the good news? Or the bad news? What's the rest of it?"

"Tibbitts also has a fantastic set of the Presidential jitters. Remember Lars Haglund—at Opa-locka?"

"Sure," Martin said. "What about him?"

"He takes a great picture apparently. He was the team leader in there. And Bernie has traced him. Old Symphony Nine now works for T.T. Tallford, and, as Tibbitts says, that starts with T and that rhymes with P, and that stands for President. Bernie's convinced that it's very big politics and potential monumental trouble. Little CIA employees may have a right to be scared."

"All right, Simon. Call him back and tell him to keep pressing. Obviously Tallford has charged off on his own here. Monckton would never let him send a White House staff man like Haglund on such a job. Monckton's too smart for that. Were there others?"

"Two."

"White House people?"

"We don't know yet."

"Simon, you've got to keep Tibbitts in full pursuit. Tell him he has no worries. He'll be a goddamn hero if he nails Tallford. Too bad about Haglund, though. I wonder how he got messed up in it."

Simon Cappell hung up his receiver slowly. "Is the old man after Monckton?" he whispered. "God help us."

At the Atherton town house Bill Martin reached

across Sally to hang up her phone. He felt her warmth on the underside of his arm. "No more calls, my love. That's just about all the good news I can stand for one night."

The Horton Hotel in Pittsburgh was built as a part of the remarkable urban rejuvenation of the so-called Golden Triangle neighborhood, at the confluence of the Monongahela and Allegheny Rivers. The clock read only ten minutes after eight. Arthur Perrine was early. He took a chair in a good location at one side of the wood-and-chrome lobby from where he would be able to see Peter Gould, regardless of which entrance he used. But after a few minutes Perrine began to feel conspicuous. The lobby was atypically empty and very quiet; he would be less obtrusive if he were reading. The newsstand did not have *The New York Times* yet; nor the Sunday *Post*. He settled for the earliest edition of the *Enquirer*. He could not bring himself to read the Pittsburgh paper. It had long ago discontinued the Ferret column in a dispute over money and he was damned if he would ever read it again.

At eight thirty Arthur Perrine folded his newspaper on his lap and looked around the lobby expectantly. Peter Gould was late. At eight forty-five he was very late. FBI men were punctual if nothing else. Perrine gestured to a bellboy to ask him for the correct time. The bellboy came over to Perrine and held out his wide, strong wrist, covered with golden hair. His wristwatch said eight forty-five too. From the young man's manner of response Perrine sensed that he had been misunderstood. He didn't need an excuse for a conversation with a young man. Arthur Perrine would meet Peter Gould, get the FBI story and be out of Pittsburgh on the last flight at ten thirty. He wasn't picking up young hustlers in hotel lobbies these days. He thanked the handsome boy for the information and made some show of picking up his newspaper and turning to the editorial section, although he had already read it. He wanted this fellow to go away. The tall bellboy stood looking at him, then turned and went back to the bell captain's stand. Arthur Perrine peered at the boy across the lobby as he turned the page; the young bastard was charming, the way he was standing there, his arms folded. Well built. A little like the lad at Martha's Vineyard that time so long ago.

At ten o'clock Arthur Perrine decided to telephone Gould. Why had he come to this forsaken place? He felt chagrined, foolish.

The bellboy watched him as he looked for the public telephones, then came up to him, smiling. "My name is Jimmy, sir. Can I help you?"

"Just looking for the phones, y'know," Perrine muttered, looking around the lobby. He didn't want to look at the boy; still he glanced, then turned his head away.

"They're around the corner, sir. Are you waiting for someone?"

"Hmmm. Thank you." The kid really is a hustler, he thought. He dialed and let Gould's telephone ring eight or nine times.

"Gould."

"Peter Gould?" said Arthur Perrine. "I'm in Pittsburgh; I expected to see you here. What happened?"

"Mr. Perrine, I'm not going to meet you. I'm sorry, but this thing is just too hot. I'm really sorry."

"Well, my God, man, I'm sorry too! You got me up here into this horrible place and now you say you aren't coming! What happened? Did Elmer Morse lean on you?"

"Mr. Perrine, I just can't talk to you. That's all there is to it. I'm sorry."

The telephone went dead. Arthur Perrine slammed the receiver into the hook in disgust. He wasn't going to spend the night in this place if he could help it. He fished another dime from his pocket and called the number on the folder that held his airline ticket.

A polite but firm young lady informed him in the most definite of terms that he could not possibly arrive at the airport in time for the last flight to Washington.

So that was it. He was in Pittsburgh, Pennsylvania, and there wasn't a damn thing he could do about it.

Well, it might not be all bad. He was in a place where no one knew him, with free time on his hands, for the first time in years. He turned to look around the lobby. He and the bellboy were the only ones there. Their eyes met briefly. It had been a long, long time; and this looked like it could be very good. Maybe a hundred dollars? Perhaps it was fate. When would there be another chance like this? The risk would be minimal. And the boy seemed genuinely attracted to him.

Arthur Perrine looked directly at the youth as he walked across the lobby.

A young woman was working through a pile of cards at the back of the registration desk. Perrine walked over to the counter.

"Miss, it appears that I am stuck, sentenced to stay in Pittsburgh tonight. Do you have a suite you can give me?"

"One night, sir?"

"Of course. Just one night."

She ran her index finger down a rack of room cards and looked up at Perrine. The bellboy was leaning on the end of the registration counter, ten feet away, listening to them.

"I'm sorry, sir. No suites. I can give you a king-size single on the river side at forty-eight dollars for one night."

Arthur Perrine nodded. The girl pushed a registration card toward him. "Will you be paying by credit card or cash?"

He glanced at the boy. "Cash," he said. He printed

the name Art Standish and his old 1952 address in New York.

"Thank you, Mr. Standish. Jimmy, will you take Mr. Standish to 1108, please?"

The boy had narrow hips. He led Perrine to the elevator, clicking the key.

"No luggage, Mr. Standish?" They were alone in the elevator. He looked at the old columnist familiarly, then licked his lips.

Perrine smiled nervously. "No. I hadn't intended to stay. But things have a way of working out for the best, don't they?"

The next morning was a quiet, clear Sunday in Georgetown. Few but the pious were abroad and so there was very little traffic.

Lars Haglund emerged from the Olive Street house at 7:30 A.M., dressed in a business suit and overcoat. He briskly walked six blocks to a corner of Wisconsin Avenue where a black Mercury sedan was waiting at the curb, its motor running.

Lars Haglund opened the rear door and dropped into the back seat. The Sunday Washington *Post* and the *Star* were fanned on the back shelf. He reached back for the papers.

"The ramp, please," Haglund grunted.

"Sir," said the Army sergeant in the light-gray chauffeur's uniform with the brocade Presidential seal on the left pocket. "The ramp. Yes sir, Mr. Haglund."

A tan Chevrolet cruising at a discreet distance behind Lars Haglund eased into a bus zone a block behind the Mercury.

As Haglund's White House car pulled into the sparse traffic the Chevrolet followed it down Wisconsin Avenue to the river, across the parkway, down E Street and into the hodge-podge of islands and lanes leading to the southwest gate to the White House grounds.

16

Captain Arnie Pittman was sincerely disappointed. He could tell himself that it didn't matter what they gave him to do, because he was sure Dick Monckton would see that he would get his admiral's star at the end. But there had been none of the glamour of foreign trips or secret assignments, as he had promised his wife, and she was giving him all that old shit again about what a failure he was. To get her off his back he finally told her about the China project he was working on. The President wouldn't trust a big secret foreign-policy breakthrough to just some old Navy hack, by God. That had shut her up; but at the same time Pittman knew that there was numbing truth in the words she had flung at him.

He would go to the Washington luncheons and receptions and meetings and everyone knew he was the DDCI, by God. As the Deputy Director of Central Intelligence he had a lot of protocol rank. But men would come up to him and talk Company business—State Department people or men from DOD—and it would often be crap he had never heard of. What the Christ was he supposed to say? These outsiders knew things about his own agency that he'd never heard of. Reporters would ask him questions about the CIA and even use Company code names. If some goddamned old lady reporter knows enough to ask a question about "Short-circuit" why shouldn't the DDCI know about it? He should at least know the code names! At least there was one subject the DDCI knew something about: the China opening.

At a dinner party at Senator Garfield Parson's home, Arnie Pittman's dinner partner, a New York banker's wife who had recently visited eastern Europe with her husband, was wondering about how effective the Russians' iron curtain really was. Were they really keeping the Hungarians in? Captain Pittman replied by telling her some stories about Romania's relations with the People's Republic of China that interested and surprised her. The stories didn't really answer her Russian iron curtain question, but it was all that Arnie Pittman comfortably knew about eastern Europe. And the Deputy Director of Central Intelligence couldn't just sit there looking dumb, could he?

At a luncheon at the State Department in honor of the Deputy Premier of Yugoslavia, the DDCI dazzled the newest member of the Board of Governors of the Federal Reserve System with an explanation of China's activities in India and Pakistan in the acquisition of raw materials.

There are many people in the city of Washington whose job it is to listen to men like Arnie Pittman who need to inflate the importance of their work. Such talk is the currency of the place, to be bought, sold or traded.

A few astute reporters began to receive odds and ends of tips soon after Arnie Pittman began the China work. Arthur Perrine printed nothing in The Federal Ferret column because he was getting incomplete bits and fragments; but he started a file based on the tentative working hypothesis that Carl Tessler had a Red China project of some kind under way.

The National Security Agency also had a file on what DDCI Pittman was saying around town about China. The NSA's thousands of Government employees are eavesdroppers who listen to other people's electronic transmissions in and out of friendly and unfriendly nations of the world; they listen to telephones, radios, Teletypes, microwaves and Telexes. From NSA's global listening the gleanings are dumped into giant computers for analysis and storage in indexed categories. One such NSA installation, in the Maryland countryside, takes particular notice of the electronic traffic in and out of the foreign embassies in Washington, feeding coded copy into special computers designed for cryptographic analysis.

Not long after Perrine first began to hear about what Arnie Pittman was saying both to dinner partners and to central bankers, an eavesdropping machine at this NSA base in Maryland intercepted a routine intelligence transmission from the Japanese Ambassador to his foreign office. Ambassador Minoru Yamasaki reported that his Minister-Counselor had participated in a conversation the previous evening with Captain Arnold Pittman at the annual Oktoberfest party at the German Embassy. DDCI Pittman was heard to observe that "other nations were often helpful to the United States in its difficult diplomatic efforts and that his friend, the President of the United States, was personally grateful for such help." The Minister-Counselor believed that Pittman was using Asia as a context, possibly referring to a resolution of the war. In a different conversation the same evening the DDCI showed a precise working familiarity with some Romanian internal governmental procedures, allowing the listener to infer that the Government of Romania was intermediating with the USSR or the People's Republic of China, or possibly both, in behalf of the United States.

The complex NSA computer program was designed to automatically select certain subjects for the attention of NSA analysts to be culled out of the vast flow of intercepted traffic. Because the Japanese transmission included three of these programmed topics, including a possible compromise of the CIA, it was automatically printed out and hand-carried to General F.R. Hill, the NSA's Director. He read the transcript through twice, then immediately telephoned Dr. Carl Tessler at the White House. Tessler listened quietly to the transcript describing Captain Pittman's obvious indiscretion of the night before, replaced the telephone slowly and deliberately, then spectacularly erupted.

A Tessler eruption was always a solo performance but it was never performed without an audience. When Hill's call came from the NSA Tessler was alone, at work on a mountain of overdue paperwork. Thinking now only of China and Arnie Pittman, Tessler shoved the piles of paper aside with his forearm and hurled himself to his door. Dr. Tessler had both an intercom and a buzzer system to link him with his administrative assistant, Junius Leach, but in times of stress Tessler simply found it impossible to remember to use them.

"Leach!" he shouted in his deep voice. "Leach, could you tear yourself away from your exalted duties to give me just a moment of your precious time?" The three secretaries in the outer office continued their typing without looking up. "Could you do me the unspeakable kindness—"

The tall, pale young man came to the door of his cubicle, brushing his long blond hair from his eyes, then shoving his silver-rimmed glasses back up the bridge of his nose. "Yes, sir?"

"Come in here, Mr. Leach!" Tessler whirled and went to the near side of his desk. Junius Leach and Tessler's secretary exchanged knowing looks of dread. As the young man went in she stepped to the door and closed it tight, repressing a grin.

"Where is it, Leach? How is one expected to work under these conditions? Will you tell me, please?" Tessler was shouting louder, having noticed that the door was closed. "You have been brought here because Governor Forville's people said you are intelligent. Your record at Harvard was good. I had the right to assume you had a good mind. I tell you frankly, I see no sign of it! With a modicum of intelligence you would anticipate the most obvious of my needs. But no, the reading to prepare me for today's appointments is not here!" He scooped up a double handful of paper from his desk and threw the pile at Leach. Most of the papers fell on the floor. The flustered aide kneeled and began to collect the debris, looking up from time to time.

"Sir," Leach began, tentatively.

"Enough! You will not do. I knew it the first day. Collect your things. There is no place for you here! Before you go, have Castle come in. Even an ignorant Southern soldier like Castle has more sense than you do."

"He's in Thailand, sir. You sent him—"

"I know where he is!" Tessler slammed the flat of his hand against the paneled wall. "Do you think I am totally unaware of what is going on here, young man? I understand; I quite understand your conspiracy to nullify my efforts to achieve world peace—you and the others on this staff. I am well aware . . ."

"Oh, sir—" Leach sounded wronged. As accustomed as he was to these tirades, he could not always silently ride them out.

Tessler waved him to silence as he dropped heavily into his desk chair. "Your stupid denials are meaningless." Tessler ran his hand through his hair, effectively disheveling it. "I am doomed to try to serve my adopted nation while handicapped and sabotaged at every turn by knaves and fools. Well, I will not have it!" He slammed his hand on his desk. "I must have some help! Why won't you help me?" A tone of self-pity crept into his voice.

Leach's tone was heavy and resigned. "I am trying, Dr. Tessler, I am trying."

Tessler picked up his telephone. "Get me the President," he said dramatically. "No—wait! Cancel the call." He looked at Leach. "Where is the NSA transcript? How can I tell the President about it? I must have it here in my hand. What have you done with it?" His voice dropped. "How much longer can I be expected to function without help?" he muttered.

"Transcript? From the NSA? I don't recall seeing one," Leach said.

"You see? It will take me all day to find it myself; but I will do so! It is vital!" Tessler leaped up and opened his door. "Carol, you must cancel all my appointments! This young idiot cannot find the transcript." He slammed the door and turned to Leach. "I do not fire you. That is too easy. You will not leave here with my affairs in such a shambles. You must repair the havoc you have wrought. I have given you a position in the White House. Where is your gratitude? How can you leave without organizing things for your successor? You owe me at least that!"

"Yes, sir," Leach said.

Tessler lowered his voice. "Please reflect upon the task I have undertaken, young Mr. Leach. It is my accepted duty to bring the contending forces of mankind into equilibrium. An era of peace. That is my legacy to the world. Now let your mind dwell on the obstacles that are heaped in my path each day. That nonstop megalomaniac down the hall; that insufferable cretin he has chosen who poses as the Secretary of State; this building full of babbling children! And you, Leach! My helper; my right hand. You are the biggest roadblock of them all! I am wrong—world peace is more important than your mother's feelings. I have decided you must go now! When she tells you her old heart is breaking, you tell her I fired you in the interests of world peace. That should console her."

There was a knock on the door and Tessler's secretary, Carol Carlson, entered holding an envelope. "General Hill's messenger just brought this from the NSA, Dr. Tessler. And the mess steward is here with your luncheon tray."

Tessler sounded like a hurt child. "Carol, how could I eat? Just put it on the desk. It will be Mr. Leach's last White House meal. Why not? He has taken everything else from me—he has sucked my blood—why should he not take my food, too? Eat, Leach! Carol, what is my next appointment?"

"It was to have been the Undersecretary of State and the Taiwan Ambassador regarding the textiles problem. But I canceled them."

"Canceled? You canceled? It is vital I see them! Get them in here. We must keep that negotiation moving!"

Miss Carlson left, smiling tolerantly. Again she firmly closed the door. Tessler tore open the envelope, sat at his desk and began to wolf a thick cut of roast beef from a plate on the tray. Leach stood watching him.

"Gott in Himmel," Tessler muttered. As the Doctor read, Junius Leach began to move quietly toward the door. Tessler fixed him with a look of fierce hatred. "Leach! You are supposed to protect me, are you not? To observe perils, to call out warnings, to anticipate treacheries? Is it not so?"

"I suppose—" Leach murmured.

"What have you done to warn me of this Pittman?" Tessler was waving the transcript, shouting again. "He will compromise the entire China effort. And have you sounded the alarm? I will tell you! You have not! Of what use are you, young Junius Leach? I know of none. Tell me if you can! What have you told me of Pittman? Speak up! Ah, you are silent. There is no place for you here, Leach. I am right about that!" Tessler began spooning up a second dish of ice cream, hunching over his desk. "Get out of my sight! You are discharged! You are of no use whatever to me. On your way out send in Carol for dictation. And find me the Romanian file. I must have it. And the textiles file—before Cooper gets here. And see to my dress suit for tonight. I assume there are fresh linens? Can you at least do that for me?"

"Yes, sir," said Junius Leach, attempting an even tone as he walked through the door.

When Carol Carlson returned, Tessler calmly dictated a memorandum to the President while holding the rumpled NSA transcript in his left hand. The lava had ceased to flow. The show was over. Carl Tessler felt better.

THE WHITE HOUSE
WASHINGTON

FOR THE PRESIDENT
From: Carl Tessler
   Mr. President: Your Deputy Director
of Central Intelligence, Captain Arnold
Pittman, U.S.N., apparently has compromised the Romanian conduit to the
P.R.C. The negotiation may be doomed in
view of China's fanatic insistence on
secrecy.
   Attached is an NSA intercept of a
Japanese Embassy transmission describing
Pittman's indiscreet conversation with
the Japanese Minister-Counselor. Aside
from this deplorable breach of security,
I have found Captain Pittman's performance at the CIA on the China project
to be uniformly poor.
   I recommend that he be removed from
the Chinese project immediately and that
he be found some other, less sensitive,
duty to perform. I do not believe him

capable of intelligence work. He should
not be at the CIA.

Ordinarily I would not trouble you
with a personnel matter of this kind.
I am doing so only because you personally participated in his selection and
appointment.

                                    C.T.

Approve_____
Disapprove_____
See me_____
Encl.:   NSA transcript
CT/cc

The memorandum was quickly typed and presented
to Tessler for him to scrawl his initials. A one-inch
square of red cardboard had been stapled to the upper
right corner of the page. When a messenger was summoned from the basement of the West Wing, Tessler's
secretary handed him a mimeographed route slip and
the memorandum for the President. Glancing at the slip,
the young black messenger went to the nearby stairway.
As soon as he was out of sight in the stairwell he read
Carl Tessler's memorandum and the attachment. Then
he tucked it under a brown manila envelope he was
carrying; he looked about innocently as he crossed the
crowded hallway at the foot of the stairs. Next door,
on the fourth floor of the Executive Office Building, the
memorandum was handed to a clerk in the office of the
Secretariat of the National Security Council. She made
two Xerox copies, stamped them with the date and hour
and an NSC log number. When an entry had been
written in a ledger and a file prepared, the clerk typed
and affixed a file label: 10939–111569–CT–Pittman–
PRC–Leak.

An NSC messenger, who was a Navy yeoman in
civilian clothes, carried the original memorandum to the

office of the White House Staff Secretary in the basement of the West Wing. He too read it as he walked. Another clerk received it, made two more Xerox copies, and went through the same logging process. Because the memorandum bore the square red tag, she then carried the original up one flight to Chief of Staff Frank Flaherty's secretary.

About forty-five minutes after Carl Tessler initialed the memorandum it was placed on Flaherty's desk in a bright red folder. Fifteen minutes later that folder rested on the table behind the President's desk, next to the bust of Theodore Roosevelt. The President was at his desk, his feet propped on its southeast corner. T.T. Tallford sat in the side chair to the left of the desk, Lars Haglund faced the President from a chair placed directly in front of the desk.

Tuckerman T. Tallford was always confident. Richard Monckton, who had a positive aversion to initials, was the only White House person who called him "Tuck." He could count on Tuck Tallford for optimistic predictions and words of reassurance when all the others on the President's staff were critical, bucking and fighting him. And Tallford was tough. He wasn't afraid of a nasty assignment if the President needed it done. Tallford had suggested this meeting with Lars Haglund, the former CIA man. It would not appear on the President's daily appointment log, of course, nor would the three men speak of it to others. But Tallford would be using Haglund more and more on the President's assignments, and he was a man the President should know and trust.

"Tuck tells me that you've managed to put a watch on Arthur Perrine," Monckton said to Haglund. "It's too bad, in a way, that we have to do that. He did help us in the campaign. But we can't allow that to make any difference. You understand that, don't you, Tuck?"

"Yes, sir, Mr. President," said Tallford. "This is a constitutional crisis. In the preservation of the Presidency some of the old friendships may have to fall away."

"Exactly." The President turned his head slightly toward Haglund and began to remove his large wristwatch. "You see, Lars, and I shouldn't need to explain this to a man with twenty years in intelligence work, but it's well we review where we are to be sure we all agree, this Government is shot through with miserable little people who do not love this country. Ideologues. They would pull down our institutions if they could; they have no real concern for the well-being of America. The only thing that motivates them is their desire for the realization of their left-wing goals, in education or health or welfare or whatever their little narrow field is. And they hate me, because they know I will try to stop them." The President buckled and unbuckled the wristwatch strap as he talked, seldom looking at Tallford or Haglund. "Oh, I don't mind their hate. I understand it. I am the first President in this century who really threatens them, and they know it. They fear me and so they hate me. And they should fear me; I intend to root them out. I don't care that they are disloyal to me, personally." Monckton held his watch in both hands, looking at it intently. "But the Federal bureaucracy must not be disloyal to the Presidency—or the country. I have concluded that their disloyalty has reached such magnitude that it seriously threatens our constitutional system, and even the nation.

"The goddamn traitors—" he looked briefly at Haglund to test his reaction to the word—"block our new programs in the departments and agencies because they disagree with the President's ideology. But *they* are not elected. Understand, the Constitution provides that the President is elected by all the people. He is the only one who is—except the Vice President, of course, who is only a goddamned tail on the kite. But the pissants in the woodwork around here block everything good we are trying to do. Tuck knows—he's been fighting them for years! Right, Tuck?"

The aide's response was automatic and strongly affirmative. "Right, Mr. President. They are insidious. They smile and say 'Yes sir,' and as soon as they are back in their little puke-green offices they cut your balls off. Until they are rooted out you aren't going to be able to get anything accomplished."

"It's just as bad on the foreign policy side," the President continued. "The miserable fags at the State Department don't like the idea of a strong White House hand on foreign policy. They hate it; so they squirm and squeal and leak all over to try to ruin it. What only the sophisticates in the White House, and a few others, realize is that they are also ruining the Presidency—the ability of the President to carry out his constitutional duties—to conduct foreign policy. Well, by Christ, we aren't going to let them bring down the Presidency! We owe it to the country to prevent that. And that's where you fellows become so important." Monckton paused and looked directly at each of them in turn. "We've got to know what the enemy is doing. And we can't rely on the FBI and the others to tell us. Unfortunately it is true, although most people would not understand this, that the FBI is not going to be of much help to us in this fight. We must never forget that my old friend Elmer Morse is basically a bureaucrat. Oh, he's loyal. He would do almost anything—I said 'almost' anything, Tuck—he would do almost anything for me." Tallford and Monckton smiled a shared joke. "You see, Lars, we had to ask you to do the columnists because we couldn't afford to put Elmer Morse in a, shall we say, conflict-of-interest situation. He has other old friendships in this town besides mine. Arthur Perrine and he were very close friends at one time. I can't afford to test Morse's loyalty to me just now," Monckton continued. "So we must have our own people to do some of these things. Is the bug on Perrine giving us anything yet?"

Tallford and Monckton both looked at Lars Haglund. He began to speak, cleared his throat nervously, and answered rapidly, "Not much on the leaks, Mr. President. Except that someone has tipped off Arthur Perrine that the FBI is tapping newspaper people and the White House staff."

"Where the hell did he get that?" Monckton exploded.

"Someone in the FBI. Perrine is still not sure of what he has though. He doesn't dare go with the story on what little he has."

"Christ! Tuck, we can't afford to have that get out. Isn't there some way to make sure Perrine doesn't get any more information?"

"I think so, Mr. President. Lars should be able to learn their FBI source pretty soon. We can damp him off, once we know who he is. And we may pick up something juicy on Perrine. Who knows what goes on in Arthur Perrine's private office these days?" Tallford smiled thinly. "We may yet be able to persuade him to do his patriotic duty."

"What do you think he does in there, Tuck?" asked Monckton.

"Well, uh, there are a lot of stories around that he's a closet queen, Mr. President. He certainly looks the part. We just might get lucky."

"Hmmm." Monckton strapped on his watch. "I've always wondered about that. Bob Bailey told me old Arthur Perrine made a pass at him one time, years ago. It could be."

Monckton swung his feet to the floor and stood to straighten his jacket, then sat again. "I wanted to talk to you," he said to Haglund, "about the Cravath situation in California. Tuck may have told you something about it, but I want to make it clear to you that I consider it a matter of the highest national security. Now why do I say that? Because it directly involves peace in the Middle East; and a war there could quickly escalate until it pits this country against the Soviet Union in an atomic war. John Cravath, as you may know, was with Eagle-Arabian Oil for many years before he retired and went into politics. While he himself is enormously wealthy, I am told that this campaign for Governor he is putting on in California is being heavily financed by the Arabs. Our Jewish friends—" Monckton glided with innuendo along the word "friends"—"will do everything they can to beat him if that Arabian connection can be proved, right, Tuck?"

"Yes, sir. Some of the strong Zionists at the TV networks, like Meyer Gold, would gut him. But we have to have the hard evidence before we can go to them for help. Cravath is very smooth and he has the California television people in the palm of his hand right now. And he's going up in the Presidential polls every day. If he wins for Governor by a big margin in California next fall he will surely take you on in two years, when you run for reelection."

Monckton looked back at Lars Haglund. "But you understand, Lars, that the political aspects of the Cravath problem are very secondary. He may be a serious candidate for President and he may not be. That makes no difference in how I conduct this office, you understand. I don't give a rat's ass who they run against me. I must decide what is right for the country. The political chips will have to fall where they may. But if the Arabs are trying to buy the Presidency through John Cravath, that is another question. I have a constitutional duty to do something about that. Or am I wrong, Tuck?"

"No sir, Mr. President. You are right. The Constitution requires you to step in and avert a subversion of the institution of the Presidency. The same as if they were trying to buy a general or an admiral."

"You see, here again," Monckton said, "it is a matter which is much too delicate for us to turn over to the FBI or the CIA. As you know, the FBI is leaking all over to the press, and if a suspicion about connection between Cravath and the Arabs were prematurely leaked I would be accused of political slander. And he would end up looking good. There can't be any leak of what we suspect unless we have positive proof. Now, how are we going to get the Cravath evidence?"

Tallford opened a folder. "Lars has put together a good little team. They have proved themselves this month, I think. One is an Italian from New Jersey, an undercover fellow we used during the campaign. And the other fellow is from Durham, North Carolina. They would be almost impossible to trace. The CIA is giving Lars the electronic gear he needs. They can start to work on John Cravath as soon as we give the word. Right, Lars?"

"Yes," Haglund replied. "But I would like to do some research on Cravath and his organization, Mr. President, and on his old oil company and Arab connections, before we begin an operation. I need to know what to look for. That might take several weeks."

"Take your time," said Monckton in a rather loud, jovial tone, "take your time. And remember that we will be interested in anything you can dig up on Cravath. He is literally a subversive, you know. Oh, not for the Russians; that's not fashionable any more. But he is going to try to subvert the Presidency for his own selfish purposes. We owe it to the country to fight him with any ammunition that we have, Lars. So get whatever you can. He's a handsome man; maybe he's a swinger. Check his secretary. And he's very popular with the movie stars—especially the liberals. Some of those Hollywood babes are like alley cats. You might check on who he's spending his nights with. And his daughter—one of them—is married to a hippie teacher at some school in Colorado. They are probably living in a commune where they swap around. We should check on all of that."

"We know a lot about the daughter, Mr. President." T.T. Tallford smiled.

Silently the northeast door opened and a rumpled middle-aged man, two Nikon automatic cameras on his neck straps, quietly slid along the east wall of the Oval Office. As Tallford humorously detailed the Cravaths' daughter's dropout lifestyle, the White House photographer did his routine job. Twenty frames of black and white and six of color were quickly taken. The President was at work with his staff and it was Willy Fuhrman's duty to be sure that every such meeting went into the filmed history of President Richard Monckton. As he silently closed the curved door behind him, the secretary on duty in the small office between the Cabinet Room and Oval Office handed him a slip of paper. It gave the date, the time and the names T.T. Tallford and Lars Haglund (staff). Only Lars Haglund noticed the photographer leave; to Monckton and Tallford he was an unremarked fixture.

"Are you sure they were married, Tuck?" Monckton asked.

"Yes, sir. That's been checked out. They had a license and everything."

"You know—" Monckton looked at Haglund—"a lot of those hippie kids just begin living together without a real ceremony. If you look at the history of great nations—I guess I've read as much history as any President except possibly Tommy Wilson—you'll find that their downfall was almost always associated with two principal causes of social corrosion: first, the use of drugs, and second, a weakening of the institution of marriage. That's why I'm so old-fashioned and hard line. If a man wants to screw his secretary, why should the President of the United States get all upset?"

Monckton wondered if he had been too indelicate. This man Haglund was a member of the staff now, of course. But it was their first conversation. Monckton often used profanity in his office, but only with certain members of the staff. Some of them could not be trusted with the President's intimacy; too much common language made them forget the great unbridgeable gulf between the President and his staff. But men like Flaherty and Tuck Tallford never tried to bridge the gulf. And so one could use some common language with them. He wondered which kind of person Haglund was.

"Why do I care that your former CIA boss, Martin, might be charged with adultery? Let me make it clear; he is a high Government official. He is Director of the CIA. Like it or not, he sets an example for the people of the country. And how our people think about the sanctity of marriage will have a great deal to do with America's survival as a great nation. The same goes for movie stars and news editors and others in the public view. That's the lesson of history, gentlemen, and we can't afford to ignore it. It's why we can't just have men like Cravath in this chair. Just look at his daughter, for Christ's sake! That tells you that Cravath doesn't understand what history teaches. Few men in public life these days do. They think it's so modern and popular to let their hair grow and run around with their secretaries and smoke a little pot at parties. All these young Congressmen—they are all leading that kind of life, aren't they, Tuck?"

"Most of them, Mr. President."

Monckton shook his head. "They should read history; it's all there. Well, Lars, it's up to you now. You are doing a fine job." The President stood; the other two followed suit. "Keep Tuck informed, of course. He and I talk twenty times a day, I guess. So I'll know how you are getting along. Tuck, be sure and keep a tight hold on that FBI leak to Perrine. That could be very serious."

"I will, Mr. President. I don't think it's anything to worry about. I can manage it."

"This is our first visit, Lars," Monckton said with a genial veneer, "and I always like to give a staff man a little memento of a first visit." He opened a drawer on the visitors' side of the Roosevelt desk and rummaged among its contents. Taking out a small white box, he slapped it into Haglund's hand. "These are the Presidential cuff links. I have them specially made up for my visitors, you know. But you don't have to worry—they are worth less than ten dollars, so you don't have to declare them." Monckton flashed his political-platform smile.

"Thank you, Mr. President," Haglund said warmly. "I'll try and do a good job for you."

"Fine, fine," said Monckton.

"Ah, Tuck," Monckton said as Tallford and Haglund neared the door, "Tuck, could you stay a minute?"

The door closed after Lars Haglund. "Yes, sir?"

"I just wanted to say that I'm favorably impressed with that fellow. He appears to be very careful."

"Yes, sir," Tallford nodded. "I think Haglund is completely reliable."

"Are we sure he's loyal?"

"He is one hundred percent loyal to you, Mr. President. He's an idealist; very unusual for a CIA agent. But I've known him since we were both at Yale. He was your type of man even then. I've seen him often over the years and I know what his thinking has been. I recruited him. I went after him because I'm so sure of him. He's a good man—and one of the best operators in the business."

"Fine," said Monckton. "That was my impression, too. But I just wanted to be sure you didn't think I had gone ahead too fast with him."

"Oh, no sir! Not a bit. You were just right with him; I'm sure he was very impressed."

"Fine, Tuck. See you later."

Lars Haglund was waiting for Tallford in the outside hallway.

"He liked you." Tallford smiled.

"Oh? That's good. But are you sure?" Haglund looked doubtful.

"Absolutely. Don't be put off by his manner. He's always pretty stiff."

Haglund seemed troubled. "No, it wasn't that."

"What was it, then?" Tallford said somewhat impatiently.

Haglund held out the opened little white box for Tallford to see. It was empty.

All through his years in the Senate Monckton and his administrative assistants had shuffled papers and appointments in response to momentary crises and pressures. In the first several weeks of his Presidency Richard Monckton had grudgingly yielded to Frank Flaherty's rigid system of priority in the use of the President's time. Almost everything could be handled by others. They agreed that it would be Frank Flaherty's principal service to his President to cull out those problems that others could solve and to arrange the rest so that the most vital papers received the President's early attention. Flaherty had the priorities color-keyed, and Monckton learned to watch for the red folders. Whatever else was going on, he found time to read them at once. Beyond these, Monckton was never sure which color was for what. There was a color for Tessler's foreign stuff, another for the domestic junk, and the yellow folder was personal: notes from the family and friends.

After T.T. Tallford and Lars Haglund left, the President returned to his desk and saw a small stack of folders arranged neatly on his back table. The President reached for the red one, carefully scanned Carl Tessler's memorandum about Arnie Pittman and stood gazing out the thick green window for a moment. Then he turned and pressed Frank Flaherty's button.

Within a minute Flaherty pushed open the west door without knocking and unhesitatingly sat in his usual chair to the President's left. As always, Flaherty looked fresh and cheerful.

"Ah, come in, Frank. Have you read this goddamned memo from Carl Tessler? The one about Arnie Pittman? Why the hell would Arnie want to go around talking about China? It's this town! All the Georgetown parties. Is that it? Has Arnie fallen for all that social shit?"

"I don't know," Flaherty said. "Isn't he the type who is inclined to play the big-shot role if he's given a chance? I can't say I really know him."

"No." Monckton hit the arm of his chair with a thud. "It's this goddamned Gomorrah of a town that does it to people. He's just a poor, simple bastard who would be dazzled by all the parties. Was he drunk? Was that it?"

"I honestly don't know."

"Well, whatever it was, I'm not going to just fire him. Is that what Tessler wants? Does he think I should just kick Arnie in the balls and throw him out?"

"No, sir. Carl suggests in the memo that we find something else for him to do."

"I agree." The President got up and began to pace the room. "It's probably time he moved to something else, anyway. Too much time over there at the CIA would drive anyone crazy. I've decided—" his voice dropped—"I think I'll make him Secretary of the Navy." A quick, false smile flicked at his face and was just as quickly erased.

Flaherty's voice reflected his incredulity. "Pittman?"

"Yes."

"Jesus H. Christ, Mr. President! That's a terrible idea! And Carl Tessler will hit the roof. That will make all kinds of problems for him over at Defense. We *have* a Secretary of the Navy. What will Carl do with him?"

"Frank, you'll just have to program Carl. This is one of those things he shouldn't come in to talk to me about. Arnie Pittman is my friend. The President should never be put in the position of defending his friends to members of the White House staff. Just tell him I have decided and I don't want to discuss it. It's final."

"But Pittman is in the Navy," Flaherty protested. "He's a captain; technically he is on active duty right now. A Service Secretary must be a civilian. He's not eligible." Flaherty settled comfortably into a rhetorical position that appeared unassailable. "The Senate couldn't confirm him," he said with finality.

"Then have him resign from the Navy, Frank," Monckton said. "There is precedent for that. Most of the FAA Administrators have been Air Force brass. They always resign and get confirmed. Tell Carl to delay the goddamn appointment until Arnie resigns and is officially a civilian. It will give him time to find the other Navy fellow something else to do. That's better, isn't it?"

"I don't know." Flaherty could smell disaster and he was wary.

"Frank, I'm counting on you to get this done. Just tell Tessler to make the vacancy and move Arnie over. It shouldn't be so hard. But he can't talk to me about it. I'll be much too busy with the China negotiations to spend the President's time bogged down in these personnel things, Frank. You and Carl must begin to save the President's energy for the big plays now, don't you agree?"

"Yes, sir." Flaherty refused to disguise his disapproval; at the same time he knew it would not deter Monckton.

"Before you go, Frank, there's one other thing I've been thinking about. Do you have another minute?"

"Of course, sir."

"Ah, a while ago I was looking at the file on the state dinner tonight for the Prince. How are they going to do the salad tonight, Frank?"

Flaherty walked to the President's back table and found the blue state dinner file, flipped it open and shuffled the papers. "I don't know—it doesn't say. Shall I find out? I presume they'll pass it in the big crystal bowls like they usually do."

"Frank, that's why I bring it up. Do you know how long that takes?"

"No, sir. Not exactly. A few minutes, I suppose." Flaherty laid his pen on the note pad and settled back into his chair.

"One night it took twelve minutes. Another time it took seventeen. For some reason it goes faster when we use the round tables. Do you know what I will be doing during those seventeen minutes? Have you ever thought of that, Frank? I'm through with my dinner. I eat very sparingly, as you know. The Prince speaks only Arabic. One of those horrible, prissy State Department interpreters will want to sit behind us. But there is only room for one waiter to slide by, back of the head table. So I will just sit beside the little Prince and we will smile at each other off and on for seventeen minutes, saying nothing. Of course, I'm willing to do that, you understand, if it's necessary. But I wonder if you could find out if they could dish up the salads out in the kitchen—could you do that, Frank? We could shorten the whole thing by ten to fifteen minutes. It would be a good example to the country, in a way. People in the United States spend too much of their time eating, you know. I only take five minutes for breakfast and sometimes less than that for lunch. Everyone would be better off if they did that. We are becoming an obese people in this nation. Does the press know that I spend less than ten minutes a day on breakfast and lunch, Frank?

It would be a good thing to get that out to the press in one of your 'Day in the life of the President' interviews, wouldn't it?"

"I don't give interviews, Mr. President."

"Well, give it to Bailey to put out. He doesn't do anything else around here. He could at least do that, couldn't he?"

"I guess so. I'll see what I can do about the salad. Does the rest of the dinner look all right?"

"The whole state dinner thing is a miserable waste of time, of course. No one likes the goddamn things except Tessler, but I suppose we have to have them. It goes with the job. But let's get it over as fast as we can."

"Yes, sir." Flaherty moved toward the door leading to the small steward's kitchen, toilet and hideaway office. He would avoid running into the President's next appointment by going through a short dark hallway that would take him into Yarnall's adjoining office. As the door slowly closed he could hear Monckton saying to the telephone operator in a loud voice, "I want to speak to Tallford."

Then the receiver smashed into its cradle.

17

Carl Tessler leaned across the narrow aisle and raised his deep voice to a shout. The inside of the helicopter had been heavily padded and upholstered to dull the engine clatter but his words still became lost in the roar. He was uncomfortably perched and strapped on a narrow, cushioned bench that ran the length of the big helicopter on the right side. Two large airplane seats were mounted facing each other beside the wide window on the left. Richard Monckton slouched in one seat with his feet propped against the other. The President held a white plastic coffee cup embossed with the gold Presidential seal; the paper napkin said Marine Air One. So did the matches, the candy and the cigarettes in the dish on the shelf beside him.

Two of the President's speech writers sat across from Frank Flaherty behind the President's chair. This was to be no Christmas vacation at Camp David. Since September, school desegregation and housing integration had plagued Richard Monckton like a toothache. Monckton had decided: This January's State of the Union address to the Congress would announce the new China policy and, at last, take a strong stand against forced busing of schoolchildren. A nice political balance.

The hard line on busing would soften the blow; it would help with the conservatives who were taking the China move very hard. Tessler and his people would write the China part of the address but Monckton would himself work on the busing section. The courts' decisions had recently exacerbated the housing-integration situation and his advisors were telling him that he would have to say something about that too; he intended to study the problem in the quiet of Camp David and make some decisions within a couple of days. Once everyone understood his position some of the controversy would abate.

Monckton was abstractedly, hypnotically watching the Maryland landscape. A fresh, unbroken December snow glared in bright sunlight, lined only occasionally by dirty-brown-gray highways. White houses and white barns blended into white fields; northern Maryland had become a pure, monochromatic plane.

"Mr. President—" Tessler spaced his words, speaking

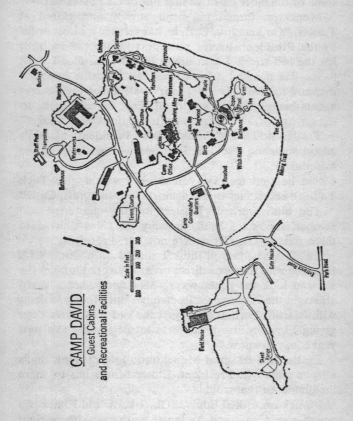

CAMP DAVID
Guest Cabins
and Recreational Facilities

Scale in Feet
100 0 100 200 300

Buckeye

Barracks

Linden

Sycamore

Hemlock

Chestnut

Hawthorn

Horseshoes

Playground

Bowling Alley

Badminton

Maple

Aspen

Pool Green

Tee

Staff Pool

Trampoline

Waterworks

Bathhouse

Dogwood

Sun Rm.

Cabin

Birch

Witch Hazel

Bathhouse

Boathouse

Camp Office

Rosebud

Hiking Trail

Camp Commander's Quarters

Tennis Courts

Gate House

Entrance Road

Park Road

Field House

Shelf Range

loudly to the back of the President's head. "I do not know very much about Bill Martin's dealings with Duncan on the declassification of the old documents, but I do know that Martin is very concerned about letting some of the most sensitive files out of his possession."

Monckton turned his head angrily and glared at Tessler. "Goddammit, Carl, he has refused a direct order by the President. I have no sympathy for the bastard; it's the last straw. I sent him a list of what files I want to see. He has had it for weeks. Oh, he came in to see me, and told me his inner fears—all about their secret agents being killed. It's a lot of crap! I'm not going to tell anyone who the CIA's agents are, for Christ's sake!"

Tessler nodded. "Frankly, Mr. President, Martin's afraid someone like T.T. Tallford will get hold of the material."

"So he told me. Do you think I would give Tuck Tallford secret files to use against the Democrats, Carl?"

The bluff worked. Tessler, looking chastened and somber, shook his head, pressing his chins down into three rolls of fat. "Of course not, Mr. President."

"Well, what do you think I should do about a CIA Director who refuses a direct order—just pat him on the ass and look the other way?" Monckton shot a sharp glance at the Professor. "Remember our other problems with Martin, Carl. It's not just the old files. He's been giving Elmer Morse a hell of a lot of trouble this past year too, you know."

Tessler looked up at Monckton. "I don't think that's all one way, Mr. President. Elmer Morse has to share the blame for that trouble."

Monckton smiled thinly. "Oh, I know old Elmer is a rough son of a bitch to tangle with. But he is right about this, you know. The CIA has been doing a terrible job. Martin is goddamn jealous of Elmer Morse, and the CIA has interfered with the FBI's work. I'm sure Elmer is right about that. Beyond that, I don't think Martin is a moral person, Carl. I understand he was living with E.S.A.'s secretary for quite a while before he married her. And now she is charging him with adultery with some Congressman's wife. How can we have a man like that as Director of the CIA? Why, he could be blackmailed by the Russians, couldn't he?"

It was not clear to Tessler whether Martin could be saved, and Tessler was seldom identified with lost causes. "Well, actually, Mr. President—" Tessler began slowly.

"Carl, I've decided," the President interjected. "Martin is finished. I want a list of new names for the job while we're up here at Camp David. I want to decide on a new Director before we come down. Do you have someone in mind?"

"No, sir. Not offhand. Give me a few days to make a list. We will start on it immediately. On another subject—I have a report from our attaché in Paris about his latest talks with the Chinese. Would you like to see it?"

"Fine." Monckton took the stiff sheets of paper and began to read. The subject of William Martin's tenure at the CIA was closed.

The farmland had begun to rise gently. At the hamlet of Thurmont the pilot banked to the left toward the high ground that Marylanders had named the Catoctin Mountains. The thick growth of now-bare deciduous trees covered the Catoctins with a gray gauze above the ground snow. A dark-green water tower protruded above the even tree mass like a fat flat-topped silo. As the helicopter flew closer Monckton put the China paper on his lap and looked out at the familiar hilltop. He never tired of picking out Camp David's landmarks as they approached. The whip antennae and radio wires were dark against the mound of snow on top of the wide water tank. Three high wire fences surrounded the hilltop. The fifty-foot no-man's land between the inner fence and outer fence had been cleared of snow. He could plainly see the electrified barrier and concertina loops of barbed wire. One of the Marine watchtowers passed under the chopper. Those poor kids would be out there now. He often took winter walks on the perimeter road and he saw them, up in those open wooden towers, all bundled up in arctic wear with their faces masked against the cold wind. It wasn't such soft duty, guarding the President of the United States.

Four high-intensity lights were flashing from pole tops at the corners of the huge grass clearing as they landed. He could see the great hangar where the helicopters would be sheltered. Two fire engines were parked on the driveway in front of the hangar doors. Those firemen in the silver asbestos suits were Navy enlisted men whose job was to drag him out and save his life in case of a crash. They didn't have a soft job up here either.

The Marine pilot gently placed the helicopter's three wheels on the three round red concrete landing targets. All the snow had been scraped from the driveways and walks, but the helicopter rotors sucked snow from the field and blew it about in dense clouds.

A Navy commander waited by a line of seven Buicks, his head ducked, holding his officer's cap on his head with the palm of his hand as the snow whipped his blue greatcoat. A Marine corporal in full-dress blues pulled the dark-blue Presidential ensign smartly to the yardarm of a ship's flagpole at the edge of the field at the instant the wheels touched the ground. The engine roar became a shrill whine as the rotors slowed and a Secret Service agent dropped the helicopter door open. The base commander moved to the steps; he stood erect, saluting, as Monckton was helped into his overcoat by the Secret Service agent. The President paused briefly to give the C.O. a ritual handshake, then walked rapidly to the first Buick. Just before ducking into the warm car he looked across the field toward a shelter which had been constructed near the flagpole, behind a wooden fence. The President waved vaguely at the press pool of six reporters and cameramen huddled under the rustic roof. They were routinely allowed to come there to observe any possible disaster in the landing; now they would retire to a motel in Thurmont to play cards and drink until the President decided to return to the White House.

The President was driven slowly through the leafless woods, along narrow asphalt roads, past the gray-green batten-and-board headquarters building and several small cabins of the same design and color. At Aspen Lodge the President alighted. He glanced about briefly but did not linger in the cold air. Camp David was best in the summer; it was several thousand feet higher than the White House and therefore always cooler. In winter usually there was snow, and a brisk wind blew steadily across the round, broad hill.

But Aspen Lodge was sound and comfortable. There were fieldstone fireplaces in the living room and in the small cozy den at one end of the building. There Flaherty had the Navy put the President's favorite old brown chair, and they had orders to keep fires going all the time. Somehow it was an even better place to work when the weather outside was cold and unpleasant.

The President usually took his meals alone in the small dining area just off the living room. A glass wall gave him a view down across the wide lawn to a far distant valley of farms and villages. It was so quiet at Camp David that when Monckton went to bed there he found it more difficult to fall asleep in that dark soundlessness than in the noise of Washington. He tried to break the silence with the radio or taped music, but they didn't help. At last, in the fall of the year, he had begun to have a few strong drinks before bedtime and he found in the alcohol the deep sleep he thought he needed. The young Navy steward who always served him in Aspen Lodge was told never to tell anyone, especially Flaherty, that he sometimes had a few drinks before bedtime. It was to be just between the President and his steward. It wasn't anybody's business what the President did at Camp David. This was his citadel— his private place. He could even have a woman if he wanted to. Others surely had. But, of course, he wouldn't.

The first night he had dinner alone; Tessler and Flaherty and the writers would eat well at Laurel Lodge. He didn't feel like seeing anyone that night. About nine o'clock the President began to take a short walk up to the top of the hill, followed by two Secret Service agents bundled in parkas. At David the agents gave him room. With the triple fence and guards and the strict clearance they put the military people through before they were allowed on the base, fifty or sixty feet was a close enough tail. He walked a few yards, then stopped, his breath condensing in the sharp air. He had forgotten how cold it became at night. He turned and went back to Aspen, where he was met at the door by the young steward in his bright-red jacket, the Presidential seal embroidered on his left pocket.

"Ah, it's cold out there, Seymour!" He shed his coat quickly.

"Yes, sir. I'm glad you came right back. You have an urgent call, sir."

The President moved toward the warm fireplace and picked up a telephone beside a chair.

"Camp David board. Yes, sir?"

"You have a call for me?"

"Yes, sir. Mr. Tallford calling, sir, through the White House board. Stand by, please." The receiver went dead in his ear, then Tallford was connected with a click.

"Mr. President?"

"Yes, Tuck. What is it?"

"Sorry to disturb you so late, Mr. President, but I didn't think this could wait."

"That's all right. I've been out for a walk in the snow. It's beautiful here. You should walk in the snow, Tuck. It does something for you."

"Yes, sir. I'm sure it does. The reason I called, Mr. President, is that I have just talked with William Martin."

"That son of a bitch," Monckton said slowly. "I've decided to fire him. Tessler is working on a list of new names for the CIA."

"Before you do that you definitely must talk to Martin, sir. I think you had better see him tomorrow."

"Why? What did he say to you?" Monckton barked.

"This is not a good line, Mr. President. I could drive up there tonight and tell you what he said, if you wish."

"No, no, Tuck. I wouldn't want you to do that. I don't really want to see anyone tonight. Isn't this something Tessler could see Martin about? I'm really pretty tied up with the State of the Union speech to do; I'll have to write most of it myself, you know."

Tallford was insistent. "Mr. President, please take my word for it. It is very, very urgent that you see Martin personally, as soon as possible. And I strongly recommend that you let him know tonight that you will see him. I can call him for you."

"All right, Tuck, I'll see him if you say I must." The President gave in wearily. "Have him come up; I'll be here at Aspen. Ten in the morning. How's that?"

"Good. I'll tell him."

"Tuck, should you be here, too? Or Tessler or Flaherty? I usually have one of you sit in any meeting with someone like Martin."

"No sir." He paused for a fraction of a moment. "Because of the subject matter, I would be the one to be there. And I don't think you will want me there. You will understand when you hear what Martin has to say."

Monckton tapped his foot impatiently. "Tuck, I can't think of anything he could bring up that would change my mind. I've decided to fire the bastard and that's all there is to it. Why do I need to see him? Can't you just tell him that?"

"No sir, I can't. He told me some things tonight that you need to know directly from him. They *could* change your mind, believe me. In my opinion the worst thing you could do right now is fire Martin. Trust me, Mr. President. Don't do anything until you talk to him. I'll set it up for ten tomorrow."

"I do trust you, Tuck. I'm sure you have only my best interests at heart. But I don't understand how it could be to the President's interest to keep a disloyal shit like Martin as CIA Director. Carl Tessler thinks the Russians could blackmail him, Tuck. We can't keep— because of his sex life, you know—we can't keep a man like that in our Administration."

A tone of pleading had crept into the aide's voice. "Just see him and listen to him, Mr. President. Then decide."

"All right, Tuck. Good night."

Monckton tapped the receiver bar twice.

"Yes sir?"

"Tessler."

"Yes sir." A silent pause blocked the line as the operator found Tessler and announced the President's call.

"Mr. President? This is Carl Tessler."

"Oh, Carl, I've just been for a walk and I was wondering if there was anything more on the CIA thing— on Martin."

"No sir. Not since we talked on the helicopter. It will take me several days to develop a list of replacements."

"Sure. I was wondering—what reasons could Martin advance for my keeping him on, Carl?"

Tessler's voice showed that he was deeply puzzled.

"Oh, I suppose the fact that he has been there for many years; perhaps that he has the confidence of our good allies, or that the CIA now has much important work in progress; it is also true that he knows the intelligence budget better than anyone—arguments along that line, Mr. President. He surely has more career experience than anyone else we have."

"Well, those are rather conventional arguments. They have all occurred to me, of course. If you were Martin, what clinching, totally winning argument could you make—something surprising—to make me back down?"

Caution made Tessler pause. He was sure something was up. "I don't know, Mr. President. So far as I know he doesn't have any such surprise."

"All right, Carl. Go back to your movie. What are you having tonight over there, a Western?"

"No. Tonight Flaherty made the choice. It's *Death of a Salesman*."

"Ah. Well, good night."

"Good night, Mr. President."

The Martin problem preyed on the President's mind and he slept badly. If Tuck Tallford had come up, it would have eliminated the mystery. What he should have done was insisted long ago that the Army install direct dial telephones at Camp David so that the goddamned Army Signal Corps operators couldn't listen in on every conversation he had. Then Tuck could have told him on the telephone what Martin had said. Instead he lay there half the night imagining what Martin's arguments could be. One thing was obvious: Martin was determined to hang on at the CIA at any cost to protect his friends and keep past mistakes covered up. It was a pure and simple case of survival. But what had Martin said to Tallford? Late into the night Monckton ruminated; it might be blackmail, but what leverage could Martin have? There were the taps, of course, but Elmer Morse would never tell Martin about something like that. And clearly they were justified; they were put on to protect the Presidency, after all. No. Tessler had put his finger on it. Martin had nothing surprising to say. He just wanted a chance to plead his case in person to the President. The President could handle that.

The sky was a milky blue at 9 A.M. when President Monckton quickly bolted down sliced papaya, toast and boiled eggs as he read the Washington *Post*. By ten o'clock the sun was shining brightly, softening the low snowbanks that lined the roads. Small streams of melting snow began to flow to the elaborate drainage system which had been installed by the military to protect the tunnels and pipes that were the anatomy of the round mountain.

William Martin's driver held a wrinkled set of driving directions in his left hand as he negotiated the sharp turns of the two-lane road up the mountain. At the Rangers' station he had been told to watch for a sign on the right at the top of the mountain, but he had noticed the tall hurricane fences and barbed wire first. "Camp David" was carved deep in the big signboard hung by chains from a rustic frame, sheltered by a narrow shake roof. Smaller metal signs warned off the unauthorized in peremptory terms.

The Marines, dressed in their tan shirts and blue pants with the red stripe, came out of the sentry house and studied the driver's identification card with great care. Two Secret Service agents looked at Martin's car through the big windows of the sentry house. One of them picked up a clipboard to note the time in his log. One Marine looked in the windows of the car, then returned William Martin's plastic CIA identity card. A heavy barricade rose hydraulically as a Marine sergeant in dark green fatigues got into a jeep and slowly preceded Martin's car. They passed through the triple fence, crossed a perimeter road and entered the thick woods. The road they were on was only the width of the car. They wound left and right, passed a frame residence with a tricycle on its side in the driveway, then a tiny wooden cabin on the right with a brown sign over the door that read Rosebud. The jeep turned right onto a slightly wider road and Martin saw a long, low office building of the same wooden design, painted the same grayish-olive drab as the house and the cabin. The roadway descended gently to the left among the barren trees, the margins widening, until they were at last in a clearing, bordered close by trees on the left but opening to a broad vista on the right. Aspen Lodge was built on the southeast brow of the mountain about one hundred feet below its summit. Between the President's lodge and the trees was a small fish pond, now frozen; beyond the near trees Martin saw several cabins and buildings. As the car door opened, Martin was aware of the presence of a number of men. Some were moving about behind the window of a building uphill; a man in a fur-edged parka stood at the far end of the lodge, the telltale wire and earpiece marking him as a Secret Service agent; a Navy Chief Petty Officer in full blue uniform, sleeves covered with stripes, talked to the Marine in the jeep; a red-jacketed mess steward held the car door. Martin was led into the lodge through a narrow vestibule by the young steward; he emerged into a living room, where he was relieved of his coat. Martin carefully held on to his thin leather briefcase.

Martin was pleased to see the pine paneling had been darkened by some process. It wasn't that typical garish yellow. The wall to the left was a gray stone fireplace. The largest colored Presidential seal he had ever seen hung over the thick mantel. Light-paneled wood bookcases filled with books took up the wall to the right. Heavy comfortable furniture was placed in front of a wall of windows straight ahead that afforded a scenic view of the hillside. The room had a subdued, informal feeling; the deep golden carpet and indirect lighting kept it from being too dark and somber in spite of the stone and the wooden ceiling beams. He counted eight telephones.

The steward brought him a cup of coffee and asked him to sign a guest book. When Martin had signed the dated page under Monckton's signature he turned back to earlier pages. There, scattered through the book, were signatures of foreign heads of state, a king, most of the Cabinet, some of Monckton's family and a couple of film stars. And the signature of Richard Monckton on page after page.

Monckton appeared in the doorway to the side of the bookcases. "Ah, Mr. Director—Bill—Tuck Tallford tells me that you want to talk to me."

The President was dressed more informally than Martin had ever seen him: white shirt and dark-blue necktie, gray slacks and a heavy brown sport jacket. As always, his shoes were black and highly polished.

"Yes, sir," Martin replied. "I appreciate your seeing me."

"Sit over here by the fire, Bill." As Monckton gestured toward a small couch by the fireplace behind Martin, he repeatedly passed his tongue along his upper lip, then dried it with the side of his thumb. His motions were abrupt and uneven, and Martin sensed the man's tension.

As they sat, Martin looked around the room and said carefully, "I don't want to talk to you here, Mr. President. I have brought some things for you to look at and I suggest you look at them here. But please do not say anything about them in this room. We should go out for a walk. We can talk outside."

"What the goddamn hell? Why all the monkey business? It's cold outside."

"It's not too bad; the sun is fairly warm. And your

lodge is constantly listened to by the Department of Defense, as I'm sure you must realize. Camp David is a Navy base, and you are the guest of the Secretary of Defense whenever you come here; I have no doubt that he could have a tape or transcript of every word we utter within minutes. I myself have seen transcripts of your conversations in this room with various foreigners. So I don't want to talk to you here."

The President's eyebrows arched in a reflection of his shock. There was no privacy, even here! The unthinkable had been thought by this fellow Martin and, worse, had been said out loud. So it now must be dealt with. That sneaky bastard Mallard Woolford had been listening to the President every time he was here. Sober, drunk, off guard and on. Monckton's mind raced back over the year of evenings in this room. But William Martin and the CIA, and what Martin had told Tallford, must be dealt with first. There would be enough time to deal with the Secretary of Defense later.

Martin was fishing in his briefcase for papers and some photographs. And Monckton forced his thought into sharp focus on this man sitting beside him.

Martin first handed the President a typewritten list of the names of those on the White House staff who had been tapped, in alphabetical order. The President looked at the page, looked up at Martin inquiringly, and began, "What—?"

Martin shook his head and held up a restraining hand. "Wait."

The second sheet was a list of the tapped reporters. The third was of the bureau chiefs. The final list named the columnists who had been bugged. Arthur Perrine's name was last. Then Martin passed Richard Monckton the photographs, one at a time, slowly. Monckton stared at each glossy 8½ by 11, without looking up, until Martin passed him another. They were arranged in sequence; the first showed the three men arriving in the blue Ford at the N Street house. The last picture showed Lars Haglund entering the White House car on Wisconsin Avenue that Sunday morning. Some of the photos made from the video tape were a little blurred but the Leica shots were crystal-clear. Martin handed the President four pictures enlarged to twice the size of the others. The first was a picture of Lars Haglund reaching high to dust Arthur Perrine's wall molding; Perrine's framed wall certificate was plainly readable in the foreground. The others were the best of those taken in the President's office when Monckton met with T.T. Tallford and Lars Haglund. Monckton looked at them for a long time. Finally Martin said, "Shall we go for a walk, Mr. President?"

Monckton's head snapped up suddenly. "Uh? Oh, yes. I want to ask you some questions about all this." His eyes were narrow. Although closed grimly, his mouth had a tired slackness about it. The President rose, again licking his lips. He moved woodenly to the vestibule and took a gray overcoat off a peg.

During the first year of Monckton's Administration the President's press secretary, Cephus Noll, had effectively sold the coolness-under-fire line to the White House press corps. Even among Richard Monckton's many journalist detractors, he was given credit for his passionless response to crises; faithful evening-news viewers could be certain that, whatever else the President might be, he was a good man to have at the helm in times of trouble. Frank Flaherty had made certain that few outsiders came near his President in times of crisis, and so the legend lived.

So, as he rode toward Camp David, William Martin expected that Monckton would be cool and calm when shown the lists of taps and bugs. Yet he briefly wondered whether the President would keep his cool when he saw the photographs of his meeting with Lars Haglund in the Oval Office. Bernie Tibbitts and the CIA's White House man had managed to get original prints, complete with the official White House photographer's date and time stamp on the back. There was no room for quibbling about their authenticity or when the meeting had taken place. Martin figured they would be the clincher Haglund was the President's man, in black and white and in glorious color as well. Monckton could not deny this indisputable proof.

Nevertheless Martin had been nervous during the drive in the snow across Maryland. As he silently rehearsed what he would say to Monckton and what Monckton would say in response, his mind inevitably strayed to the possible aftermoves. The President might try to stonewall him—he was famous for that. Then how should the bluff be played out? Would Martin have the guts to bring the whole temple down around him? The press would tear Monckton apart in revenge. It would probably destroy the President. Should he even think about such a thing? It would also weaken or destroy the FBI and drive Elmer Morse into retirement. Well, that would be a blow for freedom, anyway. He couldn't guess Monckton's reaction. The best he could do was hit Monckton hard with what he carried in Bernie Tibbitts' file and try to get a final result at once. Martin had gone back over what he would say again and again.

Aspen Lodge was a place of warmth and calm. The decor was subdued; there was not a single disquieting vibration from the old wooden duck decoys, the soft-toned watercolors, the neutral drapes and upholstery. The rooms lulled and comforted. Outside the storm doors of Aspen Lodge, however, were jarring reminders of the real world: sentry posts with guards against assassination, bomb-shelter entrances, two-way radios—and all there in the bitter cold weather. Richard Monckton hated the cold. As a boy he had done farm chores in the freezing dark before going off to school. Among his cruelest memories was the discovery of his boyhood dog, frozen to death, behind the small barn. He could never keep warm enough in an overcoat and gloves, but he would not be seen in less formal outer garments, whatever the temperature. He pretended a hearty indifference to cold weather, refusing to wear a hat or muffler as possible signs of an inner weakness. Like his constant dread of assassination, his hatred of the cold was never expressed. He dashed into crowds, apparently oblivious of danger, for the same reasons that he went out in the hated cold without a hat or a muffler. No one must ever think that the President of the United States was afraid or physically weak. He owed that to the country, and to himself.

When the President and the Director of Central Intelligence emerged from Aspen Lodge they saw only one man, heavily bundled, standing alone off to their right. He was the Secret Service agent on post near the kitchen. Perhaps because of the bright sunlight, Martin did not look closely at Elm, the small building beyond the fish pond, back in the trees. There a dark-tinted window, some eight feet across, gave the two Secret Service men in its one room a sweeping view of the approaches to the front of Aspen Lodge. A bank of television monitors permitted them to watch the Marines at the main gate, the helicopter landing area and every major road and path. Three radio systems gave them communication with the agents on the ground, all carrying walkie-talkies, with the military guards at the fence, and with the Secret Service protective service command post back in downtown Washington.

As Monckton emerged, one radio receiver crackled.

"Allen to control; Stemwinder and Martin are coming out of Aspen, moving north."

"Roger, Allen, we have him visually. Maintain normal distance."

"Allen. Roger."

Because Agent Allen had been standing at his post by the kitchen, a subconscious desire for privacy took the President on the road that went in the opposite direction. A small cabin, partly hidden by a stake fence and snow-covered plantings, could be seen down the slope to the left of the driveway. Its sign read Sassafras. Martin couldn't take his eyes off the large silver searchlights that were mounted on the ground surface to illuminate both Aspen and Sassafras at night. Then he pulled his mind back to the job at hand.

"This is an old building that we're going to take down," Monckton said, pointing to another gray-green wooden building, this one named Birch. "We will build a guest house there for foreign heads of state next spring."

"Ah," said Martin. Beyond Birch the trees closed in on the low snowbanks that marked the margin of the road. "Mr. President," Martin began, "I want to come right to the point. You and Elmer Morse, the White House and the FBI, have been engaged in some highly illegal and embarrassing operations. The lists and these pictures show that, beyond any question."

Monckton licked his upper lip, then wiped it with the side of his thumb several times. He pointed to a road intersecting from the left. "This is the road to the gate. It goes by the C.O.'s house." He pointed ahead. "But I think we'll just keep going this way. Do you ever bowl? My bowling alley is in the back of that building over there to the right. That's Hickory. All the buildings are named for trees." It was a long building of the same style.

"Mr. President, a member of your staff has been photographed bugging Arthur Perrine. He entered Perrine's house; he broke in. Your man Haglund is known to have done other jobs for you of a similar kind. And Elmer Morse has done the rest. You have a serious problem. A very serious problem."

Monckton did not look at him; Martin could sense that he was watching and listening acutely but he was unsure of the effect he was having on the President. He had no choice now but to continue—to ram it home.

"I showed these lists and pictures to T.T. Tallford last night, you know," Martin continued, raising the briefcase a little. "It was interesting. Tallford read the lists, looked at the pictures and only asked me one question. I thought that rather remarkable. The pictures have no captions; the lists have no headings or explanations. They are just people's names. Yet old T.T. Tallford asked only one question."

"What was it?" They both knew that Monckton was forced to ask the inescapable question.

Martin followed up quickly. "Tallford looked at them and the only thing he said was 'What do you want?' Not 'Who are they?' or 'What are they doing?' or 'What does all this mean?'; Tallford only asked what my price was. So I told him I wanted to see you immediately."

"And here you are."

"And here I am."

Monckton again pointed, this time to the right. "Let's go this way. This road goes on out to the big field, but there is nothing there now but the helicopter. In nice weather you can shoot skeet there. But it's covered with snow now." A jeep approached and passed by them as they turned right. The Navy driver in a khaki jacket looked surprised, recovered and saluted the President as he drove by.

"Allen to control."

"Control to Allen, go."

"We are northbound on the tennis court road. There is Navy traffic; a jeep just went by."

"Roger, Allen. We saw it. We are shutting down base traffic until Stemwinder returns to Aspen. There is a snow-sweeping crew around Laurel. Wienerschnitzel is taking a walk on the perimeter road. Otherwise the base is clear."

The guardhouse television monitor displayed the President striding unevenly beside Martin in the middle of the road. Another screen showed Carl Tessler, whose code name was Wienerschnitzel, stumping along the fence road near the helicopter pad, clouds of his cold breath forming wreaths about his head. A third screen watched four sailors scraping sidewalks under the eye of a boatswain's mate.

"I have problems, too, Mr. President," Martin said. "I know you are well aware of most of them. I am here to suggest how I can solve some of your problems, and then I will tell you how you can solve some of mine. What I propose is a plain old-fashioned horse trade."

"I don't object to trades," Monckton said flatly. "Oh, back over there on the left are the tennis courts. Of course, you can't play in this weather, but they use them a lot in the spring. I don't play tennis or golf myself. I've never had time to learn. Too busy with other things."

"I'm glad to hear you're open to a trade." Martin saw that he would have to use the same tactics as an angler playing a fish instinctively determined to avoid the net. Monckton would do anything to avoid the subject and Martin would have to keep bringing him back to it. "Now, what can I offer you? That one thing you need: total silence. Nothing need ever be said about your taps and bugs and the breaking and entering. I am the only one outside the White House who has all this information—so far. And I am willing to forget what I know."

"So." Monckton was feeling the hook. He looked behind him. There were two agents, but they were out of earshot. "And what is it that I trade—that I give you for all this silence?"

"There are several things, Mr. President."

"Ah. The price. It sounds like blackmail, you know, Martin." The fish tried to swim away again. "Oh, over here in this long building are the maintenance shops; there is an impressive installation of pumps and blowers and machinery, you know, under this mountain. All of that has to be kept in good shape all the time, of course. The Seabees do that. They are very good workmen. They tell me the Seabees can fix anything in these shops."

"I'm afraid they can't fix this particular problem, sir." The approach was too pat, too cute on the uptake, thought Martin, but he had to admit that the man was incredible with his goddamn travelogue and the personally guided tour of Camp David. As if the President thought he could make Martin forget why he came to David. "Only you and I can do that. For instance, there's the Primula Report—on Rio de Muerte, you know. I want you to destroy it."

"Ah, how can I do that?"

"It's relatively simple. I will log it out to your possession. You have a legal right to it. You can do anything you want with it. You will just never return it. It can be shredded in about twenty minutes. There is only one copy."

"Is that all? Does that solve all your problems?" Monckton's cheeks near his mouth had turned from pink to a bluish cast. His ears were very red.

"Well, not quite all, Mr. President."

"Ah, I thought not. Let's cut down here, through the parking lot. There's nothing over this way except the big water tank and the other swimming pool. The staff uses that pool. That thing over there is the big communications center, you know." He laughed harshly. "If you can get clearance you ought to look in it sometime. It's so secret they won't even let me in."

Martin swung the conversation back to the point again.

"There are several other problems to be solved, sir. One is what becomes of me. After this you're not going to want me at the CIA; it would be an impossible relationship. In fact, I wouldn't want to stay. I'll be divorced from my wife in another ten days or so and I intend to remarry right away. The lady and I have talked about what we'd like to do for the next couple of years, Mr. President, and we've decided we would like to go abroad. You might be happier with me off in a foreign country for a while anyway." He looked closely at Monckton, who was no longer striding evenly. The road took them on a moderate downhill slope and the President, briefly caught off balance, had lurched to his left. Now he was taking shorter steps in careful reaction.

"Here is where Flaherty stays. Sycamore. Over there is Tessler's cabin—Hawthorn. That cabin in between is Laurel, where they eat. I am going to build a big, new building down the hill there with a Cabinet room in it and a Presidential office. I intend to spend much more time up here and less in Washington. Especially in the good weather. So we'll need better facilities."

"Mr. President," Martin said loudly. Monckton turned his head slowly and looked at him. They were standing at a sharp curve in the road, the cabins to their right, sun-dappled trees and snow to their left. "Mr. President?"

"Yes?"

"Do you understand my suggestion?"

"Perhaps you should say it again."

"All right." Martin stood stock still and spoke very distinctly as he ticked off his list of demands. "I want to be an ambassador. Nothing heavy; not St. James or Paris. Perhaps South Africa or Mexico or some such place, until my pension is maximized. Then I'll retire from Government."

"I see."

"Now, let's talk about the CIA." They were walking again. The snow-removal crew had done their job around the cabins and had themselves been removed before the President came in sight. "You will be selecting a new Director to replace me."

"Yes, Carl Tessler is getting me a list."

"Forget Carl Tessler's list. I will give you a list right now, a list of one. The new Director will be Durwood Drew."

"Who the hell is he?" Monckton was looking down at the roadway, hands in his overcoat pockets, carefully choosing his path to avoid the rivulets of melting snow.

"He is a career employee, formerly my assistant, who is attached to the Embassy in Bangkok just now. He is a rather colorless fellow who will do an excellent job for you."

"Anything else?"

"Yes. You are to call off the dogs. No more FBI harassment."

"Are you being harassed?"

"I mean harassment of the CIA. You are to tell Elmer Morse to lay off. There is no liaison between the CIA and the FBI any more, because Morse broke it off. You will order him to reestabish it. And you will give Durwood Drew your personal backing."

"Even when he's wrong?"

"He won't be wrong often; but, yes; even when he's wrong. I'll be sitting out there watching you. If you screw the Company—the CIA—so help me God, I'll pull your chain and flush you into oblivion. That goes for the CIA budget, too. Call off the dogs and let Drew do a job. Quit this fucking corner cutting with the CIA's budget, do you understand?" Martin's emotion was getting the best of him. He reached down and scooped a handful of wet snow from the side of the road and passed it from hand to hand.

"This is interesting," said Monckton. "See those swings and the teeter-totter? That thing is called a jungle gym, I'm told. Perhaps you know that. Do you have children?" He looked intently at Martin.

"No."

"Ah. Well, William Arthur Curry had a son, you know. Billy, Junior. He put all this playground here for his son. But his wife hated Camp David; not elegant enough for her, you see. She called the buildings Arkansas motels. So she wouldn't let the little boy come up here and play with these things. I think that's too goddamned bad. The stuck-up bitch." There was a timbre of hatred in Monckton's voice.

"Mr. President, did you hear what I said about the FBI and the budget—the CIA budget?"

"Certainly. I am not deaf. I have heard all of your fucking blackmail demands, Martin."

"And?" They were approaching the kitchen corner of Aspen Lodge. They had come in a long circle, up to the top of the hill and down again. The large clearing below the lodge was down to their left.

"Look," said Monckton, pointing. A deer was foraging in the snow at the far edge of the clearing a hundred feet below them. The young red-jacketed mess steward was standing outside the vestibule, waiting to hold the door for the President and take his coat. He looked cold in his light jacket.

"And?" repeated Martin, more insistently. Time and space and advantage were running through his fingers. He felt it. It had to be now.

"And, what?"

"And what is your response? If you get silence from me? Will you destroy the Primula Report?" Martin stopped walking, twenty feet from the doorway. The steward could hear them. Martin turned. The two Secret Service agents continued to walk slowly toward them. Monckton stopped and turned away from the lodge toward Martin. Martin went on softly: "Will you destroy it, give me an overseas job, appoint Drew and call off the dogs? That's the price. Take it or leave it, goddamn you. But I want your answer now."

Monckton again licked his upper lip, made that nervous wiping gesture with his thumb, and looked down the slope at the grazing deer. Then he turned and looked at Martin. Their eyes locked for an instant, then Monckton looked down.

"I'll take it."

The President of the United States of America turned clumsily and walked toward the mess steward, fumbling with his overcoat buttons.

"Allen to control."

"Control to Allen, go."

"Stemwinder is in Aspen. All is secure here."

"Roger, Allen. All is secure. Out."

Epilogue

The official residence of the Ambassador of the United States to Jamaica was built on a low hill to catch the cooling breezes. Some wealthy predecessor had paid for the swimming pool and elaborate terrace on which His Excellency, the Ambassador, and Mrs. William Martin reclined in lounge chairs, tall cool rum swizzles in hand, watching the glowing sunset.

Martin had been confirmed as Ambassador only six weeks before; yet a month later he and Sally already felt in harmony with the pace and rhythm of the island. Sally Martin had begun to live the socially busy life of a diplomat's wife; she had made some formal calls in the Ambassador's limousine and had arranged the traditional get-acquainted reception for the growing American community on the island. It had gone very well, everyone at the Embassy agreed. Martin found the administrative duties unbelievably light compared to the CIA job. Simon Cappell had come down with them, and it was he, in truth, who did the actual work of the office. Martin's duties were primarily social and very spasmodic. The first month had been a near-perfect honeymoon.

Martin felt a little sorry for the newly confirmed Director of the CIA. At the same time it was a comfortable situation for him. Durwood Drew was at Martin's old desk, the Primula Report was destroyed and there were signs that Monckton was curbing Elmer Morse.

A white-jacketed native servant carried three newspapers to the low table between Martin and his bride. "Are your drinks satisfactory, Mr. Ambassador?" the man asked in a clipped British accent.

"Yes, Reginald. Thank you." Martin reached for the top newspaper and began to scan the front page.

Sally took a long sip of her drink. "Look at that color in the sky now, Bill. It's unbelievable. Just think what March is like in Washington. What a lovely place this is to be."

Martin gestured toward the newspaper. "Have you seen today's Miami *Herald?*"

Sally shook her head.

"Interesting. Seems a fellow on the White House staff named Lars Haglund was arrested in San Francisco last night. He and two other fellows were caught red-handed burglarizing the headquarters of a Democratic candidate for Governor there. The police caught them in the man's office."

"Was that John Cravath's headquarters?" Sally asked. Martin nodded. "Jack and I used to know him. As a matter of fact he made a pass at me once. What in the world was a White House man doing in his office?"

Martin shook his head. "The paper doesn't say. And the White House has denied any connection with the whole thing." Martin dropped the folded paper to the terrace. "I can't believe anyone could be that stupid. Not even Monckton. I'd lost track of Haglund; they should have gotten rid of him weeks ago. It's almost unbelievable."

Sally half-turned to look at her husband. She hadn't heard that tone in his voice since they'd come to Jamaica. "Why are you so upset, Bill?"

Martin slowly shook his head. "I have a feeling someone has just lit a very long fuse that leads right to me, sweetheart. Just pray to God I'm wrong."

"How could it possibly lead to you, darling?" His wife sounded puzzled.

"I'm probably paranoid—it's an old Company hangover, my love." Martin smiled, holding his hand out to her. "Come on, we've got to dress. That party starts pretty soon."

INFLAMED... IMPASSIONED...
IMPETUOUS...
*A Scorching Novel Of A Woman's
Passion Blazing From The
Pages Of History!*

by Mary Kay Simmons | 80913
$1.95

From the innocent countryside of California, past the
glitter of New York's Broadway, to the sin-swept
streets of Paris, comes this powerful story of defiant
love and forbidden lust.

Available at bookstores everywhere, or order direct
from the publisher.

POCKET BOOKS
Department SJP
1230 Avenue of the Americas, 13th Floor
New York, N.Y. 10020

Please send me_____copies of A FIRE IN THE BLOOD. I
am enclosing $_____(please add 50¢ to cover postage
and handling). Send check or money order—no cash or
C.O.D.'s please.

NAME_____

ADDRESS_____

CITY_____

STATE_____ ZIP_____

SJP-1